VEIL
OF
SECRETS

VEIL
OF
SECRETS

by

Una-Mary Parker

NAL BOOKS

NAL BOOKS
Published by the Penguin Group
Penguin Books USA Inc., 375 Hudson Street, New York, New York, 10014 U.S.A.
Penguin Books Ltd, 27 Wrights Lane, London W8 5TZ, England
Penguin Books Australia Ltd, Ringwood, Victoria, Australia
Penguin Books Canada Ltd, 2801 John Street, Markham, Ontario, Canada L3R 1B4
Penguin Books (N.Z.) Ltd, 182–190 Wairau Road, Auckland 10, New Zealand

Penguin Books Ltd, Registered Offices:
Harmondsworth, Middlesex, England

First published by Dutton, an imprint of Penguin Books USA Inc.
Published simultaneously in Canada.

First Printing, April, 1990
10 9 8 7 6 5 4 3 2

 REGISTERED TRADEMARK—MARCA REGISTRADA

LIBRARY OF CONGRESS CATALOGING IN PUBLICATION DATA
Parker, Una-Mary.
    Veil of secrets / Una-Mary Parker.
      p. cm.
    ISBN 0-453-00722-8
    I. Title.
    PR6066.A694V4   1990
    823'.914 — dc20   89-29497
                                       CIP

Printed in the United States of America
Set in Palatino
Designed by Nissa Knuth

PUBLISHER'S NOTE
This is a work of fiction. Names, characters, places, and incidents either are the products of the author's imagination or are used fictitiously, and any resemblance to actual persons, living or dead, events, or locales is entirely coincidental.

This is for Baba and Buffy,
once more, with feeling.

ACKNOWLEDGMENTS

I would like to extend my grateful thanks to those who have helped me in the course of my research and who have given me so much encouragement throughout. They include Baba Hobart, Buffy Parker, Mary de Schwarzburg-Gunther, Duncan MacArthur, Doreen Boulding, Nigel Cockburn, Howard Levene, and of course Susan Fletcher, Jackie Cantor, and my agent, Susan Zeckendorf.

'Tis one thing to be tempted, Escalus,
Another thing to fall.
—*Shakespeare*, Measure for Measure

1

THE SILENCE of the night was broken by the shrill tones of the telephone, shattering the peaceful darkness and startling Madeleine and Carl into wakefulness.

"What the hell . . . ?" Carl reached for the light switch and then looked groggily at his watch. "Who in God's name is calling us at this hour?"

Madeleine turned over sleepily, her cloud of black hair spreading on the pillows, the white muslin draperies of the four-poster bed festooned like transparent sails in the soft glow of the bedside lamp, cocooning them in a rosy oasis. "Tell whoever it is to go away," she murmured.

Carl grabbed the phone. "Hello?" His voice sounded terse. There was a pause, and then Madeleine heard him exclaim: "D'you realize it's three o'clock in the morning? . . . What? . . . Yes, there's a five-hour time difference. . . . Shall I get her to call you tomorrow?" Through half-drooping eyelids she saw his muscular legs, tanned from their regular weekends at Oyster Bay, push the sheets away. It was a hot night and his blond hair clung to the back of his neck. Suddenly he turned toward Madeleine, his brown hand cupping the receiver.

"It's your grandfather, calling from England," he whispered.

Madeleine's eyes flew open and she thrust herself into a sitting position, instantly alert.

"You're kidding!" Her heart-shaped face paled against the darkness of her hair and eyes and her expression was deeply shocked. "He hasn't spoken to us for over twenty years! What does he want?"

"He won't tell me . . . insists on speaking to you. I'm sorry, darling, but I think you'll have to talk to him—he sounds in quite a state."

Gingerly Madeleine reached for the receiver, bracing herself

as she did so. Her autocratic English grandfather had refused
to have anything to do with either her or her father since her
mother had died, and now, across thousands of miles of ocean
and twenty years of silence, he was reaching out to her from
the past as if he desperately needed her.

"Hello?" she said quietly, though her heart was thumping.

The voice was reedy, imperious and impatient, as if he'd
been kept waiting too long. "Madeleine? Is that you?"

"Yes, this is Madeleine."

"George Dalrymple here. Listen, I have to see you as soon
as possible. There are things you have a right to know, and I
don't suppose your damned father has told you everything—"

"Just a minute!" Madeleine felt a rush of anger. How dare
this old man, half-forgotten and never mentioned, disrupt
them in the middle of the night with his abusive manner! And
what did he mean about her father not telling her everything?

Her tone was cold. "What do you want?"

"I am an old man, Madeleine. I haven't long to live and it's
vital I tell you everything before it's too late." His voice was
no less querulous and demanding.

With an effort Madeleine bit back her anger, giving Carl a
glance of appeal as she did so. Responding, he reached out
for her hand and clasped it tightly.

"Listen," she said heatedly into the phone, "neither my
father nor I have seen or heard anything from you for twenty
years, and now here you are demanding . . ."

It had been 1965. She'd been three years old and they'd been
living in England when her mother, Camilla, had died. To the
best of her knowledge, Sir George Dalrymple, Camilla's father,
had refused to speak to any of them since.

"That wasn't my doing!" the rasping old voice cut in. The
conviction in his voice made Madeleine suddenly uneasy. Perhaps it had been her father, Jake, who'd refused to communicate in any way. It would be consistent with his whole
attitude toward his late wife's family. Since Camilla's death,
he'd acted as if the Dalrymples didn't exist.

As if Sir George could read her thoughts, he spoke again,
confirming what she'd been thinking.

"Madeleine, you can blame your father for the estrange-
ment. I wanted us to meet, but Jake always prevented it. Please
fly over here to see me. It is of the greatest importance, and

I just wish I hadn't left it so long." Sir George was pleading now, and the urgency in his voice alarmed her. She also knew the ring of truth when she heard it, and yet something inside her still resisted the thought of having to face the unknown, from which Jake had so obviously protected her.

Curiosity tempted her to ask: "What's it about, Grandfather? Why can't you tell me now, or write to me?"

"Impossible, impossible. I have to see you. There is too much to tell . . . to explain. I shall never rest in my grave unless you know all the facts." Sir George's voice broke on a quaver.

Alarm threaded its way icily through Madeleine's veins and she shivered. Carl, watching her anxiously, straining to hear what was being said, slid his hand up her arm and stroked her shoulder.

"Are you okay, sweetheart?" he whispered.

Madeleine nodded, her eyes troubled. "I'll have to go and see him," she whispered back.

"Are you there, Madeleine? Can you hear me?"

She directed her attention quickly back to the phone. "Yes, I'm here. I can't come immediately because I'm about to hold my first exhibition; I'm an artist, you see. But I'll come as soon as I can."

"Milton Manor, near Okehampton. In Devon," Sir George said peremptorily. "I'll be waiting for you. Come as quickly as you can, please."

"I will," Madeleine promised.

"And one more thing . . ." The voice sounded agitated again. "What is it?"

Sir George spoke with swift decisiveness. "For God's sake, don't tell Jake you're coming to see me, or he'll do everything he can to try to stop you." There was a click, the line was silent, and Madeleine realized he'd hung up. For a moment she sat very still, the receiver resting in her hand. Then she replaced it slowly, feeling deeply jarred. It was as if the past, long buried and forgotten, had been thrust upon her, stirring up half-forgotten memories and vague fears that had once filled the life of a little girl who had called out so often for her mother, and whose cries had gone unanswered. She glanced up to see Carl watching her, his lean face and china-blue eyes filled with concern. For comfort, she slid under the crook of his arm, relishing the warmth of his naked body against the sudden coldness of her own.

Her smile was wan. "How strange to hear from my grandfather like that. What can he have to tell me about my mother . . . do you think there was something sinister about her death?" It was a question she had often asked herself in the past. That might explain why Jake had always refused to discuss his wife and why he had destroyed every photograph of her and every memento. Even Camilla's portrait by the famous Philip de Laszlo, who had painted the society beauties of the day, had vanished from its place above the mantelpiece in their Beekman Place house. Madeleine could vaguely remember that portrait, although she'd been only three and a half when they returned to New York from London; it showed a fair-haired woman with pale eyes, wearing a cream lace dress. Most memorable of all were the cascading ropes of pearls that fell from round her neck, almost reaching her lap. Madeleine knew she didn't look at all like her mother; she'd inherited the Shearman black hair and eyes and white skin from her father's family. Her father's daughter, people called her; a perfect feminine likeness of the powerful Jake Shearman. But that was as far as it went. The likeness was only skin-deep.

"That call has disturbed you, hasn't it, Maddy?" Carl whispered tenderly. "Do you really intend to go all the way to England to see your grandfather?"

Madeleine turned to look into his face, thankful he was there. But then, Carl was always there for her and had been ever since they'd married four years before. She kissed his cheek, near the corner of his mouth. "I must, darling. Suppose he has something really important to tell me! I'd never forgive myself if he died and I hadn't even made the effort to go and see him. As soon as the exhibition has opened, I'll fly over. Is there any chance you could come with me?"

Carl shook his head. "Not a cat's chance in hell! With the dollar in free-fall and interest rates as jumpy as a kangaroo on a griddle, I'm going to be stuck in the bank for the rest of the year."

Madeleine sighed, snuggling closer. "Then I'll stay for only a couple of days. I can't bear to be away from you for longer than that."

Carl spoke gently. "Have you thought, Maddy, that your

grandfather might be senile and half-crazy? You could go all that way and find the whole thing was a wild-goose chase. What can he tell you about your mother that you don't already know or that Jake won't tell you?"

"That's just the point: Dad has always refused to tell me anything. You know that, Carl. As soon as my mother's name is mentioned, he clams up and acts like she never existed. Maybe my grandfather will at least tell me how she died."

"And if it's unpleasant—and maybe that's why Jake has never talked about it—do you still want to know?"

Madeleine spoke positively, though she looked distressed. "Yes. I want to know."

Carl stroked the glossy blackness of her long hair. "Wouldn't it be better to let sleeping dogs lie?" he asked softly. "I don't want you getting all upset, honey."

"I'll be okay." Madeleine lay back against the lace-edged pillows, recalling what she did know: bare facts, no more than an outline. The story of a glamorous couple who had had everything that life could offer . . . until the day disaster struck.

Jake Shearman, at twenty-five, was sure that Camilla Dalrymple was the most beautiful girl he'd ever set eyes on. On vacation from Harvard, where he'd been studying economics, he and his friends decided to drive from Nice to Monte Carlo one evening, in order to have a flutter in the casino. As the little white ball *plink-plinked* with monotonous regularity on the spinning roulette wheel under the watchful eyes of the players, and the croupiers called *"Rien ne va plus,"* Jake looked up, and through the blue haze of cigar smoke saw her standing there, watching the proceedings with a detached interest. Her cool English beauty took his breath away. Amid the more flamboyant and much older French, Italian, and Spanish women, she looked ethereal with her simply styled blond hair and understated ice-blue satin evening dress. Fragile as a spring blossom, and delicate as Dresden china, it struck Jake that she looked as if she'd break easily, as if she'd snap like fine-blown glass or glittering spun sugar.

"Faites vos jeux," called out the croupier, and like scurrying white rats, bony and bejeweled hands pushed and shoved and threw down their different-colored chips with blind compulsive abandon, and greedy faces watched avidly, some a breath

away from bankruptcy, others unknowingly hovering on the brink of a fortune. *Plink-plink* went the little white ball, and a fortune had been acquired or lost. But Jake was no longer interested in the game, so absorbed was he in watching Camilla and noting that she seemed to be on her own. No husband or escort hovered by her side as she glided from table to table, watching the play with absorbed fascination. Then Jake caught his breath; an elderly woman in a blaze of rubies and swaths of sable around her plump shoulders trotted up, and the two women smiled and started talking.

"Have you seen enough?" the older woman asked brightly. She'd been dropping into the casino for years, although she never gambled herself. To her it was a spectacle to show visitors, a little *divertissement* to while away an hour between dinner and going to bed.

"It's fascinating, Aunt Marion," Camilla replied. "And everyone's so smart! There's nothing like this in England."

"Ten years ago, when the Germans occupied France, there was nothing like this here either! But now, as you can see, everyone wears their jewels and puts on their best clothes again. It is good for morale."

Camilla gazed in wonder as men with fat wallets and women with sharp eyes continued to play as if hypnotized by the whirling wheel.

Jake rose from the table, his few remaining chips in his hand. The moment had come to make his move. Tall, well-built, and with the black hair and pale skin that typified all the Shearmans, he presented himself before the older woman with a smile and a slight bow.

She looked up, clasped her hands together, and let out an exclamation of joy. "Jake! My dear boy! What on earth are you doing here?"

Jake kissed her powdery cheek. "Lady Wantage, how good it is to see you! I'm on vacation, staying with friends in Nice. I thought I'd try my luck tonight . . ." He eyed Camilla pointedly, longing to be formally introduced, smiling his most charming smile.

"Have you two young things met?" Marion Wantage inquired with her usual vague but sweet smile. She turned to the girl. "This is Jake Shearman, my dear. His late mother and I both came from Boston and we were lifelong friends. This is Camilla Dalrymple, Jake, my goddaughter. She's staying with me at the Hotel de Paris, as her mother thought she ought to see a bit of France. She thought it would be good for her education," she added with a roguish smile.

Jake laughed. Camilla's mother could be right. Marion Wantage was an oil millionairess who had married an English baron and had then proceeded to show, not only the English but also the international set, what it was to have style. She had permanent suites at the Hotel de Paris in Monte Carlo, the Beau Rivage Palace in Lausanne, and Claridge's in London. They were all furnished with her own antiques and paintings, and she had her personal staff ensconced in adjoining suites so that they were on hand to look after her needs. Widowed now, she still entertained with flair, counting among her close friends Sir Winston Churchill, Somerset Maugham, and Jean Cocteau. Any young girl would gain a lifetime's education by spending a few weeks with Lady Wantage, Jake thought.

"So this is your first visit to Monte Carlo," Jake said conversationally, turning to Camilla. There was something very vulnerable about the way she looked up at him with her misty blue eyes.

Her voice was soft when she spoke. "Yes, it is." She looked around the richly gilt baroque room with its shimmering chandeliers and then at the desperate faces that gathered around the gaming tables, watching silently as the atmosphere grew ever more pungent with the smell of expensive cigar smoke. "But it's a bit decadent, isn't it?"

Jake laughed again. "That depends on whether you're winning or losing!"

"Shall we go somewhere quiet for a drink?" suggested Lady Wantage.

"I think that's a very good idea," Jake said, taking Camilla by the elbow.

It was a whirlwind romance. Camilla's parents, Sir George and Lady Dalrymple, invited Jake to stay at Milton Manor, their Devonshire home, and by the time he returned to the United States their engagement had been announced in the *Times.* They were married in London the following spring, and then Jake whisked his young bride back to New York, where he'd bought a beautiful gray stone house on Beekman Place, overlooking the East River.

There was also a weekend home at Oyster Bay on Long Island that Jake's father had left him, and all the trappings that belonged to one of New York's oldest and most distinguished families. Jake would one day become president of the Central Manhattan Bank, and meanwhile he enjoyed a senior position without the heavy responsibility that would one day be his. It was an idyllic existence, made all the more perfect by the arrival of their first child, Madeleine. They were feted by New York society as the "golden couple" who had everything, and it seemed as if nothing could ever happen to cast a cloud over their sunny lives. Then Lady Dalrymple died suddenly from a heart attack, and the shock affected Camilla deeply. She became chronically depressed and Jake was at his wits' end trying to cheer her up. He took her on a trip to Bangkok, suggested she do over their house, loaded her with jewels and furs, but to no avail. It was only when he was posted to the London branch of the bank that she started to brighten up. She also decided that she wanted to remain in Devon with her father, while Jake worked in London.

"But I'll never see you and Madeleine!" he expostulated. "I want you to be with me."

Camilla looked stubborn, her beautiful, vulnerable mouth set in tight lines. "Father will need me, now that he's alone. You can come down at weekends."

They looked at each other, Jake willing to do anything if it was going to make her happy again, Camilla willfully determined to go her own way.

As time passed, Jake did all he could to persuade her to change her mind, saying that if her father needed her, her husband needed her more. It was a battle he never won. Camilla remained in Devon, and eighteen months later she was dead.

"I've got to find out what happened, Carl." Madeleine rolled over in the bed so that she lay on her side, facing him. "Dad's kept me in the dark all these years, but tonight, for the first time, I really am determined to get to the truth. If he won't tell me, then I'll fly to England and find out for myself. I . . . well, I feel in a strange way that I owe it to my mother."

Carl nodded. "I understand that. Why don't you let me talk to Jake? He might find it easier to talk to another man."

Carl worked alongside Jake at the Central Manhattan Bank, as head of foreign transactions, a position he held through merit and not because he was married to the boss's daughter. From the moment Carl had joined the bank ten years before, fresh from Yale and then Harvard Business School, Jake had been impressed by him. The young man showed brilliance and flair and had a natural aptitude for banking. One day he would make a fitting successor to Jake, who had no son of his own.

"I'd rather talk to Daddy myself," Madeleine said, "but I'll wait until after my exhibition." Her first one-woman show was going to be held at the chic Midas Gallery in SoHo in ten days' time, and it was an important career move, something she'd been working toward for years. She snuggled closer, like a kitten seeking warmth. "I do wish you could come to England with me!"

Carl leaned forward and kissed her gently on the mouth. "So do I, sweetheart. I'll miss you like hell."

"Oh, Carl!" She pressed her pale slender body against his strong tanned one, and winding her arms around his neck, whispered, "I'm lost without you."

Carl kissed her again lingeringly, then leaned back, his eyes twinkling and deep laughter lines fanning out onto his cheeks. He pretended to look solemn. "You're a naughty girl, sliding up against me like this when you know I've got to get some sleep! What are you trying to do? Make me so tired I'm late for work in the morning and then have your father fire me?"

Madeleine giggled and pressed herself closer still. Her dark eyes were dancing with fun. "Now, that's a good idea! You get Daddy to sack you and then we'll be free to set off round the world on another honeymoon!" Her pale breasts were crushed against him now and she was kissing his neck just behind the ear, where she knew he was particularly sensitive.

Carl let out a groan. "Maddy," he pleaded, trying to extricate himself, "I've got to be at the office in"—he glanced at his watch—"in four hours' time!"

"Four hours!" she whispered, her tongue flicking along the edge of his jaw, her hand reaching down to stroke his thighs. "In four hours we can do it at least twice!"

"Maddy, will you stop it!"

She continued to kiss him and stroke him, knowing he didn't really want her to stop. Gradually her urgent desire transferred itself to him, so that he too became aroused, his body responding to hers so that they moved in perfect harmony. Lost in sensation, his eyes closed, he let this woman who had been his wife for four years do what she liked with him, as she had done so many times before. They were so deeply attuned to one another that they could convey their desire across a crowded room, and now, as they touched and stroked and kissed each other, there was no need for words. Madeleine's head was moving from side to side on the pillow now as she took his hand, so strong and familiar, and placed it between her legs. Carl knew her body as well as he knew his own, and he loved to bring her to a peak of excitement. She moved beneath him now, giving little cries of joy, taking him inside her body and holding him there as if she could never have enough of him, and he thrilled as he heard her cry, "Give yourself to me, Carl . . . give all of yourself to me." A moment later, with a mixture of frenzied sweetness and wrenching surrender, they climaxed together with a loving closeness, something they'd done a thousand times before, yet found as potent as the first time they'd ever made love.

Patti Ziffren sat at the Georgian desk in the library of her duplex in the Beresford on Central Park West, looking at the message her butler had taken the previous evening when she and her husband, Sam, had been out at a benefit dinner. She didn't like it. Not at all. Warning bells were ringing in her head and she had a mind to call her brother, Jake, to warn him that his ex-father-in-law, Sir George Dalrymple, was trying to contact Madeleine. But what good would that do? Jake would only get into a panic, and God knew he'd suffered enough over Camilla all those years ago, without having the whole thing brought up again. But what, Patti wondered darkly, did Sir George want with Madeleine now?

"Mallaby," she called to her English butler, who'd been with them for the past fifteen years.

Mallaby came into the room on silent feet and stood at a respectful distance. He was of stocky build, with a cherubic face and white hair, and even after all these years, he was slightly in awe of his employer.

"This message you've left on my bureau, Mallaby!" said Patti without preamble. She knew all the servants were intim-

idated by her and she did nothing to dispel their fears. Only
Sam, Jake, and of course Madeleine were allowed to see what
lay beneath the crusty surface.

"Yes, madam?"

"When Sir George Dalrymple called from England last night,
you didn't, I hope, give him Mrs. Delaney's number?"

Mallaby looked shocked and even pained. "I would never
do such a thing, madam! I merely suggested you might be
able to call him back today."

"Ummmmm." Patti Ziffren nodded thoughtfully. "Thank
you. That's all for the moment."

"Thank you, madam."

Tall, angular, and in her middle fifties, Patti Ziffren rose
from the desk as soon as she was alone again and lit a cigarette.
Her shoulders looked hunched in her perfectly cut Ungaro suit
and her hands shook slightly. The sunshine streaming in
through the long windows passed unnoticed by her. God
damn old George Dalrymple, she thought with mounting agitation. He must be kept away from her niece at all costs. But
suppose he'd gotten her number from someone else? It
wouldn't be difficult. Madeleine and Carl were a well-known
and popular couple . . . perhaps he'd already found out they
lived on Fifth Avenue.

Patti stubbed out her cigarette angrily and immediately lit
another, her mind filled with feelings of protectiveness toward
her niece. Madeleine had been a small child when Jake returned to New York from England, begging Patti to help him
bring her up. Patti remembered him saying: "I've hired an
English nanny for her, but it isn't the same as having a mother;
I need you, Patti. Someone has to try to take Camilla's place."
And of course, because she cared so much for her brother,
Patti had agreed. In a way, Madeleine came along like a late
godsend, because Patti was unable to have children of her
own.

They took to each other at once, the rich socialite with the
scratchy manner and the pretty little girl who was everyone's
friend. Patti was determined about one thing, though: Madeleine must not be spoiled or allowed to fall into the "poor-
little-rich-girl" trap. She must be encouraged to have lots of
friends, learn different sports, and be a general "all-rounder."
The first indication that she might become an artist was when

Patti found a drawing book full of sketches of their friends, lively bold drawings that were instantly recognizable, often unflattering, but very definitely the work of someone gifted.

"Look at these," Patti said to Jake one evening when he was dining with her and Sam. "The child's brilliant! You must see to it that she has the best art teachers."

Jake smiled. If Madeleine had hopped around the room on one foot, Patti would have said there was another Anna Pavlova in the family. He flipped through the sketchpad, frowned, and then looked through it a second time.

"They are remarkably clever," he said in a surprised voice. "Perhaps you're right. Maybe she ought to have special tuition."

"She must go to the Art Students' League when she's old enough, and then you must send her to the Conservatoire in Paris!" Patti said. She picked up the pad and it fell open at a drawing Madeleine had done of her. "Humph!" she snorted, regarding the thin bony face and piercing eyes her niece had given her. "If you ask me, Jake, she's too talented for her own good!"

Jake laughed outright. Madeleine's drawing of her aunt was accurate and deeply observant, even to the frown lines and birdlike way Patti held her head. But it was also faintly cruel. "Perhaps she'll be a caricaturist!" he joked.

Patti looked him straight in the eye. "Or a very good judge of character," she corrected him.

Now, all these years later, Madeleine was a portrait painter of great talent, admired by those who were not afraid to see themselves as they really were. This exhibition at the Midas Gallery would, she hoped, set the seal on Madeleine's success.

Patti lit another cigarette and, deep in thought, wandered around the library, touching things but not really seeing them, smoking absently, her thoughts miles away. Then she came to a decision. She wouldn't tell Jake what she was doing because it would only worry him. Seating herself at the desk again, she reached for the message pad and started dialing Sir George's telephone number in England.

At nine o'clock the next morning, Madeleine left their apartment on Fifth Avenue and Seventy-fifth street and took a cab to her studio on Wooster Street in SoHo. When she'd turned twenty-one, her father had bought her a studio at the top of one of the old buildings in the artists' district there. Even if she and Carl had been out late, she still left the apartment at the same time. The mornings were the best time to paint as far as she was concerned, when the light was good and inspiration flowed freely. Today she wanted to put the finishing touches to the portrait of Dustin Hoffman she was including in her exhibition.

As soon as she entered, the familiar and evocative smell of linseed oil and turpentine assailed her, sharpening her desire to work. The cozy clutter of the studio gave her confidence too; this was her little kingdom, where she could do exactly as she liked and where she could express herself in her painting. Jars filled with brushes, bottles of turpentine, tubes of paint, and boxes of charcoal lay scattered on various tabletops alongside fragments of sculpture she collected as a hobby. A jumble of canvases stood propped around, and a sofa covered with black velvet dominated the haphazard arrangement of chairs and stools and portable platforms. Above, four skylights in the roof hung like viewless windows, save for the clouds that floated overhead in a constant moving show.

Madeleine locked the door for security and then climbed the spiral stairs to the gallery at the far end. Here stood her hi-fi system, flanked by shelves of discs and tapes. A moment later the swelling chords of Rachmaninoff's Piano Concerto in C-sharp Minor filled the studio and she felt a wave of happiness wash over her that was almost as sensuous as Carl's lovemaking had been the previous night. Here, in this setting that she had created exclusively for her own use, she could reach every part of herself without inhibition, without reserve. She could tap the very source of her talent and ply her skill to her heart's content.

Walking swiftly down the steps again, she felt a heady intoxication from just being there. Perching on a high stool, she looked around at all her canvases, savoring the moment. It wasn't always like this. On days when a painting wasn't going well, the sheer frustration amounted to silent raging misery. The likenesses of her sitters mocked her from the walls, saying: *Your talent was at its peak the day you painted me! Look what a mess you're making today! You can't paint at all! You're a fraud!* And the voices in her head would go on and on, as great gulfs of self-doubting enveloped her. White with anguish, her dark eyes tortured, Madeleine would seize a palette knife and scrape away what she had just painted, obliterating her mistakes before even she could bear witness to them for longer than a moment, and all the time the voice in her head was asking: *Can I no longer do today what I could do yesterday? Has my talent gone . . . escaped . . . and left me as ham-fisted as a child with his first box of paints?* And then she would work feverishly, desperate to recapture the easy flow that came when she felt inspired. She would work until her neck and shoulders felt as if they could no longer support the weight of her head, and her face would grow tense and drawn. Bit by bit, through sheer determination and concentration on her part, the painting would begin to come right and take on a lifelike quality of its own. And only then would she relax and dare to leave the studio at night, but without a backward glance. The monster of uncertainty and lost confidence had been slain for today, but a second glance might show him still lurking, and she dared not risk it. Once home, Carl would soothe and comfort her with his tenderness and understanding, giving her encouragement, making the failures less painful.

Today it was different. Madeleine's mood was light as the sun shone in bold squares on the studio floor, and the canvases, framed and ready to go to the Midas Gallery, looked brilliantly lifelike. The chords of Rachmaninoff's music filled the studio with joy, and as she sat there she breathed the air of a summer's day. She could positively taste the sweetness of success, and although she felt a thrill at the thought of her forthcoming exhibition, she also felt awestruck at her own audacity. It had been her father's idea.

"Madeleine," Jake had said when she and Carl had dined with him one night, "you've got to get better known. How are you going to get commissions if no one knows you're a portrait painter? You must hold an exhibition, and you've got to get yourself a gimmick."

After a lot of thought, Madeleine had worked out a gimmick, although it went against her artistic nature; but then, her father was a businessman, and so was Carl, and she knew that if she wanted to become well-known, she must adopt a more pragmatic approach to her art and follow their suggestions.

She reached for her palette and started to mix the colors with a sure and confident eye. Tubes of paint lay before her in a riot of shades: lemon cadmium yellow and dark madder lake; viridian and raw sienna and Prussian blue. The very names were like poetry to her ears, suggestive of mysterious and exotic places. What crimson lake of fire was "dark madder"? What brilliant sky of blue hung over Prussia? And didn't "raw sienna" conjure up the sandy beaches of the Italian coast?

Lost in a dream world of colors and fantasy, Madeleine worked hard at the background of her painting of Dustin Hoffman, reveling in the fact that she had caught the essence of the actor himself and not the characters he'd played, for which he was so famous. Absorbed in her work, she did not notice the time passing, and at first she did not even hear the telephone ringing. At last she picked it up and answered it. There was a transatlantic click and then she heard a familiar English voice.

"Maddy? Is that you? Are you working? Oh, I'm not disturbing you, am I?" The clear fluting tones, overlaid with a bubbling enthusiasm, brought a smile to Madeleine's face.

"Jessica! How good to hear from you. How are you?"

"*Terribly* well, sweetie. I'm ringing about the party you're giving to launch your exhibition."

"You are coming over for it, aren't you?"

"Wild horses wouldn't keep me away, Maddy!"

"So, what's your problem?" Madeleine had known Jessica McCann since they'd both been eight years old, and even if they didn't see each other very often, they were always able to pick up where they'd left off, as if they'd seen each other the previous day. They'd originally met in London, at Lady Eden's school, when Jake had been reposted to the Lombard Street branch of the Central Manhattan Bank in 1970. He'd brought Madeleine and her nanny to England with him, and for two years they'd lived in an apartment in Albany, Piccadilly.

"I'm not going to be able to get to New York until the actual day of your opening. I'll still be in good time, but isn't it maddening?" Jessica was explaining.

"Is the new job working out all right?" Madeleine could just imagine her friend sitting behind her desk in the sales department of the Royal Westminster Hotel, gesticulating as she talked, gold bangles rattling, long red nails slicing through the air.

"It's fabulous!" breathed Jessica fervently. "It's hard work but I've never enjoyed myself so much in my life! I have so much *responsibility*, Maddy! You've no idea! And this hotel is the last word in glamour; you must tell all your friends to stay here when they come to London. So will it be all right if I land at two in the afternoon, on the fourteenth? It will still give me time to tart myself up before the party begins, won't it?"

"Only about four hours!" replied Madeleine, who'd been wondering when she was going to get a word in edgewise. Conversations with Jessica, as she sparkled and fizzed, were inclined to be a bit one-sided if you weren't careful. "I'll send a car to meet you at Kennedy. You can stay with us for a few days, can't you?"

"Of course! This is going to be my summer hols! Listen, is there anything you'd like me to bring over? Some little trifle that even the mega-rich Shearmans and Delaneys can't buy in New York?"

Madeleine dissolved into laughter. "Daddy loves sausages from Harrods," she replied, "and . . . oh!" She paused, struck by a sudden thought.

"Oh, no, Maddy! Please! Not oak-smoked kippers again," Jessica begged. "You know the last time I stuffed my hand luggage full of kippers, the *whole* of first class stank like a fishing trawler! I got some very funny looks!"

"I wasn't going to say kippers," Madeleine protested, still remembering the vision of Jessica coming through the arrivals gate from Europe, her nose wrinkled comically, her Gucci hand luggage held at arm's length. "I was going to ask you to look up my grandfather."

"What d'you mean? In *Who's Who*? Surely you know who he is, Maddy?" Her tone was bantering.

"Of course I know *who* he is, but I want to find out what he's like." Briefly she related her strange conversation of the night before with Sir George.

Jessica's voice was vibrant with interest. "My *dear*, how fascinating! What can he want to tell you? Listen, I'm sure I can find out a bit about the family. I know all the gossip columnists very well, and as the Dalrymples would rank as aristocracy, they're bound to have your grandfather on their files. Leave it to me."

"Do be careful," Madeleine warned. "I wouldn't want him to think I was checking up on him."

"Don't worry. I'll make the most discreet inquiries. I say, d'you suppose your mother was involved in some scandal? That would explain why Jake never told you anything. I say, how terribly thrilling!" Jessica was agog with interest.

On the corner of Wall Street and Broad Street, the Central Manhattan Bank rose in a towering block of black glass and steel, reflecting the morning sunshine in dazzling starbursts of light. Carl, getting out of the chauffeur-driven limousine, entered through the bullet-proof glass-and-steel doors, glad to be off the street, where the air was clammy with humidity. The main banking area was modern and impressive, with floors and walls and counters of black and white marble, a steel-and-lucite escalator gliding smoothly up to the second-floor gallery and an artfully arranged jungle of plants that climbed as tall as trees, illuminated by concealed spotlights. Behind the theatrical facade it was a different matter. Layer upon layer of people, one above the other, filled the glass building from street level to the twenty-eighth floor, the tellers at the bottom of the heap, above them kitchens and staff dining rooms, which opened for breakfast at eight o'clock in the morning and closed in the late afternoon, and above them floor after floor of offices filled with workers sitting at desks under harsh strip lighting, while fax and telex machines hummed out their messages from all over the world, telephones rang with maddening persistence, word processors and computers clicked and bleeped, and an atmosphere of high pressure prevailed. With transactions totaling billions of dollars a day, this great throbbing financial animal stood high among its rivals, digesting with relish the quick, the clever, and the diligent, while mercilessly spitting out those who could not take the pace.

Carl thrived in the atmosphere. From his office, which led off the gallery on the third floor, where all the executive offices were, with the exception of Jake Shearman, who had the penthouse suite, Carl had a good view of the stock exchange and the jostling and bustling on the sidewalk below. The knowl-

edge that millions of dollars were changing hands by the minute gave him an almost physical thrill. It was a special
fascination he shared with Jake. To them money was a living
thing, a plant that would grow and sprout and bear fruit;
dividends, equity, loans, and interest rates formed a major
part of their conversation and filled their thoughts most of the
time. To them money was not a collection of dry figures flashed
up on some computer, soulless and dead; it was symbols and
signs, meaningful and rewarding, telling a story or painting a
picture all its own.

Carl flipped swiftly through his mail and glanced at the first
of the day's authorizations for foreign transactions. Dollars
being transferred to Tokyo, Kuwait, Hong Kong, and Great
Britain. Pounds sterling, yen, deutsche marks, and francs coming in from other parts of the world; a fascinating, ever-
exchanging flow of money, giving a picture of trade figures
and currency regulations, deficits and profits.

Pressing his intercom, Carl buzzed for his assistant in the
adjoining office. "Averil, can we get started on this lot, please?
I'm meeting with Mr. Shearman and some clients before lunch,
so it's going to be a short morning."

"Certainly, Mr. Delaney." Averil was the perfect assistant.
She'd been with Carl for six years and she knew his ways,
down to how hot he liked his coffee. Regretfully, Carl remembered she'd be leaving soon. She wanted to move out of New
York, and nothing he'd said had been able to change her mind.
She'd had enough of city life and she wanted out. A moment
later she appeared, a pleasant-faced young woman with pre-
maturely gray hair and a gentle smile. She took a seat opposite
Carl's desk.

"Right, Mr. Delaney. I'm ready," she said.

An hour later Carl had finished and was striding to the
elevator at the other end of the curving gallery that overlooked
the bank lobby below. Stepping into its black leather interior,
he pressed the penthouse button.

Carl and Jake were close; although devoted to his own father, who was an architect in Philadelphia, he felt he had much
more in common with Jake. He was like the son Jake had
never had, and to that he owed much of his success, not, as
the gossips insisted, because he had married Madeleine. In

fact, he hadn't met her until he'd been nearly two years with the Central Manhattan Bank and, as he always laughingly reminded Jake, it had been another four years before he'd been allowed near her. "Well, hell, she's only eighteen and not finished with her education," Jake was apt to protest, although from the beginning he'd secretly hoped Carl would one day become his son-in-law.

Carl had waited, watching Madeleine from afar, growing up into a young woman of great beauty and charm, watching her progress as a painter, longing for the time when Jake would give his permission for them to see each other. In the meantime he took out lots of girls, but, looking back, it seemed that he was merely treading water, keeping emotionally afloat while he waited for Madeleine. She was everything he'd ever desired in a woman. He felt it was worth waiting until he was nearly thirty to get married.

" 'Morning, Carl," Jake greeted him as he entered the president's office. Although his hair was now gray, the years had been kind to Jake, and if anything, he was more distinguished-looking than he'd been as a young man. His eyes, almost black like his daughter's, regarded Carl with affection, and his manner was one of bonhomie. "Have a good time last night?"

Carl started, thinking of their lovemaking after the call from England, when he and Madeleine had luxuriated in each other's bodies with a rapturous knowledge of each other's needs. "Last night?"

"Didn't you have tickets for *Phantom of the Opera*? Weren't you going with Robert and Joan Allord, and then having dinner at Le Cirque?"

"Oh . . . of course!" The later events of the night had made him forget. "Yes, it's a great show! We had a very good time and the Allords sent you their best wishes."

"Good." Jake smiled. Then the phone started ringing, and after Jake had taken the call, the clients who had come for a meeting were shown into his office. For the next hour Carl became absorbed in discussing the ramifications of a loan to a shipbuilding company in Scotland. Once or twice he looked at Jake, remembering that Madeleine had told him not to mention the call from Sir George Dalrymple, wondering why Jake always refused to discuss his late wife. As Carl reminded himself, it hadn't happened yesterday, but more than twenty years ago. Surely the past couldn't be as painful as all that— or wasn't it the pain Jake was trying to avoid?

At last the meeting came to an end and Carl hurried back to his office. He had twenty minutes to catch up on some of his work before he slipped down to the directors' dining room for lunch. Averil came through from her adjoining office as soon as he settled himself at his desk. She spoke eagerly.

"Personnel has just been on the line, Mr. Delaney, to say they think they've found a suitable replacement to take over from me at the end of the month."

Carl's handsome tanned face showed a flicker of ruefulness. "D'you really have to go, Averil?"

She smiled, flattered. "Yes, I really want to leave the area, Mr. Delaney. I've been planning to go for a long time, you know."

"So what's this new girl like?"

"I don't know her personally, but I've seen her around because she's been working here for two years in the computer department. You may have seen her—she's got bright red hair. She worked for Citibank before she joined us, and I believe she's very bright."

Carl sighed. He hated change, but this one was inevitable. "Interview her for me, will you, Averil? You know what I need: someone as much like you as possible."

Averil flushed, looking pleased. "Thank you, Mr. Delaney."

Averil was as good as her word. When Carl returned to the office at two-thirty, having lunched with the chairman of a large aviation company that was starting up in Mexico, she came into his office, closed the door behind her, and spoke in a whisper.

"My replacement is in my office right now, Mr. Delaney. I've had a long talk with her, and personally I think she'd do the job very well. Her qualifications are good and she seems on the ball."

Carl asked, "Is she efficient, d'you think? Quick, with a retentive memory? You know how it drives me crazy if people forget what I've told them." He knew he was tricky to work for, and demanding too. There'd been a fast turnover of personal assistants before Averil.

"I think you'll find she's up to it. Walter Tuffin, the head of the computer department, talks highly of her. She's ambitious, I think," Averil added in an even softer whisper, "and that's a good thing. She's dead keen to work for you, Mr. Delaney."

"And you're certain she can handle the pressure?"

Averil nodded positively. "I wouldn't say so if I didn't believe it."

Carl sighed wearily. A change in his working routine and the thought of teaching a new girl to do things to his liking filled him with dread.

"Okay," he said at last. "Show her in. By the way, what's her name?"

"Kimberley Cabot."

As she rode the subway from Fiftieth to Wall Street that morning, Kimberley Cabot hoped against hope that she'd landed the job as Carl Delaney's assistant. As soon as she'd found out that the dreary, dowdy Averil Fielden was leaving, she'd gone straight to the head of personnel, George Miller, and persuaded him to recommend her for the post. She'd also made sure her immediate boss, Walter Tuffin, gave her a good reference. It hadn't been difficult. Men always ended up doing what she wanted, and George and Walter were no exception. As if to prove the point to herself, she crossed her long shapely legs with a gentle rasp of nylon stockings as the train hurtled along between stations, and out of the corner of her eye she saw three men turn their heads to follow her movements. Kimberley chuckled inwardly. They were all the same, and she was certain Carl Delaney was just like the rest of them. She'd been watching him covertly for months now, whenever she got the chance—seeing him arrive in the morning, striding purposefully across the lobby, taking the elevator to the penthouse floor, entering the directors' dining room, a tall athletic figure, far better-looking than the average banker, with sexy blue eyes and an engaging smile. She wondered how susceptible he was and came to the conclusion that happily married or not, when it came to the point he'd be as easy to seduce as all the others.

All she needed now was the opportunity to work for him and then she could start putting her plan into action, the plan that had begun to formulate in her head long before she'd ever heard of Carl Delaney, long before she'd gone to work at the Central Manhattan Bank; a plan that had taken root secretly and furtively when she'd been twelve. Now, seventeen years later, she felt as if every dream and aspiration had led her, sometimes unwittingly and by chance, other times by deliberate and careful planning, to this moment when she could make it all happen for herself.

Kimberley had grown up in the Maspeth area of Queens, the youngest of six children born to Ollie Cabot, a truck driver, and his Italian wife, Lucia, who worked in the local delicatessen and believed everything the pope said. Crammed with her family into a two-family brown-and-white clapboard house, just like all the others in the area, Kimberley didn't even see a skyscraper for the first twelve years of her life. Warehouses as ugly as aircraft hangars, yards full of trucks, acres of tombstones in the Mount Olive Cemetery, and rows of small shops like Pat's Liquor Store, Carvel ice cream, and the Lady Finesse Hairdresser for Guys and Gals made up the scenery as Kimberley looked restlessly around in search of excitement. She attended the Martin Luther High School, but made few friends. The others seemed contented to spend the rest of their lives within the confines of this area, where the most exciting thing that could happen to you would be to go into a jazzed-up Dunkin Donuts. Kimberley knew from an early age that she must get away. There *had* to be life beyond the narrow streets edged with dusty oak and maple trees and the little Holy Cross Roman Catholic Church her mother dragged her to. There must be somewhere better to live than in the tiny houses that were home to two families and which did not even boast a backyard. Not for her a life of domestic slavery like her mother's, with six children and a husband who drank most of his wage packet away.

It was on her twelfth birthday that she begged her eldest brother, Tom, who was twenty, to take her into Manhattan. Tom had a job as a porter in the Plaza Hotel and his tales of what life was like in the center of the city had long enthralled her. When they came up from the subway, she gasped, looking around her, eyes wide with amazement, little noises of wonder coming from her open lips. She felt quite dizzy. The towering buildings made her feel she was walking at the bottom of some gigantic ravine, and she clutched Tom's hand. The traffic whirled past, a police siren yelped on its blower up a side street, and the crowds jostled on the sidewalk, bumping into them. Kimberley couldn't have been more astonished if she had been dumped on Mars; television was forbidden at home and she'd never been allowed to go to the movies. Everything around her was new, and, breathless, she hung on to Tom as he led her through the dusk toward Times Square.

The sight that met her eyes dazzled her and made her heart pound. All around her the brilliant blaze of electric bulbs flashed and radiated an incandescent gaudy trail of light on every available rising surface. Glowing advertising signs leapt, glittering, up the sides of buildings and around doors and awnings: a scintillating thread of blue and gold and silver, shot with red, lacing the giant buildings together and weaving themselves into intricate patterns. Flickering, swooping, dancing, skimming; the myriads of multicolored lights had a life of their own, as they flashed and sparkled in a never-ending display. Kimberley had never seen so many lights, hadn't known so much light existed in the world. But there they were, a vivid spectacle of bright spangles illuminating the night, suggesting to Kimberley promised riches and glamour in signs that read MARLBORO, CHEVROLET, and ASTOR HOTEL.

At that moment she knew that when she was grown up she wanted to be rich, to have so much money that she'd never grow old and ugly like her mother, to have so much money that she'd be able to have anything she wanted. Anything on earth. Standing mesmerized as the traffic screeched and honked around her, she gazed at those advertisements as if hypnotized, but where others saw rows of dirty electric light bulbs, Kimberley saw chains of diamonds.

From that moment on, she was motivated to one end only: to be rich and successful. Always bright at school, she now threw herself into studying, and at sixteen, having gotten excellent grades, she left to get a job. Her mother wanted her to continue living at home and take a job in a shop, and for a while Kimberley agreed, but only because the hours allowed her to take a shorthand and typing course at the local community center. As soon as she'd qualified, she was off, living in a small downtown room, but at least it was in Manhattan. Best of all, the first job she got was as a clerk at Citibank. She'd learned the ropes fast, had been sent to a computer-programming course, and given a raise. Four years later she'd joined the prestigious and famous Central Manhattan Bank.

"I'll check if Mr. Delaney is ready to see you," Averil Fielden said.

"Thanks." Kimberley's heart was pounding as she looked around the office that she hoped was soon going to be hers. So much depended on the next few minutes. If she got this job, she'd have it made, because Carl Delaney was the key to her future. Thankful she'd decided to wear a smart but demure pale blue linen suit that enhanced her rich auburn hair and creamy skin and that showed off her figure in a subtle and classy way, Kimberley felt a deep sense of excitement. Working hard at school, slogging away at evening classes, sleeping with rich men who bought her expensive clothes and taught her how to behave in public, had given her a patina of polish over the years and helped prepare her for this moment. She didn't believe in God, not after the way her mom had gone on about the sins of the flesh, but she did remember hearing a saying: "God helps those who help themselves." Suddenly she smiled, a smile so radiant and confident that when Averil Fielden came back and said Mr. Delaney was ready to see her, Kimberley sailed into his office, knowing her moment had finally come.

Jessica grabbed the phone: "You've delivered the wrong glasses!" she stormed to the supplier on the other end of the line. "We ordered *fluted* champagne glasses, not tulip-shaped ones! How could you make a mistake like that?" Angrily she doodled on the pad in front of her with her red felt-tipped pen. "I'm not interested in your excuses. We ordered sixty dozen fluted glasses, and if they're not here by this afternoon, you can cancel the order *and* all future orders from us!" Slamming down the phone, she looked up at her colleague, Dick Fowler, with whom she shared an office.

"Damned suppliers!" she exploded, her petite frame quivering with indignation. "They're all the same. When will they ever get anything right? Remember those blankets we ordered from Hobbs? We ordered rose pink and they delivered thirty dozen in a revolting shade of peach."

Dick nodded sympathetically. "I think the worst time was

when they delivered two hundred chairs for the restaurant, all covered in the wrong fabric."

Jessica covered her face with her hands in mock despair, her lazy topknot of blond hair threatening to come undone and cascade to her shoulders. "That," she said succinctly, "is what is known as a major cock-up!"

Dick roared with laughter. Jessica, with her exaggerated way of talking and her expressive mobile little face, always amused him, and when she'd joined the Royal Westminster Hotel eighteen months before as assistant sales manager, he'd realized there'd never be a dull moment.

Jessica McCann was the eldest daughter of a retired general in the British Army, and her family had hoped she'd make a suitable marriage and settle down by the time she was twenty-two or -three; but at twenty-five she was still pursuing her career with unabated enthusiasm. Tiny, slim, with long blond hair and round blue eyes that at times made her look doll-like, she had boundless energy and vivacity, and everyone in the hotel adored her. She could soothe ruffled guests in seconds, placating them by dealing with whatever problems had upset them. Then she would pacify them further by murmuring there would be no charge for dinner in the restaurant that night . . . and there would be flowers and champagne, and fruit and chocolates in their rooms. Her genuine words of apology if anything went wrong were so sincere that most guests, especially if they were English, ended up apologizing for having complained in the first place. It was a magic formula and that was why she had been transferred from a sister hotel, the Wentworth in Park Lane, where she'd been the sales and public-relations officer, to the Royal Westminster. She'd also been promoted to being an assistant sales manager with Dick Fowler. Their boss, the director of sales, was Humphrey Peterson, a hard-faced man with ruthless ambition, who saw himself as an eventual general manager, but Jessica and Dick had such a good working relationship that they never allowed Humphrey Peterson, with his endless demands, to get under their skin. Bursts of laughter could be heard coming from their office from time to time, as Jessica did a wicked imitation of a guest or one of the staff, or Dick regaled her with stories of things that had happened before her time.

The Golding Group owned thirty-five hotels worldwide, but the Royal Westminster was their flagship and Jessica had been thrilled at the prospect of working in it. For sheer splendor and elegance it rivaled their other five-star hotels in Hong Kong, Venice, and Washington, all of which appeared in listings of the most magnificent hotels in the world.

Straddling the west side of Hyde Park Corner, and opposite the lush greenness of Hyde Park, the Royal Westminster was an imposing building, porticoed and pillared and resembling a miniature Buckingham Palace. It had been built in 1775 as the town house of the first Duke of Hastings, and was also opposite the first Duke of Wellington's former home, Apsley House, which was now a museum. Over the years, extensions had been added at the rear, where formerly stabling had provided shelter for the duke's horses and carriages. Invisible from the street, six penthouse suites had also been added, so that the hotel now had two hundred and fifty rooms, each decorated and furnished by famous designers who specialized in refurbishing stately homes. But the essence of a small palace still existed, and the Golding Group's original investment, which had turned the building from a hospital into a hotel, had paid dividends. The reported annual turnover was in the region of eighteen million pounds.

Jessica's main task at the moment was to get bookings for the principal banqueting rooms; she wanted people to hold their parties at the Royal Westminster and she knew that the way to attract them was to sell the idea that it would be like giving a party in a private house. With a large ballroom, a big reception room, and several anterooms, there was scope to give anything from an exclusive dinner party for ten to a ball for five hundred.

Jessica glanced at her page of engagements for the day and let out a yelp. "God! A Mr. and Mrs. Cyril Watkins are due any minute. They want to hold their daughter's wedding reception here, so I'm going to show them the Armitage Room." Rearranging her hair, she applied some pale lipstick and ran her hands over her neat navy-blue suit. "Then I've got to give luncheon to the managing director of CAC Computers—I'm hoping they'll hold their three-day conference here next April."

The telephone rang and she grabbed it, glancing at her watch as she did so. She ought to be down in the lobby now to meet the Watkinses. She hoped this call wouldn't take long.

"Oh, Andrew! Hi!" she said, her voice instantly dropping into an easy intimacy. Andrew Seymour had been her lover for three years and they shared his flat in Chelsea. He was a real-estate agent, and both their families took it for granted that in time they would marry.

"We're expected for dinner at eight o'clock," Andrew was saying, "and Mother wants us to wear evening dress."

"Eight o'clock!" She was horrified. "How can I possibly be changed and at their place by eight o'clock? I've got a wine tasting here this evening and I shan't get away until nearly eight. Why didn't you tell me this morning? Oh, damn, if I'd known, I'd have brought a long dress with me, and changed here!"

"Can't you leave early, for once?" Andrew sounded cross and slightly disapproving. "It *is* my parents' thirtieth wedding anniversary, you know! They've planned this dinner party for months now."

"I know." Jessica tried hard to make her voice sound patient, but it always irritated her when Andrew presumed she could drop everything in order to fit in with his plans. "And I've bought a decanter for them as a present from us both. It's just that I'm supposed to be hosting this party here, and I've only got a short day dress to change into."

"Why can't you go home beforehand to change . . . and then you could take a taxi from the hotel straight to Wilton Crescent. We could meet there," he persisted. She could sense he was getting upset, and if that happened the evening would be ruined for both of them.

"I'll work out something, babe," she said, forcing herself to sound calm and cheerful. "In any case, let's meet at your parents' house at eight o'clock. Okay? I must go now because I've got people waiting for me, but I'll see you tonight!"

"Okay." He sounded grudging.

Jessica dropped the phone back into its cradle, picked up her clipboard, and dashed out of the office and along the corridor to the elevator. If there was one thing she hated, it was being late.

She spotted them at once, standing uneasily by the reception desk: Mr. and Mrs. Cyril Watkins, down for the day from their home near Watford, a middle-aged working-class couple who had succeeded in making a lot of money from their building company. Switching on her charming professional smile, Jessica stepped forward to meet them, a tiny dainty figure, impeccably dressed, discreetly jeweled, her small intelligent face glowing with vitality. She greeted them as if they were the only people she really wanted to see that day.

"Good morning. How nice of you to come. May I get you some coffee . . . or a glass of champagne?"

They declined, shaking their heads and mumbling something about its not being long since they'd had breakfast.

"Then allow me to take you up to the banqueting rooms," Jessica said smoothly, as if she understood absolutely how they felt. Up on the second floor, she led them down wide plush, thickly carpeted corridors, crystal chandeliers blazing with many lights, silk-covered walls hung with eighteenth-century engravings of London and the occasional gilt console table laden with exotic flowers. The Watkinses followed her in awestruck silence, glancing furtively from time to time at the ornate plaster ceilings and rich hangings. It was all a long way from their modest semidetached.

Jessica flung open double doors at the end of the corridor. "This is the Armitage Room," she announced brightly, leading them into a large baroque room decorated and embellished with white plaster garlands depicting fruit and flowers against a sky-blue background. "Bars are set up at either end for a reception, but of course we have waiters circulating with trays of drinks as well." Then she walked over to the large high windows that overlooked Hyde Park. "When we do a wedding, we usually place the cake here, with pedestals of flowers on either side. It's a good position for everyone to see what is happening, and to have good pictures taken." Jessica exuded such enthusiasm, and it appeared to be so genuine, that she might have been planning her own wedding. Mr. and Mrs. Watkins were deeply impressed by the magnificence of the room and reassured by the understanding manner of this helpful young woman. Anxious to do their best for their only daughter, who was marrying a real gentleman, they were determined to make a splash on the great day.

"What d'you think, Mother?" muttered Mr. Watkins, who,

having made a pile, had so far only indulged himself by buying a BMW.

Mrs. Watkins looked at him and pressed her cream-cotton-gloved fingertips together. "It'll do very nicely," she replied quietly.

"You did say you would be expecting approximately a hundred and fifty guests, didn't you?" Jessica asked, checking the notes on her clipboard.

"That's right," Mr. Watkins said.

"Then this room is perfect for you. Of course, if you were expecting *more* guests I'd have suggested the ballroom . . . ?" She paused, dangling the temptation of something even bigger and grander before their eyes. They hesitated, Mrs. Watkins with her head cocked on one side as if she were listening for her husband to say something. Mr. Watkins studied the carpet, wondering whom they could ask to fill a bigger room.

"Why don't I show it to you anyway, as you're here," Jessica suggested, like a hostess wishing to put her best rooms at her guests' disposal. "It's only down the corridor." Setting off at a brisk walk, her high-heeled shoes sinking into the deep-piled carpet, she led them to a door on the other side of the hallway.

"This room is a copy of the corridor of mirrors in the Palace of Versailles," she said, as if to prepare them for a shock. When she opened the tall carved doors, they stood and gazed in wonder at what seemed like acres of shining polished floor, bound and held together by endless panels of antique mirrors, mottled and speckled with age, their images reflected a hundred times over, as in a darkened glass. Heavy dull-gold draperies festooned and sashed the great windows, through which a watery morning sun struggled fitfully.

"I think the other room would do nicely," Mr. Watkins commented hollowly.

Jessica nodded. "I agree. This room is better at night, when all the chandeliers are lit. Right, now, would you care to fix up all the details, seeing as you're here? It would save you having to come to London again." Gently and persuasively she asked what they'd like, while skillfully suggesting what she thought was suitable.

Thirty minutes later she was back in her office, looking pleased with herself. "Well, that's all fixed!" she said trium-

phantly to Dick. "They've booked the Armitage, plus ten cases
of vintage Bollinger, six hundred assorted canapés, eight arrangements of pink and white flowers on pedestals, a three-
tiered wedding cake—thank God I managed to dissuade them
from having a sugar bride and groom on the top!—and they
want three suites of rooms for the night before. And d'you
know something?"

Dick looked at her questioningly, amused by her
enthusiasm.

"They didn't even *blink* when I gave them the quote!" Jessica
retorted.

He laughed. "People never do. Once they've made up their
minds to give a big bash, it's all or nothing, regardless of cost!
By the way, your lunch appointment is going to be late. Here's
the message for you."

"Great!" Jessica glanced at the scribbled note. "That will just
give me time to dash home to pick up an evening dress for
tonight. Andrew and his family have got an attack of delusions
of grandeur and I've got to get myself tarted up for this dinner
they're giving."

At that moment the phone on her desk buzzed.

"Hello? Oh, Peter!" She gave a squeal of delight. Peter Thorn
was one of the *Evening Standard*'s leading journalists, and over
the years he'd become a good friend, always mentioning the
hotel if he could, and sometimes filling her in about celebrated
arrivals. "How are you? When are you coming to lunch with
me again?"

His voice was deep and rich, always on the brink of a laugh.
"Is it true Madonna's expected to stay next week . . . for her
concert at the Albert Hall?"

"God, I don't know!" she cried, aghast. "We haven't heard
anything. Have you checked with Anne Butler in the PR
department?"

"She's denying everything, but she always does, and your
reservation department says they've no one of that name expected! All very prim and proper they were, and singularly
unhelpful. Can you check it out for me, Jessica?"

"Of course I will, but you know I'll have to deny it officially,
even if it is true; that's hotel policy. Our guests have to have
their privacy protected."

"I know, I know." Peter sounded resigned. "Bloody stupid, isn't it? Her management in Los Angeles have announced she'll be at the Royal Westminster for four nights—"

"That's typical! They *want* the place swarming with the paparazzi and ten thousand fans, because it's good for her image," Jessica cut in, "but our other guests are going to *hate* it! Oh, Christ, I hope it isn't true! Security will go mad, and we don't need that sort of razzmatazz."

"You will keep me posted, though?"

"Yes, I will, Peter. Listen, I've just remembered something. If I help you on this, will you do a little favor for me?"

"Sure. What is it?"

"Do you know anything about the Dalrymple family? A friend of mine wants to find out about them. They come from Devon."

"Dalrymple." Peter paused, deep in thought. "The name rings a bell, but I can't place it."

"Sir George Dalrymple. He had a daughter called Camilla, who died over twenty years ago. She was married to an American called Jake Shearman—"

A long piercing whistle came out of the telephone receiver, startling Jessica. "Yes, I know who you mean," said Peter dryly. "Why does your friend want to know about them?"

Jessica hesitated, surprised by his reaction. "Well, she . . . she was just interested in the family," she said lamely.

"Take my advice, tell her to steer clear. There were some very nasty goings-on at the time. I was a cub reporter and I wrote a piece about it. It would be over twenty years ago now. Advise her to have nothing to do with them." For once he sounded serious, the incipient laughter gone from his voice.

"What sort of things?" demanded Jessica. "Peter, you must tell me. It's too intriguing for words!"

"It's too long a story to tell you now. Invite me to that lunch you promised me and I'll give you all the gory details. And you'll keep me posted on the Madonna situation?" It was obvious he wasn't going to be drawn any further.

"Yes, I will. Now, when are you free? Let's set up a date."

The rest of the day passed in a whirl of meetings and phone calls, including an irate customer who insisted she'd been charged for eight cases of champagne instead of six at a reception she'd held recently, and it wasn't until five o'clock that Jessica realized she hadn't been home to collect a long dress for the evening.

"Hold the fort for me, will you, Dick?" she begged. "I'll be as quick as I can, but I *must* go home and change. You don't mind, do you?" she added cajolingly. Dick smiled. Few could resist Jessica's natural and earnest manner, so evocative of a little girl in its candid yet sharp sweetness.

"Run along! I know how hard you have to work to look beautiful!" Dick teased.

"You . . . !" Jessica pretended to look insulted. "I'll have you know I was paid a compliment on my looks by the general manager last week!"

Dick smirked. "He must have wanted you to do some overtime!"

Jessica arrived at Andrew's parents' house shortly after eight that evening, to find the whole family already drinking champagne and congratulating Mr. and Mrs. Seymour.

"I'm sorry I couldn't get here before, darling," Jessica whispered to Andrew as soon as she had greeted his parents. "Do I look all right? I practically had to change in the taxi!" With one hand she dug a pin more firmly into her topknot.

Andrew slid his hand around her waist, so tiny he could have encircled it with both hands. "You look fantastic, Jessie. Here, have a drink! You could probably do with one."

Jessica rolled her eyes as he handed her a glass of champagne. "I feel pissed already!" she hissed under her breath. "You forget I've come from a wine tasting."

"But you're not supposed to *drink* at a wine tasting," he protested, laughing, "you're supposed to—"

"I know! I know!" She waggled her head from side to side. "You're supposed to swill it round your mouth and then spit it out into a bucket! Honestly, Andrew, I could never do that!" Dazzling blue eyes, half-joking, half-serious, looked up into his, and he felt his heart melt.

Andrew Seymour, twenty-eight, the son of a well-to-do company director, was a keep-fit fanatic and it showed in his physique. Well-built and muscular, he towered over the diminutive Jessica, exuding an aura of good health, his dark brown hair shining, his gray eyes clear and untroubled. Three evenings at a local fitness club every week, and games of squash and tennis whenever he could fit them in, were all part of his schedule. He was also ambitious, and since he'd formed Jason and Seymour Partnership, Estate Agents, with his best friend, Sandy Jason, he'd flung himself into his work, anxious to be part of the property boom that was sweeping Britain and so far showed no signs of slowing down. And at the center of his world of working hard and playing hard was Jessica, with whom he shared his life. One of these days he was going to ask her to marry him, although she already knew, of course, that that was what would happen. They had an understanding, as his mother told her friends. Neither was in any great hurry to marry, both being wrapped up in their careers, both happy with the way things were.

Tonight, though, Andrew felt sentimental, seeing his mother and father celebrate thirty years together. It seemed such a marvelous recommendation for legalizing living together, and his eyes grew quite misty as he saw them toasting each other and holding hands.

His voice was gruff. "We'll be like that . . . after thirty years, won't we, Jess?"

Jessica nodded, her eyes soft and her face gentle. "Of course we will," she said, and then, because she was Jessica, always ready with a flip remark or a witty barb, she added, "and won't we be *boring!*"

Andrew tried to hide the fact that he winced at her words, knowing that she didn't mean to be taken seriously, that it was just her way. He forced a laugh. "We'll be so rich by then, who'll care?" he quipped back.

Jessica laughed too. "Goodee! Talking of rich, I go to stay with Madeleine in four days' time. You hadn't forgotten, had you?"

"No, I hadn't forgotten."

"I wish you could come too," she said impulsively. "I'm going to miss you, sweetheart. Can't you get away? Sandy can manage for a few days without you."

"There are too many deals to put together at the moment," he replied, shaking his head. "We're negotiating on three houses, all million-pound properties, and I must be here to make sure everything goes through all right."

Jessica nodded, understanding, and rested her blond head

against the black shoulder of his tuxedo. "That's big business," she murmured. "So, shall I give your love to Broadway?"

Andrew hugged her closer. "You do that."

"And let's not stay too late at this party," she added with a little suggestive look.

Already Andrew felt himself getting aroused. "You bet we won't," he whispered back.

2

THE CORNER of Spring Street and West Broadway, in SoHo, was jammed with limousines, drawing up at the Midas Gallery, spilling onto the sidewalk the elite of New York society as they arrived in force to see Madeleine Delaney's first one-woman show. Photographers' bulbs flashed, a reporter from *Women's Wear Daily* jotted down who was wearing whose designs, and columnists noted who was escorting whom, seeing too often the familiar faces of well-known walkers clinging to the arms of middle-aged bejeweled women. Inside the large white room, a throng already jostled each other in their eagerness to see and be seen, and, almost as an afterthought, to look at the portraits of *Faces of the Famous.* In an atmosphere heavy with perfume mingling with the scent of towering arrangements of white lilac, waiters skimmed around as if they had no feet, carrying trays of champagne and platters of tiny grilled lobster claws.

Madeleine stood near the entrance, her deep amethyst silk dress throwing into relief her cloud of black hair and heart-shaped face as she smilingly greeted everyone and tried to hide her nervousness. Every now and again she glanced over at Carl, seeking reassurance, and he smiled back, giving her an almost imperceptible wink. Her father, Jake, was hovering supportively also, helping to introduce the galaxy of guests, who included senators and financiers, film stars, and the more prestigious members of the press. The babble of voices rose in a fever of banal greetings, but then a few people stopped to look up at the spotlit paintings that covered the walls, and gradually the tenor of the party changed. The portraits, brutally raw in their candor, impossible to ignore any longer, struck the assembled company with their electrifying quality.

"She's got real talent!" people murmured in voices that implied they'd known all along she was going to make it, and were gratified to be proved right. This, they observed, was no conventional exhibition of portraits, destined for some drawing room or boardroom. *Faces of the Famous*, depicting men only, was a collection of vibrant studies, sharply perceptive, destroying at a stroke the carefully planned public images these famous men had taken such pains to cultivate.

"I wonder where she trained?" asked a socialite, who loved "discovering" people. She opened her glossy catalog for the first time and skimmed Madeleine's biography. "Ummm. Educated at the Brearley School and then she seems to have studied at the Art Students' League before going on to Paris. I see she's won quite a few prizes; she's even had paintings in some major exhibitions. Well, I think she's quite a find. I wonder if she does women."

Her companion, reading over her shoulder, noted that a leading critic had said her portraits contained "great energy and vibrance."

"Quite a find!" repeated the woman. "I must invite her to my next party. Of course, I've known her father for years."

"I like her style," commented her companion, "even if her perception is rather cruel. Look at this one of Nixon!"

They examined the portrait, executed in colors tinged with blue, thickly applied with a palette knife, depicting with brutal clarity the inner doubts and foibles, the fears and quirks, of the man.

"Brilliant, quite brilliant."

Jake's idea of having a gimmick had worked. No one had ever given an exhibition of celebrated men, and from the commercial point of view it was a stroke of genius.

Madeleine had aimed for impact, and now, as she moved around the crowded room, she knew she had succeeded. People were eyeing her with a new respect; she was not just the beautiful daughter of a rich and famous banker who belonged to one of New York's oldest families; she was a sparkling and forceful talent in her own right, and for a moment she wondered if she deserved this much praise. She had worked hard and studied for years with a single-minded dedication, but what made her paintings special was the strange chemistry that occurred between herself and her subjects, which had nothing to do with technique or knowledge. It was as if she could read their thoughts and pick up their secret emotions, as her brush or palette knife, heavy-laden with rich burnt umber or indigo blue or carmine, jabbed at the canvas, pinning the underlying characteristics down swiftly, as a rare butterfly is pinned to a board. She had the talent; Jake had merely marketed it, with his flair for business.

Her thoughts were interrupted at that moment by the sight of a petite figure with flowing blond hair and a swish of black taffeta, hurtling through the packed gallery toward her.

"Jessica!" she cried in delight.

Jessica flung herself enthusiastically at Madeleine. "Oh, Maddy! This is all so exciting I could die! My dear, I never thought I'd get here! The flight was delayed—would you believe it?—and when I got to your apartment, you'd already left, of course . . . and . . . Oh, my God! This is so *thrilling!*"

Jessica spoke breathlessly, her exquisite little face with its English complexion flushed with excitement. Her blue eyes blazed. "Oh, Maddy! I'm so proud of you!"

Laughing, Madeleine hugged her. "I can't tell you how good it is to see you. I'd never have forgiven you if you hadn't come."

At that moment Jake Shearman joined them and Jessica flung herself at him too. "How's my favorite man?" she demanded, looking up into his handsome lined face. He was her ideal of the older man, and she frequently told him so. "Why do you never age at all?" she asked. "I can't tell you how jealous my father is of you."

Smiling indulgently, he stooped to kiss her on the cheek. "Welcome back to New York, my dear. I'm so glad you could make it; we were counting on your being here tonight. How was the flight? Did you have a good journey?"

Jessica pulled a comical face. "If you call seven hours in a plane full of screaming children, plastic food, and the worst movie I've ever seen, having a good flight, then I suppose I did. But I'm *dying* for a drink!"

Jake gave a signal, and through the chattering throng a waiter appeared.

Jessica sipped her ice-cold champagne, then let out a satisfied sigh. "Oh, bliss! Now, Maddy, I want you to show me everything. I can't wait to see what you've been up to."

Linking arms, Madeleine began steering her friend through

the crowds, pointing out the various paintings. "What do you think?" she whispered.

Jessica eyed her with genuine amazement. "For God's sake, how did you get all these famous men to sit for you in the first place? I've never seen such a collection of celebrities."

"That's what everyone wants to know." Madeleine's dark eyes twinkled with amusement. "I'll let you in on a secret. I relied on their vanity. I wrote each of them a personal letter explaining I was holding a major New York exhibition, entitled *Faces of the Famous*, and that it wouldn't be complete without a study of him. I even offered to give him the painting afterward if he liked it."

"And they bought it?" Jessica, who knew a bit about psychology from working for years in the hotel business, was impressed. Flattery—like remembering someone's name or particular favorite drink—always worked.

Madeleine nodded. "I did something else too, which was rather naughty, but it got results."

"You offered them your body at the same time!"

They both dissolved into laughter.

"They should be so lucky!" Madeleine chuckled. "I told, say, Frank Sinatra that Paul Newman had already agreed to be painted, and I told Edward Koch that George Bush had said yes. Jessica, it worked like a charm! In the end, ninety percent of them agreed because they thought all the others had accepted. I think they felt they couldn't afford not to be included!"

"You clever girl," Jessica said approvingly. Then she pranced forward again, diminutive in spite of her spike heels, exclaiming at every picture as it blazed down from the white walls, glowing under the impact of the spotlights.

"I don't believe it, Maddy! I do not believe what I'm seeing! You've got John McEnroe and Boris Becker—God, isn't he dishy!—Calvin Klein . . . now, there's a handsome man for you . . . and isn't that John Fairchild, who produces *Women's Wear Daily*? I thought so! And Bob Hope, Douglas Fairbanks . . . Maddy, who *haven't* you got?"

"Prince Charles," Madeleine replied instantly. "I'd give anything to do his portrait."

Jessica nodded knowingly. "You can't play tactics with the British royal family, but I think I know of a way you might be able to paint him when you get more established in Europe."

"You mean you know the password to get through the portals of Buckingham Palace? I bet it's impossible."

"Not really. You'd have to get a regiment or a college or perhaps a city livery company to commission you to do his portrait to hang in their building. Then they approach the private secretary at the palace, requesting that the prince sit for an artist of their choice. Actually, all the royal family get painted several times a year for this purpose, so you might stand a good chance," she added thoughtfully.

"Jessica, you're brilliant. And I'd get to go to Buckingham Palace for the sittings?" Madeleine clasped her hands together, thrilled at the thought.

"Or Kensington Palace, depending on which royal you're painting. You'd also be allowed to go as often as you liked to paint their clothes or robes on a dummy to save them posing for hours and hours," Jessica said knowledgeably.

Madeleine grabbed her arm, her face intent. "Jessica, if you could help me fix it up one day, I'd be indebted to you for life."

Jessica laughed, her blue eyes sparkling. "I'll see what I can do. In the meantime, can I have some more champagne? I'm parched!"

"Of course. Oh, I'm so glad you could come over for this party. We go back a long way, don't we?" They had moved to a corner of the gallery that was less crowded.

"How many years is it?" Jessica asked, savoring her drink. "We met at school in 1970 so that's . . . oh, Lord, I'm getting old!" she wailed.

"Seventeen years ago."

Jessica cast her eyes to heaven. "I remember hating you at first and thinking you must be spoilt something rotten because your father was so rich and you always wore such expensive clothes."

"And I remember thinking you were terribly stuck-up with your English accent and snobbish ways."

Their laughter was disturbed by Jake coming up to them, his face the color of dirty wax, his dark eyes gleaming with anxiety. Beside him Carl was hovering nervously, a deep flush staining his cheeks.

"Madeleine, I must talk to you," Jake said in a strained voice.

She looked up, startled, and then turned questioningly to Carl. "What's the matter? What's wrong?"

"I'm sorry, sweetheart." Carl shook his head, embarrassed. "I forgot you hadn't mentioned it to your father. It just sort of slipped out."

Suddenly she understood. Carl must have told Jake she was planning to visit her grandfather in England.

"I hear you've heard from George Dalrymple," Jake said sternly.

Jessica gave a sharp intake of breath and was about to say something, but changed her mind.

"Yes, I have," Madeleine said calmly. "What's wrong with that? He is my grandfather, after all, and he's asked me to visit him. I'd have told you myself, sooner or later, but I've been so busy with this exhibition."

"You're not to go, Madeleine. I absolutely forbid it." Jake's jaw muscle was twitching and she'd never seen him look so upset. Carl shuffled from one foot to the other, his face still red.

"Let's discuss this later," Madeleine whispered, aware now that people around them had stopped talking and were curious to know what was going on. Jessica eased herself out of the group on the pretext of having another look at the paintings, but Carl put his arm around Madeleine's waist.

"She's an adult now, Jake," he began heatedly. "If she wants to go and see some ancient relative, I don't see why—"

"You don't know anything about it," Jake cut in harshly. "Promise me you'll have nothing to do with George Dalrymple, Madeleine."

Madeleine began to feel angry. It was stupid of Carl to have mentioned it to Jake in the first place, without her knowledge, but at twenty-five she was capable of making her own decisions, and she'd already made up her mind no matter what her father said.

"What the hell's the matter?" She spoke so quietly that only Jake and Carl could hear, but her tone was one of suppressed fury. "Why don't you want me to go? Why have you always refused to talk about anything to do with my mother?"

Jake looked at her for a long moment, and the expression in his eyes was unfathomable. "I have my reasons," he said at last. "Please have nothing to do with your grandfather. If you do, you'll be getting into something you won't be able to handle!"

Carl left early for the bank the next morning, leaving Madeleine and Jessica having breakfast in the Oriental-style dining room of their apartment, which overlooked Central Park. Madeleine had chosen to live on this part of Fifth Avenue, up in the Seventies, because of its view; if she didn't get to see the fresh naturalness of trees and grass every day, she felt claustrophobic. Now, through the large window she watched the landscape in all its summer glory. A variety of greens, so subtle in shade she wondered if it would be possible to capture the tones in oil paints, fluttered and danced in the morning sunshine.

"Look!" she said suddenly, putting down her coffee cup and pointing.

Jessica, who was suffering from a hangover, peered, bleary-eyed. "What? I don't see anything."

"On the wall . . . running along the top now . . . see, a beautiful squirrel! They're so tame, you know, they'll eat out of your hand." Madeleine smiled with delight, watching the squirrel hop onto the branch of a tree and then climb vertically up the trunk. "Oh, it all looks so beautiful! I might go for a walk later. If it wasn't for Central Park, I'd never survive here."

"Dear God," Jessica murmured weakly, "I never expected a city girl like you to go all bucolic on me! It's cold and muddy down there, Maddy, and you'll ruin your smart shoes in fifteen seconds flat! What's brought on this sudden love of the countryside? I'd have thought your scene would be the Trump Tower atrium."

Madeleine shook her head, laughing. "It must be old age setting in. Carl and I go to Oyster Bay every moment we can to get away from the city."

"Well," Jessica rejoined darkly, "you'll never find me living in the country. I say, Maddy, have you got any aspirin?"

Madeleine rose. "Yes, of course. You must be jet-lagged after your flight yesterday."

"Jet-lagged be damned! I've got a good old-fashioned hangover, so there's no need to be so polite!"

A moment later Madeleine returned. She handed Jessica a couple of pills. "Here you are. Listen, Jessica, I meant to ask you last night, but it was so late when we got back from the exhibition. What were you going to say when my father mentioned my grandfather? You gave a sort of gasp, but then you wandered off."

"Oh, yes!" Jessica downed the aspirin with a gulp of coffee and leaned back in her chair. "I talked to a friend of mine, a journalist called Peter Thorn, who's on the *Evening Standard*. He seems to know all about your family."

"Well?" Madeleine looked at her sharply. "What did he say? Does he know anything about my mother and how she died?"

"I think he probably does. There seems to have been some sort of scandal a long time ago. He said he covered the case. It was rather peculiar, actually. He said you should steer clear of the family—"

Madeleine sat bolt upright, her expression alarmed. "You didn't tell him about me, did you? I told you to be discreet—"

Jessica cut in indignantly. "Of course I didn't mention you. I said a friend of mine wanted to find out about the Dalrymples, that's all. He implied there were some nasty goings-on about the time your mother died."

"What did he actually say? What sort of goings-on?" Madeleine felt uneasy, as if a cold hand had clutched her stomach.

"I'm sorry, Maddy, I don't know. Peter and I were supposed to meet for lunch last Friday, but he called off at the last minute because he had to cover a story about Ford Motors being involved in an industrial strike. He'd promised to give me all the 'gory details,' as he put it. But don't worry—I'll get him to tell me everything when I get back."

"Jake is trying to keep something from me, isn't he? Oh, I wish he wouldn't treat me as if I were still a child. Whatever he says, I'm going to Devon to see my grandfather."

Jessica poured herself some more orange juice from a large crystal jug. "When?"

Madeleine shrugged, her slim shoulders showing through the fine cotton of her robe. "As soon as possible, I suppose. Now that the exhibition has opened, the sooner I go and find out what it's all about, the better. At the moment, it's like having a great black cloud hanging over me."

"Why don't you fly with me when I return next Monday?" Jessica suggested.

Madeleine's face lit up. "What a good idea! I'll do that. I hate traveling alone, and I could spend a couple of nights at your hotel, couldn't I?"

"Why not!" Jessica clapped her hands together in delight. "I'll see if I can get you our Presidential Suite at a special rate."

"Thanks."

Jessica sprang to her feet, her hangover forgotten. "That's settled, then. Now, what are we going to do today?"

Madeleine stretched her arms above her head. "I know what I'm going to do. Take it easy after last night and have a walk in the park. I suppose there are no prizes for guessing what you want to do?" She regarded her friend with knowing affection.

"None at all! You don't think I've flown thousands of miles just to see *you*, do you, my dear?" Jessica bantered. "I'm off to Bergdorf Goodman, Bloomingdale's, Saks"—she ticked her fingers as she spoke—"Bonwit Teller, Tiffany's . . . and I *must* pop into Hammacher Schlemmer to see what new gadgets they've got." She gave an excited wriggle at the thought of being let loose with her credit cards.

"Rather you than me," Madeleine laughed. "How about meeting for lunch, then? One o'clock at Elaine's?"

"You're on!"

At twenty past one, Jake Shearman hurried into the Four Seasons, where he was meeting his sister, Patti, whom he'd summoned that morning to have lunch with him. He found her already seated at his usual table, spikily elegant in a Calvin Klein suit with ropes of pearls wound around her thin neck and the customary cigarette smoldering between her fingers.

She knew why Jake had summoned her to this meeting, but she wanted to find out how much he knew before she spoke about the matter herself. She ordered a very dry martini and tapped her elegantly shod foot under the table, irritated at being kept waiting.

At last Jake appeared, flurried and rushed-looking, and slightly out of breath. He kissed her briefly on her rouged cheek.

"I'm sorry I'm late, Patti. I got held up, and then the traffic was terrible."

"You're out of condition," she remarked disapprovingly. Her voice, gravelly from too much smoking, sounded hoarser than ever.

"You're a fine one to talk, with your cigarettes!" protested Jake. "Filthy habit! Shall we order, or do you want another drink?"

There was complete understanding between brother and sister. They could sound so rude to each other that people, overhearing them, flinched and thought they were fighting. In reality, a staunch affection existed that went back over fifty years, and anyone who tried to come between them faced the combined wrath of both Patti and Jake, who were fiercely loyal to each other.

"Of course I want another drink," Patti said, stubbing out her cigarette and immediately lighting another. She continued without preamble: "I hear you had a fight with Madeleine after I'd left the exhibition last night!"

Jake shot her a wary look. "Who did you hear that from?" If Patti had heard, then most of New York must know.

She shrugged. "Things get around. So what's it all about?"

"Let's order first."

"Okay. I'll have the crab mornay and a green salad—plus that second martini you promised me."

"All right, all right! You sound like an alcoholic." Jake gave the order to the waiter hovering with servility at his elbow. "And we'll also have a bottle of the Châteauneuf du Pape Blanc, 1985, please," he added.

"Come on, Jake," Patti said impatiently. "I want to know why you got me here today."

Jake sighed deeply. "Madeleine's been contacted by George Dalrymple and he's asked her to go to visit him in England. I've forbidden her, of course, but I don't think she's going to pay any attention to me."

Patti looked thoughtful. "So he got through to her, did he?" she said, almost to herself.

"What d'you mean?" demanded Jake.

"He called me about ten days ago. I was out, but Mallaby took a message. George wanted to know where he could get hold of Madeleine."

"And Mallaby told him?"

Patti snorted. "Don't be such a fool! Of course Mallaby didn't tell him, and neither did I. I called him back to say I wouldn't help, but he refused to speak to me, the arrogant old devil! It struck me then that he'd probably gotten Madeleine's number from someone else, but she hasn't said anything, has she? From what I heard, I gather that it was Carl who told you."

Jake nodded. "It was. Apparently he wasn't supposed to, and Maddy and I had a little fracas about it last night. That's when I told her she mustn't have anything to do with her grandfather."

Patti spoke with deep sarcasm. "And of course she listened to you! Really, Jake, you can't come the heavy-handed father now. She's nearly twenty-six. That's not the way to stop her going."

"Then what is? I could tell Carl the whole story, although it's the last thing I want to do, and get him to prevent her going to England. But I don't think it would do any good."

"And you'd be making a big mistake, involving Carl. Why should he bear the burden of a secret he must never tell his wife? It would put a terrible strain on their marriage." Patti dragged deeply on her Marlboro. "Come to think of it, I wonder if George Dalrymple *will* tell Madeleine anything about her mother. We may be getting in a panic over nothing. He may just want to see his only grandchild before it's too late!"

"But why now?" demanded Jake, running a hand over the lower half of his face as if checking that he'd shaved that morning. "Why, suddenly, after over twenty years, does he get in contact with her now?"

"Look at it this way, Jake. George was pretty ashamed of the whole business himself, at the time. After all, Camilla was his only child. Why should he want to stir it all up again?"

Jake sighed heavily. "I suppose you're right." The very thought of Camilla sent a chill through him, and he felt bitter that after all these years, during which he'd done his damnedest to protect Madeleine, the memory of what had happened had risen to haunt him again. At the time, he'd been driven to the brink of fear and despair by what had happened, and his only consolation had been that his daughter had been too young to understand.

Patti, aware that he was recalling the details of the catastrophe, reached across the table and put her bony and bejeweled hand on his arm. "Stop thinking about it, Jake," she commanded angrily, but her eyes were soft with sympathy. "It won't do any good. George must be very old now, and I think he just wants to see Madeleine. You can't blame him for that."

Jake remained unconvinced. "Suppose she makes inquiries in Shercombe? It's only a small village—there are bound to be people who remember."

"So what's the worst that could happen?" Patti puffed furiously on her cigarette. "If Madeleine finds out anything, she'll just have to learn to live with it, like you have. You can't protect her forever." As she recalled the past her voice became harsh.

Jake remained silent, brooding.

"You should have married again, of course," his sister continued.

"You know I couldn't."

Patti sighed gustily, and her eyes were like burning dark holes in her narrow, lived-in face. "You could have found a way," she insisted. "It was wrong of you to let the past deprive you of happiness."

"I've had a lot of girlfriends," he protested, but he knew that what Patti said was true. What had happened to Camilla had been tragic and horrifying and it had affected him deeply. But need it have prevented his finding happiness with someone else?

"I suppose you wouldn't talk to Madeleine?" he suggested tentatively. "Tell her not to go to England?"

"Do you know nothing about psychology? Forbidden fruit and all that? Really, Jake, for a grown man in your position, I sometimes think you're exceedingly foolish. Now, are you going to finish your wine or not?" she added tartly. "There's no point in your bringing me to the Four Seasons for lunch if you're going to stare into space all the time."

Jake's face reluctantly broke into a smile. "Good old Patti! It always does me good to see you."

"So I should think!" she snapped back, but as she looked at her brother her expression was kind.

Every morning a team of clerks in the Central Manhattan Bank sorted through the mail, dividing and subdividing the hundreds of letters before dispatching them to the various departments: checking accounts, savings accounts, overseas and loan accounts, requests for new checkbooks and deposit slips, and letters of general inquiry or acknowledgment—all had to be placed in the relevant baskets to be taken to the various floors of the building. Then there were bankers' drafts to be dealt with, and payments authorized by big companies, and several hundred foreign transactions.

By nine o'clock, one of the clerks had deposited on Carl's desk all the documents authorizing international money transfers for the day. There was usually a thick stack of these "yellow forms," as they were referred to, although in fact they were the color of cantaloupes. Closely printed, with boxed sections which had to be filled in by the client, stating how much money he wished transferred, they represented the millions of dollars of "flying capital," as the bank called it, from America to all parts of the world.

Carl was so experienced that a glance told him who was remitting money, into which overseas bank it was to be paid, and who would be responsible for paying the transfer charges, agent's charges, and the amount being transferred. Accuracy, diligence in checking details, judgment in gauging whether the client had sufficient funds to cover the transfer, and complete discretion were required, and Carl was pleased to find that his new assistant, Kimberley Cabot, possessed these qualities. She was quick and sharp and had an instant conceptual understanding of a situation when he explained it to her. As soon as Carl had gone through the authorizations each morning, he called Kimberley into his office and went through each transfer with her. Sometimes the Central Manhattan Bank was used as a clearinghouse, but mostly transfers were requested by companies that already had checking accounts with them. It was her job to feed each form into a special piece of equipment that would record all the details on blue film, so that at any time in the future, if there were any queries, each form could be examined on the microfiche screen.

"I also want you to make sure these companies have sufficient funds in their credit accounts to allow for the amounts they're asking to be transferred," Carl had explained when Kimberley first started.

"And when I've okayed them, then I bring the forms back to you?" she asked.

Carl nodded. "That's correct. Then I pass them on to the

president, Mr. Shearman, or one of the vice-presidents if he's not around, and the money is then transferred by computer to wherever it is supposed to go."

Kimberley smiled confidently. "Yes, I know. When I worked in the computer department, I knew the girl responsible for putting these transfers through. Only the president and the vice-presidents have the code for foreign transfers, don't they." She said it more as a matter of fact than as a question.

Carl was impressed. The girl had obviously been keeping her eyes open, learning all she could. People like her went far in the world of banking. "That's correct," he affirmed. "Even I can't put through transfers."

"Well, it's good that it's a secure system," she remarked placidly.

Carl pulled the stack of forms toward him and started scrutinizing each one swiftly and knowledgeably. When he'd checked half a dozen and entered them on the computer on his desk, he handed them to Kimberley, who took them back to her office next door and started the process of copying each form on microfilm. They worked steadily, the rhythm broken by the occasional telephone call, mostly from clients asking whether the dollar was likely to rise or fall in the next twenty-four hours.

"I haven't polished my crystal ball lately!" Carl always replied with a laugh, it being forbidden for anyone in banking to give an opinion or prophecy on such matters, in case a client held the bank responsible, at a later date, if he lost money on a foreign transaction. "Your guess is as good as mine," he continued. "If I knew the answer, I'd be a rich man!" It was his standard way of dealing with these queries, and at least the customer felt mollified by the charming way he'd been handled, even if he didn't get the answer he wanted.

Kimberley came back into his office for another batch of forms. "When I've done these, I'll go check on the credit of the ones that bank here."

"Okay. Thanks." Carl didn't even look up. All that mattered was that Kimberley seemed to be doing what she was told, and wasn't wasting his time asking stupid questions like some of the girls who'd worked for him in the past. With the exception of Averil, of course, but then, she'd been one in a million. Young women like her were rare.

At two o'clock Kimberley came into his office again. "Can I get you a sandwich or something, Mr. Delaney? You really should eat something, and it would be no trouble."

Carl looked up from his desk, where the work was still piled high as a result of the noon mail delivery, and saw Kimberley looking at him with sympathetic concern. Her pale gray eyes looked anxious, and for the first time Carl was struck by her beautiful coloring. Her rich titian hair framed the pale gold skin of her face, and the green dress she wore enhanced her prettiness.

"I'm okay," he replied absently.

"I can easily go to the canteen and get you something if you haven't time to go to the directors' dining room today," she offered.

The thought of corned beef on rye made Carl's mouth water suddenly. "Well, are you sure? What about yourself?"

Kimberley smiled and her luminous gray eyes sparkled. "I'm fine. I'm on a diet anyway. I'll be back in a few minutes."

"Thank you." Carl watched her walk out of the office and noted she had very good legs. Vaguely, as he returned to his work, he wondered if she was going steady.

In a few minutes she was back, clutching his lunch as if she'd brought him an exciting present.

"I bought you an apple as well," she said, handing him the rosy fruit. "You know what they say?"

"An apple a day . . . ?" he suggested.

Her voice was low and soft. "An apple for the teacher." Then she gave a little laugh and hurried back to her own office. Carl could have sworn she was blushing.

"I'll be gone only a week, Carl," Madeleine protested as she fastened her suitcase. "Nothing much can happen in a week."

"I wish you weren't going at all." Carl's tone was grim. "Your father had another go at me yesterday. He made it sound positively dangerous, your going to see your grandfather. I wish to God I could get away and go with you."

Madeleine came over to where he sat on the side of the bed and put her arms around his neck. "I wish you could too, more than anything, but what can go wrong? Dad's making this whole thing sound like I'm going behind the Iron Curtain! I'm only going to spend a couple of nights with my grandfather. I'll be with Jessica for the first day and the last couple of days, in London, so there's not much risk of my coming to any harm. I'll phone you if there's a problem, darling."

Carl held her close. "Why can't your father come clean with me and tell me what's wrong?"

Madeleine replied slowly and thoughtfully. "I have a feeling that Dad's never gotten over my mother's death, and since he hasn't spoken to my grandfather for twenty years, maybe he blames him. Until I find out how my mother died, we can't begin to unravel the mystery, but it's become obvious that Dad and Grandfather hate each other and that my mother is the bone of contention between them." She pulled away from him and looked urgently into his face. "I've got to go, Carl. Once and for all, I've got to find out why the subject of my mother is taboo, and this is my only chance."

Carl kissed her tenderly. "I know, sweetheart. I do understand. What worries me is that this Sir George Dalrymple sounds like a nut case. Suppose he tries to keep you at Milton Manor?"

"You mean . . . like a prisoner?" Madeleine threw back her head and laughed. "Don't be ridiculous, sweetheart! This is the twentieth century. Milton Manor may have been built in the times of Queen Elizabeth I, but times have changed since then. You're letting your imagination run away with you, and you're supposed to be the hardheaded businessman. I'm the artistic one that's supposed to have a head full of fantasies, you know!"

Carl joined in her laughter, and the tension between them broke. But he still added: "You promise to phone me if anything is wrong?"

"I promise," she replied gaily, but as she boarded the jumbo jet that evening with Jessica at JFK, she couldn't help feeling a wave of nervous apprehension sweep over her. After all, her father was not a person given to unwonted hysteria, and yet his attitude to her flying to England bordered on panic.

3

THE FIERY dawn, blazing the sky with vivid streaks of red and orange, streamed through the port windows of the jumbo jet like a celestial furnace, startling Madeleine from a deep sleep. She glanced at her watch. Six-thirty. In an hour and a half they'd be landing at Heathrow. Peering out of the window, she could see the Irish Sea below, dazzling and sparkling like a lake of fire; then the plane tilted toward the east and the fire was suddenly extinguished and the waters were dark and mysterious again. Within moments the tumultuous sunrise had faded to a misty gold and the passengers were beginning to stir. Madeleine stretched her legs and looked at Jessica, who was sitting curled up under a blanket beside her. A stewardess came bustling down the aisle looking amazingly fresh, and the compartment was filled with the pungent aroma of coffee.

"Hi," Jessica said, opening her eyes and blinking. "What time is it?"

"Half-past six. You slept well," Madeleine replied.

"It was the second dry martini before takeoff that did it. God, I look a mess!" Jessica regarded herself in her compact mirror. "I can't wait to get home and have a bath. Anyway, I'm thankful I don't have to go to work today. We can laze around and Andrew can take us out to dinner tonight."

"Yes. I'm glad I don't have to go down to Devon until tomorrow. I wish Carl had been able to come, though," Madeleine added wistfully. "I always miss him when I have to go away to do a commission or something."

"That's the worst of being a working woman. In the hotel business there are times when I don't get to see Andrew for twenty-four hours. And there's nothing I can do about it. You at least have some choice about when you're going to paint

51

someone; I have to jump-to when I'm told! The trouble is, Andrew doesn't always understand the demands the hotel makes on me. It worries me sometimes," she added with a touch of anxiety in her voice.

"But you'll get married to him one day, won't you?" Madeleine asked. To her, marriage was the most wonderful thing in the world. She couldn't bear to think of life without Carl, and she longed for her friend to experience the same happiness.

Jessica replied positively. "I'm sure we will, but not just yet. I've got a long way to go in my career before I settle down. There are a lot of things I want to achieve first."

"Such as?" To Madeleine, Jessica had gotten about as far as a woman could get in the male-oriented hotel business.

"There's so much that is still a great challenge, that's what attracts me to the business. Of course, what I'd really like is to have my own hotel. Nothing enormous, you know, but very elegant and exclusive, with only fifty or sixty rooms and a superb dining room with a chef from Paris. And I'd like to do all the little things that you can never do in a big corporation." Jessica was fully awake now, her voice eager as she spoke.

Madeleine looked at her questioningly. "What sort of things?"

"Oh, personalized writing paper for each guest, a valet on hand night and day to look after their clothes, a fully stocked fridge in each room, and I mean fully stocked. Containers of fresh sliced lemons every day, bowls of olives, as well as nuts, a variety of Twining's best tea, to go with a kettle and fresh milk and nice crockery . . . Oh, Maddy, if I had my own hotel, I'd make staying there the most memorable thing that had ever happened to anybody. . . ." Her voice trailed away, aching with yearning. Then she sat bolt upright and turned to Madeleine. "In every bathroom I'd supply terry-toweling robes, and not just shampoos and bath oil, but moisturizers, toothpaste, nail-polish remover, hair spray, all beautifully packaged in the hotel colors. Most important of all, each guest would be able to control the temperature of his own room. There's nothing worse than being stuck in a too-hot or too-cold place and not be able to do anything about it."

Madeleine looked impressed. "You've certainly given it a lot of thought, but wouldn't the work be horrendous? I mean, in a hotel, you never stop, you don't even close on weekends like a big store. Surely it would be a killer?"

Jessica's voice was vehement. "Absolutely not. When you come to think of it, Maddy, the parallel to running a big hotel is running a big house. You've got all the same elements— cleaning, laundry, marketing, cooking, dealing with staff, and lots and lots of guests. I love it," she added unnecessarily.

"I can see you do!" Madeleine smiled at Jessica's determined expression.

"I don't suppose it'll ever happen, but it's a lovely dream." Jessica sighed, then suddenly leaned forward, peering across Madeleine to the landscape just visible below. "Look! We're over England! That's Cornwall and Devon, just down there."

Madeleine looked down on the patchwork of seemingly tiny fields, visible through the drifting clouds of morning mist.

"We'll be landing soon," Jessica commented brightly. "Just time for another cup of coffee." Madeleine's heart suddenly lurched as she looked at the countryside below. By tomorrow she would be down there among those lush green fields where her grandfather lived. And by tomorrow she'd know whatever it was he wanted to tell her.

The train roared into Okehampton station and with a squeal of grinding brakes screeched to a standstill. Stepping down onto the small country platform, Madeleine paused to look around and get her bearings. She had called Sir George from her suite at the Royal Westminster the previous evening and the butler had informed her that Jenkins, the gardener, would meet her at the station. Dust and grass pollen hung heavy in the afternoon air, and as she walked toward the exit sign she could feel the heat of the tarred platform through the fine leather of her shoes. There wasn't a sign of anyone, and she was just wondering whether there was a taxi service in this remote part of the world when she spotted an elderly man wearing a tweed jacket and cap, standing beside an ancient Rover in the deserted parking lot.

"Excuse me, are you Jenkins?" she asked shyly, going over to him.

He nodded, and without saying a word took her case and put it in the trunk of the car. Madeleine climbed into the back, acutely aware of his unfriendly attitude. His manner seemed almost hostile, and as he turned out of the station yard she caught a glimpse of his profile. His mouth was closed in a grim line.

Once outside Okehampton, the roads became narrow winding lanes, edged by hedgerows eight feet high, almost blotting out the sky at times as they drove through a green tunnel entwined with a profusion of wildflowers.

"I'd no idea it was so pretty here," Madeleine exclaimed spontaneously as she caught flashing glimpses of wild myrtle, golden oxlips, and hawthorn through the car windows.

Jenkins did not respond. Gripping the steering wheel fiercely as if unused to driving, he stared stolidly ahead, his back still and forbidding.

"Have you always lived here?" she asked in an effort to make conversation.

His voice was flat. "I was born 'ere."

Madeleine leaned forward with interest. "Really? And have you worked for a long time for Sir George?"

"Goin' on forty years."

It was on the tip of Madeleine's tongue to ask if he remembered her mother, but something stopped her. An instinctual feeling that told her she was treading on forbidden ground. The back of his thick red neck and the hunch of his shoulders expressed more enmity than if he had snubbed her. She angled herself to adjust her hair in the windshield mirror, and met his eyes watching her intently. Embarrassed, she drew back and looked out of the window. There had been something disturbing about his furtive stare.

At last the car slowed down, and taking a left turn, Jenkins turned into a driveway banked by hydrangeas, their pink and blue flowering heads drooping in the strong afternoon sunshine. At the end of the drive stood Milton Manor.

The house had been built of shimmering gray limestone in the middle of the sixteenth century, its facade topped by Dutch-style gables highly decorated with scrolls scalloped out in curving lines. Madeleine climbed out of the car and stood looking up at what had been her mother's home. The house itself was E-shaped, the central porch embellished above the door with the Dalrymple coat-of-arms carved in stone. High mullioned and transomed windows, their hundreds of tiny glass panes winking like jewels in the sun, gave the place a friendly and inviting look, and for a moment she laughed at herself for having been so apprehensive. Milton Manor was nothing more than a beautiful, typically English country house surrounded by elms and oaks, the garden brimming with summer flowers, the atmosphere redolent of peace.

At that moment an elderly butler opened the heavy brass-studded front door and took her case from Jenkins.

"Good afternoon, madam. Please come in. Sir George is waiting to see you in the library."

Madeleine followed him into the large hall, cool and dark by contrast, aware that it was furnished with heavy carved tables and chairs, the walls lined with old family portraits. Hunter, as she later came to realize he was called, led her down a corridor, tapped briefly at the door at the far end, and ushered her into the library.

The first thing that hit her was the intolerable heat of the room. As if she'd opened a furnace door, a great blast engulfed her, sucking out her breath and parching her skin. Then she noticed that a blazing log fire filled the grate, and in spite of the warm afternoon all the windows were tightly shut and the curtains half-drawn. Fighting a feeling of suffocation, she walked forward and saw an old man hunched in a chair before the fireplace.

"Hello, Grandfather," she said softly, taking his blue-veined hand and looking into his face.

Sir George was small and wizened, his pale skin stretched tightly over his angular skull, a few wisps of silver hair fringing his ears. His shrunken neck disappeared into a collar several sizes too big for him, and for a moment Madeleine was reminded of a dead goat she'd seen in the desert when she'd been a child, parched dry by the sun and left to rot. Only his eyes were alive; they were pale blue and glittered with a feverish intensity, as if an explosion was about to take place in his head. He seemed to be bursting with something he could no longer keep to himself.

"I came to see you as quickly as I could," she said, drawing up a chair.

"So you're Camilla's child." The voice was a rasping whisper.

"Yes, I'm Madeleine. I believe I was a baby when you last

saw me." She spoke gently, as if to a child, so as not to excite
him more. His blue eyes searched her face anxiously.

"You were three."

"Was I? I'm afraid I don't remember."

George Dalrymple turned his head to look at the fire, and
the reflection of the flames made his eyes look like blazing
sockets in his face. Madeleine shifted uncomfortably. There
was something terrible and fearful in those eyes, as if he had
looked into the pit of hell and could not forget what he'd seen.
The heat was stifling now, closing in around her, making her
sweat, and her hair stuck uncomfortably to the back of her
neck. Suddenly he spoke, his voice stronger but his sentences
disjointed.

"There are things you should have been told . . . things that
have been kept from you. I told your father it was wrong . . ."

A sense of unreality swept over Madeleine, almost making
her dizzy for a moment. The grating voice of her grandfather,
the cloying hothouse atmosphere of the room, the mystery
that surrounded Camilla; was it only a few days ago that she'd
been the center of a sophisticated New York crowd, living a
very normal, positive life? She felt as if she'd been swept back
in time to another age and another existence. For a split second
she almost felt as if she *was* her mother.

"What have you got to tell me, Grandfather?"

He turned sharply to look at her again, taking in her pale
chiseled features, her large dark eyes, and the cloud of black
hair that framed her face.

"You don't look like Camilla," he rasped accusingly. "You
take after your father."

"I know. All we Shearmans have dark coloring. What was
my mother like?"

George Dalrymple rubbed one of his bony knees as if it
hurt—a nervous, restless gesture, a sign of inner pain. Only
his eyes continued to work, seeing things Madeleine couldn't
fathom, lost in memories of long ago.

"She was beautiful." There was so much pain in his voice
that Madeleine almost winced. "She had blond hair . . . down
to her waist . . . blue eyes, a lovely nature . . . she was a
good girl."

"You must have loved her very much."

It was as if she hadn't spoken. "My only child," he continued. "I can remember the day she was born."

Madeleine felt a great rush of pity for this old man, and her
eyes brimmed. His loss had been her loss also; the only difference was, she would never know how much she had lost,
while he could gauge it day by day, in terms of loneliness and
grief.

Impulsively she laid her hand on his thin arm. "I wish we
had met before now," she said. "I don't know why my father
didn't want us to be friends."

"I do!" he cut in harshly. "He never understood. Camilla
meant no harm. She was led astray."

Madeleine's mind worked quickly, his words conjuring up
a series of pictures she'd never thought of before.

"You mean she had a lover?" she asked. "Did she run away
with him?" That would explain Jake's refusal to talk about her.

"No! No, no, nothing like that!" Sir George said vehemently.
Then he lapsed into silence once more while Madeleine sat
there sweltering in the incandescent heat that glowed from
the fireplace, wondering if she dared ask more questions.

At that moment Hunter came silently into the room, and
bending, spoke to Madeleine in a half-whisper.

"Sir George always takes his nap at this hour, madam. May
I show you to your room?"

Madeleine followed him up the red-carpeted oak staircase
and into a large cool chintzy room where summer fragrances
floated in through the open windows. A maid had already
unpacked for her.

"I hope you have everything you need," Hunter said. "Dinner is served at seven-thirty, madam. If there is anything you
require, the bell is over there." He indicated a press button
by the side of the Adam fireplace.

"I'd like some ice water," Madeleine said immediately.

As soon as the water had been brought to her room by a
young maid, Madeleine stripped off and ran a bath in the
adjoining old-fashioned bathroom. Half an hour later, cool and
refreshed and wrapped in a big toweling sheet, she went and
leaned out of the mullioned window overlooking the garden.
A haze of soft colors, interspersed with wide bands of lush
grass, lay spread like a woven tapestry from the terrace of the

house to the encircling shelter of elm, cypress, and beech trees. Roses bloomed in profusion, mingled with phlox, love-in-the-mist, and dark blue lobelia. She could see Jenkins, in his shirt-sleeves now, kneeling by a border of dahlias, tying the stems to strong sticks. Once again she felt lulled by the tranquillity of the place. What was it her father had said? . . . "You'll be getting into something you can't handle." What was there to handle? she asked herself. A broken old man, still grieving for the loss of his daughter? A family fight that had nothing to do with her?

After a while she went and lay on the comfortable bed, still feeling the effects of her night flight from New York. Within a few minutes she was fast asleep.

A small square table, laid for supper with crisp white napery and silver, had been placed in the middle of the library. Hunter, and the young maid Madeleine had seen earlier, hovered ready to serve.

Like a stiff old crab uncoiling itself shakily from a sand dune, Sir George creaked jerkily to his feet and tottered over to the table. Madeleine slipped into the seat opposite him, suddenly aware she was ravenous. She'd had only coffee for breakfast, and lunch had been a sandwich on the train. Hunter placed the first course in front of them—lobster laced with lemon mayonnaise on a bed of delicate lettuce leaves. He filled their glasses with a fine Ladoucette au Château du Nozet, which she noticed was a 1983 vintage. Sir George hardly ate anything. While Madeleine tucked in hungrily, he picked at his food with a fork and sipped a little wine, his hand so shaky he could barely hold the glass. From time to time she smiled encouragingly, but he did not seem even to notice her presence.

They had just begun the next course, tender pink lamb with succulent vegetables, when Sir George suddenly looked up at her, his blue eyes a ferment of passion.

"It was wrong of your father to try to protect you!" he burst out querulously.

Madeleine blinked, startled by the suddenness of his attack.

"I suppose he had his reasons," she said, abashed.

"Reasons?" The rasping voice rose. "Let me tell you . . ." He broke off as Hunter filled his glass with red wine. For a moment a bewildered look moved fleetingly across his face as he looked up at the butler, and then he shrank back like a tortoise retreating into its shell. "No matter," he mumbled. "I'll tell you later."

At last dinner was over, the table cleared away, and the servants withdrawn, leaving a tray of coffee and brandy on a side table. Sir George hobbled back to his chair by the fire, which had been stoked up again with a fresh supply of logs, and Madeleine took a chair near him, hoping the time had at last come when he would tell her everything.

"You were saying my father shouldn't have been so protective of me—what did you mean by that, Grandfather?"

"He should have told you everything." The old man was rubbing his knee again, back and forth, back and forth, his blue-veined hand moving jerkily. "I know he didn't, or you'd have come before. You don't know anything about my beautiful Camilla . . ." The words were like a lament, heavy with sorrow.

"Tell me. I want to know," she urged.

"She was led astray. It wasn't her fault. None of it was her fault. She didn't mean to harm anyone." The short sentences came rattling out, sharp and grating, in mounting agitation. "Jake wasn't fair . . . he blamed her . . . but she needed help."

In spite of the stifling heat in the room, something in his tone made Madeleine's flesh tingle, as if she'd been brushed by a draft of cold air. "What sort of help?"

"She was led astray," he repeated. His breath was rapid now, his hands shaking as if from ague, and his eyes were pools of agony. He seemed to be reaching some sort of crisis.

"I'm sure she meant no harm," Madeleine said soothingly. She felt scared now, not of what he might be about to tell her, but of his obvious distress. "If you'd rather talk about it tomorrow . . ." she began.

"No! You don't understand. Time is running out, and there will be no one, once I'm gone . . ." She noticed he was having difficulty in getting his words out now, and a dull red flush stained his cheeks.

"Your mother was involved in something terrible, but it wasn't her fault. You must realize that, even though it nearly led to your death."

Madeleine recoiled, her heart missing a beat. "Don't you mean *her* death?"

He looked at her sharply for a second and then he said: "I knew you hadn't been told. No, *your* death! And when I'm gone, there'll be no one to . . ." His voice faltered and his eyes glared into hers with a look of desperation. From his throat came a long-drawn gurgling rattle.

Madeleine sprang from her chair, appalled. "Grandfather!"

Sir George made another attempt to speak, opening his eyes wide, his expression beseeching. Then suddenly he shrank and withered before her, as if retreating from life. A moment later he collapsed.

Jessica awoke to find Andrew nuzzling her, his hands sliding up inside her nightdress, his tongue flicking at the edges of her ear. For a moment she lay still, pretending to be asleep, frantically trying to remember which day of the week it was. If it was Sunday . . . Then her eyes flew open and she gave a little gasp; it was Thursday, the day the Royal Westminster management was holding a Derby Day reception and luncheon for three hundred of their most valued clients.

"God, I've got to get up!" she exclaimed, wriggling out of Andrew's arms and jumping out of bed.

"Wait a minute!" He made a grab for her wrist, but she eluded him, running to the windows and pulling back the curtains. Their apartment overlooked the center gardens of Paultons Square, in Chelsea, and at the top end she could see the red buses going up and down the Kings Road. "Thank God it's a fine day—not that it matters, as we'll be indoors, but it does make it jollier!" Now she could be assured that the ladies would be wearing pretty summery dresses and perhaps extravagant hats.

"Surely you needn't go yet? It's only seven o'clock." Andrew had awakened with a rigid erection and was annoyed at having his advances spurned.

"Darling, I must!" Jessica slipped off her pale blue silk nightdress and hurled it onto the bed. "There's a hell of a lot to do before everyone arrives at noon. This is one of the biggest days in our calendar. Now, what shall I wear?" She stood poised, naked, winding her blond hair up into a loose topknot as she surveyed the contents of her closet. Andrew lay back, marveling at the perfection of her pale petite body; her breasts were rounded like small ripe melons, her flat stomach was taut and firm, and her smooth long limbs and tiny feet reminded him of illustrations in children's books of fairies and sprites. And then he was assailed by her smell, exciting and warm, emanating from her discarded nightdress. Suddenly he was angry. This wasn't the first time she had skipped away like a naughty child just when he felt overflowing with love and desire for her. Most mornings she was out of bed and dressed before he'd even come to his senses; most evenings she was too tired when she got back from work to do anything but eat a little supper and then fall asleep.

"This is bloody ridiculous!" he stormed, clambering out of bed. "What sort of relationship is this?"

Jessica turned to look at him, her face contrite.

"I'm sorry, sweetheart! It's just that today is terribly important. Couldn't we wait until tonight?"

"No, we bloody well couldn't!" Seizing her, he lifted her up and flung her back onto the bed.

"Andrew!" she cried, annoyed. "I don't want—"

He silenced her with a kiss, holding her so close to him she could hardly breathe. She could feel the heat of his body, strong and urgent, thrusting against her, and as strongly as she had resisted him a few minutes before, so now did she find herself ignited with a passion to match his.

"No . . ." she protested with a little moan. "No, please stop it! Please, Andrew. You know I can't resist it when you do that. Oh, God!" She gave a little sob. "It's not fair!" His hand was stroking her where she was most sensitive, his face buried in her neck. With velvety fingers and silky voice he continued to arouse her.

"You've no idea how much I love you," he whispered.

Jessica found herself sinking into a whirlpool of desire, and as hard as she tried to fight against it, because today of all days she couldn't be late, her resistance crumbled like a sand castle dissolving against a rising tide. She gave a final whimper, but then, as she felt his penis thrusting hotly inside her, she clung to him, crying his name, matching her rhythm to his, unable to control herself any longer. Her ears were filled with his urgent cries and her body was flooded with his juices as she reached a shuddering peak herself. Then they collapsed in each other's arms, spent and gasping for air. For several minutes they lay like that, their limbs entwined, their breath mingling, and their eyes closed. Then Jessica opened hers and saw that the hands of the bedside clock were at eight o'clock.

"Christ!" she exclaimed, shrugging out of Andrew's arms. "Have you seen the time? Now I'm going to be seriously late." She slid off the bed and rushed into the bathroom, the passion of a moment before turned into silent anger. Andrew has taken advantage of me, she thought, and it isn't fair. He knows I can't resist him when it comes to sex. He knows . . . She caught sight of her reflection in the mirror. Her chin was red from the stubble of his chin. Damn! Now she'd have to spend more time on her makeup to disguise the telltale marks. Fuming, she dabbed her face with cold water while she ran a bath. Why the hell did he have to tempt her like that when he knew she couldn't be late for work? Knowing she was being unreasonable, yet unable to help herself, she climbed into the bath with a groan of exasperation.

At that moment Andrew came into the bathroom and stood looking down at her.

"That was a damned stupid thing to do!" she exploded when she looked up and saw him. "Now I'm going to be at least half an hour late, and Dick will be going crazy trying to cope without me."

Andrew looked distressed. "I'm sorry, Jess darling. I wanted you so much. I love you so much."

Jessica retorted swiftly. "There are lots of times when I want you too, but if you're busy or too tired . . ." Her voice trailed off. "It was taking advantage of me!" she added as if she'd only just thought of it.

Andrew's eyes opened in amazement, and for a moment he looked as if he was going to laugh. "Since when have you been a shrinking Victorian violet that *anyone* could take advantage of?" he asked carefully.

Jessica threw him a cross look. "Oh, you know what I mean. I wish you'd understand that my job is important. You deliberately set out to—"

"You didn't need much persuading, did you?" he protested, suddenly angry again. "Come on, Jess, you like it as much as I do. Don't give me this line that I forced you to have sex against your will!"

Suddenly her eyes brimmed. "I know," she said, her voice catching, "but you don't seem to understand how important the hotel is to me. They've put me in charge of all the arrangements for today, and it's crucial that I be there on time."

Andrew knelt down beside the bath, his athletic body curving naturally into graceful and very masculine lines. Gently he stroked her hair.

"I love you," he said simply. "I love you and I need you. I want us to get married one day so that we can spend the rest of our lives together. Of course it upsets me when you put your work before us, and I sometimes wonder if you still love me at all."

"Of course I love you," she replied, dabbing her eyes with a washcloth. "But you must understand I'm under a lot of pressure at the hotel. I'll be home early tonight—we could have waited until then."

Andrew rose abruptly. "I don't think we should have to make appointments to make love; it's supposed to be a spontaneous thing, like it was when we first met." Angrily he turned away and walked out of the bathroom and back to their bedroom. A few minutes later, wrapped in a bath sheet, Jessica followed him.

"I'll get back as early as I can this evening," she said in a conciliatory tone as she struggled into her clothes as quickly as she could. She was going to have to do her makeup in the taxi.

"Well, I don't know when I'll be back," Andrew replied sulkily, "so don't hurry on my account."

Jessica made a little grimace behind his back. He was going into one of his martyred moods; she'd have to work like hell when she got home tonight to jolly him out of it and reassure him she still loved him.

When she arrived at her office, Dick Fowler was already hard at work.

"I'm sorry I'm late," she apologized. "What's happening?"

Dick handed her a sheaf of notes. "Masses of calls for you. Here are all the messages. Basically, seven people have called to say they can't attend the luncheon, for various boring reasons; someone wants to bring his secretary . . . I said I didn't think there was room, which is a bit of a lie now that seven people have dropped out, but I'll leave it to your discretion.

Oh, and yes, the florist has been delayed—their van has broken down."

"Wonderful, just what I need to hear!" Jessica rejoined sarcastically. "At least all the table centerpieces will have been arranged overnight, so they'll only have to put them out when they get here." She scanned her messages, then reached for the master seating plan. A layout of their banqueting rooms, printed on a large sheet of paper, lay before it. On this the banqueting manager had drawn circles, each one numbered, to represent the tables. The larger circles were for twelve people, the smaller ones for ten. During the previous week Jessica had written the guests' names beside the table numbers, and she'd also compiled an alphabetical list linking the names with the tables they were sitting at. Now, with people dropping out, she'd have to do some rearranging.

"Number six will have only eight guests now, and number thirty-two, nine," she muttered aloud, making notes. "Oh, hell, three of those who have dropped out were all on table number twelve. I wonder if I can fill the gaps with some of the press?" Juggling the names around, she was interrupted by the phone. "People really are the limit!" she cried when she replaced the receiver. "That was the managing director of Gates Chemicals . . . you know, they always hold their conference here—saying he and his wife can come after all!"

Half an hour later she rushed with the amended list to the typist in the adjoining office. "Make these alterations on the table plan we're pinning on the easel," she said, "and have you finished typing out the sticky labels the guests are going to be given to wear?"

"Yes," said the secretary, who was already swamped with work.

Then Jessica ran along to the banqueting manager's office. He would have to inform the porters and waiters, so that they set the tables for the right number.

"Alterations, as usual!" she cried, handing him her notes. "At least it's not as bad as when we have a charity ball and some stupid titled chairman keeps on altering the numbers right up until it starts!"

Then she hurried to the scene of the action, the ballroom and the Armitage Room. This year the hotel had decided to bring all the fun and attractions of the Derby Day race meeting

into the banqueting rooms. There were stalls laden with bou-
tonnieres—red carnations for the men, pink roses for the
women. Green-and-white-striped awnings and white trellis
screens sectioned off a champagne bar and a Pimm's Cup
enclosure; tick-tack men were taking "bets" in aid of a well-
known charity, and there was a tent serving strawberries and
cream, which had been decorated with scarlet and white tulle
looped with red velvet ribbons. By the entrance, "racing" cards
and mock enclosure badges were to be handed out as the
guests arrived, and at the far end a small bandstand had been
erected, on which the band of the Grenadier Guards would
play appropriate music.

Jessica walked around checking every detail, noting that the
waiters were putting out large jugs of freshly squeezed orange
juice to go with the champagne for anyone who wanted mi-
mosas. Then she had a word with the technicians, who were
arranging enormous television screens in the four corners of
the ballroom, so people could watch the racing, live, from the
Derby. Finally she checked the thirty tables, set with their best
Limoges china and crystal glasses. The chief steward, who had
polished all the silver until it shone, was checking that everything was all right. The pure white damask tablecloths and
napkins, which had been washed and pressed in the hotel's
laundry, were virginally smooth. On each table Jessica had
also arranged for a designer she knew to do a centerpiece of
all the various racing colors, carried out in silk ribbons. The
effect was both smart and colorful, and when the bowls of
white flowers arrived, it would look better still. Pleased with
the effect, she was turning to leave the ballroom when she
saw the president of the Golding Group, Robert Scholtz, entering with the general manager hovering by his side.

Scholtz, a florid man in his fifties, had flown in from California that morning to preside over the function. He was
revered and feared by everyone in the Group, and as he approached, Jessica felt her color rise and her heart start to
pound.

"Good morning, Jessica." He beamed, shaking her hand.
The fact that he even remembered her name both impressed
her and made her more nervous. He was head of more than
twenty major hotels worldwide; why should he remember who
she was? Before she could do more than murmur "Good morn-

ing," he continued: "I hear you've done a great job getting today organized."

"Thank you, Mr. Scholtz," she replied a trifle breathlessly. "I think we're in for a big success. All our most important clients are coming, and we're expecting a lot of good press people."

"Let me see a copy of the guest list." He was still being charming, but she was not taken in by his apparent niceness. Robert Scholtz had the reputation of being a cold, ruthless operator who would not tolerate inefficiency or sloppiness.

Thankful that she had her file tucked under her arm, she whisked out the typed list. "This copy is for you," she said smoothly.

A flicker of pleased surprise registered on his red-veined face, and his small eyes looked at Jessica penetratingly. "Well, thank you." Without another word he strode off in the direction of the kitchens, obviously intent on carrying out a snap inspection there. The last thing Jessica heard him say was: "Now, about today's menu . . ."

Thankfully she slipped down to the main lobby to make sure the brass-edged bulletin board stated where the luncheon was going to be held. With any luck, she'd acquitted herself well in the eyes of the almighty president, but the day was not yet over. . . .

Andrew Seymour found it hard to concentrate on his work that day. As a partner in a thriving real-estate business, he had to be on the ball, showing people around the more up-market London houses he specialized in selling, negotiating prices in an ever-rising market. Sometimes the asking price bore no relation to the actual value of the property, and yet there was always someone ready to pay these exorbitant amounts, and to Andrew's constant surprise, the buyers were not necessarily rich Arabs or Asians, but English people who fitted into the *nouveau riche* bracket.

He'd already shown five sets of people the various properties that morning, and now he'd have to wait and see whether any of them would make an offer or not. All his persuasive charm and basic knowledge of psychology were stretched daily; he had to decide, first, when clients approached him saying they were interested in a house, whether they were genuine or not. A lot of people "house-hunted" as a hobby, because they had nothing better to do. Sometimes others were sincere but didn't have the finances and didn't qualify for a mortgage or bank loan. There were others still whose intent was genuine, but when it came to the point, they could never make up their minds. Andrew, in the six years since he'd formed Jason and Seymour, had rarely been wrong about a client.

Today, though, he was suddenly fed up with the whole business. He was tired of dashing from property to property, extolling the delights of marble fireplaces, mosaic Jacuzzis, and custom-built kitchens. He was bored with calling small back-yards with a few tubs "private gardens," and converted ga-rages "bijou residences." Most of all, he hated the sham of describing "magnificent views" from windows that actually overlooked a couple of dusty trees and a patch of scrubby lawn.

Sighing deeply, he asked one of the secretaries to say he was out next time the phone rang. The reason, he knew, for feeling so discontented was Jessica. She was the most bewitch-ing, maddening, enchanting, and thoroughly irritating woman he'd ever known, and he loved her more than anything in the world.

"What's your problem?" his partner, Sandy Jason, asked him as they paused for a midmorning cup of coffee in their Knightsbridge office. "You look as if you'd won the pools but forgotten to post your coupon."

Andrew gave a wry smile. "I think I'd like to live in the country," he announced, as if the thought surprised even him.

"You'd have to commute," said Sandy, who was younger than Andrew and liked city life. "Getting up at dawn to be here on time; going home in the dark for six months of the year. Not my idea of fun, and won't Jessica hate it?"

Andrew didn't answer. Of course Jessica would hate it. It would mean she'd have to give up her twelve-hour day work-ing at the hotel and settle down to a normal life. He didn't need Sandy to tell him that it wasn't Jessica's idea of happiness.

"Goddammit!" he exploded, pounding the desk so that his coffee spilled. "All I want to do is marry her, have three kids, and live in a nice house in the country."

"Awfully bourgeois, don't you think?" Sandy cocked a

quizzical eyebrow at him. "What about your social life? Wouldn't you miss going to restaurants and the theater and the cinema? You actually think Jessica's going to swap those high heels for green Wellies?" He chuckled loudly. "Not a hope in hell, old chap."

Andrew replied hollowly. "I know. I'm not even sure I can persuade her to get married at the moment. Oh, God, I hate all this feminist stuff—every woman thinking she can have her cake and eat it. My mother didn't put a career before my father—she was the perfect wife. Why the hell do all these girls want to be so bloody emancipated?"

Sandy rocked back in his chair, dissolving with laughter.

"You *are* in the dumps, aren't you? What's the little lady done to bring all this on? Don't forget: the reason you were first attracted to Jessica was that she's a go-ahead career girl. There's no use trying to change that now."

Andrew grinned sheepishly. "You're right, of course."

"Come on, old chap. Let's go to the pub and have a drink. Drown your sorrows. Give her a bunch of flowers or something. If she's being tricky, that'll soon bring her round."

Andrew glanced across at his partner. "You obviously don't know Jessica very well," he commented dryly.

The last of the guests had drifted away in a cloud of euphoria, brought on by a lavish luncheon, flowing drink, and an ambience of luxurious splendor. Jessica, her feet hurting in the neat high-heeled shoes she always wore, sank into a chair at one of the now-empty tables and surveyed the mess. Dirty glasses, lipstick-smeared table napkins, discarded race cards, and wilting flowers covered the surfaces of all the tables in the ballroom, but at least the occasion had been a brilliant success, and she didn't have to help clear it all away. An army of minions, still busy washing dishes behind closed doors, would see to that. A waiter offered her a glass of champagne.

"Thank you, that would be lovely," she said. It would be her first drink of the day; rule number one for hotel staff was never to drink on the job. The banqueting manager joined her, and so did Dick Fowler and Anne Butler, the director of public relations.

"Well done," Anne said warmly. "You did a great job."

"Good for business too," Dick said. "At least fifteen people told me they plan to hold their functions here again next year."

"And you'll write to them this afternoon, confirming the dates, won't you?" joked the banqueting manager.

"Thank God everyone came." Jessica had slipped off her shoes under the table. "I had a word with the organizer of the annual Flower Ball and she told me Prince Charles and Princess Diana have agreed to come to the next one. Isn't that grand?"

Anne Butler's eyes gleamed. "Give me the details when you get back to your office, will you? We can get masses of publicity for the hotel if they're coming."

At that moment, as they all sat relaxing and chatting about the success of the day, Robert Scholtz put his head around the ballroom door, accompanied by the hotel's general manager.

"Oh, Christ!" Jessica muttered under her breath, trying to get her feet back into her shoes.

"Ah, Jessica, there you are!" the president said, striding over to them. "May I have a word with you?"

"Yes . . . of course." Clumsily she got to her feet. Robert Scholtz led her to a corner of the ballroom, away from the others.

She tried not to sound anxious. "Was everything all right?"

"Splendid. Splendid," he replied, nodding. "Why don't we sit down."

They sat at one of the tables; it had just been cleared by a waiter and looked bare and derelict. Jessica eyed him nervously, wondering what he wanted.

Robert Scholtz didn't waste words. "You've been happy working here, haven't you?"

Jessica's face flamed. Oh, God, he's going to sack me, was her first thought. He thinks I'm hopeless and he's going to tell me to go. Why else would he want to speak to me alone? It was obvious he was sparing her being embarrassed in front of all her colleagues.

"I love working here," she stammered.

"Good. Good." He always repeated himself. "And you're committed to working for this company?"

Jessica looked at him wonderingly. "Absolutely," she replied firmly.

"Right. Right." He stuck out his thick lower lip and his eyes became piercing. "We were wondering if you'd be able to take on the job of director of sales. Humphrey Peterson is being posted to the Temple Hotel in Hong Kong and has to leave here sooner than expected. The situation will become vacant in three weeks' time. Are you prepared to take it on?"

Jessica sat mesmerized, unable to believe what she was hearing. She heard herself blurt out loyally, "But what about Dick Fowler? He's been here much longer than I have!"

"We think you're more suited to the job. Today you proved it."

"There's nothing I'd love more," Jessica admitted fervently. Director of sales was the top rung of the ladder as far as she was concerned, the one post she'd been striving toward from the beginning. It would offer her immense challenges and scope for her talents, and it would put her in a position of power.

She looked up at Scholtz, who was still watching her intently. "Thank you for offering me the post," she said more formally. "If you really feel I can do it, I'd be delighted to accept."

"We can go into the details later, but there is just one other thing . . . I don't know how you're placed, but . . ." He paused, his voice hesitant and speculative. It was as if he were trying to decide something.

Jessica raised her eyebrows questioningly. "Yes?"

He came straight to the point. "You would have to live in the hotel, since you'd be on call day and night. That would be no problem, would it? You're not married, are you?"

4

WITH MADDENING regularity the grandfather clock in the hall ticked on, the small noise loud in the silence that pervaded the old house. Madeleine, sitting uneasily on one of the hard carved chairs near the front door, waited with growing impatience. The doctor had been in the library with Sir George for what seemed an interminably long time now, and her anxiety was growing with every passing irritating *tick-tock*. Around her, in gloomy opulence, the polished Jacobean furniture cast heavy shadows, lit only by a brass lamp that hung from the low ceiling. Restlessly Madeleine got up and opened one of the dark paneled doors that led off the hall. Darkness and a musty smell assailed her as she reached for the light switch; a dining room with more heavy furniture met her gaze. Although spotlessly clean, it had the unlived-in atmosphere of a museum; she almost expected to see little signs indicating the period of the oak table and chairs. Madeleine turned away, shutting the door behind her, and then she crossed the hall to see what lay behind the other door. Again solid blackness lay before her, but when she found the switch, she was surprised when a warm pink glow bathed the room in a flush of light, turning it into an inviting rosy bower in an otherwise severe house. Decorated in muted shades of pink and blue and cream, with brocaded walls, delicate French furniture, and a richly woven Aubusson tapestry carpet, it was essentially a very feminine room, which she guessed must have been her grandmother's drawing room.

Fascinated by the wash of soft tints spread at her feet, she bent down to look closer at the giant cabbage roses, embroidered from palest pink to deep carmine. Against a sky-blue background the design twirled and curved into creamy stems, mingled with leaves in a variety of soft greens, and tucked among the beige scrolls and ribbons that bound the roses loosely together were little gentian violets worked in purple silk. So intrigued was she in following the pattern that it wasn't until she was in the middle of the room that she paused and straightened up. Then she gasped, stunned, her eyes moving with growing horror around the room. Every surface, from the gilt console tables to the concert grand piano, from the magnificent marble mantelshelf to the little occasional table, was covered by framed photographs of a beautiful young woman with fair hair and mocking eyes.

Madeleine blinked as a creeping coldness swept over her. She knew the face and yet she didn't know it. There was something strangely familiar about it, and yet it was unknown and alien. And the eyes, hundreds of them, watched her wherever she moved, ringing some far-distant chord in her childhood memories.

Suddenly, gripped with fear, she began to get dizzy. This overfurnished, prettily cluttered room, airless and cold, was alive with Camilla's face, for that was who it was. Paralyzed, as she stood there on the variegated embroidered roses, unable to escape the silent stare of this woman who had been her mother, a silent scream of panic filled her throat. The roses began to swirl around her feet. Camilla, in a hundred different poses and settings, seemed to be advancing on her, closing in, suffocating her with those mocking eyes. "Your mother was involved in something terrible . . ." The words filled her mind. So real did she sense danger at this moment, so malevolent did all those faces seem as they clustered, floating, pressing in on her, mocking images swirling around her head, that she fled, stumbling wildly, her hand clasped over her mouth to stop herself from screaming.

She found herself back in the hall, her heart pounding so that she felt almost sick. What had it been? She felt as if she'd experienced a tangible human assault, and had been filled with such real terror that all she could think of was escape. "Oh, Carl, I wish you were here," she whispered under her breath. "I don't understand what's going on and I'm scared!"

"Are you all right, madam?"

Startled, she looked up to see Hunter watching her anxiously.

"I'm fine," she replied, suddenly feeling foolish. "I was just looking around. Er . . . none of these rooms seems to be used much."

"Sir George often sits in the drawing room when the weather's warm," he replied, indicating the room she'd just come out of, "but the dining room is never used these days. Can I get you a drink, madam, while you're waiting for the doctor?"

"Some coffee, please," she replied.

Dr. Thurlow came out of the library a few minutes later, looking grave.

Madeleine looked at him questioningly, her heart sinking as if she already knew what he was going to say.

"Why don't you sit down, you look pale," Dr. Thurlow suggested. He seated himself in one of the carved chairs near her and spoke gently, the wrinkles around his tired eyes making him look strained.

"I'm afraid he's had a stroke. He's unconscious and I've used the telephone in the library to call an ambulance. The sooner we get him to hospital, the better, but until tests have been carried out, it's impossible to know the extent of the brain damage."

Madeleine steeled herself to ask the obvious question. "Will he recover?"

He gave her a sympathetic smile. "It's too soon to say, and of course one has to remember he's over eighty. But everything will be done for him. I understand you arrived only today, Mrs. . . . er . . . ?"

"Delaney. Yes, my grandfather asked me to come and visit him. I live in New York."

Dr. Thurlow nodded. "Yes, I see. Well, I don't know Sir George very well. I've been in this practice for just over a year and I attended him once, for mild angina."

Madeleine watched as Sir George was stretchered into an ambulance. The doctor suggested she wait at the house, as there was nothing she could do for the time being. "We'll keep in touch," he promised.

"You think he'll regain consciousness?" she asked anxiously.

"We can only hope."

A minute later the white ambulance, its red light flashing, slid away and Madeleine went slowly up to her room. Sleep was impossible. The events of the past few hours, following on her flight from New York, had left her both emotionally and physically exhausted. She climbed into bed and turned out the light, but the pictures in her mind kept flashing vividly before her, disturbing her deeply. Most of all she felt bewildered by her experience in the drawing room below. It was almost as if she'd been physically threatened by something. But what? A room full of old photographs was nothing to be afraid of. Perhaps jet lag, combined with the shock of her grandfather's collapse, had caused her imagination to play tricks. As an artist, of course, she was perhaps more aware of people's faces, and especially their eyes, and maybe being confronted with dozens of photographs of her mother had been more traumatic than she'd realized.

Switching on the light again, she reached for her book and started reading. Now was not the time to let her imagination run away with her.

The next morning, the doctor drove over to Milton Manor himself to break the news to Madeleine.

"I'm afraid your grandfather died in the early hours of the morning," he said gently. "They did everything they could, but he had suffered a massive stroke."

Madeleine felt a deep pang of regret, although she'd half-expected the news to be bad. The old man had looked so frail, except for the glittering feverishness in his eyes. And hadn't he begged her to visit him because "time is running out"? It seemed he might have guessed himself that the end was near, and that was why he'd been so desperately anxious to see her.

"Thank you for your help," Madeleine said.

"I'm sorry I couldn't do more."

When he left, Madeleine went to the kitchens to tell the servants Sir George had died. Hunter and the household staff took the news gravely, but Jenkins wept, slow tears trickling down his withered cheeks.

"I'd like you all to know that although my grandfather has died, I will see that you are all taken care of. I'd like you to stay on here until further notice, and as soon as I can, I'll let you know what's happening," Madeleine said to reassure them. Maybe Sir George had left everything to her, and maybe he hadn't; whatever the outcome, Madeleine didn't want the servants to worry about their next paycheck.

"Thank you, madam," Hunter said, acting as spokesman.

"That's very kind of you. Will you be staying on yourself?"

"Certainly until after the funeral," Madeleine replied.

Carl was in Jake's office when Madeleine's call came through later that day.

"Hi, sweetheart," Carl greeted her. "How's it going?"

"Grandfather died early this morning," he heard her say.

"Christ! Wasn't that a bit unexpected? What happened?"

Jake looked up sharply from his desk. "What's going on?"

Carl explained briefly.

". . . so it's all been a bit traumatic," Madeleine was saying.

"Is she all right?" Jake demanded. "Here, let me speak to her." He seized the phone from Carl. "Madeleine? What's happening? Are you okay?"

"I'm fine, Daddy. Just a bit sad that Grandfather died before I could get to know him, and before he could tell me anything. You're going to have to tell me why—"

"You're coming home right away, I hope?" Jake interrupted.

"How can I?" Madeleine said. "There's the funeral, and there will be things to see to. Listen, you've got to tell me what's been going on. Grandfather said my mother was involved in something terrible . . . something that nearly led to my death. He was starting to tell me all about it when—"

"He was senile, Madeleine. He imagined things, that's why I didn't want you to visit him," Jake cut in quickly.

"He wasn't senile!" Madeleine protested. "I'm certain of that. He said there was something I must be told, because once he was dead there'd be no one. You must know what he meant. He said you should have told me years ago. Come on—for goodness' sake, I'm not a child."

"Madeleine, your grandfather's mind went when your mother died."

"Then why did you tell me I'd be getting into something I couldn't handle if I came to see him?" she challenged.

"For that exact reason! I wanted to protect you from the demented wanderings of an old man," he retorted.

"Daddy . . ." Jake could hear the doubt in her voice. "Daddy, if it's the last thing I do, I'm going to find out about my mother. May I speak to Carl again, please?"

Jake handed back the phone, feeling immensely relieved. With old George Dalrymple dead, the chances of Madeleine's finding out what had happened were fairly remote. Of course, there were always the village people, but he doubted they'd talk. They, too, had lived in fear at the time, and would wish the past forgotten.

Carl stayed late at the office that evening because he had a stack of work to get through, and besides, he didn't much like the idea of going home to an empty apartment. Madeleine had said she was going to be away longer than expected, and the prospect of being on his own for the next week or so didn't appeal. What had he done with himself when he'd been a bachelor? Already he'd forgotten. There had been girls, of course, lots of girls, and they'd gone to the movies and out to dinner, he supposed; occasionally there'd been a party at a friend's place, and sometimes a group of them had sat up all night drinking and talking. But mostly he'd ended up in bed with the girl he was dating.

Looking back, he found it hard to reconcile the carefree young man he'd been with the responsible banker he was today, and just for a fleeting moment he wondered what it would be like to recapture that hedonistic pursuit of pleasure that once he'd taken for granted.

Kimberley was working in her office next door, and idly he wondered what she did with her evenings. An attractive girl like that must surely have a busy private life, he thought. Immersed in work, he forgot about her again until he heard her come into the room.

"Are you off now?" Carl asked conversationally.

Kimberley was cradling a small plate in her hands, which she brought toward him, like a child offering a gift.

"I wondered if you'd like a piece of my birthday cake," she said. A slice of chocolate cake filled most of the plate, which she set before him on the desk. "The girls in my old department gave it to me at lunchtime," she added. A smear of creamy filling had stuck to her finger, and carefully, like a cat, she licked it clean.

"Is it your birthday today?" Carl felt very remiss. He should have known; he should have gotten her a small but suitable present and a card. Jake always gave his secretaries presents on their birthdays and at Christmas.

Kimberley giggled. "Yes, but who wants to advertise she's a year older?"

Carl eyed the cake, wondering how he was going to avoid all that cholesterol without hurting her feelings. "Going anywhere nice tonight?"

"No. Just home," she said lightly.

"Ah, a family party. How nice." Carl rose, thinking that if she was leaving now he could dump the chocolate cake down the can and she'd be none the wiser.

"I live alone," Kimberley said simply. "I thought I'd watch TV and then have an early night."

"On your birthday?" He stood looking at her, amazed.

"I had planned to go out with some friends, but one of them got ill, so the plan was scrubbed." Kimberley smiled at him, not a trace of self-pity on her face.

Carl felt embarrassed. Not only had he not realized it was her birthday, he hadn't gotten her a present, and now she'd told him she was going to be alone.

"Say, let me at least get you a drink," he said quickly.

"No, really, it doesn't matter," she protested, still smiling.

Carl had a brilliant idea. He went to the built-in fridge in the corner of his office, where he always kept a selection of both hard and soft drinks for important clients, and took out a bottle of Moët & Chandon. It was ice-cold.

"I hope you like champagne." Suddenly he was rather glad of an excuse to have a drink and a talk with someone. It would help ease his own loneliness, and also pass the time. He poured the wine into two tulip glasses and handed her one.

"A very happy birthday," he said, raising his glass, "and may you have many more of them."

Was it his imagination, or did Kimberley seem less servile, less the willing little assistant at that moment, and more a woman of confident assurance? She'd dropped into the chair in which his clients usually sat, her long legs crossed, her head thrown back in a gesture of expectancy, her gray eyes regarding him with languid interest.

"Thank you," she said. "This is very nice of you."

"It's the least I can do," Carl replied, suddenly noticing that her cleavage was like a valley, a cleft between two snowdrifts. He dragged his eyes away and went back to sit behind his desk. "I hope you're happy here in the bank," he said. "We like everyone to be happy." It was all he could think of to say, and even to his ears it sounded trite and banal.

"Sure, I love my job." Kimberley nodded confidently. "I always wanted to work in a bank, ever since I was a little girl."

Carl asked her about her family and noticed that she was not very forthcoming. The conversation was stilted and awkward, and Carl refilled their glasses. He and Kimberley had so little in common, except for their work, that bridging the gap between them conversationally was proving more difficult than he'd thought. Maybe it had been a mistake to offer her a drink after official working hours. Now that dusk had fallen, there was something unusually cozy and intimate about his office, in a now almost silent building with only the night security people patrolling the corridors. Down below, on Wall Street, the evening rush was over, and the sidewalks were silent and deserted under a lavender sky. For a moment he felt as if he and Kimberley were the only people left alive.

"Here, have some more to drink," Carl said, refilling their glasses and breaking the awkward silence between them. He didn't usually drink much, but tonight he felt like it. After all, there was no Madeleine to go home to and no engagements to keep. He was a free agent, and the wine was lifting his spirits to the point that he was feeling quite elated. He decided to open a second bottle.

"Your wife is away in Europe, isn't she?" Kimberley asked, shifting her position in the chair so that her tight skirt rose higher, exposing her thighs.

Carl looked at her legs, and to his surprise, felt himself getting aroused.

"That's right, and I heard today she's going to be away for at least another week or so," he said, hearing through a faint roaring in his ears the regret in his voice.

"That must leave you at rather a loose end," Kimberley remarked, looking at him with an unnerving directness. "What are you going to do with yourself while she's away?"

Carl knew instantly what she meant, and, suddenly embarrassed, he averted his gaze. "I don't know." He laughed awkwardly and took another gulp of his drink. It was a long time since a girl had propositioned him, and, half-flattered, half-shocked, he rose and went to look out the window. It would never do to get involved with someone in the bank, and besides, there was Madeleine, he thought. He'd always been faithful to her, and they had a great sex life together.

He felt a hand at the small of his back, and turning sharply, saw Kimberley standing by his shoulder.

"What would be the harm? Who would ever know?" she whispered, and he could smell the scent from her hair, heady and exciting as she moved closer.

"No, Kimberley," he heard himself say, but a voice in his head said: Who *would* know? What *would* be the harm? The champagne had really gotten to him now, and he felt as if he could do anything—break all the rules and not get caught, have himself a ball and escape the consequences. He could do as he liked, and he needn't be answerable to anyone.

"No, Kimberley." His voice sounded almost pleading. She was pressing herself against him now like a cat, insinuating herself against his side. Why am I arguing? he asked himself. Why the hell am I saying no? My mind is saying no, but my body is saying yes. . . . I can't resist you, Kimberley. Yes, I want you. . . . Yes, I need someone tonight.

Carl's mouth sought hers, and found her lips softer than he'd expected. She kissed him back with a gentle sweetness, almost a childlike trust, and he put his arms around her and held her close. As he closed his eyes, his mouth on hers, the complaisant thought passed through his head that here was a girl who would be no trouble; here was a girl whom he could trust to be discreet.

Kimberley eased herself out of his arms, her eyes never leaving his face, and slowly started to undress. Carl went quickly to the door of his office, looked out into the corridor to make sure no one was about, then locked both his office door and the one that led to Kimberley's office. When he turned back, Kimberley had gone into his adjoining private washroom.

"Come and join me?" she called out, and he heard her switching on the shower. Struggling out of his clothes, his wild elation mounting, he entered the little washroom, which was in semidarkness. Kimberley stood underneath the warm spray of water, her red hair loosened so that it fell damp and clinging to her white shoulders. In her hands she held a bar of soap, which she was twisting around and around between her palms, until they were creamy with suds. Then she reached out for Carl, drawing him into the circle of water with her, smoothing the slippery lather over his chest and down to his hips, while he stood spellbound, mesmerized by the magic she was weaving. Steam rose all around them, misty and soft in the dim light, and all Carl could think of was that he wanted this moment, so full of exciting anticipation, to last forever.

"Do you like that?" she whispered so softly he could hardly hear.

"Kimberley . . ." He buried his face in her streaming red hair, sucking the white skin of her neck, sliding his hands around her buttocks, where the flesh was yieldingly soft. Her hands had slipped down to his groin now, manipulative and coaxing, gentle and unhurried.

"I need you. God, I need you badly," he groaned. "Take me inside you?"

"Soon," she promised, then slipped out of his arms and slid around to the back of him, pressing herself close, stroking him with soapy hands from behind and in front.

Carl raised his face into the jet of warm water and felt as if he was being borne down swirling rapids, half-drowning, his mind lost in the sensuality of the moment, his body throbbing with the most piercing pleasure he had ever known. He was being carried on a journey of flooding turbulence, of hot whirl-pools and rivers bursting their banks. Great waves surged him onward and upward uncontrollably, on a tide whose currents swept away all else with the ecstasy of the moment, and turning, he lifted her off her feet and thrust himself inside her. Impaled, Kimberley clung to him, her head thrown back so that her red hair flowed in the water like a trail of blood, her white throat working on the brink of a cry. Savagely, with the desperation of animals tearing each other to pieces in a pre-historic act of lust, they possessed each other, while the steam rose about them and the warm jet of the shower played a dance on their naked bodies.

Sir George's funeral took place at the nearby village church of St. Olaf's. Madeleine, accompanied by Mr. Marks, of Spindle, Coutts, and Marks, her grandfather's lawyers, drove the short distance through the narrow winding village streets of

Shercombe and arrived just as the coffin was being lifted out of the hearse. Gathered outside the entrance to the church were groups of village people, mostly women with shopping baskets and toddlers in their arms. They stood in respectful silence as the oak casket was borne aloft, a wreath of white flowers from Madeleine resting on the lid, while the bell in the church tower tolled its solemn song. As soon as Jenkins drew up at the gates and Madeleine stepped from the car, she was aware that the local interest shifted sharply from the coffin to her. Dozens of people turned to stare, their mouths expressionless but their eyes flickering with furtive interest. Was it her imagination, or did the figures seem to huddle closer as she approached? Madeleine had the unpleasant sensation of being more than a local curiosity. When she looked into some of the faces, acknowledging their presence with the hint of a polite smile, eyes were instantly averted, feet shuffled; there was a perceptible drawing back among the front ranks, like animals sensing fear. She turned to look at Mr. Marks to gauge his reaction, but he seemed not to be noticing and returned her look with a friendly smile.

The vicar greeted her on the porch, shaking her hand and leading her up the aisle to a pew in the front, where Mr. Marks joined her. The servants from Milton Manor sat behind, Hunter ramrod stiff and dignified, Jenkins strangely clean-looking in a shiny dark suit. The organ was thundering richly, reverberating through the twelfth-century church, and she recognized the strains of Bach. The place was musty, damp-smelling, and dark, the only light coming in through narrow medieval windows, while two ineffectual candles sputtered on the altar.

Madeleine picked up her prayer book and was once again aware that she was being closely observed. Turning slightly to see if any of the villagers had come into the church, she noticed an elderly woman, beautifully dressed and with a sweet lined face, looking in her direction. Beside her sat a dark-haired man in his early thirties; he too was looking at her.

Then the woman smiled, a charming smile that lit up her face, so that laughter lines became deeper, fanning onto her cheeks. The young man's smile was more diffident, but he inclined his head in a friendly fashion, as if he, too, knew who she was. Madeleine nodded back, not having any idea who they were.

The service was short, followed by the interment in the churchyard. Madeleine noticed that the plot had been dug beside her grandmother's grave: "Emily, beloved wife of George Dalrymple and mother of Camilla. 1900–1946." Then she looked around, wondering if her mother had been buried here too.

It wasn't until they were out of the churchyard, watched again by the villagers who had maintained their vigil, that the older woman approached Madeleine, her hand outstretched and an expression of compassion on her face.

"My dear, you won't remember me," she said. "My name's Alice Stewart . . . this is my son, Philip. The last time I saw you, you were only two or three, but I'd have recognized you anywhere. You had large dark eyes and that wonderful dark hair even then."

"How do you do. You must have been a friend of Grandfather's," Madeleine replied, smiling back. She had liked the look of this woman from the moment she'd set eyes on her in the church, and her son seemed pleasant enough too.

"I've known George for over fifty years. He was a wonderful person, always so kind. So kind." For a second she gazed into the distance dreamily, as if remembering past pleasures. Then she looked at Madeleine again, her bright blue eyes soft and affectionate.

"And of course Camilla was my best friend," she said.

Madeleine's eyes widened. "You knew my mother?"

"Of course I knew your dear mother! We used to play together as children. Oh, we had such fun! We were debutantes the same year, and we went to all the parties together. Ah, those were happy days."

"I'd love us to meet again sometime," Madeleine said impulsively. "I'll be here for a while longer. Could I call you? Maybe you and your son could come over for lunch."

"We'd love that, wouldn't we, Philip?" Alice Stewart turned to her son, who had been listening to his mother's reminiscences with amusement.

"Sounds great," Philip agreed, catching Madeleine's eye.

"Then that's fixed! I'll call you tonight. I'm sorry I can't ask you back to the Manor now, but I've got to talk to grandfather's solicitor." She indicated Mr. Marks, who was waiting by the car for her.

"Of course you have, my dear," Alice said, patting her arm, "and we shall look forward to hearing from you. I can't tell you what a pleasure it is to see you again after all these years. Camilla's little girl! George must have been very proud of you." With a wave of her white-gloved hand Alice Stewart walked gracefully away.

Philip gave Madeleine a broad grin. "See you soon, then."

Back at the Manor, Hunter had set the table in the library as usual, and stood ready to dispense drinks. Mr. Marks asked for "a small sherry" and Madeleine had vodka and tonic. Drained by the morning's events, she wanted to get everything settled so that she could decide what to do with the old manor house if, as she strongly suspected, her grandfather had left it to her.

"Let's take our drinks into the garden," Madeleine suggested. "It's such a lovely day."

"That would be very nice," replied Mr. Marks. He was a prim-looking man in his forties, with receding sandy-colored hair and pale blue eyes that frequently blinked. When he looked at Madeleine, he blinked even more. Her beauty, emphasized by her simple black dress and the blackness of her hair, riveted him. He had never seen anyone quite like her. Clutching his briefcase, he followed her out onto the terrace and to a wooden bench under a spreading cedar tree.

"I have Sir George's will with me," he said eagerly. "Shall we get the business out of the way now, before lunch?"

Madeleine smiled at him and nodded, aware of the effect she was having on him. His sandy eyelashes flickered madly, like moths beating their wings against a window, as he withdrew the document from his case.

"It is really quite straightforward, Mrs. Delaney. Sir George made this will in 1967, and apart from a bequest of five thousand pounds to a Wilfred Arthur Jenkins—"

"He's the gardener," Madeleine interrupted.

"Apart from that," Mr. Marks continued, "he has left Milton Manor, all its contents, lands, effects, livestock, stocks, and shares, et cetera, to his only child, Camilla Mary Shearman, née Dalrymple, of Beekman Place, New York City."

Madeleine started, hearing her mother's name spoken as if she were still alive. Not noticing her surprise, Mr. Marks continued: " 'In the event of Camilla Mary Shearman predeceasing me, her daughter, Madeleine Elizabeth Shearman, on attaining the age of twenty-one, shall inherit my estate in entirety.' "

"That's me," Madeleine said unnecessarily. "My mother died when I was a child."

Mr. Marks raised his eyebrows and then took a swift sip of his sherry. The funeral, the presence of this beautiful young woman, and the heat of the sun as they sat in the garden were too much for him; he felt quite unsteady and rather emotional.

"Then you are the sole heir, Mrs. Delaney," he quavered. "I hadn't realized your mother had died, but then, I've only been with the firm for the past eight years and I don't think we've had any dealings with Sir George in that time. He obviously didn't think it necessary to make a new will when your mother passed on, as he'd already made provision for you."

"Yes, I see," Madeleine said thoughtfully. What Mr. Marks said was perfectly reasonable, but she still thought it strange.

"Will you be living here?" Mr. Marks asked.

"I don't think so. My husband and I live in New York, where he works with my father. I'm a painter, so it doesn't matter where I live, but Carl won't get transferred to England for several years yet, so I think I'll sell the house."

A tinge of disappointment cast its shadow over Mr. Marks's face. "Well, if I can be of any help, let me know. I can put you in touch with several land agents, but of course you do realize that nothing can be done until after probate has been agreed."

Madeleine looked bewildered. "Probate?"

"That is the assessed value of the property," Mr. Marks continued, "and when probate has been fixed, there will be the capital-transfer tax on the value of the estate to pay. It could be as long as a year before you will be able to put Milton Manor on the market."

"As long as that?" Madeleine had no experience of these things and had imagined she could have everything settled within weeks. "Do I keep the house open and running until then?" she asked.

"It will be easier to sell when the time comes, if you do. Empty houses do not have the same appeal to buyers," Mr.

Marks explained. "Of course, too, before anything can be done, it will be necessary to obtain a copy of your late mother's death certificate in order to prove your claim."

"Can you do that for me?" Madeleine asked, suddenly experiencing a feeling of helplessness. All her life she'd had things done for her, and she'd never had to think about business because all her interests and all her energy went into her art. Jake had looked after her and arranged everything for her ever since she could remember, and in the last few years Carl had taken over. She knew what a bank statement looked like but she didn't think she'd ever seen a tax form in her life.

As if sensing that she felt out of her depth, Mr. Marks leaned forward, his face alight with eager helpfulness. "If there's anything I can do at any time," he murmured in a rapt voice, "please feel free to call on me, Mrs. Delaney."

"I will," Madeleine replied, smiling with relief. "In the meantime, is it all right if I tell Jenkins about his inheritance?"

"Yes, of course. Quite all right."

When Mr. Marks left an hour later, Madeleine wandered back into the garden in search of Jenkins. The afternoon had become golden and languid, the air so still and the silence so heavy that the persistent humming of the bees, hovering dizzily above the lavender bushes, was the only sound to be heard. Sweetly pungent, the scent of new-mown grass drifted toward Madeleine as she paused, standing to look around her at the immaculately kept flowerbeds and hedges. It seemed a pity to sell this beautiful old place, she thought, and yet she knew she didn't want to stay here.

Jenkins was kneeling by the herbaceous border, pulling out weeds. He'd changed out of his shiny suit and was wearing his usual brown corduroy trousers and an open-necked shirt.

"Jenkins," Madeleine said gently, knowing he must be feeling the death of her grandfather more than any of them, "I thought you'd like to know that Sir George has left you five thousand pounds in his will."

Jenkins paused in his weeding for a moment, staring at the rich brown soil, his face flushed.

"Thank you, ma'am," he said at last.

Madeleine stood watching him for a few more minutes, wondering how she could bring the conversation around to her mother. "Since you've been working here such a long time,

Jenkins," she said, suddenly feeling nervous, "I expect you've seen changes in your time, haven't you?" A breeze came ruffling through the trees as she spoke, and she raised her hands to her head, trying to control the dark curls that fluttered around her face.

"No, ma'am. Nothing much changes in these 'ere parts." His thick workman's hands tugged at an obstinate dandelion root.

"But you must remember my mother," Madeleine said reasonably. "After all, if you've worked here for forty years . . . you see, I don't remember her at all, so it's nice to meet someone who must have known her." She tried to sound casual, as if it didn't matter all that much to her, but her heart was pounding in her rib cage as she felt herself drawing nearer to the truth.

"I remember her," Jenkins grunted grudgingly.

"What was she like? Tell me about her."

Jenkins' voice was flat in its finality. "There's nothing to tell."

Madeleine felt taken aback by his surliness. "But Sir George wanted me to know about her—that's why he asked me to fly over from America!" she exclaimed. "What happened to her, Jenkins? You were here then—you must know!" A hint of desperation had crept into her voice.

The old gardener rose to his feet, rubbing the earth from his thick fingers for several moments. Only then did he look at Madeleine, his eyes veiled, his mouth stern. "Some things are better left alone," he said, and with that he turned abruptly away, walking in the direction of the kitchen garden. His dismissal of her was absolute, the broad chunky outline of his receding figure so forbidding that she froze, unable to run after him. At that moment it hit her that the mystery of Camilla went far deeper than she'd realized. It went beyond Jake and his refusal to discuss her; it went beyond an ordinary family feud. Something had happened that Sir George had wanted her to know, and whatever it was, Madeleine was convinced that Jenkins was somehow involved.

5

JESSICA CAME rushing down the front steps of the Royal Westminster shortly after seven, gesticulated wildly at a passing cab, and jumping in, gave the driver her address in Chelsea. Her mind was in a turmoil. To have been offered the job of director of sales by Robert Scholtz was so fantastic, so unbelievable, that she felt quite breathless. But, oh . . . ! She put a hand to her mouth and closed her eyes for a moment. What on earth was she going to say to Andrew? How could she possibly breeze home and say to him, "Oh, by the way, I'm moving out, as my new job will require me to live in the hotel"? Jessica groaned inwardly, imagining his reaction. On the other hand, she couldn't turn down this opportunity either. It was a chance in a million, and besides, if she did, it would give all those chauvinistic directors of the Golding Group a perfect opportunity to cite her as a typical example of a girl who could have had a brilliant career but didn't because she put her private life first.

"Blast and damn!" Jessica muttered under her breath as the taxi rattled down Sloane Street. Why is life so unfair? she asked herself. Men didn't have to choose between their work and the women they loved. Why should she?

As soon as she let herself into the apartment she could hear television blaring in the living room. Andrew was watching a panel game, nursing a whiskey and soda, the evening newspaper on his knee.

"Sorry I'm late," she said gaily, trying to smother her feelings of guilt. Flinging off her spike heels, she flopped onto the sofa beside him.

"D'you want a drink?" he mumbled, never taking his eyes off the screen.

"Not for the moment," Jessica replied. "What would you like for dinner?" As she said the words she knew the role of housewife, on its own, would never be enough for her. She needed the stimulation of working in an exciting job; she loved the tensions of living in the fast lane, with every day bringing new adrenaline-charging challenges. The thought removed all lingering doubts from her mind; she *had* to accept the post Robert Scholtz had offered her.

Andrew wrenched his eyes away from the TV. "What's all this domesticity bit? I thought you'd be tired after your big do at the hotel, so I've booked a table at L'Escargot."

"Oh, Andrew!" Jessica felt deeply touched, because it was so unlike him. Usually she cooked something from the freezer or he went out and bought a Chinese takeout. "What a lovely surprise! I adore L'Escargot." She slipped her arm around his neck and kissed him on the cheek. "We'll be able to celebrate . . ." she began, and then stopped. Her innate sense of timing told her that this was not the right moment to tell him her news. ". . . to celebrate the fact I've got the whole weekend off," she ended instead.

Andrew took her small slim hand and squeezed it. "I'm sorry about this morning," he said gruffly.

Jessica responded swiftly. "It was my fault too. I was really uptight. So much depended on today going well."

Andrew didn't ask how her day had gone. Instead he launched into a lengthy description of how he'd shown a two-million-pound house in Regent's Park to an Arab who'd declared it was too small for all his wives and children.

"We did get an offer for the broom cupboard, though," he added.

Jessica's eyes widened. "What d'you mean, the broom cupboard? Not a real broom cupboard?"

"A real broom cupboard," Andrew insisted. "You know Haversham House, that block of flats near Harrods? The owners have converted what used to be the janitor's room on the third-floor landing, where he stored his cleaning materials and vacuum cleaner, into what is referred to as a 'London *pied-à-terre.'* "

"You have to be joking!" Jessica started laughing, not taking him seriously.

"I kid you not. It has a shower, an electric kettle, and a sofa bed, and we sold it for what it would cost to buy a two-bedroom cottage in Essex!"

"Andrew!" Jessica looked quite shocked. "That's dreadful!"

"So are prices in the most fashionable parts of town, but who am I to complain? If I'm going to keep you in the luxury to which you've become accustomed, I've got to make a killing while I can. Surprisingly, there's always some bugger stupid enough to pay!"

Jessica looked away quickly, then reached down to pick up her discarded shoes. "I'll go and change before we go out," she said quietly, slipping from the room.

In their bedroom, which she'd decorated with green-and-pink Laura Ashley fabric three years ago, her guilt deepened. It was as if she were betraying Andrew by planning a whole new life for herself that did not include him. Worse than that, she hadn't even the courage to tell him now. Ever since Robert Scholtz had spread at her feet a future so glittering, so fantastic as to be almost unbelievable, she had known what she had to do. It wasn't a question of choice, really. The only choice left to her was when to tell Andrew.

L'Escargot, in the heart of Soho, was crowded as usual when they arrived, and while they waited for their table they sat in the bar area, drinking aperitifs. Andrew was still going on about the houses he and Sandy Jason had on their books, and how the property boom was going on and on in a seemingly endless upward spiral.

"Houses are the best investment in the world," he declared stoutly. "Stocks and shares are dicey, even gold and silver have their ups and downs, but bricks and mortar go on forever!"

"Yes, Andrew," Jessica said patiently, her eyes flickering around the dimly lit bar and into the restaurant beyond. "Someone should clear that table of dirty glasses," she said fretfully. "I hate it when tables aren't cleared immediately. Don't you think we should ask for the menu? We could be deciding what we want and giving our order while we wait. Someone should have brought us one."

Andrew regarded her with a smile that masked his irritation.

"Sweetheart, can't you be off duty for just a little while? How this restaurant's run is no concern of yours, as long as we get a decent dinner."

Jessica looked abashed, not realizing she was still acting as if she were in charge of everything.

"I'm sorry, Andrew. It's habit, really. I'm so *aware* of everything in a restaurant or a hotel—it's second nature to have my eyes everywhere, checking that the staff are doing everything properly."

"Well, I'm sure the manager here is perfectly capable of running the show without your help." He spoke flippantly, and even jokingly, but Jessica got the point. She was out with him and she ought to be relaxing and putting him first.

"You're right—it's a very bad habit!" she scolded herself mildly. "I must remember: I AM HERE TO RELAX AND ENJOY MYSELF!" She made it sound like a slogan.

Andrew regarded her fondly. "At these prices, sweetheart, you certainly are. Never mind, Jess, once we're living in the country you'll get out of the habit. You know, I was thinking . . ." He went on to describe the type of house he had in mind for them, stressing the necessity of a large garden "for the children to play in."

Jessica said nothing, her eyes fixed on the piece of lemon floating in her gin and tonic, unable to look him in the eye and tell him she'd be moving into the Royal Westminster within the next three weeks, and that she'd be living there for the foreseeable future.

Feeling like a traitor, she let him ramble on while she sipped her drink and began to wish she'd never been offered the damn job in the first place. She ought to tell him, but how could she ruin his evening, when he was being so sweet and generous, thinking he was giving her a glorious time? He'd never understand, now or at any time, that she needed to fulfill her ambitions and to feed the starving desire to be an achiever that consumed her day and night.

"What will you do if we live in the country?" Jessica asked at last, because this was a part of his Grand Scheme that he never seemed to consider.

Andrew grinned. "I shall be the Lord of the Manor! A gentleman farmer! The local squire!" he joked.

When she'd stopped laughing, she said, "I suppose you could still be an estate agent, dealing in country properties instead of London ones."

"That's what I had in mind, while you work for the Goose

and Gander Inn instead of the Golding Group, Inc!" he quipped.

Jessica tried very hard to look amused, but she felt jarred by his mockery. It underlined his basic feelings: he would continue to pursue his career while she settled for any job, even if it was second best. Never before had she realized how much her future in the hotel meant to her: if she didn't realize her full potential, she'd never forgive herself.

Dinner was rather strained as she tried to steer the conversation back to generalities, and for once there were yawning black pits of silence between them; but when they got back to Paultons Square, Andrew took her to bed and made love to her gently and sweetly, as if to obliterate his rough and demanding treatment of her that morning. It was almost as if, in an unspoken way, he understood the complexities of her nature, although she knew he didn't. Andrew didn't understand her at all. He was like all men, convinced that his occupation was much more important than any woman's; convinced also that the old-fashioned values his mother had modeled herself on were the only right ones. She ached with tiredness and longed to curl up and go to sleep, but Andrew was being so loving that she hadn't the heart to tell him how she felt. And I do love him, she told herself as she submitted to his embrace . . . but I will love him less if I can't follow my own destiny.

The next morning Jessica awoke cold and stiff, the duvet having slipped over to Andrew's side of the bed, as a pale gray dawn filtered through the Laura Ashley curtains. Outside, a chorus of London birds shrilled away, rivaling their country cousins with their lusty singing. Getting silently out of bed, Jessica knew she had to get to the Royal Westminster and submerge herself in its atmosphere before Andrew awoke and her resolve of last night vanished. She knew she couldn't face him with the truth yet, but neither could she bear to lie to him for much longer.

Having dressed in a navy-blue dress and high-heeled shoes, she put on a minimum of makeup, brushed her hair, and leaving it hanging loose, crept out without disturbing him. Breakfast would have to wait until she got to the hotel, and then, for once, she'd spoil herself and order the full menu from the chef: grapefruit, eggs and bacon, croissants, toast and marmalade, gallons of coffee—the lot. It wasn't every day she could indulge herself like this, and she decided it was her reward for getting in to work two hours before everyone else; but in her heart she knew it was "comfort eating" because she was worried.

When she arrived, the whole place seemed to be slumbering, bedroom curtains drawn and lights dimmed, but behind the scenes she knew the day's activities had already begun. Many of the staff of three hundred would have already arrived; the chambermaids would be collecting the linen and towels from the laundry rooms, which were steamy warm and sweet with the smell of starch; the goods entrance at the back would already be bustling with activity as the produce for the day, ordered from the chef's market list, was delivered. There'd be fish from the North Atlantic, its flesh firm and the eyes checked to make sure it was fresh. If the eyes were sunken it would be sent back with anything else that was less than perfect. Then there'd be lichees from China and cherries from California; onoki mushrooms from Japan and ripe avocados from Spain. A cornucopia of the world's finest products. The kitchens would begin to fill up with all the most exotic fruit and vegetables obtainable. Truffles came from the king of truffles in France, Mr. Pebe, and chocolates from the house of Godiva. Baby corn from Thailand and miniature bananas from Jamaica were unpacked for spot checks on weight and quality; the finest beef from Ayrshire in Scotland and the most succulent lamb from New Zealand were placed in the walk-in refrigerators. Oysters and escargots, venison and guinea hen, sun-ripened apricots and tiny wild strawberries arrived in profusion, so that the air grew sharp with the tang of mingled smells.

Cleaners, waiters, florists, and maintenance people would be arriving, and slowly the hotel would be waking up to another long day. Soon guests would be having their breakfast trays taken to their rooms, complete with posies of flowers in little Limoges vases and the daily newspapers. Reception would be busy checking arrivals in and departing guests out, and as the morning progressed, the tables in the restaurant would be laid for luncheon, the bars would be restocked, and down in the cellar the sommelier would be checking his stock of 250,000 bottles of various red wines and his 80,000 bottles of assorted white wines, fewer in number because hotels didn't have to invest, long-term, in white wine as they did in red.

As Jessica made her way up to her office, she felt a sudden and enormous pride in the whole place. It epitomized true excellence with elegance and its reputation of being London's top hotel was not without justification. From its marble lobby to its penthouse swimming pool it ran as smoothly as silk, and that was because everyone pulled together, she thought, with one object in mind: to make the guests welcome and keep them happy.

By ten o'clock she felt as if she'd done a day's work, so advantageous had her early-morning start been. When the phone rang she was well into her stride.

"Sales Department," she said crisply.

"Is that you, Jessica?" asked a hesitant voice.

"Maddy! How good to hear from you. How are you?"

"Great! You sounded so fierce, I wasn't sure it was you."

Jessica laughed. "Sorry, I was expecting a business call. What's happening? Are you coming up to London?"

"I'm flying back to the States early next week because there's nothing I can do here until probate has been agreed, and that could take months, and I'm desperate to go home."

"Missing your dearly beloved?" Jessica teased. "You old married couples are worse than the people who come here for a dirty weekend!"

"I shall ignore that remark, Miss McCann," Madeleine declared, pretending to be offended. "I was going to invite you and Andrew down for my last weekend here, because I'd love to see you, but now I'm not sure if you deserve it!"

"Maddy! You beast! We'd adore to come."

How much easier, thought Jessica as she replaced the receiver a few minutes later, to tell Andrew about her new job while they were staying with Madeleine.

"I'm going to make a list of the things I'd eventually like shipped to the States," Madeleine told Hunter. "Do you think you could get out all the silver for me to see?"

"With pleasure, madam," Hunter said. He was enjoying there being a young mistress around the place, although it was only for a few more days, and he and the rest of the staff felt enormous gratitude to her for saying she'd keep them on at Milton Manor, even if it was a year before the house could be sold. "Shall I set it out in the pantry, madam? There is quite a lot of it, stored in the strong room in the cellar."

"That would be fine." Madeleine smiled at the butler, hoping the new tenants, whoever they were, would want to keep him on. Hunter had been so helpful to her since she'd arrived, getting hold of the lawyer for her, contacting the undertaker, and arranging many of the details of Sir George's funeral, and she felt very grateful. Jenkins she was not so sure about. After her encounter with him in the garden two days previously, he'd seemed to be avoiding her, leaving cut flowers for the house on the kitchen table and then scuttling back into the garden before she could say anything to him. Madeleine decided not to press him further about Camilla. It was, after all, Jake's job to tell her what had happened, and she intended to see that he did so as soon as she got back to New York.

Meanwhile, armed with a notepad and pencil, she started to take stock of the contents of Milton Manor, deciding what she'd sell with the house and what she'd take home. A lot of the furniture would have to remain; it was far too large to fit into their apartment and would not blend with the light modern decor. But some of the smaller pieces would go well in the weekend house at Oyster Bay, which Jake had put at her and Carl's disposal when they got married. The paintings were a different matter. She would definitely keep them. Many dated back to the sixteenth century and were portraits of her Dalrymple ancestors—stiff stylized paintings, so unlike her own work, but immensely valuable and of great historical interest. Listing them carefully, she authenticated a Gainsborough, two Lelys, a Joshua Reynolds, and a priceless sketch by Inigo Jones. Her grandfather's art collection, she reckoned, must be worth in excess of eight million dollars. Persian rugs, some fine pieces of Dresden china, and a beautiful brass candelabrum were added to the list. That left only one room in the house to examine. The drawing room. Madeleine had managed to avoid going into the room of a thousand eyes since the night of her grandfather's collapse, and she still shuddered whenever she thought about it. The incident had shaken her so badly that she'd dreamed about her mother's face every night since then, seeing again those mocking eyes closing in on her.

"Hunter," said Madeleine, keeping her voice light and non-chalant, "could you open up the drawing room for me?"

"Yes, madam. Will you be using it when you have guests this weekend?" he asked hopefully.

Madeleine seized the chance to act as if it was just another room in the house and of no special importance to her. "That's right. Open all the curtains and shutters and give the place a good airing. And put some flowers in there too. I'll have a look at the furniture and paintings tomorrow."

"Very well, madam." Hunter withdrew, a look of delight on his face, as if he couldn't wait for the weekend.

That evening, after Madeleine had eaten a light supper in the library, she decided to have a look at the books that filled the shelves from floor to ceiling, in ranks of gold-tooled-leather bindings. There must have been thousands of them, she estimated as she pulled the mahogany library steps into position and climbed up to look at the upper shelves. Her hand smoothed along the spines of the works of Sir Walter Scott, Charles Dickens, and Jane Austen, all first editions. On the shelf below were books on history, and further along, a collection of illustrated books about wild animals. As Madeleine continued her exploration, noting books that would be of special interest to Carl, she found a treasure trove of literature. Never in her life had she seen so many valuable books in one collection, or so many fascinating ones. She reached out and lifted from the shelves a copy of Milton's poems. He was her favorite poet and she decided to take this volume home with her, in spite of Mr. Marks's saying nothing must be removed from the house until it had been valued for probate. Who's going to miss one little book? Madeleine thought, tucking it under her arm.

She was just about to rearrange the remaining books on the shelves so a gap wouldn't be obvious, when she spotted a black volume, old and dog-eared, tucked away at the back. Withdrawing it and blowing away the dust that clung thickly to it, she saw it had no title on the spine or on the front cover either. Flipping it open and realizing it was handwritten, sometimes in ink, sometimes in pencil, she climbed down the steps and went and sat on the sofa. A cloud of dust arose, making her sneeze as she clapped the covers together to get rid of the cobwebs. It was obvious it had been hidden at the back of the shelf for years.

Opening the first page, she saw the handwriting was large and rounded and difficult to read; but it seemed to be some sort of journal, although there were no dates anywhere, nothing to indicate what day or month or even year it had been written. An entry caught her eye: "Tonight we met in the barn, where the crossroads used to be: The King of Darkness, Power of Power, was in our midst."

Feeling suddenly uneasy, Madeleine skimmed through a few more pages, able to make out only certain words: "Pagan rite" . . . "spirit of hellfire" . . . "allegiance to Satan"—and then a horrifying passage, written in red ink: ". . . covered in oil and smeared with the blood of a hare, the spirit entered my body. . . ."

Madeleine involuntarily threw the book away from her, hurling it toward the fireplace, where it landed with a thud by the brass fender. Whoever had penned that journal had been involved in witchcraft and black magic, something she greatly feared. When she'd been at school, a lot of her friends had become fascinated by the occult, and had frightened each other to death with tales of sticking pins in wax images in order to harm an intended victim, or being able to cast spells over people by obtaining locks of their hair or even photographs. When their teacher found them playing with a Ouija board one day and learned about their morbid interest in malfeasance, he hadn't been so much angry as full of warning. Madeleine had never forgotten him saying that to play around in the spirit world was highly dangerous: "If you dial a telephone number and get it wrong, you can always hang up," he explained, "but if you should make contact with an evil or mischievous spirit, there's no hanging up. You're stuck with it."

Madeleine shivered as she looked at the evil little book lying on the hearth. She didn't even want to touch it again, so strong was her superstition, and she wondered if her grandfather had realized it was up there tucked behind the volume of Milton's poems. And what was she going to do with it now? she asked herself. She couldn't leave it there, flung down so violently that it had landed open and facedown. Hunter would wonder what on earth she'd been doing. Then she rose to her feet, telling herself she was being stupid. How could a book hurt her? She didn't plan to read it, or be influenced by its contents, and if it was as old as she thought, it could be of local historical interest. Bending down, she picked up the volume and placed it on a side table.

The next day was Friday, and having breakfasted in her room, Madeleine went down to the kitchen to go through the weekend menus with the cook. Jessica and Andrew would be arriving in time for a late supper, and she wanted to give them something light. Hunter had just finished laying out the silver in the pantry.

"Good heavens, I'd no idea there was so much!" Madeleine exclaimed, looking at the collection of glittering pieces that covered the large pantry table and were also laid out on a side dresser.

"A lot of it is Georgian, madam," Hunter explained, "and there are also some very fine Queen Anne salt cellars. Of course, this tray is only Victorian, but it is very pretty, isn't it?" He picked up a large silver tea tray edged and handled with intertwined ivy leaves, the Dalrymple family crest engraved in the center.

"Very pretty," Madeleine agreed. "How did my grandfather come to have so much, though? There's enough here for a dinner party at the White House."

Hunter smiled. "I believe Sir George entertained a great deal in the old days, when Lady Dalrymple was alive. I should say, madam, that most of this silver has been in the family for several generations. These candelabra are particularly beautiful, I think." He indicated four matching candlesticks, each two feet high, embellished with cherubs and garlands of leaves and grapes, the five candle branches shaped like the stems of a vine.

"They're exquisite. My God, my husband will be thrilled when he sees all these things; he loves silver." Madeleine continued to examine the treasure trove. There were butter dishes shaped like scallop shells, ornate tea and coffee pots, minute cream jugs and sugar bowls lined with sapphire-blue glass. A collection of entrée dishes with lids blazed as a ray of sunlight coming through the window caught their polished surfaces. Then, like a conjurer demonstrating his favorite trick, Hunter unrolled a length of green baize, displaying dozens of shining forks and spoons.

"It's too amazing for words," Madeleine said. "I've never seen so much silver in one place in all my life. You'd better put it away for safekeeping, Hunter. I'm not sure if it's insured."

"I'll lock it up again, madam. The drawing room is ready, by the way, if you wish to use it now."

"Thank you, Hunter." Madeleine went into the corridor that led to the hall, and was passing the open library door when she saw a movement, no more than a flickering shadow by the fireplace. The French windows were wide open and, conscious of security after seeing all that silver, Madeleine hurried into the room to see who it was. She glanced around quickly, but the room was empty, the only movement the gentle swell of the draperies as a sudden gust of wind whipped across the lawn and through the open windows. Nothing seemed to have been disturbed, and yet she was sure someone had been in the room. Shrugging, she closed the windows and then made her way to the drawing room.

Hunter had obviously been hard at work, for the curtains and wooden shutters had been opened, letting in the fresh morning air, and there was a smell of lavender furniture polish and full-blown roses. Madeleine walked to the center, breathing steadily, waiting for some reaction, testing the atmosphere as a bather tests the temperature of the water. Her gaze shifted from the swirling roses in the tapestry carpet, up to the brocade-covered chairs and sofas, and then higher still to the black grand piano that stood in the corner. Fixing her eyes on the array of framed pictures that cluttered its surface, she looked unflinchingly into the face of Camilla, challenging the mocking eyes and the beautiful face to scare her. It was almost an anticlimax when she felt nothing. All that stood before her in a silver frame was one of many black-and-white photographs of a woman's face, looking over her shoulder into the lens, the features clear-cut and delicate, the eyes direct, the mouth half-smiling. Relief swept over Madeleine, coupled with a feeling of foolishness. This whole business was causing her to let her imagination run away with her, and she'd been getting fanciful. Laughing a little at herself, she wandered around looking at the other photographs, picking up little objets d'art that lay scattered about, taking stock of the room as a whole. It was a very pretty room, in fact, and there was nothing sinister about it at all. It must have been the shock of her grandfather's collapse that first evening, coupled with jet lag and general apprehension, that had led her to feel that this room was filled with evil, she thought. On the other hand, there were too many pictures of her mother for anyone's taste; the room was overpowered by them. Deciding to put most of them away in the drawer of a Queen Anne chest that stood against one wall, she stacked them up in twos and threes, being careful not to damage the frames. Gradually the room began to look larger and seem airier, the mirror above the mantelshelf reflecting the pastel blues and pinks and gilts that harmonized so perfectly with the colors of the carpet.

There were only a few more pictures left to put away. Madeleine went over to the table by the window, and reaching out for the largest, which was gilt-framed, she picked it up. A second later she let out a yelp as if she'd been stung, and the photograph went crashing to the floor, the glass exploding in a shower of brittle shards that stuck to the carpet like tiny quivering arrows. Camilla's face stared up at her, and for a moment Madeleine thought she was going to faint.

Hunter came hurrying into the room. "Madam, are you all right? I heard a crash . . . Oh, dear, I hope you haven't cut yourself!"

Automatically Madeleine looked at her hands, although she knew she wasn't hurt. Then she turned away from the window, realization making her head spin and her throat dry up. "No, no, I haven't cut myself. Could you clear away this . . . this mess, please . . ." she stammered, then rushed out of the room, her trembling legs hardly able to carry her.

For how could she tell Hunter that the scrawled inscription on the photograph—"To Father, with love from Camilla"— was written in the same hand as the journal she'd found the previous evening?

Jessica and Andrew arrived late that evening, having taken a taxi from Okehampton station because Jessica wasn't sure which train they were catching.

Madeleine went to greet them, her black hair tied off her

face by a ribbon, her casual white slacks standing out in the velvety purple twilight that was rapidly enshrouding the silent countryside.

"Am I glad to see you both!" Madeleine exclaimed with feeling as they entered the house.

"Finding the countryside boring, sweetie?" inquired Jessica.

"Boring, no. Nerve-racking, yes," replied Madeleine. "Anyway, come and have a drink, and we'll talk later."

"This is a lovely place you've inherited," Andrew remarked as they settled themselves in the library, where Hunter had arranged a cold buffet supper, with freshly caught lobster and salad. "Do you really want to sell it?"

Madeleine nodded. "I most certainly do. Nothing would induce me to live here now."

Jessica, who looked slightly drawn and pale, gave Madeleine a quizzical glance. "Have you found out how your mother died? Was it here, in this house?"

"I don't know, but I do know what she was up to before she died," Madeleine replied grimly.

Andrew raised his eyebrows and looked at her inquiringly. Jessica leaned forward, anxious not to miss a word. "Why, what was she up to?" she asked.

"Black magic."

"*What?* Oh, for God's sake, Maddy!" exclaimed Jessica.

"It's very upsetting," Madeleine said seriously. Then she told them what had happened, including what her grandfather had said before he died. "When I realized today it was my mother who'd kept a journal about her experiences . . . well, I can tell you, I freaked out! Ever since that time at school . . . My God, Jessica, I can understand now why my father didn't want me to know anything when I was a child."

"And you really think she got involved in witchcraft and that sort of thing?" Jessica asked, her blue eyes as round as saucers. "I thought all that sort of thing went out in the Middle Ages! You *can't* have got it right!"

"I promise you I have. I just knew something was wrong that first evening. I remember Grandfather saying she'd been led astray and that Jake didn't understand—"

"I don't suppose he would," Andrew said dryly. "Don't tell me you two girls honestly believe in this sort of thing?"

"I certainly do," Jessica said emphatically.

"So do I," agreed Madeleine. "I know from the articles and books we read at school that the power of evil is one of the strongest forces there is."

Andrew leaned his head back in the armchair, his legs stretched out in front of him, and his laughter filled the room.

"I don't believe it!" he chortled. "Intelligent, educated women like you, with careers . . . Oh, God, you have to be joking! You can't believe in all that twaddle."

Jessica and Madeleine smiled at him in a condescending manner.

"Witches' covens are springing up all over the States," Madeleine said. "It's no laughing matter."

"Black magic is rife in this country too," Jessica added. "But to think your mother was involved . . ."

"Okay," Andrew said reasonably. "Let's have a look at this journal."

"That's the strange thing—it's vanished," Madeleine said.

"Vanished!" exclaimed Jessica.

Andrew smirked and said nothing. Madeleine looked at him, wishing he'd take the situation seriously.

"I left it on the table, over there, last night. This morning, when I passed the door, I was sure there was someone in here, but when I came into the room it was empty. Later on in the day when I came to look for it, out of a sort of morbid fascination, it had gone. I'm sure whoever was in here this morning took it." Madeleine indicated the table on which she'd left the journal.

Jessica gazed over at the table, which stood in a side window, as if she expected to find an answer. "So it could have been seen by someone passing the window, from the garden?" she suggested.

"Ah, a budding Agatha Christie!" Andrew teased.

"Oh, do shut up!" Jessica said. "I'm only trying to find a rational explanation. Have you any idea who could have taken it, Maddy?"

"I think it was Jenkins. He's been the gardener here for the past forty years, and I'm convinced he knows the whole story. And I can tell you something else: he sure as hell doesn't want me to find out anything. He clammed up completely when I tried to ask him about my mother."

"This is absolutely fascinating!" Jessica crowed, her tiredness vanished. "You've *got* to find out what it's all about."

Later, after supper and several glasses of wine, Madeleine took them into the drawing room, where Jessica begged to be allowed to look at some of Camilla's photographs. With Andrew scoffing gently, Jessica pored over the framed prints, but Madeleine looked away, busying herself by having another look at the little silver snuffboxes and trinkets that lay scattered about. All she wanted now was to get home to Carl and a life of normality.

"Let's go up to bed," she said at last.

"Suits me," Andrew said with a grin. Then he turned to Jessica and gave her a playful smack on the bottom. "Are you going to walk up the stairs . . . or fly up on your broomstick?"

The heavy rain started to fall at dawn, obliterating the countryside as it lay bleakly under low-lying gray clouds. Jessica was awakened by heavy splattering on the bedroom windows, and as she lay listening to it she planned what she'd say to Andrew. The thought made her stomach contract nervously because she knew he was going to be absolutely furious. If only I'd told him earlier in the week and got it over with, she fretted, glancing over at him as he lay slumbering. It never failed to surprise her how young he looked when he slept; almost boyish, his face smooth and relaxed, his mouth tilting up naturally at the corners. He's going to be hurt too, she reflected. For a flashing moment Jessica contemplated turning down Robert Scholtz' offer, seeing herself and Andrew continuing as they were, enjoying their comfortable lives in their smart London flat; each going to work in the morning, and then coming home at night, sure of each other's affections, confident in their future together. The picture was rosy and contented, and also safe. That's the trouble, thought Jessica, easing herself into a sitting position in the bed. It's too contented, too safe. As the rain continued to hiss on the terrace below the window and the gentle sough of the trees grew stronger, Jessica knew it wasn't enough; not while she had the chance to soar to the peak of her career, to enjoy the power and the satisfaction the future held for her. In ten years' time, maybe. She'd be only thirty-five then and there would still be plenty of time for getting married and and even having a baby.

Women of forty had babies these days, she reassured herself.

Jessica lay down again, her mind finally made up. She couldn't put off telling Andrew any longer.

By ten o'clock the rain had turned into a blinding deluge, drumming on the windowsills of the Manor, turning the lawns into a squelching carpet, and running in muddy streams down the pathways.

They sat in the library, Madeleine and Jessica chatting while Andrew slouched in an armchair reading the *Daily Telegraph*. From time to time he looked out of the windows as if hoping the storm would magically cease.

"Not much chance of going for a walk in this weather," he commented bleakly.

Jessica glanced up quickly, breaking off in the middle of saying something to Madeleine. Something in the disconsolate tone of his voice made her heart quicken, reminding her again of what she had to do.

"Oh, Andrew!" she said, as if she'd just remembered something. "I've been meaning to tell you—Robert Scholtz, you know, the president of the Golding Group, was over from the States a few days ago and . . . well, he's offered me the job of director of sales." Jessica pressed her hands together to stop them shaking. "It's the most wonderful opportunity—of course it means much more money too—and it's a terrific feather in my cap! It's one of the top positions in the hotel." She was aware she was gabbling, her words running one into the other.

Andrew put down his newspaper, a pleased expression on his face.

"Well done, Jessie," he said quietly.

"Congratulations! Why didn't you tell us before?" Madeleine asked. "I know you hoped you'd be made director of sales one of these days, but isn't this much sooner than you expected?"

"Yes, it's because the person who is doing it now is being transferred to another of our hotels in Hong Kong. It's not official yet—I think there'll be an announcement in a week— but in the meantime, no one at the Royal Westminster knows. It's going to be a bit of a shock for Dick Fowler, whom I work with, but that's life, isn't it?" Jessica gesticulated, her gold bangles chinking as she talked. She was sitting very upright now, her tight jeans emphasizing the slim vibrance of her body, her feet in the inevitable high-heeled shoes tucked beneath her.

Andrew regarded her with lazy approval. "And so when does this new job start, darling?"

Jessica looked across at him, her little face suddenly tight, her eyes defiant. "In about three weeks, I think. There is just one snag that's not going to thrill you . . ." She gave a forced laugh, brittle and tense. "They want me to live in. It's part of the hotel policy: all senior management have to be on-site twenty-four hours a day."

There was a stunned silence. Madeleine was the first to break it. "Live in? You mean live in the hotel?"

"That's right. I'll be given a room, probably on the top floor. It won't be a suite or anything grand like that, but it doesn't matter because I'll only be using it to sleep in," Jessica replied. Now that she'd actually told Andrew, she felt her courage and conviction returning.

"Thanks very much for consulting me before you accepted!" Andrew said angrily.

Jessica flushed. "Well, how could I refuse a chance like this," she said defiantly. "Come on, Andrew, it's not the end of the world. I will have time off, and some weekends too. It doesn't change anything between us."

"Oh, you don't think so?" he said bitingly. "Well, I think it changes everything." Then, without another word he rose, flung down the newspaper, and strode out of the room. A moment later they heard the front door slam.

"He can't have gone out in all this rain . . . can he?" Jessica rushed to the library window and looked out. "It's still pouring. Oh, what a fool! He'll catch his death of cold."

"You can hardly blame him, Jessica," Madeleine said reasonably. "It must have been an awful shock for him. Didn't you think he'd be upset? God, Carl would kill me if I announced I planned to sleep at my studio in future because I wanted to get on with my painting." Her heart-shaped face looked pale and shocked and her eyes were laden with concern.

"That's different—you're married!" Jessica wailed, throwing herself back onto the sofa. "I knew Andrew would hate it. I've been dreading telling him, but, Maddy, it *is* my life. How could I possibly turn down an opportunity like this, I ask you?" She brushed her eyes angrily with the back of her hand, her voice breaking on the edge of a sob. "It's not going to alter our relationship."

Madeleine regarded her with quiet amazement. "Of course it is, Jessie, dear. When will you see Andrew? Occasional evenings, sometimes on weekends? After three years of living with you, it's pretty hard on him to find you're suddenly moving out."

"From Chelsea to Hyde Park Corner is hardly the other side of the world, for God's sake!" Jessica's voice rose to a querulous squeak. "I thought you'd understand, Maddy. That's why I waited until this weekend to tell Andrew, because I was sure you'd back me up."

Madeleine shook her head. "Sorry, Jessica. I'm with Andrew on this one."

For the rest of the weekend the atmosphere was strained. The rain continued to fall in a slanting curtain, and the house seemed filled with a chilling dampness that seeped through the skin to the bones. Forced to stay indoors most of the time, they read, watched television, and conversed in a stilted fashion. Jessica began to pray for Sunday evening, when they were due to return to London, because Andrew's cold fury was getting her down. Never one to harbor grudges herself, she sparkled and fizzed again within minutes of having a fight, and couldn't understand why he didn't also. At last it was Andrew who suggested they catch an earlier train.

"What a pity, but with the weather so miserable, I think you're right," Madeleine said understandingly. "I'd come back to London with you now if I could, but I've got a final meeting with Mr. Marks, the solicitor, tomorrow morning, before I fly home on Tuesday."

As they got into the waiting taxi to take them to the station because it was Jenkin's day off, Jessica turned and flung her arms around Madeleine.

"It's going to be ages before I see you again!" she cried. "Wish me luck in my new job, Maddy!"

"Of course I wish you luck," Madeleine replied warmly. "It's your life, honey, and I really hope everything works out for you."

Jessica fought back emotional tears.

Madeleine kissed Andrew on the cheek. "Good-bye, Andrew, and thanks for doing a valuation on the house. When I get around to selling it, maybe you could handle the sale for me."

"Of course I will, Maddy dear." Andrew looked at her fondly. "Take care of yourself and don't let this business of your mother get you down. After all, it's all in the past."

"I know."

"And give my best regards to Carl."

"Yes, give Carl my love and a big kiss from me," Jessica chimed in, sticking her head out of the taxi window.

"I will. Good-bye." Madeleine watched as the taxi drove off, its tires sending out sprays of muddy droplets. Then she went back into the house to start packing.

At nine o'clock the next morning Mr. Marks arrived, a drab beige raincoat a couple of sizes too big for him protecting his dark suit from the steady drizzle that had now replaced the heavy rain. His blinking eyes reminded Madeleine of a mole coming out of the darkness, confused by the light. She led him into the library and offered him coffee. He appeared to be slightly agitated.

"There is a slight hitch in the proceedings," he said as he sipped his coffee, light, with sugar. "It's causing a delay in proving your claim on the estate, and I shall have to get some details from you."

"What sort of details? What do you need to know, Mr. Marks?"

"Well, the problem is, Mrs. Delaney . . ." Here he paused to stare into her face, his eyes blinking rapidly. "So far, we have not been able to find any trace of your mother's death certificate."

6

CARL LEFT the Central Manhattan Bank shortly after six, telling his chauffeur he wouldn't be needing him. Then he hailed a cab to take him to Kimberley's apartment, La Premiere, on Fifty-fifth and Broadway, a towering monolith opposite a popular diner that did a good imitation of being a forties restaurant. That morning she'd suggested he spend the night with her, and, spellbound, knocked out by her sexuality, he agreed, telling her to go early so they wouldn't be seen leaving the bank together. Already, he thought with amazement, I'm slipping into the games some married men play. He was appalled at how easy it was.

When he arrived, Kimberley had already changed into loose silk pajamas, her feet bare, her red hair cascading around her shoulders like burnished copper. She'd lit the apricot-shaded lamps in her luxuriously furnished living room, throwing into relief the dark brown suede sofas and chairs and cream fur rugs, all presents—as the apartment itself had been—from previous lovers. As Carl stepped into the room, he felt as if he'd walked into a box of delicious chocolates—rich, dark and tempting. Kimberley padded over to the wet bar, her legs visible through the green silk, her bare arms creamy and smooth.

Carl had been fantasizing about this moment all day.

When Kimberley handed him his drink, he put it on a side table and took her in his arms. This was what he'd come here for, his senses told him—to lose himself in the warm body of this voluptuous woman with the white skin and the titian hair. Without saying a word, he pushed her down onto the fur rug, pinning her beneath him, tearing away the clinging silk of her pajamas. Kimberley curled herself around him, welcoming him with little moans. Demented, losing control, Carl ripped away the last of the silk, revealing her perfect body and flawless skin. Without even bothering to remove his own clothing, he took her savagely, his breathing heavy; he was desperate to possess this woman who had so suddenly bewitched him. His passion reached flash point, maddening him that there was something elusive about her that he was unable to capture. She was giving nothing of herself away. At last, with a final surge, Carl poured his life into her, desperate to have her and hold her and make her his; but as he raised his eyes to look into Kimberley's, all he saw was an expression of smiling detachment. He buried his face in her neck, unable to bear what he saw.

"You're hot," she said brightly. "Would you like a drink?"

Carl shut his eyes tighter, feeling ready to weep in this moment of acute anticlimax. He had started out wanting a purely sexual thrill, an affair on the side, a diversion from his loneliness while Madeleine was away, but somehow in the past few hours he had hoped for something more from Kimberley. Now, he realized, she had nothing more to give. It was obvious, looking around the apartment, that she could not have afforded to furnish it so lavishly from her earnings; she didn't make enough at the bank to even pay the rent. Painfully aware that he was one of many, he accepted her offer of a drink and felt foolish at his own naiveté.

While Carl lay fast asleep, his mouth slightly open and his breathing deep and regular, Kimberley slid out from between the brown satin sheets and crept, naked, to the kitchen. It was four o'clock in the morning and the humidity of the city, still noisy and active at this hour, made her feel sticky. Going to the refrigerator, she got out a can of Seven-Up and jerked back the metal tag. A loud hiss penetrated the heavy silence of her apartment and she paused, listening, but Carl did not stir. Kimberley's mouth curved in a smile. Let him sleep . . . while he could. Soon he'd be too worried to even want to go to bed!

Perching on a kitchen stool, her bare feet swinging clear of the cork floor, she leaned forward until she could rest her elbow on the windowsill. From here she could look south, down Broadway, and watch the constant ebb and flow of traffic and the dazzle of lights that now, from the twenty-fourth floor, looked like tiny pinpricks. She remembered another night, a long time ago, when a little girl had stood in Times Square, and all around her the lights had sparkled and shone in gold and silver, red and green, and shimmering blue. They'd spun a promise of excitement and untold wealth that was soon going to be fulfilled. Not long to go now, she assured herself, and then all her dreams would become a reality. She'd have everything she'd ever wanted—the jewels and furs, the exquisite clothes, a lovely house and cars. . . . Soon now it would all be hers, thanks to Hank Pugsley; and also thanks to Carl Delaney, although he didn't know it yet.

Twelve months before, while sitting in a singles bar one night, Kimberley had met Hank Pugsley. Not met, exactly, although that's what she'd tell her friends, but been picked up by Hank. He was middle-aged, married, and exceedingly rich. He was also very fat and unattractive, with lank greasy hair and small eyes, but that didn't bother Kimberley. He might be good for a dress or even a fur, so she wasted no time inviting him back to her apartment, and in doing so, ditching another man she'd agreed to meet that night. People like Hank were "fillers-in," as she described them to herself, someone who would fill in the time until her lucky break came along. Meanwhile, men like Hank had allowed her to live in a nice apartment and dress smartly.

Kimberley discovered that Hank owned a company called Brandt's Motors. They sold spare parts for cars and trucks and operated in New Jersey. Hank ran a small office in downtown Manhattan, but the reason for that, he explained leeringly, was that it gave him an excuse to stay in town some nights instead of going back to his wife. It was a story Kimberley had heard a thousand times before, and she shrugged, bored. Men were all the same, from her father onward, and they sickened her.

"I've got a big outfit, you know," Hank declared, disappointed by her lack of interest in him, "and I make a stack of dough."

"Oh, yeah?" She studied her long nails, painted a frosted pink, and wondered when he'd go.

Anxious to impress her, and puffed up with his own importance, he helped himself to some more of her brandy and started bragging.

It was the greatest mistake he was ever to make in his life.

"D'you know how I get away without having to pay much tax?" he demanded proudly.

Kimberley looked up, her interest instantly engaged. He might, she thought, have something useful to say. "No. How d'you do that?"

Hank leaned back on her brown satin pillows, his sweating shoulders staining the fabric almost black, his cigar filling the air with its pungent stench.

As Hank explained, Kimberley became more and more attentive, making mental notes of everything he told her, memorizing details with a mind like a trap.

"It's my money, after all," he concluded smugly. "I'm not robbing my customers, and I reckon I should be able to keep as much of my own money as I want. After all, I've earned it. Why should I let the fucking IRS get it all!"

"How clever," Kimberley said slowly, and she meant it. She rolled over on to her stomach so that she was facing him, her breasts swinging large and pendulously. "Have a little more brandy, honey," she said affectionately.

Flattered, and pleased by his own ingeniousness, Hank told her more, his small beady eyes gleaming with cunning.

What held Kimberley's particular interest was that the millions of dollars he was transferring, to a numbered account in Switzerland, initially went through the Central Manhattan Bank, where his company had an account. Probing gently, being careful not to appear too interested, because he thought she was a budding model and models didn't usually bother with high finance, Kimberley finally got out of him everything she wanted to know.

Over the next few months she was able, surreptitiously, to check out what he'd told her. Sure enough, every couple of weeks large amounts were transferred from Brandt's Motors to Zurich. Kimberley started to formulate a plan, and that was where Carl came in.

Madeleine walked Mr. Marks to the front door and stood talking with him on the steps of Milton Manor.

"I'll get the details from my father," she told him. "You say that if we had the exact date and place, it would help trace my mother's death certificate?"

"Exactly so." Mr. Marks still looked slightly agitated. It was a reflection on the good name of Spindle, Coutts, and Marks that they were unable to do a simple thing like trace a death certificate, and under the circumstances, highly embarrassing.

"I'm just so sorry that it will delay things even more . . ." he continued, his voice drifting away as if he didn't know how to finish the sentence.

Madeleine shrugged. "It can't be helped. I'll get the information to you as soon as possible. In the meantime, thank you for all you're doing."

"Oh, not at all. Please don't mention it." He darted her a grateful look under his quivering eyelashes and got into his car. "We'll be in touch, then, Mrs. Delaney?"

"We will," Madeleine promised with a smile.

It wasn't until later in the morning that she realized she would probably be able to get her questions answered sooner than she'd expected. Alice Stewart and her son, Philip, were driving over for luncheon today. Alice would be sure to remember when and where Camilla had died.

They arrived at one o'clock, with Philip at the wheel of his Aston Martin. Alice Stewart, unperturbed by the speed at which her son drove, emerged from the vehicle unruffled, an elegant figure in a silver-gray dress, her white hair curly and fluffy around her face.

"My dear Madeleine! It is sweet of you to invite us over," she said, holding out her hands in greeting as Madeleine came forward to welcome them. Alice glanced up at the Dutch-style gables and scroll-carved stonework of the old house and smiled.

"My goodness, it's a long time since I've been here. George used to entertain a great deal, but when he became a widower, he found it more difficult."

Madeleine led them into the drawing room for drinks before luncheon. Alice, she noticed, had turned small talk into an art form, and charmingly and captivatingly kept the conversation going with her reminiscences of bygone days when Milton Manor had been the setting for many a lavish party.

"I can even remember Camilla's coming-out ball here; there was a pink-and-white marquee in the garden, and your grandmother had arrangements of big white michaelmas daisies everywhere," she recalled. "It all looked so pretty."

Hunter announced lunch and they went through to the

stately dining room, which now sparkled with use and smelled of sweet-scented stock from the garden.

"You must have missed my mother when she married Daddy and went to live in the States," Madeleine observed as Hunter placed plates of fresh asparagus in front of everyone before filling the glasses with wine.

"Yes, indeed!" Alice nodded vigorously, her pearl drop earrings shimmering as she moved her head. "But then of course I got married myself and went to live in London until my husband inherited our place from his father."

Madeleine leaned forward eagerly. "Were you living here when my parents returned to England in 1965 . . . when I was three?"

"No, we were still in town then, but we often came down for weekends, and sometimes I'd bring Philip over to play with you."

Philip looked at Madeleine and smiled. She smiled back politely, but it wasn't Philip she was interested in at this moment. She spoke with sudden urgency: "And were you here when my mother died?"

Madeleine wondered what she'd done wrong. Alice had almost recoiled and was now ashen-faced, her pale lipstick taking on a mauve tone.

"What did you say, my dear?"

Madeleine spoke carefully, never taking her eyes off the older woman's face; it was as if a mask had been pulled down over Alice's features, wiping away and blanking out all color and expression. "I asked if you were here in Devon when my mother died?" she repeated clearly.

"Oh, yes . . . I mean, no . . ." Alice was looking at her strangely. "It's . . . it's such a long time ago, I can hardly remember," she added lamely. Madeleine glanced at Philip, who was watching his mother with a puzzled look on his face. Alice fiddled with the long ropes of pearls that hung around her neck—like the pearls, Madeleine thought suddenly, that she remembered being around her mother's neck in the portrait by de Laszlo.

"But did she die here, or up in London?" Madeleine persisted. "The solicitor told me this morning they can't trace her death certificate. If I knew exactly where and when she'd died, it would be a great help."

Alice's manner had changed. The talkative, outgoing woman full of vitality and friendliness had suddenly become withdrawn, almost furtive-looking. "You must ask your father about all that." In spite of the quaver in her voice, she spoke with finality. Then, with astonishing panache and social dexterity, she plunged straight into a dissertation about the roses having mildew this year. Philip, obviously relieved that what looked like a sticky minute had passed, offered his suggestions, and the conversation turned to gardening.

Madeleine, leaning back in her chair, felt both disappointment and growing disquiet. Whatever had happened to her mother, Alice Stewart wasn't going to talk about it.

Carl had been in a meeting with Jake all afternoon, and now, when he returned to his office he found Kimberley waiting for him, her translucent gray eyes as clear as cold marbles, but her mouth tilted into its accustomed smile.

"Do you have a minute?" she asked, standing opposite him as he sat at his desk sorting out papers.

Carl looked up warily. The last two nights had been a great mistake, he'd decided. No harm had been done, but nevertheless he'd been extremely foolish to fall into the cliché of the boss-and-secretary affair. Now he planned to extricate himself gently and pleasantly, as if he were sure their fleeting relationship had meant no more to her than to him.

"Sure, but I'm a bit busy, as you can see . . ." he began in a friendly fashion, but something in her expression cut him short.

"This is important, Carl." Kimberley no longer called him Mr. Delaney when they were alone. She sat down on the chair opposite him, looking businesslike with her hair swept back into a neat chignon and wearing a black-and-white-checked "power" suit with padded shoulders.

"What is it?"

"I have a friend, Hank Pugsley. He owns a company called Brandt's Motors in New Jersey, and he banks here, with us."

Carl's mouth tightened. If Kimberley was going to have the gall to ask him to arrange a loan for one of her lovers, she had another thought coming to her. "So?" he snapped.

Undaunted, Kimberley went on to explain Hank's method of tax dodging. "It's quite neat, really," she explained. "Some

time ago he started a phony company in Switzerland, called
Michaux Internationale. Every two weeks Hank is sent a fake
invoice from Zurich, sometimes amounting to hundreds of
thousands of dollars, for machine tools and various spare
parts. He then sends the money to Zurich, but of course it
goes into his numbered account, as Michaux Internationale
doesn't exist.''

"I'm not with you, Kimberley," Carl said, frowning. "Why
are you telling me all this?"

"Because I've thought of a way of stopping him."

Carl was taken aback. "By reporting him to the feds, you
mean?" He thought for a moment. "That could be a problem,
especially from the bank's point of view. We would be using
privileged information and that would constitute a breach of
trust." Then he looked up at her. "Apart from which, why do
you want to spill the beans on a friend of yours?"

Kimberley smiled, amused. "I have a much more interesting
proposition to put to you than that."

"What are you talking about?" Carl's stomach contracted
uneasily and a prickle of fear shivered down his spine. "You
don't intend to blackmail him?"

"You're head of foreign transactions, right?" Kimberley continued, as if she hadn't heard him. Carl nodded, mute with
apprehension. Kimberley continued, "Whenever you receive
one of Hank's instruction forms authorizing money to be transferred from his business account at the Central Manhattan
Bank to Switzerland to pay Michaux Internationale's invoices,
you have to pass it to Jake Shearman after you have done the
initial paperwork. I know you've been receiving them, because
I've been watching." She paused to let the words sink in.
"Jake Shearman and two of the vice-presidents are the only
people who have the code for transferring large amounts of
money by computer to foreign countries. I trained in computers and I'm a computer programmer, so I do know what
I'm talking about," she added, her voice an urgent whisper
now.

Carl was watching her as if hypnotized; her cold clear eyes
held a hint of fanaticism, binding him to her, immobilizing
him so that he sat still, almost mesmerized, his brain reeling
as the implication of what she was saying penetrated.

"You have access to Jake's office. I want you to borrow the

computer tape that has the key to the foreign-transactions code and I want you to let me have it for an hour. In that time I can make a copy and then you can put the original back in Jake's office."

"I still don't understand, Kimberley," Carl said heavily. But a voice inside his head said: *You understand only too well*. But he had to play for time while he decided how to handle this situation. He felt caught off-balance, unprepared. Kimberley was in control of the position at the moment, and she knew it. She'd deliberately chosen a moment, during working hours in the bank, when she knew he wouldn't be able to make a scene. She leaned toward him now, her eyes fixed on his face. Carl felt himself recoil as she spoke.

"This is my plan, Carl," she said. "Every time you get instructions from Hank Pugsley to transfer money to his Swiss account, you give it straight to me. I will put it though the computer, using my copy of the tape with the coded key, only instead of transferring it to Hank's account, I will be transferring it to a numbered account at a bank in Zurich that I opened six months ago."

Carl closed his eyes, shock and fear turning him ice-cold, making his heart pound. He knew what she was going to say before she said it. He'd made love to her in the shower . . . in her apartment . . .

"Don't think of refusing, Carl. I doubt if your wife and your father-in-law would appreciate receiving a copy of the tape recording I made of you screwing me in my apartment last night."

The silence in his office was palpable, locking them together in a fearful conspiracy. Her words thundered in his head, holding him in a vise of torment. He'd let himself be maneuvered, by the oldest trick in the world, into a situation where he was ripe for blackmail, and unless he could think of a way out, he would only fall deeper and deeper into Kimberley's clutches.

"Let's make a deal," he heard Kimberley say. "We'll split the money, because neither one of us could pull this off single-handed. That's fair, don't you think?"

Carl sprang to his feet, anger and panic engulfing him. "You're off your trolley!" he whispered furiously.

"No, I'm not. There's no way we're going to get caught.

Hank isn't going to find out the money isn't reaching his account because he never receives bank statements from Switzerland; he told me himself it would be too dangerous if they fell into the wrong hands. Even if he did find out, what can he do about it? He's acting illegally himself, pretending to pay for tools that don't exist, in order to defraud the government. He wouldn't dare squeal. Believe me, Carl, we can cream off several million dollars and no one will know.''

"If you think I'm going to go along with this crazy scheme . . .'' Carl muttered, running his hands through his hair. What scared him most of all was that he knew Kimberley's plan could be made to work. He *was* in a position to ''borrow'' the computer tape for a short while from Jake's office, provided he did it in the late afternoon, after Jake and the two vice-presidents had left the bank; and Kimberley knew what she was doing, so she would have no problem making a copy. After that, all he had to do was pass over Hank Pugsley's instruction forms to Kimberley for processing, instead of to Jake, and as she'd said, Hank was unlikely to make a scene even if he did find out what was happening.

Carl looked at Kimberley, realizing she'd worked everything out, down to the last detail, and in a moment of self-loathing he wondered how he'd ever thought her attractive. Fool! Fool! How could he have let himself get caught like this? For a moment he contemplated telling her to go to hell; he even contemplated rushing up to Jake's office to tell him what had happened, but he knew that if he did, he'd be finished. Madeleine might forgive him an indiscretion, although she'd be deeply hurt, but Jake wouldn't. Jake lived by a rigid set of moral rules, especially where the bank was concerned, and sleeping with a member of the staff and thereby putting oneself in a vulnerable position would, in Jake's opinion, show a severe lack of judgment; and a sense of judgment, in banking as in politics, was essential.

"You really haven't got any option, have you?'' Kimberley was saying. "You've got to be part of my plan—or your whole future lies in ruins. You can kiss the prospect of being the next president of Central Manhattan Bank good-bye if you don't go along with it.''

Her words hit Carl like a physical blow. He would lose everything he'd worked for if Jake were to find out, and if her scheme went disastrously wrong he'd lose everything anyway. Carl went to his washroom, shuddering as his eyes caught the shower, remembering her standing there naked. Splashing cold water on his face, his mind spinning down into a bottomless void that was filled with horror and anger, he cursed himself for being such a fool as to have succumbed to his mindless lust for a pretty girl.

Carl awoke at five o'clock, his head throbbing and his limbs rigid with tension. For two nights now he'd slept only fitfully, spending most of the time on his back gazing up at the ceiling while his mind reeled in a frenzy of worry as the slow hours ticked away. How could he have ever gotten himself into this situation? The question chased itself around and around in his brain until he thought he'd go mad. He cursed himself for his moment of weakness and thanked God that Madeleine was not there to witness his torment. And yet he longed for her too. None of this would have happened, he thought unhappily, if she hadn't gone away. In the four years of their marriage he hadn't so much as looked at anyone else, although they'd often been apart for days at a time if she was away on a painting commission. Yet this time, during that one crazy irresponsible moment, he'd wrecked everything. The guilt he felt about Madeleine even overshadowed the events of yesterday afternoon, when Kimberley had demanded he get the computer tape from Jake's office. Feeling sick with fear, he'd knocked on the door of Jake's office and, finding it empty, walked in and gone straight to the safe where the tape was kept. He knew how to open it in seconds. When he'd married Madeleine and become "family," Jake had made him privy to a lot of highly confidential material, and that included the combination to his private office safe.

Holding his breath, he turned the knob twice clockwise until it rested at six. Then he turned it once counterclockwise, stopping at nine, and clockwise once again until the tiny arrow got to five. A final turn and the door opened. Carl's mind raced as he reached for the tape, at the same time extracting some other papers, as a cover, in case he was caught. Then he closed the safe and hurried from the room. Kimberley was waiting for him in his office. Without a word she took the tape from him. Drenched with sweat, Carl sank down on the chair behind his desk and watched her go back to her own office. He tried to work but found himself shuffling papers about, as the longest hour of his life began. Whenever the phone rang he jumped with fright; when anyone knocked on his door wishing to see him, he felt himself tense with fear. He could imagine Kimberley copying the tape in the computer department, spinning some lie, no doubt, to explain what she was doing, if anyone asked. For a moment he was almost grateful that she was so adept at lying and so skillful at deceiving. Anyone with less wits about them would surely get caught.

At last she returned, a satisfied smirk on her painted lips. Carl grabbed the tape from her, collected the papers he'd also taken from Jake's safe, and within five minutes had returned everything. No one had seen him, as far as he knew, going into Jake's office either time, but the strain of the afternoon had left him with a blinding headache.

Slowly now, as if his mental agony had transferred itself to his body, he eased himself out of the four-poster bed and padded into the adjoining bathroom, which Madeleine had designed in soft shades of pink marble. Relaxing in a tub of very hot water, which he felt would help him unwind more than a shower, he planned to get to the office before Kimberley. It was imperative that he do something to put an end to her scheme before everything got out of hand. Suppose he offered her money. Persuaded her to leave the country. But how much money would it take? Carl shook his head in silent anguish. She'd want millions, because that was what she'd said she could get from robbing Pugsley. Where the fuck was he going to get millions to give her? He didn't *have* millions, and he couldn't go to Jake or Madeleine because of course they'd want to know why he needed it. Suppose he borrowed it from someone else. But that was no use; he'd have to provide collateral, and that would involve Madeleine and her father again. In a gesture of furious despair, Carl picked up a flask of perfume that stood on a ledge by the bath and flung it at the opposite wall. In a shattering of glass, a pungent trail of Claude Montana scent drifted toward him, bringing Madeleine's presence into the room as strongly as if she'd been standing there.

"Oh, Jesus," he groaned, stepping out of the bath carefully so as not to cut his feet. Picking up the shards of glass, he wrapped them carefully in tissue and dropped them in the wastebasket. Madeleine would be home very soon now, and he wondered how he was going to face her.

An hour later Carl strode into his office.

"What the hell . . . ?"

Kimberley, standing by his desk, turned to look at him coolly. "Hank should be putting through a transfer to Zurich anytime now. I was going through your morning mail to see if there was any sign of it."

"How dare you touch my things!" Carl stormed. "What the fuck do you think you're doing?" He found his hands were trembling and he'd broken out in a sweat.

Kimberley looked at him insolently. "Keep calm. It hasn't arrived yet in any case. But I'll keep a look out for it, so don't think you can go slipping it to Jake Shearman behind my back."

"God damn you!" Carl looked at her with revulsion, hating himself even more than he hated her. What had he ever seen in her? "I'd like to kill you!" he breathed in her face.

"Or fuck me?" she scoffed crudely.

"Enough people have probably done that already!" he snapped, turning to leave the office. He walked along the corridor, blind with rage, bile rising sourly in his throat. When he came to the second-floor gallery he paused to look down on the main banking area. Clerks were arriving for work; nice, simple men and women bent on doing a good job, content to receive their paychecks at the end of the week and go home to their families every evening. For a long moment Carl envied them their uncomplicated lives, and then he wondered at the turn of fate that had sent him a secretary in the shape of Kimberley Cabot. Down among the stretches of black-and-white marble and chrome and Lucite, ordinary decent people were going about their work, while in his office a she-devil had taken possession. Carl suddenly wished with all his heart that he could turn the clock back to even a couple of weeks ago.

Madeleine hurried out of the arrivals terminal at JFK and into the waiting car. It had been more than two weeks since she'd seen Carl, and now that she was nearly home the longing for him intensified, making her wonder how she'd managed without him for so long. She glanced at her watch, which she'd altered to New York time before disembarking. At this rate she'd be back in her apartment by two-thirty; too late to call Carl and suggest they meet for lunch.

Settling herself in the back of the limousine, she tried to plan her day, but her thoughts kept straying back to Carl. They'd talked constantly on the phone, of course, almost every day, but it wasn't the same. She closed her eyes, imagining his arms around her, his mouth demanding, his body pressing against her. Aroused, she opened her eyes again wondering if she could persuade him to leave the bank early.

When the familiar outline of Manhattan appeared on the horizon, her heart gave a little twist of excitement. Only another twenty minutes and they'd be on Fifth Avenue, drawing up outside number 944.

The empty silence of the apartment depressed her, as she went from room to room as if to reassure herself everything was all right and nothing had changed. Why, she asked herself, did she have this feeling that something was wrong?

At that moment Teresa appeared to take charge of her luggage. Madeleine greeted her and asked for some coffee.

"Right away, ma'am. Did you have a good trip?"

"Yes, thank you, Teresa. Has everything been okay here?"

"Yes, ma'am." The maid didn't seem to want to linger, and picking up one of the suitcases, added: "I'll get your coffee and then I'll do the unpacking."

"Thanks." Madeleine went back into the living room to phone Carl. At least she could talk to him, even if she couldn't see him until this evening.

The wintry sun streamed in through the two large windows, dazzling and highlighting the all-white room, where the Thai silk festooned curtains resembled thick whipped cream and the carpet was like a drift of soft snow. White was piled on white, in thick cotton and silk upholstery, in pleated muslin lampshades and bleached ash furniture. The only colors in the room were in two portraits, one of Carl and one of Jake, which she'd painted some years before. The one of Carl, looking impossibly blond and handsome, hung above the white marble fireplace, and the one of Jake was on the opposite wall above a writing table. Madeleine glanced at them as she entered the room, wondering with a fresh eye, brought about by her ab-

sence, if they weren't too strong for such a delicate room.
Especially the portrait of Jake. She'd forgotten how totally
dominating it was, depicting her father sitting at his desk in
the bank, his face composed in serious lines. She went over,
idly, to have a closer look, and was suddenly struck by something she'd never noticed before. His eyes had the same mocking watchfulness that she'd seen in the eyes of Camilla's
photographs. The chilling look was not as pronounced as in
the photographs, but it was definitely there: a wariness, a
guardedness—and a knowledge. But a knowledge of what? A
shared experience? A secret known only to them? Madeleine
put her hand to her face in a gesture of bewilderment, wondering if it was only she who could sense these things. Maybe
this gift of reading a person's soul was what made her the
painter she was. Maybe her artist's eye saw something that
others didn't see. With a little shudder she turned away. The
portrait was much too strong for this room, she decided.
Maybe she would give it to her father as a present.

That evening Carl was home early, wiping out her depression by arriving with an armful of pink roses. She hurried
across the hall to greet him, her arms outstretched.

"Hi, Maddy. Welcome home." Carl kissed her tenderly.

"It's so good to be back, you've no idea." Madeleine ran
her hand through the thickness of his hair at the nape of his
neck. "I'll never stay away so long again."

"You couldn't help it, sweetheart. Is everything all right . . .
do you have to go back again?"

"At some point I'll have to supervise the sale of the house,
but it won't be for ages yet." Madeleine took his arm and they
walked slowly into the living room, where she'd already put
a bottle of champagne in a silver ice bucket. "I've missed you
so much, Carl. You've no idea. I wish to God you'd been with
me."

"So do I!"

Madeleine looked at him sharply, wondering if anything was
wrong. She'd had such a strange two weeks, overcast by death
and doubt and mystery, that maybe she was letting her imagination run away with her; but he'd spoken with such
vehemence.

"Well, thank you, honey. I didn't know you missed me *that*
much!" she joked coquettishly.

Carl flushed, and grabbing her again, kissed her long and hard. "I'll show you how much I missed you," he said lightly as he released her.

"I was hoping you'd say that," Madeleine replied with a wicked grin. "That's why I've given Teresa the night off."

"Scheming woman." He pretended to spank her bottom, but he put up no resistance as Madeleine drew him in the direction of the bedroom. Suddenly she stopped, and turning toward him, put her arms around him again. Pressing her cheek to his, she whispered, "Oh, I love you, Carl, and I need you so much."

"I need you too," he whispered back as he buried his face in her hair, and he was glad she couldn't see the deeply troubled look in his eyes.

"Can we meet for lunch, Daddy?" Madeleine asked Jake when she phoned him the next morning.

Jake seemed to hesitate for a moment and she knew he was trying to delay her confronting him with demands for the truth about her mother. But after a moment he said, "Yes, of course, my dear. I can't manage today, but how about tomorrow?"

"That would be fine."

"La Caravelle at one?"

"Perfect. I'll see you then. 'Bye, Daddy."

When Madeleine entered the restaurant the next day, in a simple white suit with gold jewelry, there was a flutter of interest and heads turned, elbows nudged, and voices dropped to whispers as she joined Jake at the bar.

They made a handsome couple, father and daughter, both tall and slim, as they were seated at one of La Caravelle's best tables, reserved for VIP's only. Madeleine's black hair framed her exquisite face in a riot of fluffy curls, while Jake's gray hair and lean tanned face gave him a distinguished air.

"It's good to see you again," Jake remarked smilingly when he'd given their order. "How was England?"

Madeleine looked at him askance. "England was fine; pity I can't say the same thing about my grandfather."

"That remark's in rather poor taste, isn't it?" Jake remarked mildly. "I'm sorry you had to suffer the shock of George dying just after you'd arrived."

"But you're not sorry he's dead," Madeleine observed.

Jake raised his eyebrows and looked at his daughter in surprise. "What a strange thing to say. George was an old man and he'd been slightly crazy for years. I would have thought his death, to use a cliché, was a merciful release. I warned you not to go to see him, Madeleine. I knew it would be no picnic."

Madeleine leveled her gaze at Jake, her voice steady. "Daddy, there's no point in your trying to hide anything from me. I found out a lot of things when I was staying at Milton Manor, but I need you to fill in a few details. I want to know what happened to my mother."

Jake gave a false laugh and threw his arms wide in a gesture of bravado. "Why are you so obsessed with the past?" he demanded. "It's over and done with, and now that George is dead, that's the end of the chapter. The end of the Dalrymples."

"It's not, Daddy. You forget, I'm half Dalrymple, and Grandfather has left me a wealth of family heirlooms. Just because my mother's dead, we can't pretend the family never existed!"

Jake didn't answer.

"My mother was involved in black magic, wasn't she?" Madeleine challenged.

"Where did you hear that nonsense?" Jake had paled, but he did not falter. "From George, no doubt. Surely you don't believe—"

"I found her journal in the library, hidden behind some other books. It described a Black Mass . . . and other things." Madeleine broke off, shuddering. "Jenkins was involved too, wasn't he? He stole the journal the day after I'd found it, and when I asked him about my mother earlier, he refused to say anything. He was obviously trying to cover up the truth."

"Jenkins?" Jake repeated, shaken. "Good God, is he still around? I thought he'd have died years ago. Now, listen to me, Madeleine . . ." He leaned across the table in a confidential manner, his voice lowered. "There *was* some talk of a witches' coven or some such stupid thing going on in the village of Sherston years and years ago, but your mother was certainly not involved. I believe she was a bit intrigued; she may have jotted down notes of what she'd heard, but that was all. As for Jenkins, he was just the gardener. I don't know what sort of trash George filled your head with, but as I've told you, he was senile. He probably didn't know what he was saying."

At that moment the waiter interrupted them to serve the poached salmon they'd ordered and to refill their wineglasses. Jake looked around the restaurant, waving casually to a few friends he saw at the other tables, obviously anxious to change the conversation.

"There's Oliver Strong," he remarked. "Did I tell you, Madeleine, that he's going to run for Congress?"

"I'm not interested in Oliver Strong," Madeleine said mutinously. "I don't care if he's going to be President! Grandfather said that at one point my life was endangered by what my mother was doing. . . . Now, for God's sake, Daddy, I have to know what happened. It's important to me."

"Keep your voice down. People are looking at us," Jake said tensely. "I don't want to hear any more of this nonsense!"

"Well, there's one thing you're going to have to tell me," Madeleine said. "I need to know exactly when and where she died, because there's no trace of her death certificate."

Jake hurried around to his sister's Beresford apartment as soon as he'd said good-bye to Madeleine and seen her into the waiting car. Patti Ziffren, who was about to leave for a bridge party, greeted him with her customary acidity.

"Really, this is most inconvenient! Couldn't you have called me first?" Her voice was more gravelly than usual, and a haze of blue cigarette smoke surrounded her like an aura.

"I'm sorry, Patti, but I had to talk to you urgently."

"Oh, well, you'd better sit down, then." She waved him to a chair in her large cluttered living room. "What's the matter?"

Briefly Jake repeated his conversation with Madeleine.

"Oh, my God!" Patti sank onto one of her pale pink sofas, more angular than ever in a sharp navy-blue Chanel suit and a plethora of gold chains. "What are you going to do?"

"I don't know," Jake said wretchedly. "Why the hell didn't George make a new will after . . . ? Patti, I wish to God you'd stop smoking!" Irritably, he waved his hand, trying to disperse the smoke.

"Do stop being so neurotic, Jake." Nevertheless, she stubbed out her cigarette in a large marble ashtray. "I think you're going to have to tell Madeleine everything," she said reflectively. "You can't hide the truth from her now."

"I can't, Patti, I can't. She's found out enough as it is. Christ, how I wish George had just gone and died quietly without involving Madeleine in the first place, then she need never have known anything at all."

Patti eyed him sympathetically, although she still spoke harshly. "Pull yourself together, for goodness' sake. Why don't you call up this lawyer—what did you say his name was . . . Marks?—and tell him in confidence what happened. He'll understand why you don't want Madeleine to find out the truth, and then let him worry about the legal side of George's will. No one's going to dispute that Madeleine is the rightful heir to her grandfather's property."

"I suppose I could." Jake sounded doubtful.

"Of course you can. Stop being so negative." Patti's restless hands reached for her jeweled gold cigarette case. "You've gone this far to protect Madeleine, why can't you go further?" She lit her cigarette and dragged on it with obvious pleasure.

Jake looked at her, his face still anxious. "Jenkins is the danger," he said quietly. "Thank God he apparently clammed up when Madeleine questioned him about Camilla. But can he be trusted not to talk in the future? Madeleine says she's going back to Milton Manor to deal with the contents when she sells the house."

Patti puffed thoughtfully. "Couldn't you silence him with a nice fat check?"

Jake looked startled. "That's not quite my style, Patti. I don't think I've ever paid out hush money in my life."

"There are times," Patti said severely, "when you should forget you're a banker and try to act like a normal human. If the thought of paying off Jenkins makes you squeamish, *I'll* damn well do it. Now, I must go or I'm going to be late for my bridge party."

"I'll think about your suggestions," Jake said as they left her apartment together.

"I know you'll do what's best for Madeleine." Patti's eyes twinkled a moment before she added, "And next time, Jake, telephone before you come rushing here for advice!"

7

"HAVE YOU heard the latest?" Dick Fowler barged into Jessica's large new office, which bore the sign "Director of Sales" on the door. He was doubled up with laughter.

"What's happened?" Jessica looked up from her desk, glad that they were still friends. Her promotion over Dick could have caused a rift between them, but he had been the first to congratulate her when her appointment had been announced, and he seemed genuinely glad for her.

"Room service have just phoned through to say that the client in room two-oh-two has ordered four breakfasts!" Dick chortled.

Jessica looked perplexed. "What, for him and his wife?"

"Wife be blowed! He's a single booking. The waiter who's on duty for that floor is on his way down to report to you."

Jessica's expression was a mixture of amusement and exasperation. "Security haven't noticed any hookers patrolling the corridors again, have they?" she asked. Six months before, in spite of the stately grandeur of the Royal Westminster, they had been forced to run a purge on prostitutes who slipped into the hotel late in the evening and then cruised up and down the corridors tapping on any bedroom door where a form ordering only one breakfast hung from the doorknob.

In one night security had rounded up eighteen of these ladies of the night, and from then on hotel policy had changed. Single women entering the hotel were politely approached by a member of staff now, inquiring if they needed assistance. Genuine women guests liked the courtesy; hookers took the hint and left, and the word soon got around that their presence was not welcome. There hadn't been any trouble for months now, thought Jessica, hoping it wasn't all going to start again. That sort of thing gave any hotel a bad name.

There was a tap on her office door. A young Italian waiter, smartly dressed in black trousers and a spotless white top with a mandarin collar, entered at Jessica's request and stood respectfully before her desk.

"I hear two-oh-two has got company?"

"Yes, miss."

Jessica tried to hide her amusement at the young man's obvious embarrassment. "Yes?" she said encouragingly. "Who's in his room with him?"

There was a long pause as the waiter swallowed with difficulty. "Three young ladies," he said at last. "All in the bed."

Jessica started, visibly surprised. "Three?" she exclaimed. *"Three?"* She turned to Dick Fowler, whose self-restraint had broken down and who was leaning back in his chair roaring with laughter.

"This isn't funny," Jessica said, trying to sound severe. "We'd better get Mr. Powell to deal with this."

"He's on sick leave . . . remember? And Mr. Wolfson's at a two-day hotel conference in Paris." Kenneth Wolfson was the general manager, and Dennis Powell was his assistant.

Jessica swore silently and looked back to the waiter. "Thank you for letting us know. That will be all."

"Thank you, miss." He scuttled out of the office as if relieved.

Dick looked speculatively at Jessica. "That leaves you . . . or would you like me to handle it?"

Jessica responded immediately in her usual gutsy fashion. "Oh, I'll deal with him. If he thinks he can use this hotel like a bordello, he's got another thought coming. Anyway, I can't wait to see what this Casanova of the corridors is like."

For a moment it crossed her mind that Andrew would really enjoy hearing all about it tonight, but then with a pang she remembered there was no more Andrew in her life. When they'd returned from staying with Madeleine in Devon, he'd issued an ultimatum.

"It's me or the hotel, Jess," he'd said, and from the sadness of his voice she knew that he'd already realized what her choice would be. Jessica had wept copiously, arguing for hours that

she could manage both, but Andrew had been adamant. The
hotel was going to consume her, twenty-four hours a day, and
they'd hardly ever see each other—just for odd nights here
and there and the occasional weekend.

"You must see it can't work." Andrew's voice had been
quiet and reasonable.

"But I love you!" Jessica had wailed. It was no use. She
couldn't turn down this chance, and Andrew knew their relationship couldn't continue while she insisted on working at
this level. On the day she'd moved out of his Chelsea flat,
taking just her clothes with her to the hotel, while her parents
stored the rest of her possessions in their house, she'd wept
as if her heart would break. That the pain she was going
through was self-inflicted did nothing to alleviate her sorrow.
After three years of living with Andrew, it was over, and she
had never in her life felt more torn—between wanting to stay
and wanting to go. For a long moment she was bitter at the
price she was having to pay to further her career, and she just
hoped to God that in the long run it would be worth it.

Jessica looked up at Dick, then jumped to her feet and
straightened her slim shoulders. "Okay, I'm ready to do battle
with this oversexed stud. What's his name?"

Jessica leaned across the reception desk to speak to the clerk.
"Can you tell me which gentleman is Mr. Stratford Stevenson,
when he comes down from his room?"

"Certainly, Miss McCann." The uniformed clerk glanced
around the lobby. "Here he is now, coming out of the
elevator."

Jessica spun about, and a look of incredulity spread across
her face. "What . . . *him?* Are you sure?" she croaked.

"Absolutely certain. He booked into room two-oh-two two
days ago."

"Right!" Jessica strode across the lobby, her high heels click-
ing on the white marble flooring.

"Mr. Stevenson? Good morning, I'm Jessica McCann, director of sales. May I have a word with you, please?" With
distaste she shook Stratford Stevenson's hand and led him to
the seating area, where low sofas and brass-edged coffee tables
stood clustered under an oasis-style arrangement of tall plants.

Jessica sat facing him, thinking that never in her life had

she seen such an unattractive man—short and greasy-looking, with dark strands of hair plastered over his bald head. His ferret eyes slithered to and fro as they traveled all over her body.

"What can I do for you?" he asked throatily, his thick lips barely moving.

Wondering how much he had to pay to get a girl, not to mention three, Jessica tried to hide her revulsion.

"I understand you have three . . . er . . . guests staying in your room," she said.

"So what?" Mr. Stevenson shrugged and looked at her boldly. "They're my guests and I can have whom I like in my room."

"Certainly you can," she informed him pleasantly, "but by law, all persons staying overnight must register. We need a record of all guests in case of fire or any other unforeseen happening. Apart from which"—here she drew a deep breath, determined to remain in control of the situation—"our policy at the Royal Westminster is to charge for all guests who stay here."

"I'll pay for whatever they have to eat or drink."

"I'm afraid you'll do more than that, Mr. Stevenson. The accounts department will be adding the overnight charges for your three guests to your bill," Jessica said firmly.

Mr. Stevenson made a sickly attempt at smiling. "Oh, come on, be reasonable. My little friends aren't doing anyone any harm," he protested.

"I'm sorry, but it's hotel policy."

He leaned forward and looked at her insolently. "That's like charging me corkage for screwing!"

Jessica rose, dignified in spite of her diminutive height. "If you choose to put it that way, Mr. Stevenson, that is *exactly* what we are doing. Thank you for your time. Good-bye." Then she turned away, leaving him standing, gaping after her.

"And *so*," Jessica asked as she regaled Dick back in her office, "shall we charge him corkage at beer rates or champagne rates?"

For the rest of the morning Jessica was busy putting the finishing touches to the "Glorious Twelfth" special dinner she was organizing for August 12. The first batch of grouse to be shot that morning would be flown down from Scotland and served in the hotel's Fantaisie restaurant, where she had planned a Scottish theme for the evening. Salmon, caught in the River Dee near the Queen's Scottish residence, Balmoral, was on the menu, and Jessica had gotten the chef to order haggis from Edinburgh. The tables were going to be covered with tartan tablecloths, and in the center of the room there would be a magnificent free-standing decorative arrangement of stuffed grouse, which she'd hired from a local taxidermist, strutting on a bed of heather, thistle, and bracken.

"The restaurant is fully booked for the evening," the restaurant manager had informed her the previous day.

"Thank God for that," Jessica replied. "I sent out six hundred expensively printed notices to everyone I could think of. It's a relief to hear they've responded."

Satisfied that she'd done everything she could to ensure that the evening, which was in three days' time, would go well, she glanced at her watch, and gasped when she saw it was already twelve-thirty. In fifteen minutes she was meeting her friend from the *Evening Standard*, Peter Thorn, in the cocktail lounge. Taking the elevator up to the sixth floor, she ran along to room 217 and, opening the door, flung herself across the room, whipped a packet of tights out of the chest of drawers, and started to change. Room 217 was now home to her, a neat impersonal space furnished with a bed, an armchair, and some plain furniture suitable for staff. Adjoining it was a tiny bathroom in which, she told her friends, it wouldn't merely be impossible to swing a cat—there wasn't room to swing a mouse either. Jessica spent as little time in there as possible. Sleeping alone depressed her, and she wasn't used to it yet. There'd been many mornings when she reached out for Andrew as she awoke, only to find her hand hitting the bedside table. Then she would wonder if she'd done the right thing. Everything had happened so quickly and with a finality she hadn't expected. It was still a shock to realize that she and Andrew were no longer together and that her home was now the Royal Westminster Hotel.

A few minutes later, holding her Filofax and hotel bleeper, she hurried into the bar.

"Peter!" she greeted him rapturously, kissing him on both cheeks. "It's been far too long since we last met. Come and

sit down and we'll have a jolly strong drink before lunch."
Bubbling and fizzing, Jessica ordered champagne cocktails,
asked for menus so they could take their time deciding what
to order, and carried on a voluble conversation with Peter at
the same time.

"How's the new job?" Peter asked when he could get a
word in. "You're quite the business executive these days,
aren't you?"

Jessica laughed, her eyes glowing. This was what she liked—
meeting people, entertaining, being in luxurious surroundings,
organizing special sales events, having the power to make
things happen.

"It's divine!" she said fervently. "I've got so many ideas for
attracting people to come here. D'you want to know what my
latest plan is?"

"I doubt if I shall be able to stop you."

Undaunted by his teasing, she continued: "I'm going to
introduce a special Christmas scheme, for couples who don't
have children. They'll be given a stocking full of little presents
with their champagne breakfast in bed. We'll have a traditional
lunch in the restaurant, and I'll have jugglers and fire-eaters
and other entertainers. We'll put a giant tree in the lobby and
show a really good film in the ballroom, and at night there'll
be carol singers, followed by dinner and dancing."

"And the next day guests take out a bank loan to pay for it
all, I suppose." Peter grinned. "Sounds a fun weekend to take
a girlfriend on . . . I'm not so sure about a wife."

"Peter, you're *wicked*. Oh, that reminds me." Jessica collected her thoughts quickly, so she could give Peter an edited
version of her weekend at Milton Manor, without involving
Madeleine. "You were going to tell me about the Dalrymple
family. I heard a rumor when I was down in Devon the other
day, that one of them was involved in black magic. Is it true?"

Peter looked at her askance. "Is the pope a Roman Catholic?
You bet it's true! I told you I had to cover the story—about
twenty years ago, it was. Jesus, it was awful!" Then he leaned
toward Jessica, and quietly, so that he couldn't be overheard
in the crowded bar, told her what had happened.

"Oh, my God!" breathed Jessica when he had finished. Her
face had gone pale, and she looked horrified. "Is that really
true?"

Peter nodded. "Witchcraft still exists all over the country, you know, even in this day and age. But that was a particularly nasty episode. It gave me the creeps, I can tell you. I read that old Sir George Dalrymple had died recently. Of course, he claimed at the time that he'd no idea what was going on, but I'm not so sure."

Jessica glanced at her menu so she wouldn't have to meet his eyes. What he had told her was so appalling that she felt quite shaken. And one thing was certain: there was no way she could ever repeat it to Madeleine.

Carl froze as he looked at the form on his desk. Kimberley had already gone through his papers before he'd arrived, and she'd placed this one right on top. With sickening dread he picked it up, scanning the authorization for three hundred and sixty thousand dollars to be paid by Brandt's Motors, Inc., New Jersey, to Michaux Internationale, Zurich. Hank Pugsley's signature was scrawled along the bottom of the form, to which was pinned an invoice charging for machine tools imported from Switzerland.

Kimberley came briskly into Carl's office at that moment. Her face didn't show a trace of emotion. She nodded when she saw he was examining Hank's form.

"I'll go back to my apartment at lunchtime and pick up the copy of the coded tape I made," she said in a whisper. "I'll put the transfer through the computer at about five o'clock, when everyone's gone. If anyone should see me, I'll say I'm checking up on a client's current account to see if he's got sufficient funds to cover a foreign transfer."

"You've got it all worked out, haven't you?" Carl said hollowly, knowing that nothing was going to change Kimberley's mind now. She was quite determined to embezzle Hank's money, and although he knew her scheme was as foolproof as any scheme could be, the slight element of risk made him feel quite ill.

"Of course I've got it all worked out!" she snapped. "This is not a job for amateurs."

Carl went through the morning's mail, giving Kimberley instructions on the dozens of other transfers that were going through. At last he leaned back in his swivel chair, his shoulders aching with tension, his head throbbing. Kimberley sat opposite him with her notepad on her knee, watching him closely all the time. If he so much as reached for the phone, her eyes darted to his face, trying to gauge what he might be about to do. In an atmosphere heavy with distrust and dislike, he tried to concentrate on his work, but it became more difficult as the morning wore on. What astounded him more than anything was that he had been fool enough to be taken in by her seductive little-girl manner at the beginning. As he looked at her now, cool and calculating, with her hair drawn back into a neat chignon, it seemed impossible that this was the same girl who had drawn him to her in the shower and set him afire with her sexuality, transporting him into a fever of desire. It rankled to know he'd been one of many and that he'd allowed himself to be used and manipulated by her. Anger and wounded pride, mingled with fear, squirmed bitterly in his mind.

It was painful, but he had to know something, had to ask her one more question while steeling himself to hear the answer.

"Do you still see Hank Pugsley?" he blurted out awkwardly.

Kimberley's full mouth curved into a smile. "Jealous, are you?"

Carl flushed deeply, and she looked more amused than ever. Her translucent eyes sparkled with malice.

"Why should I be jealous? You meant nothing to me," Carl retorted.

"That's not what you told me when we were in bed!" Kimberley rejoined swiftly. "But to answer your question . . . I stopped seeing Hank after he'd told me about his scam. He thought I was a model, and at that point I didn't want him to know I worked in this bank, of all places."

The phone buzzed on Carl's desk, making him jump. He pressed the key to line one. "Hello?"

"Jake here. Can you come to my office?"

Guilt flushed through Carl in a tidal wave. "Sure, Jake. I'll be along right away." Then he caught Kimberley's eye.

"I don't know why you're looking like that, Carl. We haven't even done anything yet," she said mockingly.

"I know." Carl sighed heavily, feeling as terrible as if they'd already committed the felony. Jake had put his trust in him from the beginning, guiding him through the intricacies of high finance, investments, backing loans, and banking practices, encouraging him every step of the way, grooming him to take over eventually; and here he was, about to betray the man who had been like a father to him. Then there was Madeleine. Carl closed his eyes for a moment. To think about it was more than he could bear.

Jake wanted only to discuss the financing of a new aircraft factory in Ireland. The Central Manhattan Bank had agreed to lend sixty million dollars for the project, but as Carl sat listening to his father-in-law, he felt as if his and Kimberley's sordid involvement was written clearly all over his face. Shifting uneasily in his seat, hardly able to concentrate, he oozed guilt from every pore.

"Are you all right?" Jake asked at length.

Carl started. "I'm fine. Just a bit of a headache, nothing really."

Jake's lined face creased into a kind smile as he looked at Carl benevolently. "Why don't you and Madeleine go down to Oyster Bay this weekend? You could do with a break, and you haven't had much of a chance to be with her recently."

"Yes, I'd like that. I'll talk to her about it tonight." A couple of days by the ocean, staying in the rambling holiday house with its garden leading onto the beach, might take his mind off the mess he was in, for a short time anyway.

"That's settled, then," Jake said. "Now, about this scheme . . ."

Carl looked up swiftly, his heart pounding through his head again. "What?"

"The scheme to launch this aircraft factory," Jake explained patiently. "You'll have to arrange the transfer of dollars to Dublin, and I want you to be at the directors' meeting next week. They're flying over on Tuesday to discuss the final details with us. Is that all right with you?"

"Oh . . . oh, sure," Carl said hurriedly.

"Right. Now, don't forget to mention the weekend to Madeleine. You look tired and you could do with a break." Jake placed a hand on Carl's shoulder as they walked to the door of Jake's large office.

"I'm fine, but thanks anyway," Carl replied.

When he got back to his office, he still felt shaken.

* * *

Kimberley sat at her desk watching until the hands of the brass wall clock in her office reached five o'clock. That was when the clerks went home and the computer room would be deserted. It was now ten to five. She slipped her hand into her purse and extracted the tape. It fitted snugly into the large patch pocket of her suit. She added a pack of cigarettes, so if anyone noticed a bulge she could make a joke about smoking too much. Then, with closed eyes, she ran through the program she'd have to feed into the computer to get access to her account in Zurich. Her account number she knew by heart: 23007 4810 66792, followed by the code word HURRY. Provided she wasn't interrupted, it was going to be a cinch.

"Working late?"

"That's right." Kimberley, entering the computer room, acknowledged Liz, one of her former colleagues. Liz was still at her desk fiddling with a computer printout. "They're a bunch of slave drivers around here, aren't they?" Kimberley added jokily. The tape felt as heavy as a brick in her pocket, and twice as large. She shuffled the handful of papers she was carrying. "Can't stop to talk. Mr. Delaney wants something checked out right away."

"Anything I can do to help?" Liz asked. She was a heavily built girl with a florid face and strong body odor. Kimberley had always disliked her.

"Don't worry," Kimberley said breezily, "it won't take long, and it's rather nice to be back in here again." She went over to an empty desk and pretended to be checking her papers in order to play for time.

"I'm not in a hurry," Liz persisted. "What do you want to check?"

"No, it's all right, really." Her hair was sticking to the back of her neck now, and her hands trembled. *Go, Liz, for Christ's sake, go,* her mind implored as the fat girl sat there in a broad-striped dress that resembled awning fabric, a bland smile on her face.

"What's it like working for Mr. Delaney?" she asked, settling down for a gossip.

"Look, honestly, he's waiting for me upstairs, and I must get on with this," Kimberley said desperately, yet anxious not to appear rude. That would arouse Liz's suspicion. "Let's meet for lunch one day soon, and then we can have a good talk."

"Well . . . if you're sure . . ." Liz sounded mollified, though still reluctant to leave. Slowly and laboriously she gathered her things together in her chubby hands, watching Kimberley all the time.

"Sure I'm sure!" Security would be making rounds at any time now, and it was vital she switch over the tapes, enter the transfer, and put the original tape back before the computers were switched off for the night.

Liz started walking slowly toward the door, and then she stopped and turned back to Kimberley. "Did you hear that Julie's boyfriend had left her? D'you know, he just packed his bags and went . . . didn't even leave her a note. Did you ever hear anything as dreadful as that?"

Sweat was pouring down Kimberley's back now, and she felt as if she could scream. This goddamn fat ugly boring girl seemed determined to stick around, and she felt like hitting her. Time was running out. And the transfer had to be put through today.

"Don't tell me now . . . save it for when we have lunch together," she said, forcing a smile. "I've got to concentrate on this or Mr. Delaney's going to be furious at my taking so long."

"Okay," Slowly Liz lumbered away, and Kimberley waited, listening, until she was sure she'd really gone. Then, with her heart in her mouth, she seated herself swiftly at the main computer and removed the tape containing the program for clients' current accounts. In its place she put the tape from her pocket. The green screen flickered off and on again and then sprang to life in a flurry of numbers and figures. Her copy tape was working perfectly. Gasping with excitement, her heart pumping violently, Kimberley knew, at that moment, that her scheme, planned and plotted for so long, was really going to work. Concentrating with intensity, she tapped smoothly and knowledgeably on the keyboard. ACCESS GRANTED spelled itself out on the screen . . . and she took a deep breath, forcing herself to keep calm. With Hank's authorization on top of her pile of papers, she began to enter the details. First she had to feed in the number of his account at the Central Manhattan Bank. The screen responded without a hitch. Then she tapped out the amount to be withdrawn from Hank's account. Again the result flickered up with perfect accuracy. This is fantastic, she thought exultantly. It was going better than in her wildest dreams. The next thing she had to do was transfer the money to her own Swiss account, instead of his. She entered the code for the Zurich Banque Internationale, and the irony that it meant tapping out HURRY was not lost on her. Her fingers flew over the keys, every nerve straining in her body, listening in case anyone was coming. Her heart was hammering so hard she could barely breathe now: HURRY—and then a wave of pure physical pleasure when the screen flashed up the details of her own Swiss bank account. Not long now. . . . She leaned forward, the unearthly green glow of the screen reflecting on her pale skin and translucent gray eyes. For a moment she looked as if she was at the bottom of the sea, the clear green waters holding her still in a breathless moment; but the illusion was broken as she shifted her position, frowned, and then tapped out the number of her account. There was a pause and then she entered the amount. Another pause, a flicker, and then the words CREDIT RECEIVED flashed up.

Kimberley hardly remembered what happened in the next few minutes; all she knew was that the precious tape was back in her pocket, she'd replaced the original one in the computer, and she was hurrying up to her office, not stopping until she was safely behind her desk again. There she leaned back in her seat, regaining her breath and composure, wishing her heart would stop thudding. Not that it mattered. She was now three hundred and sixty thousand dollars richer.

8

MADELEINE LAID down her hog-hair brush and stood back, her head tilted to one side, her lips pursed. The portrait was shaping up nicely; Dwight Lasmo, president of Phoenix Oil and an Opec minister, looked back at her from the canvas with a florid libidinousness that matched the figure sitting in the carved chair opposite her. At the last sitting she had outlined his features in a wash of burnt umber mixed with turpentine and linseed oil, and just in that one session she had captured the essence of the man. Now, as she mixed the right paints to form the basis for flesh tones, she felt the strange but familiar chemistry between herself and her subject stirring within her again. It was as if she was in tune with what was going through his mind, intuitively picking up his thoughts and feelings. The finished portrait was going to surprise quite a few people, she thought as she started to work on his eyes. No one would guess, meeting him casually, that the cold, ruthless exterior hid a man consumed by self-doubt and a sense of inferiority. She spotted a vulnerability in his expression when he didn't think anyone was looking at him, and she guessed he found keeping up a protective public image a great strain. Nevertheless, she would paint him as she found him, even if it did mean exposing something he'd rather keep hidden, because her artist's integrity did not allow her to lie on canvas.

"Would you like to listen to some music?" she suggested. He was beginning to flag, and his eyes were growing blank from boredom. Music would give him something to concentrate on.

"I'd like that very much, but won't it distract you?" Dwight asked.

Madeleine shook her head, laughing. She put down her palette and brushes and went up to the stereo in the gallery, a slim vibrant figure in a tightly belted white boilersuit, a white bandeau holding her hair off her face. "I don't even hear it when I'm painting," she admitted honestly. "Which do you prefer? Pop? Classical? Opera? I've got most things here."

Dwight ran the tip of his tongue tentatively across his bottom lip and spoke with sudden diffidence. "Have you any of Frank Sinatra's records . . . or Andy Williams'?"

Madeleine suppressed a smile. "Of course. No record collection would be complete without them," she said gaily. She might have guessed he'd choose an oldie and a goodie like Sinatra or Williams—a safe, familiar choice that would remind him of when he was a young man.

With the strains of a well-known love song filling the studio, she went back to work and was soon in her own world again, unaware of everything except the face before her. And then a thought slanted its way into her brain, making her pause, wondering, for a moment. She'd suddenly remembered that first night at Milton Manor, when she'd come across all the photographs of her mother and had experienced a profound inner knowledge of what Camilla had been like. It was the same when she painted a portrait. She would look at a person and intuitively know what his inner self was like; insecure as Dwight Lasmo was, or corrupt, or avaricious, or lecherous, or even just plain stupid. It was all there, in their eyes; it was like looking into their souls and seeing their very beings. She might glimpse it for only a fraction of a second, but once observed, it stayed in her mind and became transferred, through her hand, onto the canvas. Madeleine paused for a moment, her brush poised, her brow furrowed. No matter how hard she tried to dismiss her memory of that first night at Milton Manor, it was an undeniable fact that she had seen an expression of evil in her mother's eyes. . . . Or could it have been fear? Madeleine felt confused now, her powers of recall blunted by the passing of time. Perhaps her imagination was playing tricks . . . had played tricks with her that night. Perhaps Camilla had been frightened of something, all those years ago, and that fear had transferred itself to Madeleine through the photographs. . . . Was it terror and not evil that had transmitted itself to her? The thought took hold, gripping her mind in a paralysis that made her put down her brush, unable to continue painting.

"Do you mind if we stop now?" she asked Dwight Lasmo in a small voice. It was nearly time anyway; she'd been painting for almost two hours.

Dwight looked relieved. "I don't mind at all. It's more tiring than I thought, being painted, isn't it?"

Madeleine nodded distractedly. "Yes . . . yes, it is tiring," she agreed. She started cleaning her brushes in a jar of white spirit. The sharp smell filled the studio, as much a part of her life as the Claude Montana perfume she always wore. Dwight Lasmo took his pocket diary out and riffled through the pages.

"I have another sitting next Thursday at noon—is that right?" he asked.

"That's right." She smiled briefly. "I'll look forward to seeing you then."

He approached the easel. "May I have a look?"

"Of course." She stepped aside so he could see better. "It's coming on very well."

Dwight stood before the canvas, his face filled with awe. "That's amazing . . . that's exactly how I feel!" He turned to her with a look of wonder, tinged with suspicion. "How do you know what I'm feeling . . . what I'm like inside?"

Madeleine shrugged. "I don't know myself, but I suppose it's what enables me to paint portraits."

Dwight studied the canvas again. "It's quite uncanny. I've never even seen a photograph of myself that made me feel it was really me, but this is exactly how I see myself."

Madeleine smiled. "Good. I'm glad you like it. It will be even better when it's finished. We'll do a lot more next Thursday. Now, if you'll excuse me . . . ?"

"Of course." He gave the painting a final pleased look. When he had gone, she tried to do some more work, but her day had been ruined. The thought, so sudden and unexpected, so horrifying she dared not even name it, had now taken hold and she knew she would not be able to rest until she found out if she was right. She must seek out the truth now, no matter how terrible the revelations might be. It stood to reason, she told herself, wondering why it had never occurred to her before, that if no death certificate could be found for her mother, then there could be only one answer.

*   *   *

Patti Ziffren was exhausted. Last night she and Sam had attended the annual fall Fantasy Ball, in aid of cancer research, and this morning she regretted going. Once she'd enjoyed dressing up and going to parties every night, but now, she decided, she was too old for that sort of thing. Sam still enjoyed socializing, but then, it was different for him. He settled himself in a corner with his brandy and cigars, surrounded by all his old cronies, talking business until the early hours. That, to Sam, was like being drip-fed with the essence of life itself. Patti had to keep up with all the other women, and that could be hard work; being the best-dressed and most bejeweled; being the wittiest and best-informed; being the most brilliant, because that was the standard she'd set for herself when she'd been Patricia Shearman, the young and beautiful daughter of Henry Shearman, who owned the Central Manhattan Bank. That was a very long time ago, she reminded herself now, as she applied her lipstick. Her father was dead; the bank was now a public company. At least Jake was its president, and being his sister still had a certain cachet.

Patti sat at her dressing table looking at the reflection of a pale, drawn woman with severely arranged dyed blond hair, and she didn't like what she saw. How had she arrived at this moment in her life? she wondered wearily. Where had all the fun gone? She was tired of the whole eternal social round, the shopping for clothes each season, the regular trips to fashionable resorts, the ladies' lunches and the bridge afternoons. And she was bored with seeing the same faces and eating the same caterers' food and looking at the same florists' arrangements everywhere she went. Absentmindedly she reached for the blue enameled cigarette box, wondering how she could avoid going out to dinner tonight. She watched herself in the glass as she lit the cigarette, the skin around her lips puckering into a concertina of tiny folds. Her eyes looked hollow, and with a tiny stab of panic she was suddenly aware of her own mortality. That cough . . . it wasn't any better. She smoked too much, she knew, but it brought her an immeasurable amount of comfort. In fact, she couldn't contemplate a life without cigarettes; from the first one in the morning to the last one at night, she enjoyed every puff. She didn't care what people said, smoking was her one pleasure in life and she wasn't going to give it up.

Slipping her slender black stocking feet into smart black high-heeled pumps, she went to the dining room and found Sam already seated at the breakfast table, reading the New York *Times*.

Patti helped herself to coffee, strong and black, and with it she took a couple of aspirin. A fresh cigarette smoldered in an ashtray beside her cup.

Sam glanced over at her. "Hung-over?"

She looked at him with some asperity. "I didn't drink that much," she snapped. "I just have a headache. I think I'll cancel lunch today."

Sam nodded noncommittally. He was a short rotund man with a cheerful round face and thick white hair. Nothing ever seemed to irritate him, and he was renowned for his joviality, a quality that sometimes drove Patti crazy.

"I'm off to Hartford to look at some interesting real estate that's become available, but I'll be back this evening," he said, folding the newspaper. "Do we have anything on tonight?"

Patti seemed to shudder. "Dinner—but I think I'll cancel. I'm beat."

"Why?" Sam inquired blandly. "We weren't late last night."

Patti took a deep drag of her cigarette. "I don't care whether we were late or not, I'm beat," she repeated. Then she started coughing, a deep rattling cough that sounded as if her lungs were being torn apart.

"Nasty cough," Sam observed, rising to leave the table. "You shouldn't smoke so much, Patti."

"You! You can talk!" Patti sputtered, her eyes watering with exertion. "I never see you without a great fat cigar—" The rest of her words were lost as she coughed and wheezed.

"But I never inhale. Never."

"Well, bully for you!"

By noon she felt better and was helping herself to a martini, when she heard the doorbell to her apartment ring. A minute later she heard Madeleine's voice in the hall. Patti went to greet her.

"Just like your father—always arriving unexpectedly!" she remarked tartly. "Now that you're here, you'd better stay for lunch, I suppose."

"Hello, Aunt Patti." Unabashed, Madeleine kissed her pale

cheek. "You're looking very smart. Are you sure I haven't come at a bad moment? Are you going out?"

"I wouldn't have invited you to stay to lunch if I'd been going out." Patti's gravelly voice was huskily welcoming. "What would you like to drink?"

Madeleine glanced over at the wet bar. "I'd love some Perrier."

"Huh! Designer water! What next? Well, come and sit down and tell me what you've been doing—and how is that divine husband of yours?" Patti lit a cigarette and perched on the edge of an upright chair as if she was about to jump up again. "You're getting too thin," she observed sternly.

"Can we talk?" Madeleine blurted out as soon as the butler had left the room.

"I didn't suppose you'd come here to discuss the stock market. What's the matter, Madeleine?"

Madeleine hesitated, as if she didn't know where to start. Then she said, "I suppose Daddy's told you all about my trip to England?"

Patti nodded. "I gather your grandfather died as soon as you arrived. Rather bad timing, I must say."

For once, Madeleine didn't smile at her aunt's abrasive manner. "The thing is, Aunt Patti, a problem's arisen over Grandfather's will. The lawyer can't trace my mother's death certificate, and I find that very strange. And Daddy won't give me any of the details, like when she died, or even *where* she died."

Patti's mind worked quickly, forming what she was going to say. She'd plead ignorance, of course; say she was in New York when it all happened and that she wasn't sure of the details. But that wasn't going to make the problem go away; nor would it satisfy Madeleine.

"Surely," Patti said reasonably, "if someone's been dead for more than seven years, it doesn't matter whether the certificate can be found or not."

"I don't know," Madeleine replied, spreading her hands in a helpless gesture. Then she looked at her aunt, her eyes wide with anxiety and bright with unshed tears. "Why am I being kept in the dark, Aunt Patti? I had a terrible thought this morning when I was in the studio, and you must tell me if

I'm right. I really can't take the strain of not knowing any
longer."

Patti stiffened. Surely Madeleine couldn't have hit upon the
truth? No, that was impossible. From what Jake had said, she
had only the vaguest idea of what had happened, certainly
not enough to have drawn any conclusions.

"You must remember that I was here in New York, living
my own life at the time," Patti said with asperity. "I don't
know that I can help you." She stubbed out her half-smoked
cigarette and automatically lit another.

"If there is no death certificate," Madeleine said slowly, "and
my mother's death is shrouded in such obvious mystery, then
I can only conclude that . . . well . . ." She floundered, hardly
able to put into words what she was thinking. ". . . perhaps
her death was never reported," she concluded.

Patti watched her closely, observing the emotional struggle
that Madeleine was trying to control.

"Never reported?" Patti repeated. "What do you mean?"

"I mean, was her death kept a secret . . . has my father
refused to talk about it . . . because she was murdered? Is that
it, Aunt Patti? Was my mother murdered? Did my father kill
her?"

The telephone buzzed on Jessica's desk. It was Kenneth
Wolfson, manager of the Royal Westminster.

"I'm calling all department heads for an emergency meeting
this morning, Jessica," he informed her. "Be in my office at
nine-thirty."

"I'll be there," she promised, wondering what had happened. Every morning there was a brief meeting in the manager's office to discuss any points arising out of the day's
program, such as a banquet with a member of the royal family
attending, in which case extra security would have to be arranged, or the arrival of a VIP who might need extra looking
after, or something as mundane as a broken boiler that needed
repairing; but that usually took place at ten o'clock. Heads of
departments met only once a week, to report on the bigger
issues, and that meeting had been yesterday.

Jessica shrugged and, rising from her desk, went into Dick's
office next door.

"Do you know what's up? Why are we being summoned by the great white chief?" she asked.

Dick grimaced. "I've heard a nasty rumor, so it probably has to do with that."

"What sort of rumor?"

"I've heard that the unions are threatening to bring out all the hotel staff on strike unless we meet their new overtime-pay demands within twenty-four hours. This time tomorrow, we may be making the beds and serving in the bar . . . and even cooking in the kitchens ourselves. Don't you just long to see Kenneth Wolfson and Dennis Powell down on their hands and knees scrubbing the floors!" He laughed. Dennis Powell was the assistant manager.

Jessica looked dumbfounded. "You've got to be joking!"

"I wish I was! It's true, Jessica. I popped into the kitchens earlier this morning, and everyone's abandoned the utensils to paint placards with slogans like: 'We're not slave labor' and 'Management is exploiting us.' "

Jessica looked startled. "My God, they're not going to lobby public sympathy, are they? That would be very bad publicity for the hotel."

"As far as I could tell from the mutterings, they plan to parade around the front hall and in the street outside the entrance," Dick replied.

Jessica clasped her head, appalled. "Oh, Dick, this is serious! I can just see all those Portuguese and Philippine chamber-maids jabbering away with the French and German waiters. And the Italians—they get hysterical at the least provocation. No wonder Kenneth Wolfson has summoned us all. Do you really think we're in for a serious strike?"

"I hope not, but it's a tricky position."

"If only we were a smaller hotel, then we could sack the lot of them and employ nonunion workers."

Dick agreed. "They don't seem to understand in this business that there's no such thing as work-to-rule. If there's a job to be done, you stay and do it until it's finished."

"As if I didn't know! But management can't give in over this, Dick. If they do, every hotel in the Group, from Bahrain to Turkey, will be under threat of a strike from the staff, demanding higher overtime pay."

"I know, I know," Dick replied, shaking his head.

At nine-thirty all the management personnel were squeezed into Kenneth Wolfson's office. The atmosphere was tense. Jessica, seated next to the banqueting manager, Mike Lyle, raised her eyebrows questioningly.

"Any news?" she whispered as Kenneth Wolfson shuffled the papers on his desk, cleared his throat, and prepared to talk to them all.

"No," Mike murmured, "except that there's to be a meeting with the union spokesman at noon."

"Maybe something will be resolved," Jessica said hopefully.

Mike replied dryly, "I very much doubt it. They mean business this time."

Wolfson was brief and to the point. "We have a serious problem on our hands, with a staff walkout threatened at noon tomorrow unless we meet their overtime demands. The staff are on a go-slow today, and we need all of you to do everything you can to keep this place running smoothly."

There were nods of approval from everyone.

Kenneth continued: "Should we not be able to come to a satisfactory settlement with the unions, then you must all be prepared to help keep the place running as best you can. There will be a rota of those of you who will be put onto bedmaking and cleaning the rooms, those of you who will look after the front office and guests' luggage, and then of course there will be the kitchens and bars to be manned. We have a day in which to make these contingency plans, should the strike go ahead, and I would like each of you to return to your office now so that you can plan for your individual departments."

Amid a scraping of chairs and muted mutterings, the management rose, their faces grim. All of them had the interests of the hotel at heart, or they wouldn't have been in the positions they were. To keep everything running smoothly, from fresh flowers in the vases to fresh sheets on the beds, was of paramount importance to them all. The golden rule of running a hotel was that no matter what, the guests' comfort must come first.

Jessica rushed straight down to the reception desk in the lobby to see if any VIP's were due to arrive within the next twenty-four hours. If necessary, she'd have to get them into another hotel if the Royal Westminster couldn't look after them properly. Anne Butler, from the public-relations office, went with her. It was going to be her job to keep the story of the strike out of the newspapers, and she was deeply angered by this disruption.

"What d'you want?" she asked Jessica, almost crossly, as Jessica joined her at the reception desk.

"I want to see if we've got any VIP's arriving," Jessica replied. "They wouldn't exactly relish finding this was a do-it-yourself establishment."

Anne didn't smile. She looked at Jessica as if she were a skittish schoolgirl. Comtemptuously she said, "Why bother asking reception? I have the list of celebrities due to check in. Tomorrow it's the president of CBS television arriving from New York for a couple of days, and the day after, there's some actor from California."

At that moment Dennis Powell, the assistant manager, came hurrying up to them. "Ah, there you are, Jessica," he said, smiling in spite of the situation. Dennis had been with the Golding Group for twenty-five years, much of which he'd spent working in their hotels in the Middle East. He'd been at the Royal Westminster for eight years now and was renowned for his charm, whether he was talking to one of the maids or to a celebrated guest.

"Good morning, Mr. Powell. Is there anything I can do for you?" Jessica asked, while Anne just stood there, saying nothing but looking harassed.

"There *is* something I'd like you to do for me, Jessica," he said warmly. Jessica was a great favorite of his, and they shared a sense of comradeship. "We've got Bernard Scheller arriving on Thursday for a ten-day visit."

Anne cut in with a hint of I-told-you-so: "That's the actor I was telling you about."

Dennis Powell turned and looked at Anne with sad eyes, as if he pitied her effort at knowing what was going on. "He's not an actor," he said, "he's a famous composer and conductor. He's over here from the States to give a concert at the Royal Albert Hall," he added mildly.

Anne flushed angrily and shrugged, but Jessica's face lit up as she exclaimed, "Oh, how fantastic! I've got all his records. I'll see if I can get him into the Dorchester or Grosvenor House, in the event of the worst happening."

Powell looked at her gratefully. "Make contingent plans for him, because he's a very important client. He will only ever stay in five-star hotels, so we don't want him upset in any way. He's a rather demanding guest, Jessica, and I want you to keep an eye on him the entire time he's here. He entertains a lot, mostly in his suite, so make sure he has everything he wants."

"I will," Jessica promised. "It will be a pleasure . . . I've admired his work practically all my life."

Dennis smiled. "I wouldn't tell him that," he joked. "It'll remind him of his age!"

"And don't ask him if he's in the Top Twenty because he doesn't write that sort of music!" rejoined Anne with a bitchy laugh. It annoyed her that although she was the press officer, it was Jessica who got the nice jobs, like looking after the more important of the hotel's guests.

"I'll see that he has everything he needs," Jessica said, ignoring Anne, "and I'll check all the details now." She sped over to the reception computer and tapped out the name on the keyboard. Bernard Scheller. There was a pause of a couple of seconds, and then the screen read: "Arriving Heathrow, 7:45 A.M. Wednesday 17 June. Hotel's Rolls-Royce to meet him and bring him to hotel. Expected time of arrival: 8:30 A.M." Then there were some details giving his American Express card number and home address, which was in Sardinia.

Jessica hoped the strike would be averted so he could stay. She'd met many so-called VIP's in her time, but rarely one as talented as this.

The silence in the room was almost palpable and Madeleine was sure Patti could hear the thundering of her heart.

"Is that what happened?" she asked, her voice heavy with dread. Now that she was about to find out the truth, she suddenly wished she'd taken her father's advice and pushed the whole thing to the back of her mind. What good was the truth going to be to her now, anyway? It wouldn't bring her mother back. It wouldn't redeem her often lonely childhood—in spite of Aunt Patti's devotion. It wouldn't bring her peace of mind; in fact, it would only serve to underline the sense of loss she'd always felt. Worse, the truth might reveal something about her father that she'd rather not have known.

Patti Ziffren exploded in a shower of cigarette ash and billowing smoke. A racking cough tore into her lungs.

"Good God, child!" she spluttered. "Of course your mother wasn't murdered! What on earth gave you that idea?" She was deeply shocked. This was all Jake's fault. If he'd handled the situation better, Madeleine's imagination would never have run away with her like this, allowing her to conjure up terrible visions.

"How could you think your mother had been murdered?" she demanded when the worst of her coughing fit had subsided. "I've never heard of such a ridiculous thing in all my life! . . . And to suggest it might have been Jake! Really, Madeleine, you're getting carried away by this whole thing. Your stupid old grandfather has filled your head with nonsense. Why, Jake wouldn't hurt a fly, and you know it!"

"I was wrong to think that Daddy might have had anything to do with it," Madeleine admitted, "but something sinister did happen, and I'm quite certain about that—something so terrible that Dad won't even talk about it. It's driving me crazy, wondering . . . not knowing . . . and now not being able to find a death certificate."

Patti, in her anxiety to reassure Madeleine, and yet unwilling to tell her everything, sounded harsh. "Oh, for goodness' sake, pull yourself together! You're getting obsessed!"

"I'm sorry," Madeleine said contritely. "I never used to think about my mother all the time, but recently, since my trip to England . . ." Her voice drifted off and Patti felt a deep wave of compassion for her. Madeleine had been too protected all her life, and now she was being half-exposed, in the worst possible way, to a situation she did not understand, with half-truths getting mixed up with sheer fantasy and only a little knowledge. What the girl needed, she thought to herself, were some hard facts, but they could come only from Jake.

"Listen to me," she scolded, as if her niece were a little girl again. "I'm sure your trip to England was upsetting, but there's no need to make a major drama out of it. Whether Camilla's death certificate can be found or not is immaterial. You have inherited your grandfather's estate and in due course I gather you're going to sell it. That's it. End of story."

Madeleine remained silent, toying with her glass of water,

her long black eyelashes casting a fringed shadow on her pale cheeks.

"I know exactly what's the matter with you," Patti suddenly said sharply. Madeleine looked up.

Patti was sitting very upright, lighting another cigarette. "This whole business," she began, "has suddenly made you realize you haven't *got* a mother. As a child you never asked about her, you know. You were perfectly happy with your father and all your toys and the time you spent with me. You accepted the situation which, for some reason, you are refusing to accept now. It may be sad, but it's something you've got to come to terms with sooner or later. All this hoo-haa with your grandfather has merely made you see, perhaps for the first time in your life, what you've missed."

Madeleine nodded slowly, recognizing the wisdom and truth of Patti's words.

Patti looked at her directly. "Now, let me tell you something. You don't have a monopoly on being motherless, so you must stop feeling sorry for yourself. You have a father who loves you very much, a fantastic husband, and for what it's worth, you've got me." Her eyes were tender now, belying the abrasiveness of her words.

Madeleine's eyes swam with unshed tears. "Oh, I do realize, and I am grateful, and I'm especially grateful to you for all you did when I was small." She gave a deep sigh. "Perhaps Daddy was right when he said I shouldn't have gone to England. I do feel more confused and disturbed than before, but of course my curiosity has been thoroughly aroused."

Patti snorted. "Well, you know what they say: 'Curiosity killed the cat.' Now, do me a favor and put away that wretched glass of water and have something decent to drink! Lunch will be ready in a few minutes, so you can pour me another martini. Then I want you to advise me on my bedroom. I'm going to have it redecorated. I hear Chinese yellow is the 'in' thing this year . . . but do you think it will go with my complexion?" Artfully she diverted Madeleine, and was pleased to see a little color returning to her cheeks. Later in the day she would get hold of Jake and tell him that things couldn't continue as they were. Madeleine was going to have to be told *something*, even if it wasn't the whole truth.

*   *   *

The atmosphere in the hotel was strained and Jessica could feel trouble in the air like a brooding storm about to burst. In the lobby and kitchens, the go-slow was snarling up the normal smooth-running efficiency; the upstairs beds remained unmade so far, and room service was taking an hour to produce a pot of coffee. As she hurried back to her office, she saw a group of porters and house electricians clustered in the corridor, deep in discussion. A few of them glared balefully at her as she passed, and she tried to ignore them, but it was difficult. Of all the hotel staff, these were the ones with whom she sympathized. They worked all hours, often having to dismantle and clear the ballroom at three o'clock in the morning, only to reset it with tables and chairs for a breakfast conference or exhibition. Heavy sofas and grand pianos and stages had to be trundled around, spotlights had to be reangled and microphones set up and tested. Sometimes these men worked for forty-eight hours at a stretch, with only a three- or four-hour break while a function was' actually in progress—not long enough to go home but too long to be hanging around without a comfortable place to sit.

Jessica crossed her fingers, thinking of Kenneth Wolfson, at this moment in talks with the union spokesman. By this time tomorrow either an agreement would have been reached or they'd all be working flat-out, no matter how menial the task, ensuring that the Royal Westminster kept running. It would be a major calamity and cost the hotel thousands of dollars; it would also be bad for its image, and Anne, in the public-relations department, was going to have her job cut out in dealing with the press. But nothing, Jessica knew, would force them to close, even for a few days. The three hundred and eighty staff members might go on strike, but management was going to have to keep the show on the road somehow.

Two hours later Dick put his head around her door, a jubilant grin spread across his face.

"I've just heard—it's all over! The strike's off."

Jessica jumped to her feet, arms waving, bangles rattling. "That's terrific! What happened?"

"Management has offered an increase of twelve percent on overtime pay, and the union was satisfied."

"Thank God for that. Now I can get to meet Bernard Scheller. We were going to have to send him to another hotel if the worst had happened."

"Bernard who?"

"Bernard Scheller. Oh, Dick, you must have heard of him?" Jessica looked scandalized. "Didn't you see *Beneath the Shadow* or *Ring of Light*? He composed the theme music for them, and masses of other films as well."

Dick shrugged. "Never heard of him, but I'm not a great one for music myself. So, what's he doing staying here?"

Jessica gave a little wriggle of excitement. "He's flying in from Boston, and while he's in London he's giving a concert at the Albert Hall. Mr. Wolfson has asked me to look after him and see that he has everything he wants."

"Oh, yes?" Dick grinned, his tone full of innuendo.

"Don't be silly! He's at least a hundred and three." She giggled. "He's been composing and conducting for *years*."

"Well, I'd wear two pairs of tights when I met him if I were you—I've heard all about these composer chaps."

"Dick, you're disgusting!" Jessica shrieked. She grabbed a sheet of paper from her desk, screwed it into a ball, and threw it at him. Dick, laughing loudly, ducked and shadowboxed. The relief at hearing the strike had been averted made them feel quite childishly lighthearted, and they were still playing when the door opened and Anne came into Jessica's office, her lips pressed together with disapproval.

"I came to tell you the strike's officially off," she said in a schoolmistressy way.

Jessica and Dick tried to smother their laughter.

"W-we know," spluttered Jessica.

Anne drew herself up and spoke pettishly. "Then some of us can get on with our work, can't we?"

"Oh, yes, that's right," Dick agreed, pretending contrition. "Now that I don't have to be chief washer-upper in the kitchens, I'd better get back to the boring things of life."

"And *she*," Jessica muttered under her breath as she watched Anne depart, "is a calamity looking for a disaster."

"But the big white chief must think a lot of her," Dick observed. "I heard she'd been given a raise . . . and a dress allowance."

Jessica smiled sweetly at him. "Really? I wonder what she spends it on?"

Two days later, Jessica was down in the lobby by twenty past eight to meet Bernard Scheller. Dressed in a chic little dark blue suit with navy tights and high-heeled navy shoes, she'd done her makeup with extra special care that morning, and for once her topknot was smoothly and securely fixed. Taking a seat in the oasis of tall plants, from where she could watch the entrance, she longed for a cup of strong coffee. Room service didn't apply where live-in staff was concerned, and she usually had coffee and croissants at her desk, but today that would have to wait. Tapping her foot nervously, she kept her eyes on the revolving glass doors so that as soon as the car appeared she could alert reception of the great composer's arrival.

At this hour the lobby was still and empty, the white marble floor gleaming like an ice rink, the towering arrangement of fresh flowers on the center table the only touch of color amid the elegant gray decor. It would be a different scene within an hour. Stacks of luggage would be coming and going as guests arrived or checked out, and the air would be filled with foreign accents and all the phones at reception would be ringing and everyone would be hurrying to and fro.

At that moment the smooth lines of a Silver Cloud Rolls-Royce glided up to the main entrance and a chauffeur in gray uniform jumped out to open the passenger door.

It was Jessica's first glimpse of Bernard Scheller as he got out of the car and hurried through the revolving glass doors. She had an impression of a tall man, immensely broad-shouldered, exuding charisma and a sense of power that made her falter momentarily as she went forward to greet him. He looked younger than in his photographs, with a lean hawklike face and a mane of hair graying at the temples. What struck her most were his eyes. Slightly hooded, they were the most incredible shade of dusky dark blue, like a twilit sky.

Stepping forward, she extended her hand. "Good morning, Mr. Scheller. I'm Jessica McCann, director of sales. Welcome to the Royal Westminster." It was her usual greeting, an automatic patter that came to her without thinking, but this morning she wasn't even aware she was speaking. Bernard

Scheller's eyes seemed to be catching hold of her senses, paralyzing her as she stood looking up at him.

"Good morning," he replied courteously, without smiling.

Porters were rushing out to the car to unload his luggage,
and the receptionist was poised and alert, an ingratiating smile
on his face.

"What can I get you to drink, Mr. Scheller, while we check
you in?" Jessica asked as she led him over to the desk. "Coffee,
tea, perhaps a mimosa?" She was aware of him handing over
his American passport and being given a registration form to
fill in.

"I'll have herbal tea, please."

Jessica signaled to a hovering waiter, seated Bernard at a
nearby table so he could write in more comfort, and discreetly
and without fuss arranged for the porter to take his luggage
up to the Roxborough Suite, which she had already stocked
with champagne, a bowl of exotic fruit, and a large box of
liqueur chocolates, compliments of Kenneth Wolfson. Bernard
Scheller was to be given the VIP treatment for the duration of
his stay, and she was determined nothing would go wrong.

Madeleine and Carl arrived at Highwinds at Oyster Bay, on
Long Island, late Friday evening. The white slatted house,
with its veranda and wooden steps down to the beach, had
belonged to the Shearman family for many years, and it was
here that Madeleine had spent weekends and vacations when
she was a child. A resident housekeeper kept the place in
order, with the help of a gardener, so that at any time Jake or
Carl and Madeleine could announce their impending arrival
and everything would be in readiness.

Madeleine went out onto the veranda as soon as they arrived, where Long Island Sound lay quiet and peaceful, the
waters hardly seeming to move, the last light of day descend-
ing gently on Locust Valley and Bayville. It was her favorite
view—always the same, always there. Carl came out to join
her, his hands in the pockets of his cream linen trousers, his
attitude one of forced casualness.

"Can I get you a drink or anything, honey?" he asked.

Madeleine turned to smile at him. She'd been looking forward to this weekend ever since he'd suggested it, and she
was determined not to mention her mother, or Milton Manor,

or any of the things that had been preying on her mind lately. Carl seemed to have worries of his own, and he looked deeply strained, so she had made up her mind that these precious two days together, on their own, were going to be perfect.

"A nightcap might be nice," she replied softly, "before we go to bed."

Carl looked out to sea, nodded silently, then went back into the house to fix their drinks. When he came back, Madeleine drew him down onto a swing sofa and slipped her hand into his.

"This is the life, isn't it?" she murmured with a contented smile.

"Ummm. We should come here more often," Carl replied, gazing out to sea.

They sat in companionable silence until he rose slowly and stretched. "I think I'll go for a short walk," he said, and she thought he sounded awkward, as if he felt guilty for not inviting her to join him.

"Okay, sweetheart," she replied mildly. "I'll have a long lazy bath . . . and then we can go to bed when you come back, can't we?" She reached out to catch his hand and press it to her cheek.

"Sure, honey."

"Will you be able to see? It's almost dark . . . don't go falling into the sea!"

Carl gave a little laugh. "No chance of that. I won't be long."

Madeleine watched him go, longing for him filling her heart. If anything were to happen to him . . . She dismissed the thought, banishing it because she couldn't bear to think of a life without Carl and his love. He filled her life in every way; even the success of her painting owed much to his reassuring support. She thanked God, with every fiber of her being, that she had never had to worry about him cheating on her. In an age when philandering husbands were looked upon as the norm, she counted herself one of the luckiest women in the world because Carl had always been faithful to her.

A shimmering cold dusk hung like a gray veil over Oyster Bay as Carl walked slowly by the water's edge. He'd taken off his shoes, and the sand oozed spongily between his bare toes as the breeze ruffled through his hair. He'd had to get away from Madeleine for a little while, the feverish torment of his mind making it difficult for him to be natural with her. One word hung in the air before him: regret. It ate into his mind night and day, driving him crazy. Regret . . . regret. He kicked savagely at a stone, hurting his toe, almost rejoicing in the pain because it was a different type of pain. *How could he have let himself be seduced by Kimberley?* It was unthinkable. Unbelievable. He licked his lips and tasted the salty air on his mouth; salty as the tears he could not shed. In one wild unguarded moment he'd ruined his life. The thought was so shattering, he paused and turned to look to the horizon, but with unseeing eyes. Even if Madeleine never found out, even if he and Kimberley got away with embezzling Hank Pugsley's money, he'd ruined his life because he'd let himself down. That was as bad as betraying both Madeleine and Jake and the bank. He'd done something that could only earn him a feeling of self-loathing, and for the rest of his life he would be treading a knife's edge, until . . . Until when? Until Kimberley had stolen enough money? Until Hank or Central Manhattan Bank found out?

As he stood there, the waves spending themselves in lacy frills about his ankles and the darkness closing in around him, he almost wished he could step forward into the sea and keep walking . . . the waters getting deeper . . . He could feel the waves closing over his head, pressing down on him, filling his lungs, while a heavy blackness bore him away into oblivion. . . .

With a strangled cry of anguish, Carl turned and started walking back to Highwinds.

Madeleine was sitting up in bed reading when he got back.
"Had a nice walk?"
"Great!" He tried to keep his voice light and steady. "You should have come too, lazybones!"
Madeleine laughed. "Lazybones yourself! I bet you I'll beat you at tennis tomorrow."
"You're on!"
"Carl . . ." She reached out to him, her eyes tender and her mouth soft. A moment later he was in her arms, and they were holding each other close. "You smell wonderful," she murmured, pressing her face against his. "Like the seashore."

She trailed her fingers through his hair, closing her eyes, so all her other senses were aware of him.

"My love . . ." The words were wrenched from his throat as he started to take off her nightdress. "My darling love . . ." At last she lay naked on the coverlet, her smooth curves catching the light in dark hollows and pale hillocks, her breasts twin pinnacles and her hair a cloud of blackness on the pillow. Carl thought he had never seen anything more beautiful.

Madeleine clung to him, responding and wondering why there was such heartbreaking urgency in his movements and pain in his face. For once he was rising to an early climax, as if unable to control himself, and there was a certain desperation in his manner too. Madeleine decided not to try to ride the same wave of passion. Although deep, her arousal did not match his, and so tonight she decided that she would give of herself only for his pleasure. Sometimes it happened like that, and she didn't mind, for the mental satisfaction she derived from making him happy was at times almost as joyous as seeking her own physical release. Holding him in her arms, blending and shaping her body to his frantic one, she felt as old as womanhood itself; as old as the earth or the sea that lapped on the shore, and as old as the moon that cast a silvery glow on the sands. She felt like a mother comforting her troubled child, holding him safe within the circle of her love: but then Carl climaxed violently, so that he bucked and reared his head up as he plunged about in her hot wetness, and as he cried out her name, Madeleine knew suddenly, instinctively, that something was dreadfully wrong.

9

"Is THERE anything else you want, Mr. Scheller?" Jessica asked, sitting perched on a chair in his suite, a notepad on her knee. "I've made all the arrangements for your press conference in the Armitage Room tomorrow morning at nine-thirty, and I've ordered a car to take you to your rehearsals after that."

Bernard Scheller had been staying at the Royal Westminster for three days, and as Kenneth Wolfson had warned her, he was a demanding guest.

"I told you I'd invited some friends over for drinks this evening, didn't I?" he asked in his faintly mid-European accent.

"Sixteen guests at seven o'clock, for champagne, here in your suite," Jessica replied immediately without having to consult her notes. "And you would like the chef to make some phyllo-pastry parcels filled with a hot chili mixture, and also some grilled baby lobster claws and a large dish of *crudités*."

Bernard nodded, his expression, as always, serious. He was a man with a permanently guarded manner, a barrier to protect himself from the adulation of the general public, who flocked around him in sycophantic adoration and would have bled him dry if he'd allowed them to. Only after three days was he becoming relaxed with Jessica, whose manner was so utterly professional.

"We'd better have some whiskey as well," he observed. "Not everyone likes champagne."

"Right." Jessica made a note on her pad. Bernard intrigued her, although nothing was going to induce her to reveal her curiosity. All she knew about him was that he was Austrian by birth and that he'd studied at the Curtis Institute in America

before going on to become a world-famous composer and conductor with the Boston Symphony Orchestra. That much she
had gleaned by reading a short biography on the back of a
record sleeve. It had gone on to say he was a first-rate pianist
as well, and had made many television appearances and re-
cordings with the New York Philharmonic and Vienna Philharmonic orchestras.

Bernard passed a weary hand over his hooded eyes and let
out a great sigh. "God, I'm tired. This touring is too much."

"Where will you be going this year?" asked Jessica, a hint
of sympathy in her voice.

Bernard shrugged. "Milan, Tokyo, Moscow, Sydney . . .
God knows. I shall be flying to a dozen capitals within the
next few months."

"That must be very unsettling."

He raised his thick dark brows. "Unsettling, but I'm afraid
very necessary. When I return to Boston in two weeks' time,
I have an important concert. The President and his wife are
flying in for it, and the evening is going to be relayed on live
television. And so it goes on," he added, spreading his hands
expressively. "Month after month I tour the world. It is important to my career."

"And where is your home? Where do you go between
tours?" Jessica asked, fascinated.

Bernard's expression changed, grew softer and more relaxed. "I have a house in Sardinia. Ah, there I find peace and
quiet. That is where I do my composing. It is so wonderful,
after months and months of traveling and living in and out of
suitcases, and always being on show . . . to live in a swimsuit
and feel the freedom of my own house. To be near to nature
is necessary for my creative powers. I go to Sardinia to recharge
my batteries and cleanse myself of the pollution of city life."

Jessica nodded, impressed. Beneath the superficial glitter
that surrounded him, Bernard was obviously a very sincere
person, and she liked the unspoiled way he spoke. Here was
somebody, she told herself, who had not let success and fame
go to his head.

"May I ask you one other thing," she heard Bernard say as
she prepared to go back to her office. Jessica's heart sank. It
was all very well being helpful and seeing that as a VIP in the

hotel he was being looked after, but she had a mountain of work on her desk, and there was no doubt about it: Bernard Scheller was time-consuming.

"Yes, of course," she said brightly. "What can I do for you?"

His reply took her completely by surprise. "I'd like you to have dinner with me after my guests have gone tonight."

Jessica looked at him and found herself mesmerized by a pair of twilight-blue eyes looking at her intently.

She flushed. "That's very kind, but I'm on duty," she said, suddenly embarrassed, while her mind reeled. Why would he want to have dinner with her?

Bernard shrugged. "So what? Presumably you've got to eat, so why can't you eat with me downstairs in La Fantaisie?"

"Well . . . yes . . ." she floundered.

A glimmer of amusement showed in his eyes. "Then that is settled, and I hope you'll join my other friends for drinks up here first."

"Thank you." A sudden thought occurred to Jessica. "How many shall I book the table for?"

His look was penetrating, and for the first time since she'd met him, the corners of his mouth were quirking up at the corners in a rather attractive fashion. "Just for two," he said smoothly. "There'll be just you and me."

For some reason Jessica couldn't account for, her heart started hammering in her chest.

Jessica dressed with care that evening, up in the little hotel room that was home to her now. When she entered Bernard's suite, he greeted her with appreciative eyes before introducing her to his friends. Jessica glanced at the assembled company and knew that Anne Butler from the press office would have killed to be present tonight. There was a famous television talk-show host, a best-selling author, a well-known Hollywood film producer, and a man-eating actress in a fake snakeskin dress that plunged to her navel. Standing by the bar, a celebrated journalist and the chairman of a large newspaper chain were demolishing a plate of canapés, proving her point that the richer people were, the greedier they were. In her time at the Royal Westminster she'd seen whole buffets, piled high with food, being stripped bare in minutes by a group of millionaires, as if they hadn't eaten for months.

More people were arriving, and Bernard was introducing her as "my friend Jessica McCann," which she found very gratifying, as he could so easily have referred to her as the hotel's sales director. The women guests were kissing Bernard on both cheeks and the men were giving him bear hugs and slapping him on the back, and Jessica saw what a popular man he was. Sipping her champagne, she mingled happily, aware that the other guests were wondering where she fitted into Bernard's life. She could see the speculation in their eyes and hear their curiosity as they asked how long she'd known the great man.

"You're English, aren't you?" asked a German industrialist's wife. It sounded like an accusation.

Jessica opened her doll-like blue eyes very wide as she smiled back innocently. "No, as a matter of fact, I'm not."

"No?" The woman's drop emerald earrings wagged aggressively. "Then what are you?" she added rudely.

"I'm Scottish." Jessica smiled sweetly. "The McCanns come from Ayrshire." She turned to find a scruffy-looking young man in black leather with a straggle of greasy hair hanging to his shoulders. Jessica thought with amusement of what must have passed through the head of the commissionaire downstairs when he saw this apparition coming through the revolving doors.

"Good evening," she said, hoping to make him feel at home. "My name's Jessica McCann. What's yours?"

"Ignacio Herrera," he replied shyly.

"Of course!" Jessica felt herself blushing. He was the most famous flutist in the world, even more famous than Bernard Scheller. "What brings you to London?" she asked, feeling weak. I mean, she said to herself, there are VIP's and VIP's, and this is all too rich a mixture, even for me. I prefer to be behind a desk doing the administration, not having to meet all these living legends.

"I'm playing in Bernard's concert at the Albert Hall," Ignacio replied. "You're coming to the concert?"

"Of course she's coming to the concert," Bernard butted in as he joined them, flinging an arm around Ignacio's shoulders. "You are coming, aren't you? I have a ticket for you," he added, looking questioningly at Jessica.

"If I can get time off, I'd love to," she replied, thrilled.

"Then it is settled!" Bernard moved on, his charismatic personality filling the room as he talked to friends in the way kings talk to courtiers.

At last the party was over and everyone had departed in merry groups, leaving Jessica and Bernard alone in a suddenly silent suite. It was at that moment that it struck Jessica: Bernard was a deeply lonely man. She could sense it in the lines of his serious face and in the droop of his broad shoulders; like a lot of famous people, she realized intuitively, he had a thousand acquaintances but few real friends, and it was obvious he couldn't bear to be by himself. Disconsolately he was pottering around the room now, straightening things that had already been straightened by the waiters, fiddling with the empty glass in his hand.

"Our table will be ready—would you like to go down to the restaurant now?" Jessica suggested, feeling sudden sympathy for this great man who was so basically alone. She knew that empty feeling when the party was over and everyone had left. Since she'd split from Andrew, she'd had many such moments.

"Yes. Yes, that would be good," he replied, glancing at her.

In the muted lighting and hushed tones of La Fantaisie, they were shown to a table in an alcove intimately tucked away from the melee of other diners, discreetly placed so they could see but not be seen. Bernard took control of the menu and wine list, and Jessica let him. It was rather nice for once not to be in charge.

"That was a good party," Jessica remarked, in an effort to make small talk. "I think everyone enjoyed it."

"I hope so." Bernard seemed slumped in gloom. "Too many of them are sycophantic, though. Forgive my language, but they are what we call star-fuckers."

Jessica nodded, understanding him. "But you must have a lot of real friends."

"From the early days . . . yes, but when you get to my age and you are never in one place for long, it gets harder to make new friends. I see my real friends from time to time, but we are all working hard—you know how it is." His hooded eyes gazed sadly at the other diners, mostly couples. "Sometimes one has the feeling," he added, "that everyone has someone, except oneself."

How well she knew what he meant. In fact, everything he was saying seemed to find an echo in her heart. It was as if he were expressing in words the thoughts and feelings that had sometimes come to her in the middle of the night, and yet it was she who had chosen to put her career first. There was no one to blame but herself. As if Bernard could read her thoughts, he spoke again.

"It's the loneliness that I find so hard to bear," she heard him say. "I have no wife now, you know. My marriage ended in divorce, and I find it very difficult having no one to share my life with."

It flashed through Jessica's mind that she'd heard that line before and that it was a very old one, but on this occasion she couldn't help but be touched by his words. Suddenly he smiled, the twilight-blue eyes lighting up unexpectedly.

"Corny, eh?" he mocked in a self-deprecating tone. "I know. The corniest story in the world, but it just happens to be true. My existence is so nomadic it's impossible to form permanent relationships, but like all men, I need someone by my side, someone to love." Bernard grew serious again. He glanced at her left hand. "You're not married, I see."

Jessica tried to give a light laugh, but it didn't quite come off. "Not in this job, I'm not! No husband would stand for the hours or the fact that I now have to live in the hotel." For a moment a shadow crossed her face as she thought of Andrew. He hadn't been prepared to stand for it.

Bernard sighed deeply. "You must be lonely too, sometimes?"

Jessica shrugged, sensing that she was getting into deep waters.

"I don't have the time," she lied. "The days go so fast . . ."

An uneasy silence fell between them as the waiter served their first course of consommé Fedora.

Bernard was the first to speak again. "Do you think we could console each other a little? Ever since I met you, I've been fascinated by—"

Jessica broke him off by sitting very upright and shooting him a sharp look. "Certainly not!" Her expression was deeply offended.

"Please don't get me wrong," Bernard protested, looking distressed. "I didn't mean: Can I whisk you up to my suite after dinner and take you to bed? What sort of man do you think I am?"

Jessica was beginning to wonder. So far, the script for the evening was following the lines of a cheap romantic novel: "Prominent rich celebrity whisks hotel sales director off her feet and tries to carry her off to far lands."

"I don't know what sort of man you are, Mr. Scheller, and I don't propose to find out," she said evenly. "I'm here to do my job of seeing you are properly looked after in the hotel. Nothing more."

"Oh, Jessica, I understand. I've expressed myself badly." He ran a hand across his forehead in a gesture of distress.

You sure have, she thought crisply.

"Of course I'm attracted to you," he continued. "I wouldn't be a normal man if I weren't, but there is something more." His hooded eyes held hers for a moment. "I think I'm falling in love with you," he said slowly.

"Well, that's not very sensible! You'll be gone in a week and you'll never see me again." Her voice rose, half-joking, half-serious, as she tried to control the sudden trembling of her limbs.

"I know." He looked down at his plate. "But do me one favor, please. Just one thing. You will come to my concert, won't you? I'll give you a ticket, and you must come to the party afterward. Please?"

Jessica spoke evenly. "I'd like that very much. Thank you."

"Good." Bernard raised his wineglass and toasted her. "Here's to your coming to my concert."

"Here's to your concert," she said pointedly.

The letter arrived in the morning mail, propped up against the silver coffeepot on the breakfast tray Teresa carried into Madeleine and Carl's bedroom. Carl was already in the shower, but Madeleine, relaxed after their weekend at Oyster Bay, still lay in bed, in no hurry to get up. The weekend seemed to have done Carl good, she thought as she reached lazily for the letter. The tension of the first night, when he'd made love to her so frenziedly, seemed to have passed by the next morning, and as they swam and played tennis and listened to music in the evenings, watching the changing moods of the sea from the veranda, he'd begun to unwind. And there was something else: he'd never been so openly loving and devoted. It reminded her of the days when they'd first been married, only this was better. There seemed to be a greater depth to Carl's feelings as he talked to her, and his lovemaking had been ardent, as if he couldn't do enough to show her how much he loved her. It was the difference, she thought, between the passion of a new love, which always holds an element of selfishness in it, and the selfless giving of a love that is deeply consolidated and full of understanding and a special knowing. Madeleine smiled contentedly to herself, still basking in the afterglow of their weekend together. With Carl's love to support her she knew she could handle whatever the future might hold as far as Camilla was concerned.

She looked at the letter more closely; it was from Mr. Marks, the lawyer from Okehampton. Pouring some coffee, she shrugged. The weekend had taught her that the most important thing was her marriage, and if that was all right, the mystery surrounding her mother was of little importance by comparison. Ripping open the envelope, she took out the typed letter.

It was, of course, couched in legal jargon, a lot of which she didn't understand. For example, Mr. Marks had written: "The said Mrs. Madeleine Elizabeth Delaney, née Shearman, must prove her mother's death, as her claim to the inheritance is *per stirpes*." What the hell did that mean?

"Carl," Madeleine called out, and at that moment Carl came back into the bedroom, his wet blond hair the color of tawny sand, a blue terry-cloth robe about his shoulders.

"Carl, what does *'per stirpes'* mean? It sounds like a dreadful disease."

Carl raised his eyebrows and then caught sight of the letter in her hand.

"It means 'progenitor of family'—an ancestor."

"Ah!" Madeleine glanced back at the letter. "The lawyer says I've got to apply for a court order of presumption of death: 'see probate rule sixty, clause one'—oh, for goodness' sake, why can't he write in layman's language?—and that 'an order for leave to swear to the death will be made by a registrar of the principal registry, under section one of the Supreme Court Act of 1981.' Carl, I don't understand a word of this. What am I supposed to do?"

"Let me see." Carl sat on the edge of the bed and skimmed through the letter. "Nothing for the moment, darling. Mr. Marks says he will keep you informed, so it looks as if he can make the claim on your behalf."

Madeleine sank back against the pillows in relief. "Thank God for that. The last thing I want to do is have to go back to England. Meanwhile, I suppose I can't sell Milton Manor yet?"

"I'm afraid not."

"What a nuisance. Andrew—you know, Jessica's ex-boyfriend—called me on Friday to say he thought he had a buyer."

Carl rose and started dressing. As she watched him, Madeleine could see he was getting tense again. Tight-lipped and silent, he was selecting a tie from the closet, choosing a pair of cufflinks from the little alligator jewel case she'd given him, and deciding which shoes to wear.

"Have you got a very busy day ahead of you?" she asked gently. She'd have to talk to Jake soon, if pressure of work was having this effect on Carl. Although he seemed in a hurry to get to the bank, she could also detect a hint of dread in his attitude, and that was uncharacteristic of him. Usually he was brimming with enthusiasm about his work. Suddenly the weekend seemed like a long time ago.

"No busier than usual," he said, almost coldly.

A few minutes later he was gone, his breakfast almost untouched, the strain in his eyes clear as he bent to peck Madeleine on the cheek.

Folding Mr. Marks's letter and putting it back in its envelope, Madeleine decided to drop into the bank at lunchtime and show it to Jake. If only she could get him to talk, just give her a few details—such as the date of her mother's death, or whether it had occurred in Devon or in London—she might be able to stop what was obviously going to be a long, drawn-out case. She also made up her mind to tell him that Carl was working too hard.

At ten o'clock she had a meeting with her frame maker, the man who could enhance or ruin the look of one of her portraits by producing something too heavy or too light, the wrong shade or the wrong texture. The importance of having exactly the right frame was essential. Madeleine and Leo Parramon would spend hours with sections of planed or carved wood, plaster casts, different shades of paint, from soft gray to dull gilt, and often fabric to stretch tightly over the wood. Sometimes, of course, she would pick up antique frames in Christie's or Sotheby's, rich ornate gilt affairs with scrolls and twirls and baroque swags, suitable for old-fashioned formal studies. Madeleine herself preferred to have Leo make modern-style frames. His most revolutionary were of Lucite, designed so cleverly that they glittered like clear water with shards of brilliant light filtering through it.

"What shall we do with Dwight Lasmo?" she asked, laughing, as she and Leo sat on one of the sofas in her studio and looked at the finished portrait of the oil baron. Leo sat with a large pad on his knee, making little sketches, his eyes narrowed, his head on one side.

"You've used a lot of dark rich tones," he noted. "Browns, greens, blacks. What sort of room is he going to hang it in?"

"The boardroom of Phoenix Oil. It's a dark-paneled room, with ceiling lights and dreary furnishings. Gilt would look hideous. How about ebony?"

Leo, bearded and arty-looking, raised his brows, impressed. "Ebony's not a bad idea," he agreed. "With maybe a narrow fillet of bronze?"

"I like it!" Madeleine exclaimed.

"Okay. Now, what else needs framing?" He turned to several more finished canvases propped around the studio.

Together they worked for a couple of hours, designing between them a variety of frames for all her most recent works.

"I suppose you want most of these by yesterday?" Leo asked as he at last rose to go.

Madeleine laughed. "What's wrong with the day before? Seriously, Leo, the only one that's urgent is Dwight Lasmo's. I've promised him he can have it in a couple of weeks."

Leo groaned. "A couple of weeks, she says! No, there's no hurry, Leo! A couple of weeks will do just fine!" He leaned forward and kissed her on the cheek. "You're a slave driver, Madeleine! Okay, a couple of weeks it will be. I'll get all the others to you as soon as I can."

"Got all the dimensions?" she called after him as he hurried off down the street.

"What do you take me for? A fool?" he shouted back merrily.

Madeleine grinned after him. Leo was a great guy and a

good friend. Whatever happened, she knew he'd deliver on time. Then she glanced at her watch. If she was going to catch Jake before he went to lunch, she'd better hurry down to Wall Street right away.

The meeting to discuss the sixty-million-dollar loan to the new aircraft factory in Ireland was drawing to an end at last. Jake, seated at the head of the table in the boardroom of the Central Manhattan Bank, looked smilingly at the directors, squared up the papers before him, and spoke: "Then we're agreed to lend the money, under the arrangements we've discussed?"

They had spent more than an hour going over all the figures, and Carl, his head aching, longed to get back to his office. Another authorization from Hank Pugsley had arrived that morning, asking for three hundred and twenty-one thousand dollars to be transferred from Brandt's Motors to Michaux Internationale in Switzerland, and he knew Kimberley was aware of the fact. At five o'clock she'd be going down to the computer room again to divert the money to her own Swiss account, and he felt as if his head would split from anxiety.

Carl heard the other directors agreeing to Jake's proposal, and the decision to lend the money was finalized.

Business over, everyone rose, gathered up his papers, and left the boardroom. Carl was just turning to go himself when Jake called out.

"Carl, can you spare me a moment? I'd like to have a word with you."

"Sure." Carl looked at his father-in-law, his heart skipping a beat. "What can I do for you?"

"I'm going to lunch now with the president of Citi-Telecom, but I'd like to discuss the transfer of money to that car plant in Italy. I'm not happy with the arrangements at the moment. Shall we say three o'clock in my office?"

A wash of relief swept over Carl. God, he thought, if I don't get a grip on myself, I'm going to be flipping every time any little thing comes up.

"Fine, Jake." He tryied to keep his voice steady. "I'll be with you at three."

As Carl turned to leave, he caught Jake's eye and gave a slight forced smile. Was Jake watching him strangely? He couldn't be sure, but the feeling of uneasiness lasted as he returned to his own office.

Kimberley came up the steel-and-Lucite escalator from the main lobby, where she'd been dealing with a query, and found Carl had just returned from the board meeting. Together they entered his office and she immediately shut the communicating door to her office so they could not be overheard.

"Everything all right?" she asked immediately.

"So far," Carl replied tensely.

"Right. I'll go back to my apartment on my lunch break and bring back the copy of the computer tape so I can put the transaction through, as usual, when everyone's gone home."

Carl groaned. "Can't you give it a miss this time?"

"Oh, for Christ's sake!" Kimberley's voice was low and impatient. "You only have to countersign Hank's transfer and put it through the normal channels. I had to take the risk of making a copy of the computer tape; you only had to sneak it out of Jake's office for an hour. And it's I who have to go down to the computer room, switch the tapes over, and put through the transactions, while you sit up here on your ass twiddling your fucking fingers!"

Carl dropped heavily into the chair behind his desk, his face a gray mask of anxiety. "Hank Pugsley's going to find out sooner or later. The man would be a fool if he didn't notice hundreds of thousands of dollars missing from his account."

"How often do we have to go through this, Carl? I've told you Hank doesn't get bank statements from Switzerland. He's never going to know his money's missing until he goes over there to get it, by which time I'll have as much as I want. There's nothing to fear from Hank." Kimberley perched on the edge of his desk in a familiar fashion, her long black-nylon-clad legs crossed. "Anyway," she continued, "you know as well as I do that Hank can't do anything about it, even when he does find out. He's not going to want to go to prison for tax evasion. There's no way he'll squeal."

Carl looked at her with loathing. He'd done everything he could think of to put an end to her scheming, including agreeing that she could keep all the money she'd stolen if only she'd stop now; but it was no use. Yet he had to give it one more try.

"You've taken over a million dollars from Hank's account already. Isn't that enough? Do *you* want to go to prison, when we could stop right now and no one would be any the wiser?" Carl demanded. "Why push your luck?"

Kimberley looked at him for a moment, her gray eyes cold and reptilian, her red hair afire from the sunlight that streamed in through the windows. Then she laughed in his face, a laugh that sent a shudder through him.

"Quit now?" she mocked. "You're out to lunch! This is the neatest little scam ever thought up, and if you'll only quit panicking, we'll end up with millions."

Carl closed his eyes as the inevitable stared him in the face: Kimberley had no intention of quitting, and she was going to drag him along with her.

"Christ, I wish I'd never set eyes on you," he burst out hoarsely.

"You should have thought of that before you fucked me!" she shot back venomously. "You couldn't get enough of me in the beginning, could you? You were begging for it . . . in the shower . . . back at my apartment. You were quite happy to get involved with me then and have your fun. But of course it's different now, isn't it? You're having to pay the price for your little fling, and so you want out. Well, no chance, buster, we're in this together, and we're going to go on until I say so." Kimberley raised her head defiantly, her eyes never leaving his face.

Carl jumped to his feet, enraged. "I'd let you damn well *broadcast* that tape of us in bed, if it wasn't for my wife," he stormed. "There's only one reason why I'm doing this—to protect her. I care for her more than anything else in the world. That's the only goddamn reason I'm letting myself be blackmailed; otherwise I'd go straight to the police."

"Too late to do that now," Kimberley retorted sardonically. "You're as implicated as I am, so we'd go down together. I knew you'd never go to the police, not even at the beginning. You're too interested in protecting yourself, so don't give me that trash about your wife."

Carl spun on her, his fists clenched, his eyes bulging with rage. "Get out of my office!" he cried harshly.

Kimberley shrugged. "I'm going anyway. Have you forgotten we've got another of Hank's transfers to put through? I'm going back to my apartment now to pick up the tape." She strode purposefully to the door that led to her office, where she collected her handbag. Then she went down in the elevator to the lobby. Once on Wall Street, she hailed a passing cab and gave the driver her address.

A minute later, Carl left his office too; if he didn't get out of the building for a short while, something in his head was going to explode. Quietly he shut the door behind him.

His office remained still and empty for a few minutes longer, the atmosphere still charged with tension, the sun laying a warm band of light across his desk. The phone rang several times, but then cut off as there was no one to answer it. Dust motes in the still air hovered uncertainly. Then the door leading to Carl's washroom opened slowly and silently, and, half-fainting, Madeleine emerged, holding on to the wall for support.

When Jessica arrived at the Royal Albert Hall, the vast domed building was already swarming with people, blocking the traffic with their cars, pushing their way into the many entrances around the circumference of the building, and standing in groups waiting for friends. Large posters on the front hoardings announced 'Bernard Scheller in concert . . . conducting the Royal Philharmonic Orchestra.' Across them were stickers announcing SOLD OUT.

Jessica, in a pale yellow evening dress, her golden hair falling loosely down her back, joined the crowds getting swept along by the atmosphere of excitement. This was Bernard Scheller's second London concert in ten years, and more than five thousand people of all ages were cramming into the hall to hear his music. In the vestibule she joined a long line to buy a program, listening to the snatches of conversation around her, suddenly feeling very proud that she actually knew him. He had given her a front seat in one of the grand-tier boxes. As she took her place, the view was breathtaking, surprising her—although she'd been to the Albert Hall before—by the richness of its gilt baroque ornamentation and red plush draperies. The hall was built on the lines of a Roman amphitheater, and thousands of people sat on rows of gilt chairs in the well of the auditorium, and in row upon row of raked seats that stretched up to the first tier of boxes. Three more tiers, like velvet-lined jewel cases, rose, spreading upward to the roof, where those who could not afford expensive seats stood or walked around the circular gallery. Tonight the place was packed, and there was a buzz of expectancy as people chatted in undertones or read their programs. The orchestra members were taking their seats now, under banks of brilliant lights that made their instruments shine brassily, and soon the air was filled with strange muted notes as they tuned up. A frisson of excitement ran tingling down Jessica's spine. She consulted her program. The first item was the score Bernard had written for the award-winning film *Silver Apples of the Moon*.

The audience seemed to be settling now as Jessica looked around, and the musicians seemed poised, ready to begin. At that moment a dazzling white spotlight pierced the semidarkness and Bernard Scheller strode forward from the wings and a tremendous roar of welcome erupted from the gallery to the pit, so that the very building seemed to shudder.

Jessica's breath caught in her throat as Bernard surveyed the vast audience that stretched from his feet upward to the gods, and then he bowed, his stage presence holding everyone's total attention. The power he exuded was like the sun bursting forth over a dark landscape, and his personality seemed to fill the hall as he held five thousand people in his thrall by just standing there. And this is the man, she thought wryly, who confessed to being lonely.

The music started, and, mesmerized, Jessica sat back and let it carry her on a journey of such exquisite pleasure that she forgot where she was. It transported her to forests lushly carpeted by a mist of bluebells, to a meadow where wild poppies quivered in a summer breeze, to a shoreline where jagged rocks glistened as waves came pounding in from some distant ocean, to a sunset that dipped away and faded with intolerable sadness, marking the end of a day, a year, a lifetime. The throbbing music soared with such unbearable sweetness that Jessica found herself aching, hurting, thrilling with emotions that wrung every fiber of her being.

When Bernard Scheller laid down his baton, tears were coursing down Jessica's cheeks.

The giant dome of the Albert Hall seemed to lift, the walls expand, the little lights in their silk shades shiver, as a thunder of applause rocked the building, and Jessica dabbed her eyes in embarrassment. The ovation lasted several minutes, while Bernard acknowledged the acclaim, still immaculate in his white tie and tails. The audience would have been content to go on clapping, but at last Bernard picked up his baton and a hush descended as everyone settled down to listen again.

Jessica remained transfixed, marveling at Bernard as he controlled this huge orchestra, bending it to his will, coaxing it, commanding it, ruling it with a power that was absolute. With strong hands beating a tempo and dark blue eyes darting to and fro, he brought the music to life and took the audience with him in an unforgettable journey of sound.

When the concert finally ended in a tumultuous surge of applause, Jessica sat exhausted and drained. The music had moved her so deeply that as she made her way to the large reception room where the party was to be held, she felt as though she were moving in a dream, languid with emotion, transported to another world.

The room was already full of people and she recognized several of them from the cocktail party in Bernard's suite. The great man had not yet appeared, timing his entrance to the exact moment when he knew it would have the greatest impact. Jessica found herself with a glass of champagne in her hand, talking to an elderly couple who seemed to know him well; but all the time, her eyes were straining to observe his arrival, to see him face-to-face again, and to marvel at his sheer genius.

At last he stood in the doorway, as perfectly dressed and groomed as if he were just setting off for his first engagement of the evening, his twilight-blue eyes surveying the crowded room with satisfaction. Instantly he was surrounded by a mob of well-wishers, kissing him, patting his shoulders, fawning over him in a wave of adulation. Jessica, holding back, watched as he slowly made a circuit of the room, edging foot by foot, as people gathered close, hanging on to his arm, eager for a word. He got to Jessica, gave her a brief smile, and then was swept past her by a rush of new arrivals. A moment later he had gone, only the top of his head visible as he was almost jostled to the far end of the room.

Jessica experienced an unexpected feeling of deflation as she found herself standing alone in his wake, looking after him. It was as if she'd gained something marvelous from the night, but somehow lost it too as she watched his receding figure.

Confused and unhappy, she slipped out of the Albert Hall and into the darkness of the night. Bernard's music had invoked a terrible yearning in her—for what, she wasn't sure—and when she got back to her small hotel room she sat on the bed for a long time, gazing out at the rooftops of London, which glowed a soft amber from the streetlights below. Her mind was telling her one thing and her heart was telling her another, and, deeply perplexed, she thought about Bernard and his music and tried to understand her own feelings.

Madeleine's first thought, almost animalistic in its instinct to run away and hide, was to get to her studio as quickly as possible. Hurrying down to the lobby from Carl's office, hoping against hope she wouldn't bump into him or her father, she rushed into the street and managed to give the driver of the cab she hailed the address on Wooster Street in SoHo.

Shock stunned her senses. She couldn't even cry. Unawareness, born of numbness, took hold of her, and before she knew it they were outside her studio and the driver was hollering, "That's three and a half dollars."

Dazed, she handed him a five-dollar bill. "Keep the change," she mumbled as she got out and fumbled for her keys.

All her brain could do was repeat over and over the things she'd heard Carl and Kimberley say. Surely this was a nightmare; surely she'd wake up in a moment, safe in bed, encircled by Carl's arms, to find this whole thing was a bad dream. But what they had said to each other kept stabbing at her mind, indelibly committing itself to her memory.

Carl and *Kimberley?* It's impossible . . . it can't be true. As she sank trembling onto the studio sofa, every part of her cried out in rejection. And they were embezzling money from one of the bank's clients! What was she going to do . . . to say to Carl? The horror of what she had discovered sent her mind spinning and tumbling in fragmented directions as she tried to grapple with a situation that an hour previously would have seemed utterly impossible. Carl and Kimberley? Madeleine rejected the thought violently, swerving away from it with revulsion. There *must* be a mistake . . . she couldn't have heard right. Carl loved her. She knew it through and through. Carl was honest too; never in a million years would he commit a felony . . . and yet with her own ears she'd heard him discuss the money they were embezzling. Then she recalled something else, something Carl had said: *There's only one reason I'm doing this: to protect her.* Kimberley is blackmailing Carl, Madeleine thought. She's forcing him to steal, because if he doesn't . . . Then the tears sprang to her eyes and she rocked herself back and forth, hugging a cushion. Carl *did* love her. He was doing this only to protect her. Madeleine forced herself to concentrate on this, because it was what mattered most. To protect her from finding out that he'd been to bed with Kimberley, he'd allowed himself to be blackmailed. And then she remembered Carl saying: *I care for her more than anything else in the world.* That was what she had to believe; that was what she had to hang on to if she was going to avoid falling apart. Nevertheless, she became racked with uncontrollable sobbing for a love betrayed and a trust broken. She cried for a long time, and then, dabbing her eyes, she wished with all her heart she'd never gone to the bank today. When she'd arrived, Jake's secretary had told her he was in a meeting, and so she'd gone along to see Carl, only to find his office empty. Thinking she'd freshen up in his washroom while she waited for him to come back, she'd suddenly heard angry whispers between Carl and Kimberley. Why hadn't she made her presence known then? Because, as she caught what they were saying, she'd become paralyzed by a terrible fascination to hear more, and it was at that moment that she realized Carl was in very real danger. If this Hank Pugsley—she marveled that she remembered the name—were to find out he was being robbed blind, the scandal involving the bank would rock New York and Carl would get a long prison sentence; Jake would be disgraced as well. The implications were too terrible to contemplate, Madeleine thought as she blew her nose and tried to pull herself together. Perhaps it was a blessing in disguise that she *had* gone to the bank. Grief at Carl's unfaithfulness to her became swamped with anger toward the woman who could bring about his downfall and who had tempted him and then gotten him into this mess. Revenge filled her heart, now coupled with a strong desire to get even. She loved Carl and she would do anything to save their marriage. Positive action was what was needed now, she told herself as she rose from the sofa and went to make some coffee. Carl had gotten himself into this, and she didn't want to probe the whys and wherefores; she just wanted to get him out of it so that things could get back to the way they'd been before. But paramount in her mind was another thought: Jake must not find out what had been going on, or he'd never trust Carl again.

10

"JESSICA, HAVE you checked this proof?" The assistant general manager, Dennis Powell, stood over her desk flapping a sheet of white paper before her.

Jessica glanced up nervously. Proofreading wasn't exactly her forte, but she'd pored over the wording of an invitation the hotel was sending to people for a promotional breakfast party, and she was sure it was all right.

"Yes, why? Is something wrong?"

"Thursday isn't spelled T-h-i-r-s-d-a-y!" Dennis said crossly.

Jessica clapped her hand to her cheek. "Oh! My God, is that what it says? I think they employ complete idiots at that printing firm. Sorry, I'll change it." She grabbed the proof from him and made the alteration with a red pen.

"You're sure everything else is okay? The new menus and wine lists?" Dennis queried, his voice heavy with doubt.

Jessica flushed. This was the third mistake she'd made in two days, and her self-confidence was shaken. Usually she was so careful about checking proofs; she'd never forgotten the disaster when she'd worked at the Wentworth Hotel and the press office had passed a proof giving the wrong date. Two hundred and fifty people had turned up a day early for a dinner-dance.

"Of course I've checked everything else," Jessica said brightly, "but I'll go over it one more time, just to make sure."

"Please do."

When Dennis left her office, she tried to concentrate on the latest sales figures before her, but the numerals jumped around the page and after a few minutes her concentration slid away and she found herself thinking of Bernard Scheller again. Ever since the night of the concert, that unforgettable figure standing on the podium as he filled the Albert Hall with the sound of his music had been in her thoughts. Jessica hadn't seen him since that night, and now that the concert was over, she doubted she'd have to do anything more for him except see him off when he left in two days' time. The thought filled her with unaccountable depression. Bernard had made a deep impression on her, and, confused, she tried to analyze her feelings. One thing was certain: she'd never felt like this about Andrew. Theirs had been a gradual love, built initially on mutual tastes and a foundation of friendship. They had grown into each other during the months before they started living together, so that it had seemed a natural thing to do. This obsession of hers with Bernard was something else. She felt as if he'd cast a spell over her.

This is crazy! she told herself, throwing her pen down on the desk with characteristic impatience. I don't even know Bernard. I don't know anything about him, except that his music thrills me to the core.

Somehow Jessica managed to get through her work that day without making any more mistakes. At six o'clock she was due to welcome another arriving VIP, aging film star Lynette Herbert, who was in London to promote her newly published biography. Just as Jessica was greeting her, she saw Bernard come out of the elevator and go into the bar. He was alone.

"Can I get you a glass of champagne while you check in, Miss Herbert?" Jessica asked, trying to keep an eye on the entrance to the bar and look after Miss Herbert at the same time.

"I never drink. That's why I've kept my looks," Lynette Herbert replied with an expansive smile.

Jessica smothered her amazement that this elderly woman still considered herself beautiful. She'd had so many face-lifts that her skin was stretched into a parchment mask, and her heavily mascaraed eyelashes made her eyes look like aspic-covered orbs in a nest of spiders. Laboriously Lynette Herbert started filling in the registration form, her passport held tightly so that no one would see her date of birth—doubtless earlier than the one claimed in the biography.

Jessica tapped her foot, trying to curb her impatience, watching the bar entrance all the while. Bernard might come out at any minute, and she was longing to see him again. She glanced at her watch. He'd been in there only about five minutes; if she got this wreck of bones and silicon up to her suite quickly, Bernard might still be there when she got back.

"Let me take you up to your suite, Miss Herbert," Jessica said pleasantly when the last of the formalities had been completed at the reception desk.

Lynette Herbert wasn't to be hurried. When they got to her second-floor suite, she insisted on Jessica showing her how to work the remote control on the TV, how to dial for room service, and how to unlock the refrigerator. "And remember to tell them," Miss Herbert commanded in a reedy voice, "that I only like Melbix toast for my breakfast."

"I'm sure that can be arranged. Now, if you'll excuse me . . ." Jessica was practically hopping from one foot to the other in her urgency to get away. Bernard might have left the bar by now; he might even have left the hotel to go out to dinner.

"Can someone press my suit?" The aged voice was plaintive. "I'm appearing on breakfast television tomorrow, and I must have my suit pressed."

Swiftly Jessica rushed to the bedside table, and picking up the receiver, dialed nine. "Please send the ladies' maid to room two-oh-one," Jessica said as soon as she got through. Then she hurried to the door, intent on escape. "There'll be someone along in a moment to see to your suit, Miss Herbert, and if you want anything else, just dial five. Now, if you'll excuse me, I have to get to a meeting." Without waiting for a reply, Jessica slipped out of the suite and ran down the corridor to the elevator.

Bernard Scheller was standing in the middle of the lobby, looking out through the revolving doors as if he were waiting for someone. Jessica gulped, and started walking across the lobby, trying to look casual.

"Oh, good evening!" She put on a surprised voice as soon as she got level with him. It suggested he was the last person on earth she had expected to see at that moment. His dark blue eyes turned to look into hers, and she could have sworn Bernard Scheller looked relieved.

"Hello, Jessica. I saw you here a few minutes ago, but you were with someone. I was looking for you."

"Oh!" There was a whole gamut of emotions in the way Jessica said it. Then she added in a professional way, "Is there anything I can get for you?"

"Maybe there is." He regarded her seriously, his mouth unsmiling.

"Yes?"

"I'd like you to have a drink with me." Bernard spoke slowly.

Jessica answered simply, "Thank you. I'd like that." Inside her, something had begun to tremble.

"Let's go up to my suite—it's too noisy in the bar," he said firmly.

"All right." Well, why not? Jessica asked herself defensively. It's unlikely he wants to give me dictation or ask me to put a call through to Timbuktu, but what the hell! In her present restless mood, she felt a sudden need for adventure. Patting her pocket to make sure she had her bleeper with her in case she was needed urgently, she followed Bernard into the elevator.

The view from his suite was spectacular, and gave Jessica something inconsequential to chatter about. A few people on horseback were cantering along Rotten Row as the early-evening sun filtered through the lush greenery of Hyde Park, and mothers were gathering up their children to take them home, and a couple of boys were walking their dogs.

"What will you have to drink?" Bernard asked, cutting across Jessica's banalities about the nice evening.

"Vodka and tonic, please."

Silence fell like a smothering blanket as he poured the drinks. Jessica shifted her position nervously on the large white sofa.

Suddenly Bernard swung around and looked at her. "I asked you to have a drink with me because I want to talk to you, Jessica."

"Oh!" Again she packed a lot into the monosyllable.

"Is that all you can say—'Oh'?" he mocked gently, and then smiled, a smile of such rare warmth that his face lit up with an inner radiance.

"Well," Jessica said, stumbling, confused, "what do you want to talk about?"

"I want to tell you why I haven't seen you for the last couple of days."

"I expect you've been busy."

"No, Jessica, I have not been busy. I've been thinking. I've been trying to work out in my mind what I should do about you."

Jessica's hand began to shake at the directness of his words. She was also amused. In this age of feminists, no Englishman would have dared to make such a remark. She regarded him silently with her round blue eyes.

"Jessica . . ." Bernard reached for her hand and held it tightly in both of his. "I know this sounds crazy because we've known each other for such a short time, but I'm in love with you." His voice was richly tender. "I told you I was lonely, but that isn't my reason for wanting you now. Please believe me. I love you, and I think you love me, although you may not yet realize it."

Jessica averted her gaze, confused and unable to face the directness of his.

"I don't know," she said with complete candor. "I simply don't know, Bernard. I've only just ended a relationship that had lasted over three years . . . and that was a terrible wrench . . . but you see, I love my life here in the hotel. I love my work. That was why Andrew and I . . . How can I have fallen in love with you when I hardly know you?"

His smile was secret and knowing. "But nevertheless, you have," he said softly. "Remember that first morning we met? As soon as I saw you standing there like a little bird about to take flight, I knew we were right for each other. I love you, my darling, and I want to be with you more than anything else on earth."

Jessica found herself listening, rapt in spite of her reservations, to this powerful man who could dazzle and confound by the sheer brilliance of his personality. Then some hard core of resolve inside her started to melt, making her wonder if she really *was* in love with him. She ached inside, but was it for him or the emotions his music aroused? Or was she merely suffering from an inner loneliness by living in the impersonal atmosphere of a hotel instead of with Andrew in an apartment?

Then she looked up at Bernard. He was standing, feet apart, looking searchingly down at her, and all at once some knot in her stomach loosened and she felt the last shreds of caution break up and scatter. This was a man she couldn't resist. And didn't want to resist. Leaning forward, he took both her hands and pulled her gently to her feet. A moment later they were in each other's arms, pulled together as if by a magnet, while Jessica seemed to hear the clash of cymbals and the roar of drums in her ears. Bernard *was* his music; all the passion and the pathos, the exultation and the bitter sweetness, were what made up this incredible man, and as he kissed her deeply, her senses swam and she felt faint.

"Bernard . . ." she gasped, looking up at him, the top of her head coming barely to his shoulder. She suddenly felt scared. Could she bear this much emotion? Her bones were melting, her insides turning to a torrent of fire. Dizzily she leaned against him, trying to catch her breath, knowing that she had never felt like this before.

Bernard looked down at her with moist eyes and slowly started to undress her, as he did so, stroking her breasts and hips and thighs with hands that were both strong and gentle. As if he were handling a precious instrument, he caressed her body, tuning it finely, preparing her for the moment when he would take her and possess her and make her his. Surrendering to the domination of his mouth and hands, Jessica found herself filled with physical rapture, as he had filled her soul with music on the night of the concert. When the pressure had built up in her so that she could bear it no longer, she cried out for him, wanting him with a desire that was consuming her.

Bernard entered her with a quick hot thrust, lifting her to greater and greater heights of ecstasy as he plunged wildly, until, like a searing, crashing crescendo, Jessica cried out as orgasm after orgasm convulsed her and sent her mind spinning off into space.

It had been a week since Madeleine had overheard the conversation between Carl and Kimberley in his office, and it had been the most agonizing week of her life. Carl still had no idea she knew anything. With superhuman effort, explaining away her manner by saying she'd caught a flu that was going around, Madeleine struggled through each day, spending most of her time at the studio. At night she went to bed early, complaining of headaches and tiredness, and so far Carl had believed her. How long she could keep this up, she had no idea. All she knew, in a kind of blind terrified way, was that she didn't want Carl to find out she'd discovered what was going on; not until she'd decided what to do, and how to do it. A half-formed plan was taking shape in Madeleine's head and, amazed by her own feelings of revenge toward Kimberley, she lay awake in bed at night long after Carl had fallen asleep, plotting just when she'd make the first move. It would have to be soon, because the longer Kimberley embezzled funds, the greater the risk to Carl . . . and the likelihood of Jake finding out. Hour after hour it all went around in Madeleine's mind as she tossed and turned, her mind in a fever, her heart breaking. That was what really hurt, of course—the fact that Carl had gone to bed with Kimberley Cabot. Madeleine knew that was why she was taking an almost diabolical relish in planning to bring about the girl's downfall. Madeleine cared about the reputation of the Central Manhattan Bank for her father's sake, but she didn't give a damn about the money that was being embezzled, nor did she give a damn about Hank Pugsley. What she did care about was wreaking revenge on the woman who had seduced her husband and in whose hands he could be ruined.

Oh, God, Carl, how could you? her mind screamed in the dark. *How could you have betrayed me, even for a moment, even if it meant nothing to you* . . . and then the tears would flow, hot and salty, into her pillow and she would stuff the quilt into her mouth to deaden the sounds of her sobs.

Saturday dawned wet and humid. One of those days when clothes cling clammily to the skin and the atmosphere is stifling. Madeleine arrived at her studio early; Carl had gone to play golf with friends and wouldn't be back until early evening. The day stretched before her like a thousand other Saturdays, only this one was going to be different.

At two o'clock she entered the lobby of the apartment house La Premiere, on the corner of Fifty-fifth Street and Broadway. It hadn't been difficult to find out where Kimberley Cabot lived, and a call from a street telephone a few minutes before had assured Madeleine that she was in. A security man sat behind a desk, heavyset and watchful. He was talking to a couple as Madeleine slipped quickly to the elevators before he had time to question her. To her relief, the elevator doors opened as she reached them, and two women, chattering loudly, got out. A moment later the doors slid shut and she was alone in the claustrophobic container that rose up through the building as swiftly and silently as a snake, hissing when it drew to a standstill on the twenty-fourth floor.

Apartment 279 was on the right of the landing, and as Madeleine stepped forward, trying to quiet the thumping of her heart, Kimberley's door seemed like a black and forbidding face. She pressed the bell and waited. A muffled movement on the other side of the door made her aware that Kimberley was peering through the spyhole. Madeleine looked steadily into the little glass lens, aware that she was eyeball to eyeball with her deadly adversary.

"I'd like to talk to you, Kimberley," she said in as calm and level a voice as she could muster. "It really would be to your advantage if we met, and I know you're there, because you answered the phone a few minutes ago."

The silence that followed was stunned and hollow, and then after a few moments Madeleine heard the rattling of security chains and bolts. Then the door opened very slowly, and there stood Kimberley. Today there was no makeup on her face, nor fancy clothes to give her a look of cheap allure, but a freshly scrubbed young woman in faded jeans and a T-shirt, her riot of fiery curls held back by a scarf.

"What do you want?"

Madeleine fancied she sounded more fearful than insolent. "Do you mind if I come in? I think it's time we had a talk."

Reluctantly Kimberley opened the door wider and stepped aside. Her gray eyes were alert now, sharp and shining like anxious marbles. With a sideways jerk of her head she indicated that Madeleine should enter.

By daylight, the living room that Carl had thought resembled the inside of a box of chocolates looked more like a litter basket for the used wrappers. Newspapers, magazines, clothes, overflowing ashtrays, and dirty cups and glasses were strewn around. On one wall an untidy assortment of books was stuffed onto a couple of shelves.

Carefully, Madeleine picked her way across the room to the sliding glass screens that led onto the balcony. Pushing one further open, she stepped out, as if to seek fresh air. The implied insult was not lost on Kimberley.

"What do you want?" she asked harshly.

Nonchalantly, taking her time, Madeleine picked at the flaking paint on the railings without looking at Kimberley. At last she said, "I overheard you and my husband talking when I was at the bank last week. I know exactly what you're up to."

Kimberley's head jerked up and her face flamed. "What the fuck . . . !"

Willing herself to stay calm, Madeleine continued, "I was in the washroom adjoining my husband's office when you both came in and proceeded to discuss the embezzlement you are carrying out at the bank. I must say, you didn't leave out a detail!" The dryness in Madeleine's voice was grating.

In the pause that followed, the only sound was the muffled roar of the traffic hundreds of feet below. Madeleine's face was as pale as the other's was scarlet. Then Kimberley swore obscenely, and her hands started working nervously.

Unmoved, Madeleine continued, "I heard all about the money you are stealing from Hank Pugsley's account."

Kimberley's eyes nearly popped out of her head. "You *know* him?" She stared disbelievingly at Madeleine, who shrugged, letting the girl think what she liked.

Smoothly Madeleine persisted. "I also heard how you blackmailed Carl into taking a coded tape for the computer from my father's office so that you could make a copy of it, and I heard how you go down to the computer room late in the afternoon, when everyone's gone, to put through the false transaction. Actually, I don't think there's much I don't know."

Madeleine watched as Kimberley, just inside the room, slid down onto one of the brown suede sofas, noticing how marble white she'd turned now, so that her breasts, revealed by the low-cut T-shirt, resembled blue-veined cheese. She knew she had the upper hand now. No matter how much pain this girl had caused her, Madeleine could, if she wished, have her begging for mercy.

"I suppose you know it's only a matter of time before you're caught? It's a terribly dangerous game you're playing."

An expression of wild defiance crossed Kimberley's face. "It wasn't dangerous until you fucking came poking your nose in," she cried angrily. "Now I suppose you're going to go running to your fucking daddy!"

Madeleine's dark eyebrows rose a fraction as she stood looking coolly down at Kimberley. "That's why I'm here, Kimberley, to tell you I've no intention of saying anything to my father." She looked away, momentarily unable to bear looking at this woman, imagining Carl in bed with her . . . kissing her . . . taking her into his arms and making love to her. . . . Below, to the south, Broadway lay like a glittering ribbon, winding its way through the rigidly square blocks of New York, and for a moment the scene blurred as she fought for control. When she spoke again, her voice was steady.

"I'm here because I want to protect my father, and by protecting him I shall be inadvertently protecting you and my husband."

"Does Carl know you've come to see me?"

"Carl has no idea I've found out what's happening."

Kimberley sounded unbelieving. "How come?"

"He left his office shortly after you did that day. He had no idea I was in the washroom."

"So now what? D'you plan to blackmail *us?*" Kimberley gave a short harsh laugh and Madeleine had to dig her nails into the palms of her hands to prevent herself from hitting the girl. Something about Kimberley, as she sat on the sofa, her legs sprawled wide and her breasts swelling out of her T-shirt, filled Madeleine with revulsion. The girl reminded her of a vixen in a permanent state of heat.

"Could we have some coffee?" Madeleine said, ignoring Kimberley's question. "I could use some . . . and I expect you could too."

Kimberley looked at her, startled. "Fuck the coffee! Why the hell are you here?"

Madeleine turned away from the balcony railings and reentered the living room of the apartment. "It's so much easier to talk over a drink," she responded smoothly.

Uncertainly, and looking deeply disgruntled, Kimberley rose and went into the small kitchen across her central hallway. Noisily she poured water into a percolator. A few moments later Madeleine followed, her hands in the pockets of her suit, a relaxed smile on her face. She spoke casually, as if she'd dropped in to see a friend. "Nice place you've got here. Have you had it long?"

Kimberley shot her a venomous look. "Over a year."

"Ummm. I've always liked this part of town." Madeleine glanced around the neat kitchen, which was obviously more used for assembling food and drink than cooking. Rows of expensive crystal glasses, from champagne flutes to tumblers, were arranged along two high shelves, from under which hung man-size coffee cups. At one end of the counter a wine rack was fully stacked with Bordeaux and Burgundys and several bottles of Dom Perignon, and beside it were jars of cashew nuts. When Kimberley opened the refrigerator to get some milk, Madeleine noticed it contained nothing but cocktail snacks and bowls of ice cubes. A hooker's kitchen, she thought, with everything a hooker needs for entertaining. But Kimberley was no ordinary hooker; she was a highly intelligent young woman, ingenious, manipulative, and cunning. Also highly dangerous.

"Oh, you've got a microwave oven!" Madeleine suddenly exclaimed. "Are they any good? My housekeeper's always urging me to get one, but I wasn't sure how useful it would be."

Kimberley swung around on her in a sudden burst of fury, her voice an explosive screech, her eyes blazing. "What the fuck are you playing at? You barge in here uninvited, tell me you know what's going on, and then you start waffling on about fucking ovens as if this was a tea party! What the hell's your game?"

Madeleine looked at her with a smile, maddening in its serenity.

"Well?" Kimberley yelled.

Madeleine's fingers smoothed the folds of one of Kimberley's tea towels, which had THE BIG APPLE printed all over it in scarlet lettering.

"I believe in carrying on in a civilized manner at all times," she said coolly. "There's no good getting rattled, Kimberley. If you've any sense, you'll keep on the right side of me. I know enough to put you away for a long time."

"Your precious husband's in this as much as I am!" Kimberley retaliated sharply. Then she fell silent, glowering at the percolator, knowing the truth of Madeleine's words.

Madeleine continued to admire the kitchen fittings as if nothing had happened, watching Kimberley all the time out of the corner of her eye. She fiddled with a bottle opener, the handle shaped like a banana, and she examined a cookie jar with a picture of a naked dancing girl on the lid. The coffee had another minute to go before it was ready, so Madeleine wandered back into the living room, as if bored. When Kimberley brought in the two steaming cups, she found Madeleine sitting on the brown suede sofa powdering her nose from a gilt compact, her initials set in diamonds on the lid so that they glinted in the light.

"Right," Madeleine said, as if she'd suddenly made up her mind to get down to business. "As I told you, my main concern is to make sure my father never finds out what is going on, but I also want to prevent Carl from getting caught for his part in this business."

Kimberley continued to maintain a sullen silence while she scrutinized Madeleine's face, as if looking for clues.

Madeleine went on, "To enable me to protect the two people I care about most, I must ask you *not* to tell Carl I've come to see you today." Kimberley opened her mouth to protest, but Madeleine raised her hand to silence her. "It's vital Carl doesn't know I'm aware of what's going on, because if he did, he'd blow the whole works and you'd be for the high jump."

"Crap!" Kimberley cried.

"I do know Carl better than you," Madeleine said coldly. "If you want to stay around, this meeting between us never happened, okay?" Her dark eyes flashed and her tone was commanding. Madeleine was amazed by her own strength. Where had this sudden rush of self-confidence come from? A week ago she'd have been a quivering mass, begging Kimberley to leave Carl alone; now she felt strong enough to face anything, and with a flash of insight she knew it was because she loved Carl so much. She would do anything for him, even face this tough little cookie who hadn't a scruple in her body.

Kimberley reached for a pack of menthol cigarettes and, lighting one, dragged on it deeply. "Okay. I don't give a damn whether Carl knows we've met or not. What I want to know is, what's your angle? If it concerns Carl, he'll have to know, and since we're lovers, it will be difficult keeping anything from him."

Madeleine felt a slow burn of anger building inside her, but with a supreme effort she quelled it, knowing she must remain calm at all costs or she'd play right into this girl's hands. "Since you are *not* sleeping with my husband," she said succinctly, "my only concern is what is going on at the bank."

"Ah-h-h!" Kimberley dragged out the word sardonically. "If it isn't blackmail . . . it's a cut you're after!"

Madeleine rose with dignity and stood looking down at Kimberley. "There seems little point in continuing this conversation," she said icily. "I was going to offer you a large sum of money if you'd stop putting through these fraudulent transfers, but it seems you have a nice little—though totally unrealistic—fantasy in your head which you'd rather pursue. A pity," she added reflectively, "because when I arrived I intended giving you a large check, and the opportunity to leave the bank without anyone finding out what had been going on." She could see the inner conflict tearing Kimberley apart as she wondered if she hadn't blown an easy way out. Madeleine didn't give her the opportunity to say anything, though. Curtly she said, "It's too late now, of course. As far as I'm concerned, you can go on embezzling funds until you're caught."

Kimberley sprang to her feet, chagrin, fury, and regret written all over her face. "You . . . !" she began explosively.

Madeleine turned at the door to make her parting shot. "Remember. Don't tell Carl I've been here today. If you do, I'll go straight to my father and tell him everything. Every single thing," she added clearly.

The door slammed behind Madeleine, and Kimberley sank onto the sofa, her legs suddenly weak, her brain reeling with shock. At that moment she could have killed Carl for being so fucking stupid! Imagine not knowing his wife was in the washroom while they talked! Rage and fear swept through her, paralyzing her thoughts and making coherent reasoning impossible. She lit a cigarette with trembling hands, trying to remember everything Madeleine had said, but it didn't add up. The fucking crazy bitch had talked in riddles—and why had she come to visit in the first place? To offer hush money? To beg Kimberley to leave Carl alone? It hardly mattered, Kimberley thought. Madeleine, powerful with knowledge, was in a position to blow them all sky-high. She wouldn't, of course, because she wanted to protect Carl . . .

Today had been a game of cat-and-mouse, but where was it leading?

Slowly and distractedly Kimberley started cleaning her apartment, remembering she had someone coming to see her that
evening. She piled clothes into the closet and stuffed empty
soda cans, old newspapers, and the contents of overflowing
ashtrays into the trashcan. But all the time, her mind was
spinning in spirals of panic, wondering whether, in spite of
Madeleine's warning, she ought to tell Carl what had happened.

At last, as if in need of comfort, like a child counting the
money in his piggy bank, she slid her hand behind the bed's
padded headboard and, groping, felt for the large envelope.
Unlike Hank Pugsley, she'd asked the bank in Zurich to send
her monthly statements because she needed the reassurance
of knowing her account was steadily increasing. The statements made real all those fantasy dollars that merely flashed
across the computer screen as she keyed in the transfers. In
a way, the knowledge that she had so much money secreted
away made her seem more real too. A Woman of Wealth. A
Somebody, after a lifetime of being a Nobody.

Kimberley unfolded the latest bank statement and felt an
almost physical pleasure as she read the balance at the bottom
of the right-hand column: one million, five hundred and sixty-
three thousand dollars. She let out a sigh of rapture. Soon it
would be two million dollars . . . and then three—provided
that goddamn wife of Carl's didn't screw up everything.

For a moment Kimberley contemplated getting out of New
York now, right this minute. Pack a small case . . . she had a
valid passport and enough cash on her for a one-way ticket
to Zurich . . . she could be there tomorrow and no one the
wiser. Carl certainly wouldn't go looking for her, that was for
sure. The idea took hold and grew; better to get out with less
than two million dollars, she reflected, than wait to be caught
with three. She even got as far as opening her closet to decide
which clothes she'd take with her.

But then she remembered something, something so tempting she couldn't resist closing the doors firmly again and abandoning the idea. For the moment, anyway.

Hank Pugsley was due to put through another transfer in
the next week to ten days. It could be for as much as three
hundred thousand dollars. Kimberley decided to wait. If Madeleine hadn't done anything so far—and she must have known

for nearly two weeks—then she was unlikely to do anything immediately. Kimberley decided to take a chance. She'd wait for just one more transfer before getting the hell out of New York.

Madeleine walked briskly up Broadway to Central Park, and in spite of the winos and vagrants who raved and ranted at the park's perimeter, she decided to walk back to her apartment on Fifth Avenue. In her present frame of mind, the sense of danger, the risk of being mugged or attacked, or even assaulted, was what she needed to cleanse her from the feeling of sleaziness she'd experienced in Kimberley's apartment. She glared angrily at a drunken bag lady who looked as if she was going to cause trouble, and quickened her pace. She felt contaminated and more emotionally assaulted and upset by seeing Kimberley than if she'd been physically attacked. The last hour had drained her, and yet it was beginning to sink in that she'd actually scored. Kimberley had been left bewildered and confused; there was no doubt about that in Madeleine's mind. The girl hadn't known what was happening, and Madeleine's mission had been totally successful. Yet the memory of Kimberley made her flesh crawl. How could Carl have . . . ? She closed her eyes and tried to shut off the visions that came to haunt her all the time now. She must concentrate on the positive aspects of the task she'd set herself, and now that she'd completed phase one of her plan, she must go ahead with phase two. It wasn't going to be such a walkover either. Phase two was going to be dangerous and tricky.

For a second Madeleine's heart sank, wondering if she had the strength to carry on, but then she thought of Carl. If I didn't love Carl so much, she thought, this whole nightmare would be impossible, and if I wasn't sure he loved me too, in spite of everything, I wouldn't be able to carry on.

She could see her apartment house through the trees now, and with a rush of thankfulness she broke into a steady jog, oblivious of the passersby who wondered at the elegant young woman in a gray linen suit and high-heeled black shoes trotting briskly along.

Home was a haven. Madeleine wanted a hot shower to rid herself of the last essence of Kimberley, so that when Carl got back from his golf she'd be as calm and composed as possible.

"There's an urgent message for you, madam," said Teresa when she let herself into the apartment. "I've written it on the pad by the phone."

"Thank you." With her heart skipping a beat, Madeleine's eyes flew to the notebook she always kept on the hall table. Could Kimberley have discovered . . . ? She snatched it up, frightened for a moment, then let out a long sigh of relief. It was from Jessica. Please call her urgently at the Royal Westminster. She had something amazing to tell Madeleine.

Smiling now, grateful for any distraction, Madeleine went into the living room and started dialing Jessica's number. Typical Jess, she thought as she waited to be put through to the sales office, to dramatize the most trivial situation. She'd probably been given a raise, or was having her office redecorated!

Five minutes later Madeleine sat dumbfounded, hardly able to believe what her friend had told her.

11

"WE REALLY would be very sorry to see you go, Jessica," Kenneth Wolfson was saying in a stunned voice. "Are you sure you've given this enough thought?"

Jessica sat in the office of the general manager, feeling slightly stunned herself. The past week had been the most extraordinary of her life, and she hardly recognized herself by her actions. Swiftly and with barely a backward glance she was doing a complete turnabout, throwing to the winds all her previously adamant views on work versus a private life. Where was the old Jessica, who had given up Andrew and the prospect of a secure marriage and future because her job prospects at the Royal Westminster were more important?

After Bernard had made love to her the previous week— was it only a week ago? . . . it seemed like years to her now— he'd asked her to stay with him forever. Just like that. Jessica-I-love-you-and-I-want-to-spend-the-rest-of-my-life-with-you. And to her amazement, Jessica had heard herself agreeing with a wholehearted rush of emotion that left her dizzy. Never in her life had she felt such heady ecstasy as when she was with Bernard, and her feelings were obliterating everything that had mattered to her previously. There was no past, nor present either; the future was all she could see now, stretching before her like a glorious avenue into infinity. And that future was totally filled by Bernard.

"Of course I'll stay with you, darling," she'd whispered as a cold blue dawn stole over the rooftops of London. "I'll stay with you forever." What was she saying? She didn't care. All she knew was that she'd found a paradise within the circle of Bernard's arms, a heaven she couldn't resist. Then he had hugged and kissed her with a wild abandon that had thrilled every cell in her body, and together they had lain close, planning the future.

It was only during the following day—as she rushed about the hotel giving lunch to a restaurant writer, setting up meetings to discuss forthcoming events, greeting VIP's in the lobby, and sending out invitations for a reception—that the full impact of what she was planning hit her forcibly. Bernard's last words, as she slipped out of his suite before breakfast, suddenly rang in her ears with appalling clarity:

"First we will be going to Boston, my darling, then on to Washington and New York, and after that Moscow, Paris, Tokyo, and Sydney. Then, when the tour's over, we'll spend the next four months in my house in Sardinia, where I do my composing."

It all sounded fantastic, but as she tottered along the corridor to get to her own room, it dawned on her that by going with Bernard she'd be leaving her job in the hotel. The thought took her breath away—but then, so did Bernard. Overcome by this turn of events that made her feel as if she were being whisked along on a big dipper that had gone out of control, she was overcome by conflicting emotions. She'd broken off with Andrew so that she could give her all to the Royal Westminster, yet here she was about to chuck the chance of a lifetime in the hotel business for a man she'd known only a matter of weeks! It was crazy. She needed to have her head examined! But . . . Sitting at her desk, she also knew that the most wonderful, glorious, and fantastic thing had happened to her. She'd fallen in love with a man in a million . . . and he was in love with her! All her life, in everything she'd done, she'd let her head rule her heart; she'd made sensible decisions and afterward been grateful that she had. This time, the temptation to let her heart rule her head, and lead it where it would, was so strong she had no desire to fight it. Why not give way to these glorious emotions? Just for once?

All morning Jessica's moods swung from wanting to go away with Bernard, to wanting to stay and follow her career. There was no reality in the thought that she was going to go to Kenneth Wolfson and hand in her resignation, but there was no reality in her dreamlike future with Bernard either.

How can I be doing this? she asked herself distractedly, her lazy topknot of blond hair coming loose as she shook her head, her small fists clenched on her desk. I'm about to give up everything I've spent six years working for. It's lunacy! Oh, but what delicious lunacy! Her mind and body still reeled from Bernard's lovemaking the previous night; four times she'd surrendered to his ardent passion, letting him take her again and again, as if he couldn't have enough of her. Virile enough for a man half his age, skilled as only a man of experience can be, Bernard had awakened her to delights she didn't know existed. Where, Jessica demanded as she picked up her pen, am I ever going to find a man like that again? She'd be a fool to turn her back on such a rampant, consuming love that was burning her up even as she sat at her desk. At lunchtime she came to a decision. She'd go and see Kenneth Wolfson and tell him she was leaving.

"Of course I've thought about it, Mr. Wolfson," Jessica said, sitting as taut as a jack-in-the-box before the lid was lifted. "I know it's very sudden . . . and I'm very sorry to inconvenience you like this . . ."

"Frankly, Jessica, I think you've had a brainstorm," Kenneth Wolfson said. He spoke kindly, and in a fatherly fashion, but there was concern in his eyes. "You've known Mr. Scheller for only a short time, and you don't know anything about him. Don't you think you're being unwise in wanting to give up your career—when you have such a brilliant future—on what I can only describe as a wild infatuation?"

"It's *not* an infatuation!" Jessica said indignantly. "Don't you believe in love at first sight? That's what's happened for both of us, and I'm not a starry-eyed eighteen-year-old, you know, Mr. Wolfson. I do know what I'm doing, and although it may seem a bit fast off the mark to others, it feels *right* for us!" Her gilt bangles chinked as she gesticulated, anxious to get her point across.

Kenneth Wolfson remained silent, looking at her with a worried expression.

"I realize I must work out my notice, of course," Jessica continued hurriedly. "I wouldn't want to let you down by just walking out this minute. But I am determined to live with Bernard. You've been so good to me, but"—she spread her hands in a gesture of helplessness—"what else can I do?" Her piquant little face looked genuinely puzzled.

"If we weren't so frantically busy here," Wolfson said, shaking his head, "I'd suggest you take three months' leave of absence so you can get this . . . this thing out of your system, but I'm afraid it's impossible right now; and I'm afraid there can be no question of our keeping your post open, should you change your mind."

"I won't change my mind," Jessica said firmly. "I've always adored my job, but this is something else."

He spoke dryly. "It certainly seems to be. Very well, Jessica, with great reluctance I'll accept your resignation and I'll have a word with Dennis Powell. Maybe we can find a replacement immediately, which would mean you could leave quite soon."

"Really?" Jessica's blue eyes blazed with delight.

Wolfson, in spite of his feelings of misgiving, smiled indulgently at her. She looked like a little girl who'd been promised a treat.

"I can't promise, Jessica, but I'll see what I can do."

"Thank you, Mr. Wolfson. I'd be terribly grateful. You've been so understanding." Jessica sprang to her feet, looking vibrantly alive, and brimming with enthusiasm.

It was in the evening, while she was changing to dine with Bernard, that Madeleine returned her call.

"You're what?" Madeleine gasped when Jessica told her the news.

"It's true!" Jessica chortled. "I'm madly in love! Oh, Maddy, I'm absolutely *dying* for you to meet Bernard. He's the most fantastic man that's ever lived! And guess what? . . . We're going to the States. Well, he leaves tomorrow, and I'm following as soon as they've found a replacement for me here. We can see lots of each other!"

"It'll be wonderful having you in the States," Madeleine was saying in a shocked voice, "but, Jessie, isn't this all awfully sudden?"

"Don't *you* start!" exclaimed Jessica. "I've already had it out with our general manager: Do I know what I'm doing? What do I know about Bernard? Oh, Mr. Wolfson gave me the whole works, telling me it was all infatuation. How can he know?" Her voice rose plaintively.

"Well, you've always been an obsessive person, Jessie."

"What do you mean, obsessive?" Jessica sounded quite offended.

Madeleine laughed. "I mean, whatever you do, you go for it hell-for-leather. One hundred percent. There are no half-measures with you, are there? You threw yourself into the hotel business as if life didn't exist outside the Royal Westminster, and now you're doing the same thing over this new boyfriend! Are you going to give up work altogether?"

"Well, I'll have to, won't I?" Jessica was deeply disappointed that Madeleine was not sharing in her euphoria. "I'm going to be living in hotels, not running them, all over the world for eight months of the year, and all my time will be taken up looking after Bernard."

"Ummm." There was silence on the line.

"I thought you'd be excited for me," Jessica wailed. "You've no *idea* how much I'm in love."

"I'm sorry, Jessie. Of course I'm pleased, if you're happy. I'm in shock still, I suppose. Somehow I'd always imagined you staying in the hotel business—you've always seemed so dedicated to it."

"Well, that was *then*. This is *now*," Jessica replied, relying on her own form of logic.

"Have you told Andrew what's happened?" she heard Madeleine say.

"I haven't talked to Andrew for weeks. Anyway, it's got nothing to do with him. Remember, it was Andrew who really broke off our relationship because he couldn't stand my working so hard. I wanted us to carry on as usual, but he wouldn't have it."

She heard Madeleine sigh deeply.

"Maddy . . ." Her voice caught fractionally. "I'm going to be all right, you know. Don't sound so upset. I want you to be happy for me!"

"I'm not upset, honey, just a bit worried for you. I couldn't bear it if you ended up having regrets."

"I promise you I'm doing the right thing . . . everything's going to be fine," Jessica pleaded. It meant a great deal to her to feel she had her best friend's blessing, especially as she still had to face her parents and break the news to them. They'd been very upset when she and Andrew split up.

"Jessie, I wish you all the happiness and luck in the world," Madeleine said warmly, "and I can't wait for you to come over."

An instant beam spread over Jessica's face. "I'll let you know as soon as I do. Anyway, how are things with you? Painting any more famous faces?"

"I'm fine . . . and busy."

"And that *divine* man you're married to . . . how is he? Still making fortunes?"

"Carl's fine."

Jessica's ever-mobile and expressive face changed from a grin to a faint frown. Madeleine sounded . . . well, sort of strange. Could the shock of hearing about Bernard have affected her that much, or was she upset about something else?

"Are you all right, Maddy?" she demanded.

Madeleine's voice came across the line stronger now, as if she were making an effort. "Yes, everything's great, and I'm longing to see you again."

"You're sure you're okay?"

"Of course!" Madeleine protested stoutly.

"Right, then. I'll be in touch."

"Good luck, Jessie."

Jessica replaced the receiver, her brow still puckered. Madeleine was keeping something back.

Jessica spent the night with Bernard again, and it reaffirmed in her mind that no matter what anyone said, she was doing the right thing. They hardly slept at all, passing the dark hours in deep and wonderful conversation, planning their lives together, in between making love. Bernard was flying off in the morning, so every moment was precious, because she wasn't sure when she'd see him again.

"I'm going to write a symphony when we get to Sardinia," Bernard whispered as the song of the dawn chorus from the birds in Hyde Park filtered through the open window, "and I'm going to dedicate it to you."

Jessica felt lost for words. It was the most beautiful thought she'd ever heard, and emotionally she reached out and clutched his hand.

"My little angel, my little love," Bernard murmured, his twilight eyes looking deeply into hers, thrilling her so much she felt the mounting pressure of sexual arousal again.

"I can't live without you," she moaned, running her hands

over his broad shoulders. "Oh, God, I hope I can get to America soon."

"I'll be waiting," he promised, slipping his hand between her legs, touching the seat of her excitement, stroking her with strong yet gentle fingers as the tension built up inside her. Then she slipped her legs around his hips, drawing him closer, her eyes glazed, her mouth partly open.

"I shall *die* if you don't come inside me," she cried out, clinging to him. "Oh, Jesus . . . Bernard, oh, oh, Jesus . . ." She rocked her head from side to side on the pillow, half-crazed with desire, straining to feel his strength filling her, pushing up hard inside her . . . hard . . . hard . . .The world turned upside down amid an explosion of blazing stars, and the heavens were torn apart as she let out a scream, rocked to her depths by a searing climax.

Later that day, as she tried to keep awake at her desk, Jessica received a call from Kenneth Wolfson. Her position as director of sales had been filled. She was free to leave the hotel within a week.

It was Monday, two days after Madeleine's visit to Kimberley's apartment. Carl left for work as usual, and Kimberley, on the lookout for another transfer from Hank, was already in his office when he arrived.

She glanced at him as he entered. "How was your weekend?" she asked with a touch of insolence.

Studiously Carl avoided looking at her as he took his seat behind the desk. "Fine, thank you," he replied with icy politeness.

"Really?" Kimberley drew out the word, her voice flat with doubt, her pellucid gray eyes looking searchingly into his.

"Yes." Carl glanced up at her, genuinely surprised.

"Well, aren't some people lucky!" she rejoined, shrugging. Then she turned away and went next door to her own office. Carl frowned at her retreating figure, wondering what she was carrying on about. Had something happened? He glanced through the stack of transfers to be dealt with on his desk and noted with relief that there was nothing from Hank Pugsley. Had Kimberley seen him over the weekend perhaps? Could

Hank have discovered what was going on? Carl's heart started
to thump heavily and unpleasantly and his hands felt clammy.
Torn between the desire to question her and find out if there
was anything wrong, and the fear that if he did he wouldn't
like what he heard, Carl remained at his desk trying to work,
avoiding contact with her as much as possible. But even her
presence in the adjoining office felt threatening. Like an unseen
menace breathing poison into the atmosphere, Kimberley went
about her work, while Carl was forced to breathe the same air
and listen to her voice on the phone and to her typewriter as
it clacked; and all the time there was the redolence of deep
fear between them. They were united in executing a serious
crime, and now they could not even communicate with each
other, so great was the antipathy between them. If they were
partners in crime, they were also the bitterest of enemies.

At twelve-thirty Carl heard a light tap on his office door. A
moment later Madeleine entered, her arms full of shopping
and her manner cheerful. Seeing he was on the phone, she
mouthed: "Hi, Carl!" before dropping her parcels on a chair.

Carl put his hand over the mouthpiece. "I'm talking to Tokyo. I'll be with you as soon as I can," he whispered.

"That's okay," she whispered back, smiling. Through the
open doorway into the adjoining office she could see Kimberley
working at her desk. At that moment Kimberley looked up,
as if conscious of being watched, and the two women's eyes
met and locked. Madeleine held the stare coldly, and after a
moment Kimberley's eyes flickered away and her gaze
dropped back to her work.

Carl hadn't noticed any interchange between the two
women, and Madeleine thought how tired and haggard he
looked as he sat hunched over the phone, quoting figures to
some businessman in Japan. Madeleine had come to his office
today hoping to find it empty. Carl lunched with someone
almost every day, and she was sure Kimberley took her lunch
break to go shopping. Now she would have to rethink how
she was going to carry out phase two of her plan. She needed
just a few minutes alone in Kimberley's office, because she
was sure the answer to getting the girl finally out of their lives
lay there. Carl was still on the telephone. Madeleine wandered
around looking at the pictures on his walls, as if they were a
source of profound interest. Then, out of the corner of her eye

she saw a bank clerk enter Kimberley's office and say something to her. She strained to listen.

". . . can you go to his office right away? He wants to give you the details of the dollar transfer to Kuwait for the Voltex Construction Company," the clerk was saying.

Kimberley swore loudly. "That'll take hours! I wanted to go to lunch now!"

"Sorry. Mr. Watts said it was urgent."

"Oh, hell!"

Madeleine tensed, straining to hear what was happening. If Kimberley were to leave her office now, while Carl was still on the phone . . . God, she'd have to act fast—and there was a terrible element of risk—but she might just have time.

Carl was gesturing to her to sit down. "I'm going to be some time yet," he whispered, putting his hand over the mouthpiece.

"Don't worry about it," Madeleine replied softly. The longer, the better, she thought. Strolling nonchalantly toward the door to Kimberley's office, she was just in time to see her backside flouncing out with obvious irritation, banging the outer door after her.

Madeleine didn't waste any time. With a backward glance to make sure Carl was still engrossed in the papers before him, from which he was quoting, she slipped through the open door and made straight for Kimberley's desk. She knew exactly what she was looking for, because she'd seen it in Kimberley's apartment—a black leather Filofax very like her own. She hadn't been able to examine it then, but now, as her eyes swept feverishly over the clutter on the desk, she knew that it was vital to find it. With every nerve straining to listen for either Carl ending his phone call or Kimberley returning for some reason, she looked around without disturbing anything. Files, papers, ledgers, and transfer slips were stacked on every surface. She saw a memo signed "Kimberley Cabot" lying on the desk. Swiftly she folded it in half and stuffed it into her pocket. It wasn't what she was looking for, but a copy of Kimberley's signature would certainly be useful. She continued her search. The office was a mess and there were even some files heaped up on the floor on one side of the desk. Then she saw it! The black diary-file, together with Kimberley's purse, on the floor by her swivel chair behind the desk. Madeleine grabbed it and undid the stud clasp, her heart pounding and her hands shaking. Was there time now? Should she slip it under her jacket and go to Carl's washroom, where she could examine it without fear of being disturbed? But then she'd have to put it back where she found it, and if Carl had finished his call . . . No, she decided. It was now or never.

Because her own Filofax was identical, Madeleine knew the layout by heart—where the ordinary diary section was, and the address-book section, the parts devoted to "Accounts," "Projects," "Finances," "Daily Planner"; there was also an index for classified listings like the telephone number of the TV repair company, or the electrician or the carpet-cleaning company, and this was followed by an index headed "Restaurants." Madeleine knew what she did if she wanted to jot down something confidential; the question was, did Kimberley's mind work in the same way? Carl always teased Madeleine about this, saying no man's mind could ever be as inventive—and illogical—as a female's. Who but a woman, he joked, would put the number of her bank cash card under S for "Shopping"? He'd fallen all over himself with laughter the day he'd discovered that. Automatically Madeleine flipped open the address section of Kimberley's Filofax at S—maybe for "Switzerland"? Her pulse quickened. Spritza Cool Bar. Stanton's Garage. Bunny Steinberg. Josh Stanton. Nothing. Then she turned to C—for "Cash," perhaps? Car Rental. Chanterelle Couture. Nancy Clavell. Madeleine's eyes skimmed the entries; nothing. She continued her search, a frantic feeling of the minutes ticking away filling her with desperation. M for "Money"; nothing. D for "Dollars"; nothing.

Sweat was breaking out all over her body now and her hands were sticky. Please, God, let it be here, she implored under her breath. Give me a break, God, before anyone comes into the room and discovers me riffling through the diary of Carl's assistant. How would that look? What the hell would I say? At that moment she was struck by a brainwave. Oh, why hadn't she thought of it before? O for "Overseas" or "Offshore"! That must be it! When she looked at the O listings her heart nearly stopped. Orthodontal-insurance number indeed! Grabbing a scrap of paper, she jotted down the row of numbers: 23007 4810 66792. Then she closed the Filofax and replaced it carefully beside Kimberley's purse again. Checking that she'd left everything as she found it, she was already standing in the doorway of Carl's office as he hung up the telephone. She tried to look cool, but beads of perspiration were plastering the black curls to her forehead, and her clothes were sticking to her.

"I don't think your air conditioning's working properly," she observed. "It's terribly hot in here."

"Is it, sweetheart?" Carl replied vaguely. He was busy making notes.

"I think I'll freshen up. How about some lunch, if you've got time?" Madeleine braced herself to enter the washroom, forcing herself to control her emotions, because the last time she'd been in here her world had fallen apart.

"Sure. I'd like that," Carl said, looking up and smiling at her. "Are you all right, Maddy? You look very flushed."

"I'm fine," she replied with forced gaiety. "I'm hot because this place is like an oven!"

They lunched at a nearby fish restaurant, with Madeleine keeping up a flow of light chatter so that Carl wouldn't suspect how worried she was about him. She longed to reach across the table and tell him that soon, with any luck, it would all be over; but caution prevented her. The nightmare was far from over yet, and it was vital that he not suspect the part she was playing in bringing about Kimberley's downfall. If he knew, if he had even an inkling of what she was up to, he'd get edgier than ever and then Kimberley would notice, and the whole thing could blow up in their faces.

It wasn't until Carl suddenly made a remark during lunch that Madeleine realized she'd been absorbed in this terrible business to the exclusion of everything else.

"Have you heard any more from that fellow Marks?" he asked.

"Who?" For a split second she stared at him blankly. The names that had been running through her mind lately were Kimberley Cabot, Hank Pugsley, Brandt's Motors, and Michaux Internationale. "Marks?"

"How many Mr. Markses do you know?" Carl teased. "You couldn't think of anything except the mystery surrounding your mother's death and your grandfather's will, and now you don't even remember who I'm talking about!"

"Sorry, darling." Madeleine flushed. "I've been so involved

with my painting, and you know how everything else goes out of my head when I've got a lot of commissions," she lied.

"Even so, Maddy . . ." He looked incredulous. "What's happening over your mother's death certificate? Has Mr. Marks applied for a court order of presumption of death?"

Madeleine shook her head. "I don't know. I'll call him tomorrow and find out what's happening." She didn't want to talk about it right now. There was nothing she could do for the time being anyway, and the lawyer had said he would keep her informed and let her know when her claim had been granted in the British courts. Far more important was what she had to do next: find out where Hank Pugsley hung out and go and see him.

"You're so kind!" sobbed Jessica. "Thank you all so much." She wiped away the tears as the general manager, Kenneth Wolfson, his assistant, Dennis Powell, Dick Fowler, Mike Lyle from banqueting, Adolph, the restaurant manager, and even Anne Butler from the press office toasted her with champagne as she clutched the going-away present they'd all chipped in to give her. It was a beautiful dark red leather jewel case, the inner compartments lined with cream suede.

"It's beautiful!" Jessica gasped. "I just hope Bernard gives me some jewelry to put in it."

Everyone laughed at her comical expression.

"Well," said Dennis Powell, patting her shoulder, "you know what will happen the next time you come to this hotel, don't you?"

Jessica looked mystified.

Dennis explained, "There'll be someone in the lobby to greet you with a drink while you check in, and Mr. Bernard Scheller and Miss Jessica McCann will head our list of visiting VIP's, and you'll be given the full treatment."

Jessica looked appalled. "Oh, no! I don't want to be treated any differently, and knowing me, I'll probably forget anyway and start rushing around checking all the other bookings and seeing how many events we've got in banqueting."

"Oh, I'm sure you'll take to the life of a lady of leisure without any trouble," Anne Butler interjected, a hint of spite in her eyes.

"Don't worry—I will!" Jessica retorted spiritedly.

"So where are you actually going to be based?" Dick asked. He was going to miss Jessica like hell; even in a crisis she was good for a laugh.

"In Sardinia, I suppose, where Bernard has a house, but it's lucky I like hotel life, because I'm going to be moving from one to another for eight months of the year."

Anne's eyes narrowed. "You poor thing. How unsettling for you!" Her insincerity was not lost on Jessica, who smiled sweetly and replied, "A nomadic existence, my dear. Goodness knows how I'll survive."

"Jolly exciting, though," interjected Dick, missing the point.

"Fascinating," Kenneth Wolfson said. "I know the Far East very well, working for the Golding Group out there, but I'd love to travel around Europe."

Anne had one more barb to hurl at Jessica. "When are you actually getting married?"

"Married?" Jessica echoed, pretending shock. "Goodness, what a bourgeois idea! I don't know if we'll *ever* get married, but then, I never did think a bit of paper made any difference to a relationship."

Anne's lips tightened in anger and her eyes looked flat and sullen.

"Well, we're certainly going to miss you," Dennis Powell said hastily. "The old Royal Westminster isn't going to be the same without you."

"Don't say that, or you'll make me cry again," Jessica implored. "If Bernard wasn't a man in a million, you wouldn't be getting rid of me so easily."

At last the drinks in Kenneth Wolfson's office came to an end and Jessica was kissing everybody good-bye—even Anne Butler—and hurrying up to her room to finish packing. In an hour's time she was leaving the hotel and going down to Guildford to spend her last night in England with her parents. Early tomorrow morning her father would be driving her to Heathrow, where she'd catch the flight to Boston; and Bernard would be waiting for her.

An hour later a porter came up to collect her luggage, and having taken one last look at the small room that for a short time had been home to her, she followed him down in the elevator.

As soon as she stepped into the lobby an enormous sense of loss enveloped her, making her throat dry and her eyes sting. This lobby was to her the heart of the hotel, and she remembered the first time she'd entered it, feeling terrified because she'd just been transferred from the Wentworth, and this new job at the Royal Westminster was so important to her. It had seemed so vast and strange, with its stretches of marble flooring, the long reception desk, the elegant oasis of furniture and plants, and the sweeping staircase that led up to the second floor. She remembered all the thousands of times she'd crossed this lobby on her way to the bar or the restaurant or to meet a guest; and those Christmases when the center table of flowers was replaced by a giant tree shimmering with little lights. She remembered the glamorous occasions when they'd had a grand ball or dinner, like the time the Prime Minister had attended a Conservative-party banquet, and they'd placed vases of blue flowers everywhere. And then there were the thousands of people she'd met, right on this spot, many of whom had become her friends.

The tears slid down her cheeks as she realized a chapter had closed in her life. Never again would she know the changing moods of this public place which had become as familiar to her as her old home: still with expectancy through a thousand dawns; clamoring with people and voices and shifting luggage at high noon; quiet as a mausoleum at dead of night. She would never belong in this spot again, or be any part of its day-to-day activity. Already she felt she'd left it all behind and that she was a mere shadow standing here now blending in with arriving guests and departing tourists, and no longer belonging. Unnoticed and invisible. Only her memories lingered now.

Jessica moved swiftly to the revolving glass doors and into a waiting cab as if she could not bear to hang around any longer. Her career in the hotel business was over forever.

The telephone rang just as Madeleine was getting out of the bath.

"It's for you, Mrs. Delaney," Teresa said, tapping on the door. "It's a Mr. Andrew Seymour, calling from England."

"Tell him I'll be right there." Madeleine grabbed a bath sheet, and wrapping it around her sarong-style, hurried to the phone by her bedside. She had a strong feeling she knew what he was calling about.

"Hi, Andrew. How are you?"

He sounded agitated. "Maddy, do you know what's going on? I rang Jessica at the Royal Westminster because I wanted to know what she'd like me to do with a box of tapes she left in my flat, and they told me she'd left! Left to get married!" The hurt and shock in his voice were painful to hear.

"Oh, I'm so sorry," Madeleine said sympathetically. "It all seems to have happened so quickly . . . and I don't know if she's actually getting married," she added, hoping that might soften the blow.

"I don't believe this is happening," he said slowly. Then there was a silence on the line, as if he were bracing himself to ask the next question. His voice croaked. "Who is he?"

"Bernard Scheller," Madeleine replied quietly.

"Bernard Scheller? Isn't he . . . ?"

"That's right. The composer."

"Jesus! He's old enough to be her father. What the hell's going on?"

"Andrew, that's all I know. I was as surprised as you are when I heard. It seems he was a guest in the hotel—"

"Where can I get hold of her?" he cut in.

"I don't know."

"Oh, come on, Maddy!" She could sense his fury mixed with anguish. "You're her best friend—you must know. And I'll find out sooner or later, so you might as well tell me now."

"I'm not being evasive, Andrew. I honestly don't know where she is at the moment, except that she was due to join Bernard in Boston before going on to Washington and New York. I'm expecting her to get in touch with me. Shall I get her to call you?"

Andrew groaned heavily. "I don't suppose she'll want to. Christ, I wish she had let me know what she was doing before going off like that. What I don't understand is, why has she given up work? That hotel meant everything to her. Hell, she even turned me down because of it! Then this bastard comes along . . . How long has she known him?"

"Two weeks."

"Two weeks!" Andrew yelled. "Couldn't anyone stop her? She must be out of her mind! It'll never last!"

"Andrew," Madeleine said gently, "I do know how you're

feeling, but Jessica is a grown woman. She has to be left to make her own decisions."

"Oh, I know, but it's all my fault, really. I should never have forced her to choose between me and the hotel. God, what a fool I was! But even when she did, I sort of hoped she'd get tired of it in time, and we'd get together again."

"I know. I'd rather hoped the same, for both your sakes."

"Oh, well . . ." He sounded dispirited, his voice hollow. "Tell her I called, will you, Maddy?"

Madeleine's heart ached for him. Andrew had taken a gamble and lost, and for a moment she felt quite angry with Jessica for being so unpredictable and flighty. But that was Jessica all over: part maddening, part lovable, as dazzling as quicksilver, but with a heart of gold. Jessica probably thought Andrew no longer wanted her and that was why she hadn't told him about Bernard. Certainly she would never have set out to hurt him intentionally.

"I'll tell her to call you the minute I hear from her," she assured him. The last thing she wanted was to get involved, or start acting as a go-between, but at least she could pass on Andrew's message. After that it was up to Jessica.

Andrew replaced the receiver slowly and gazed out his office window, ignoring the fact that there were two people waiting to talk to him on other telephone lines. They could wait; he had to collect himself before he could talk to anyone. The shock of hearing what Jessica had done was a bitter blow, doubly painful because he blamed himself.

"Are you all right, old chap?" Sandy inquired from his desk opposite.

"I'm okay." Grimly Andrew took the first waiting call, dealt with a minor query, then took the second.

An uneducated woman's voice came on the line. "I saw your board outside an 'ouse on the corner of Eaton Square," she said. "I'd like to look over it."

Andrew winced at the flat vowels and the dropped H's. She was obviously a working-class woman and he felt he ought to warn her about the price. It would certainly be beyond the range of anyone but a rich American or an Arab.

"Certainly, madam," he replied politely. "I know the one

you mean. It's a freehold property, though, and the price is three million pounds."

"I wants to see it," the woman said doggedly.

"Very well, Mrs. . . . er . . . ?"

"Latimer," she said, almost crossly. Her tone seemed to say: Stop messing me about.

"Mrs. Latimer. Would this afternoon at three o'clock be convenient?" Andrew cast his eyes to heaven as he spoke. This was going to be a complete waste of his time, but not for nothing did they call themselves "an agency that takes a personal interest in our clients' wishes."

"Yes." Mrs. Latimer hung up abruptly.

"I bet she just wants to see what the inside looks like," Sandy remarked when Andrew told him. The house in question had been featured in the *Evening Standard* a few days before and had aroused much interest, having a swimming pool on the lower ground floor, and a garden with trees and a little stream full of goldfish on the roof. It was a coup for the Jason and Seymour Partnership that they had been appointed sole agents by the owners, who lived in Spain, and who Andrew suspected made their money by drug pushing.

"D'you want me to show the house for you?" Sandy asked Andrew. "You look beat."

Andrew shook his head. "I'll live. If I can just get Jessica out of my mind, I'll be fine. Goddammit!" He pushed himself away from the desk on his swivel chair with a violent movement. "What have I done, Sandy?" he groaned. "How could I have been such a bloody fool? Jessica and I were made for each other . . . and I let her slip through my fingers. Oh, God! What a mess!"

Sandy, who had overheard Andrew's conversation with Madeleine and who had gathered what had happened, looked cynical.

"If she's as flighty as she sounds, could be you're better off without her," he remarked.

Andrew flushed with anger. "She's not flighty at all! How could she have held down a job like she did, if she was flighty? It's obvious she's been seduced by this old man, who must have some hold over her."

"Humph!" Sandy snorted. "If you believe that, you'll believe anything. Forget her, Andrew. That's my advice. There are plenty more fish in the sea!"

Andrew paced up and down their smart pale-blue-carpeted office, so filled with bitter regret and anger that he could hardly speak.

"It's nearly three o'clock," Sandy reminded him.

"What? Oh, hell." Picking up his car keys, he strode out of the office without saying another word.

When he arrived at the large, imposing porticoed house in Eaton Square, he double-parked his car, risking a fine, and went to wait on the doorstep for Mrs. Latimer. The wind gusted along the pavement, sending leaves spinning into whirlpools of dust, while overhead an uneasy sky pressed down on the city. Jessica, why didn't you talk to me before you rushed off like that? Jessica, did our years together mean so little to you? Lost in his anguished thoughts, Andrew did not at first notice a large gray Rolls-Royce, driven by a uniformed chauffeur, glide up the street and stop. A minute later the chauffeur was holding open the passenger door for a buxom woman in her thirties, who alighted and tottered forth on thick legs and high stiletto heels.

"Are you the agent?" she demanded, looking at Andrew.

Andrew recovered himself in time to smile politely and acknowledge that he was.

"I'm Mrs. Latimer," she announced unnecessarily. "I wanna see round the 'ouse."

"Of course." Andrew had changed his mind about Mrs. Latimer's ability to afford three million pounds on a London house. She was plump, with a mane of dyed blond hair, a too-short blue skirt, and a tawny-colored fox jacket. Her coarse, heavily made-up face bore the hostile expression of a woman who knows she is not socially acceptable, although she has enough money to be so. And Mrs. Latimer did have enough money; that was for sure. Her diamond earrings and solitaire ring, with a stone as big as a lump of sugar, assured Andrew that here was a possible buyer. How she had come upon her money, he didn't want to know. He was merely there to make the sale. He proceeded to show her around the house.

For someone who had probably started life in a slum dwelling, with damp running down the walls and an outside lavatory, Mrs. Latimer showed typical superciliousness when it came to the finer points of carved cornices, Adam fireplaces, and parquet floors. Andrew gritted his teeth and longed for the days when only the educated and cultured had the money to buy historic old houses. But then he remembered the three percent he and Sandy would be making out of the deal, and he gave Mrs. Latimer a sickly smile. After all, business was business.

At last they finished the tour of ten bedrooms with bathrooms *en suite*, four reception rooms, large kitchen and utility rooms, and all the "mod. cons." of this "des. res.," not forgetting the swimming pool, sauna, Jacuzzi, and roof garden complete with two London sparrows.

Mrs. Latimer stood in the spacious marble hall, her hand on her hip, her expression that of someone who has entered a bar and is waiting to be served.

"I suppose it'll do," she remarked grudgingly. "'Ave to be painted over, like. Colors are dull, but it'll do. I'll 'ave it."

Andrew was still reeling with shock when he got back to the office. "It's sold . . . to the most ghastly woman, but at least it's sold!" he told Sandy. "God knows what she's going to do with it. Probably decorate the drawing room in leopard-skin-patterned fabric and the bedroom in purple satin, but who cares?" The sale had cheered him up. "Not a bad afternoon's work," he added modestly.

"There's a message for you on your pad," Sandy said. Something in the forced casualness of his voice made Andrew look at him anxiously.

"Jessica called," Sandy said breezily. "She left her number, so you can call her back."

Madeleine poured a couple of drops of linseed oil on to the blob of white paint on her palette and worked it in with the tip of her brush. When she was satisfied with the consistency, she leaned forward and very carefully, with a feather-light touch, added the highlights to her portrait of Pearl Ermintrude, one of New York's leading socialites. This was the part she liked best. Adding those little dots and streaks of white that brought the face to life and gave it added depth. Especially the eyes. It was amazing what a tiny blob of glinting white, painted on the iris, could do. Then she added a touch of yellow and pink to the white paint, and started adding touches to the bridge of the nose, the forehead, the chin, and along the cheekbone. She stood back to see the effect. Mrs. Henry Ermintrude II, Pearl to her friends, was going to be thrilled out of her tiny mind. The portrait was destined to hang in the Ermintrudes' Dakota apartment, and Pearl had specially worn a pale green silk dress to be painted in, "because the color will go so perfectly with our decor."

Madeleine grimaced, and then signed the canvas with a flourish, in dark brown paint. She gave it one more appraising look, then started to clean her brushes. It was only lunchtime, but she wouldn't paint anymore today; she had something more pressing to do. She checked the address where she was going: Tenth Avenue and Twenty-sixth Street, not too far from Penn Station, a place called the Altman Building. She didn't have an appointment. She could only hope he'd be there and that she'd get to see him.

The Altman Building turned out to be a tall tower housing over fifty companies, their names listed by the elevator in the lobby. Not a smart building, by any means, she observed, running her eye down the list of occupants, who mostly seemed to be in the construction or machine-tool business. Taking the creaking elevator to the eleventh floor, she stepped straight into a small cluttered reception area, the walls lined with battleship-gray metal filing cabinets, a couple of battered desks, and a film of grime clinging to everything like a patina of poverty. In one corner an ancient coffee machine gurgled lethargically, as if it, too, was depressed by the surroundings.

A blowsy-looking girl with bleached hair tortured into an artful concoction of curls piled high on top of her head sat at one of the desks, a telephone receiver wedged between shoulder and jaw. She was deep in conversation.

" '. . . Aw, gee, honey,' I told him straight: 'I don't like it that way!' I said: 'I'm not going to date you again unless you treat me like a lady' . . . and what d'you think that bastard said? He told me I was frigid! Me! Frigid! Well, then I told him he can shove it up his own ass for all I care!"

Suddenly the girl looked up, a resentful expression on her face at having been disturbed. "Yeah?" she asked Madeleine.

"I'd like to see Hank Pugsley, please."

Insolent brown eyes looked her up and down. "Is he expecting you?"

"No, but please tell him it's very important," Madeleine said firmly.

The girl gave a sigh of irritation and spoke into the phone again. "Dorothy? . . . Yeah, sorry about this. Will ya hang on a minute . . . I'll be as quick as I can." Flashing Madeleine another reproachful look, she pressed the button on the office intercom.

"Hank, there's someone here to see you," she bellowed.

Madeleine winced, and the girl addressed her again.

"Name?"

"Delaney. Madeleine Delaney."

Another pause after the girl had repeated her name, and then another question, sharp and unfriendly. "What's it about?"

By now Madeleine was trying to keep her temper in check. One thing was obvious: Hank Pugsley ran a shoddy, cheapjack outfit, and the girl probably got paid peanuts. But then of course he wasn't into reinvesting in Brandt's Motors; he was too busy feathering his own nest in Switzerland.

"Tell Mr. Pugsley," said Madeleine with a hint of aggression, "that I have to talk to him on very important business, and I won't go away until he sees me."

The girl looked taken aback, but not for long. Her voice twanged nasally. "She says it's important, Hank." There was a pause and then she looked up at Madeleine again. "Last door on the right, along the corridor," she said grudgingly.

"Thank you," Madeleine replied with pointed politeness. As she strode away along the corridor, she could hear the girl on the phone say: "Dorothy, are you still there? . . . Sorry about that! As I was saying . . ."

The wording painted on the door was grandiose compared to the conditions of the office: "President. Hank Pugsley. Brandt's Motors." Knocking, Madeleine entered to find a large man in shirtsleeves, his red face bloated with fat, his bare forearms covered with black hairs. From between his teeth a cigar protruded, so much a part of him that she wondered if he slept with it clamped between his lips like a baby with a pacifier. Small wary eyes regarded her sharply as he remained seated.

"Well?" Hank Pugsley demanded.

Madeleine stepped forward, an incongruously elegant figure in a simple cream dress. She pointed to the chair facing his desk and asked with exaggerated good manners, "May I sit down?"

Hank watched her with widening eyes and a slackening of the lower lip. "Sure. What can I do for you?" he asked with a touch more deference.

"My name's Madeleine Delaney," she began, "and I have something to tell you which I think you ought to know." Her heart was fluttering wildly now, wondering how he was going to react. At all costs, she reminded herself, she must keep Carl's name out of this.

Hank looked alarmed, and Madeleine could tell he was guilty of a dozen misdemeanors by the way his eyes were registering varying degrees of anxiety as thoughts passed through his mind. She could guess he was thinking: Has my wife found out I've been going out with hookers? Has the Department of Trade discovered I'm producing inferior goods? Worst of all, is the IRS onto me?

Madeleine let him simmer for a moment, allowing the obvious jumble of panic in his mind to settle and subside.

"What sort of thing?" he asked in a hoarse voice.

Madeleine leaned forward confidentially and dropped her voice.

"First, I must ask you to respect the fact that I am talking to you in complete and utter confidence, and that I will not answer any questions as to how I came about finding the information I am going to give you."

Hank took several seconds to digest this.

"What's . . . er . . . what's it about?" he gulped.

"Do you agree not to question me about my sources?" Madeleine insisted.

He shrugged his great shoulders and spread his spatulate-fingered hands on the desk. He hesitated. "It depends."

"I'll tell you everything I know, and it is to your advantage, Mr. Pugsley, I assure you, but that's *all* I can tell you."

The desire to be put out of his suspense, coupled with his acute curiosity, made him reply: "Okay. Whatever you say."

Madeleine took a deep breath. "I believe you know a girl called Kimberley Cabot."

A shot of fear went through his eyes. "Are you a private dick? Has my wife sent you?"

"Nothing like that," Madeleine said. "This has nothing to do with your private life. But you were unwise enough to tell Kimberley that you were evading paying all your taxes by transferring dollars to a phony company in Zurich."

That did it. Hank shot up two feet in the air, his face gray, his eyes terrified.

"I deny it!" he blustered breathlessly. "Who the hell d'you think you are, barging in here—"

"Listen, Mr. Pugsley. It's no concern of mine what you do with your money!" She spoke sharply. "I'm not from the tax people, or any other official department, for that matter. I'm here because Kimberley Cabot is ripping you off and I think you should know about it."

Confusion, relief, suspicion, and finally incredulity passed like changing masks across Hank's face. He sank back heavily into his chair. "What the fuck are you talking about?" He sounded weaker.

Madeleine explained swiftly and in a decisive voice. She told him exactly what Kimberley was doing, describing it as a one-woman operation so as not to involve Carl. "I can't tell you how I found out," she concluded. "All I know is that every time you arrange to transfer dollars to Switzerland, she diverts them to her own numbered account. I even have the number of that account."

Convinced at last, Hank sat slumped, and again she could see his brain trying to work out what he could do. Report Kimberley to the FBI? Complain to the Central Manhattan Bank? Have it out with Kimberley in person?

Madeleine saved him the trouble of trying to find a solution. She spoke earnestly. "There's nothing you can do about it, because you'd be in big trouble with Internal Revenue yourself, and Kimberley knows it. She's banking on your silence if you find out. That's why she's sure she can get away with it."

"The fucking little cunt!" Hank exploded. "And I thought she was a model! Some model!" He spat in disgust. "What am I gonna do? D'you know how much of my money she's stolen?"

"How often do you put through a transfer?"

"Every coupla weeks . . . around three hundred thousand dollars each time." He groaned despairingly.

Madeleine raised her eyebrows and did a quick calculation. "Then she's probably taken more than a million dollars by now. Maybe a million and a half."

"Holy shit!" Hank sat stunned, gazing blindly at the papers on the desk before him, not seeing them, but visualizing his precious money being stolen from him. "I could do with a drink," he mumbled. Fumbling in a drawer of his desk, he produced a half-full bottle of Scotch, the glass of the bottle blurred with imprints of sweaty fingers.

"Want one?"

"No, thanks."

He poured the amber liquid into a paper cup and gulped noisily in the silence of the dreary little office, his eyes registering pain. For a moment Madeleine felt quite sorry for him.

"There is something we can do, if you'll cooperate," she ventured.

"Tell me something first . . . No, two things."

Madeleine shook her head. "I told you at the beginning that I can't tell you how I found out."

"But you can tell me what's in it for you," he shot back.

"There's nothing in it for me except to see justice done—maybe a very rough sort of justice, but nevertheless I'd like to see Kimberley Cabot put out of action . . . probably as much as you would," Madeleine replied evenly.

"Has she been screwing your husband?" His little eyes suddenly went shrewd with understanding.

Madeleine averted her gaze, as if the subject was distasteful, but inside she felt a pang. His remark was unnervingly accurate, and she had to cope with her emotions for a few seconds before she could reply. Then she turned to him with a calm smile.

"My father happens to be the president of the Central Manhattan Bank. I want Kimberley stopped, because sooner or later she'll bring disgrace on the bank, and that would hurt my father. Nothing like this has ever happened before, and it would affect him deeply." *And Carl. And me*, she thought to herself.

Hank sniffed loudly. "So what are you proposing? We get

a hit man to take care of her? I don't like the idea. Once you get in with the mob—"

"Nothing like that!" Madeleine was shocked. "My God, no! That really *would* be fatal!"

"So what are you suggesting? Oh, Jesus Christ, I've just remembered!" He slammed the palm of his hand to his brow, and there was the loud slap of flesh on flesh.

"What's the matter?"

Hank looked grayer than ever, his skin a dirty bleached color now. "I sent off another transfer first thing this morning, for three hundred and thirty thousand bucks! Fuck, how can I stop it? I'd better call up the bank and say—"

"It's all right," Madeleine said urgently. "Don't do anything! It will make her suspicious if you cancel it now, and anyway, she won't be able to put it through."

"How d'you mean?"

For the first time Madeleine gave a satisfied smile. "Unless I'm very much mistaken, she won't be able to divert your money to her own account anymore, not unless she can think up another way of doing it. This time your money will end up where it's supposed to: in your account instead of hers."

"Yeah? How did ya fix that?" Hank asked skeptically.

"I can't tell you, but I do think your money's safe, now and in the future. In the meantime, Mr. Pugsley, how would you like to get what was stolen back again?"

Hank drained his paper cup of whiskey, filled it up again, and took another swig. "Lady, you make me nervous. I'd like you to stop talking in riddles. You look like a classy dame, but how do I know you're on the level? And why should you want me to get my money back? How do I know I can trust you?"

"You've nothing to lose by trusting me, have you, and you can easily check that I'm Jake Shearman's daughter. The way I see it, I'd like to put to rights the loss you have suffered at the hands of an employee of the Central Manhattan Bank, and I'll be frank: I'd like to see Kimberley deprived of that money."

Suddenly Hank seemed to be on Madeleine's side, and his attitude toward her changed. They had a purpose in common now, a desire to get even with Kimberley Cabot, and Madeleine could sense a new respect in his attitude.

"So what do we do?" he asked.

Madeleine outlined her plan. Hank's expression changed to one of total agreement and approval. "Jeez!" He whistled through his teeth. "You're quite a dame, aren't you?"

"So you'll help me?"

"Sure! It'll be my pleasure!" The hint of a smile filled his flushed face. "This has given me the fright of my fucking life. I'll never risk doing this sort of scam again. Christ, you don't know who you can trust, do you?"

Madeleine's smile had a touch of irony in it as she agreed with him.

A few minutes later she left Hank's office and went along the corridor to the elevator. The girl at the reception desk was still telling Dorothy the horrors of her life.

"Is that you, Jessica?" Andrew braced himself to hear her voice again, knowing its light, dulcet tones would cause him pain.

"Andrew!" She sounded shocked, although she must have been expecting him to return her call. He could imagine her going pink in the face, hands gesticulating wildly. "Oh, Andrew! Did Maddy explain that I left London in such a rush I barely had time to even say good-bye to my parents? Are you terribly angry with me? Was it a terrible thing to do? I'd no idea you'd be upset! . . ." Breathlessly, in a way Andrew knew so well, Jessica rattled on, hardly allowing him a word.

". . . and then, when I landed in Boston and telephoned Maddy, she said you'd been in touch," she concluded. "Anyway, how are you?"

"I'm okay." He was determined to resist that overwhelming charm of hers that was as natural and uncalculated as a child's, and yet could have such devastating effect on other people. For a moment, actually, he had a strange sensation that they were still together, that the last few months had been nothing but a silly quarrel, which they were about to patch up. "And you're well?" he asked.

"I'm fine."

There was an embarrassed silence where once there would have been an easy intimacy, reminding Andrew that they were no longer together, that Jessica was now thousands of miles away with someone else.

"Good," he said. "So . . ." The silence became an eternity of unspoken words and unformed thoughts as Andrew recognized how deep his loss was. He wanted to ask Jessica: Why? Why did you give up your entire career for this other man, when you couldn't even give up a little bit of it for me? Why were you able to turn your back on the three years we had together for someone you hardly knew? But all he was able to say was: "You'll be doing a lot of traveling now, I suppose."

Jessica spoke hurriedly, as if glad the lull in the conversation was over. "That's right. I'll be living out of suitcases from now on. It's lucky I like hotel life, I must say . . ."

I'm glad she's not talking about *him*, Andrew reflected as she chatted on. Then he thought: This is hurting much more than I thought it would. I can't believe I was such a fool as to let her go. He closed his eyes and heard her talk about visiting Moscow and how she was looking forward to it. "That'll be interesting," he heard himself say, while the pain ripped through his heart with lacerating swiftness and his mind cried out in silent anguish.

Andrew didn't remember much about the rest of their conversation. When he hung up, he felt sick with a cold misery and a feeling of utter defeat, made all the worse because he was convinced it was all his own fault.

As soon as Madeleine left Hank Pugsley's office, she went straight back to her studio, not to paint but to sit down and quietly assess the position. Luck had been on her side so far; incredibly, she'd managed to get into Kimberley's apartment to talk to her, and she'd also had good fortune on her side when Kimberley had been called out of her office and she'd been able to examine her Filofax. And now she'd had her meeting with Hank Pugsley. Everything was going her way so far, but she wondered how long that could last. The next thing she needed was an excuse to go to Europe without awakening either Carl's or Jake's suspicions and curiosity, and that might prove difficult.

Madeleine stayed for several hours in her studio, gazing absently at the canvases hung around the walls or stacked on the floor. Occasionally she glanced up at the skylights, where, through the glass, white clouds could be seen scurrying across a blue backcloth like an ever-moving picture; but then she would glance at the faces of all the men and women she'd painted—some famous, some not; some beautiful, others quite ordinary; all bearing testimony to the years of hard work she'd put into her career. But her eyes weren't focused, and nothing around her seemed real, because all she could really see was a pale feral face framed in a mass of red hair, the mouth lewd, the eyes coldly brutal. It was as clear to her as if she had painted it. The face of Kimberley Cabot.

With shock, Madeleine realized she was in the grip of revenge. She wouldn't rest until she had brought about Kimberley's downfall, and for a second she felt a pang of shame. Doesn't this lower me to her level? she asked herself. Then she remembered hearing somewhere that you had to fight like with like. This was not the time to turn the other cheek and be forgiving. Her whole future with Carl was in jeopardy while Kimberley was allowed to get away with what she was doing. All Madeleine had to do now was find a plausible reason for flying to Europe.

The problem solved itself. When she got back to the apartment, there was a letter from Mr. Marks, saying she was urgently needed in Devon.

12

"DINNER AT the White House! But I've nothing to wear!"
Jessica wailed. They were sitting in their very English suite at
the Ritz-Carlton in Boston, and Bernard was calmly reading
aloud his itinerary for the coming few weeks. Jessica had arrived two days before, to a rapturous reunion with him, but
now she was trying to come to grips with the day-to-day
routine that would be her future life. Strangest of all was
finding that although she was still living in a hotel, she'd joined
the ranks of the rich and privileged and was no longer concerned with the running of the place. Suddenly her mildest
wishes had become someone else's most pressing duty, with
Bernard ordering everyone around them with the same command that he used to conduct an orchestra. Miss McCann
wishes to have her hair done . . . her dress pressed . . . her
shoes shined. Certainly, sir. Miss McCann would like an extra
pillow . . . another drink . . . a little snack. Yes, sir. Certainly,
sir. No sooner had Jessica muttered that it would be nice to
have something than the figurative conductor's baton was in
action again, and Bernard had everyone running around in
circles.

With the unerring instinct of someone who relishes life to
the full, Jessica flung herself into her new life with the velocity
of a bullet, but she greatly missed not being in control anymore. She'd been so used to giving orders at the Royal Westminster, and to being responsible for the smooth running of
the place, that now she felt disconcertingly disoriented, and
strangely lost.

"The President and his wife are having one of their huge
dinner parties," Bernard was explaining, "when anyone who
is anyone gets to go, and this time that includes me and my
lovely lady friend!"

Jessica pulled a little frown. "Bernard, I hate being referred to as your 'lady friend.' It's an awful expression. The next thing, I'll be referred to as 'your constant companion.' "

"You could do worse, my darling," Bernard demurred.

"And I could do a lot better!" Jessica flashed back. "What's wrong with 'girlfriend'? She almost added as a joke, "Or fiancée or wife?", but Bernard seemed to have lost a little of his sense of humor since she'd arrived in Boston. Instead she said seriously, "Darling, what shall I wear for this dinner? Will it be terribly formal?"

Bernard looked up at her as she paced their suite, her small feet in their spike heels almost high-stepping like a pony in her agitation. Suddenly she felt unsure of herself, and very nervous. Everything seemed to be beyond her control now.

"You must have something suitable," he observed mildly.

Jessica spun around, looking unhappy. "I haven't got anything that would be right. Oh, if only you'd told me before I left London, I could have got something at cost; I know all the designers at home."

"We are 'at home,' " Bernard said pointedly, "or as much at home as we'll ever be. You'd better get used to it, Jessica, because we'll never be more settled, except when we're at my house in Sardinia."

Jessica stood still for a moment as the words registered. Of course, what he said was true. She'd known when she left London that for the rest of her life "home" would be wherever Bernard was. Mistaking her silence for sulking, he rose angrily to his feet.

"Good God, what a fuss over a dress!" he suddenly roared. "Every city has dress shops. Go out and look! There are plenty of dress shops in Boston, for Christ's sake!"

Jessica stared at him, taken aback by his manner. She had to admit she was making a fuss, but it was because she wanted him to be proud of her, and it wasn't every day that one got to have dinner with the President of the United States.

"Okay, I'll go!" she said brightly. "I'll go right now and come back with something that will stun you." She went to get her coat and purse from their bedroom. When she returned to the living room, Bernard was absorbed in the score of the symphony he was conducting that night with the Boston Philharmonic. Jessica realized he'd completely forgotten she was there.

"Fine!" she said to herself with a comical expression. "And enjoy yourself, Jessica! Get yourself a nice dress, Jessica! Have a nice day, Jessica!"

Leaving the Ritz-Carlton, which she'd heard described as the grande dame of Boston hotels, she walked along Arlington Street, where on the opposite side of the road fine public gardens blazed with summer flowers and grass as green as emeralds. She had to find a store where she could buy a stunning dress, and maybe shoes and a purse to match, and she was just about to ask an incredibly handsome young policeman she'd spotted where the main shops were, when something suddenly struck her with unpleasant force.

In the past, she had lived on her earnings, sharing the cost of running the apartment with Andrew and being financially independent. From the age of nineteen she'd paid her own way, proud of the fact she didn't have to ask anyone, not even her parents, for money. But what was going to happen now? She'd saved a few thousand pounds of her salary while she'd been living in at the Royal Westminster, but that wouldn't last her long, especially if she was supposed to buy expensive clothes to go with Bernard's life-style, and there was no way she was going to be able to work again with the constant touring. A fragment of her newfound euphoria crumbled away as she walked slowly on, she knew not where. Why hadn't she thought of the money side of living with Bernard before? Would he give her an allowance, or would she have to ask every time she wanted a pair of tights? The thought was galling. It would make her feel like a kept woman, and she hated the idea.

When Jessica got back to the Ritz-Carlton nearly two hours later, having spent much more than she wanted to on a simple white crepe evening dress, she had worked herself into a state of great agitation. She must know where she stood, and the sooner she discussed it with Bernard, the better. She found him where she had left him, sitting in the living room of their suite. He was talking to someone on the phone.

"*Sí*, Prague!" bellowed Bernard into the mouthpiece, "and after Prague, I go to Madrid. *Sí!*"

Jessica went through to their bedroom, hung up her new dress, and waited until she heard him replace the receiver. Then she rushed back into the living room, her expression a mixture of anxiety and anger.

"Bernard, I must talk to you," she began.

"Hush!" Bernard lifted the receiver again and asked the hotel switchboard to get him a number in Paris.

Jessica hovered about impatiently, watching him as he talked, wishing she could get the matter settled quickly. This whole scene is too humiliating, she thought distractedly. I'm not used to being so dependent on anyone. I'm a working woman who has always got a kick from having my own money and . . .

Bernard hung up. Jessica flung herself on the sofa beside him. "Bernard, I *have* to talk to you!"

He looked slightly surprised at her vehemence, but she could tell his mind was still miles away.

"I realize I can't work now, and so I wondered what I'm going to do about money," she blurted out, knowing it sounded crass but desperate to get his attention before he started to make more calls.

"Money?" Bernard looked at her so blankly she might have been talking about nuclear energy or splitting atoms. "What do you mean?"

"Money! For buying clothes and . . . things!" Jessica had flushed so deeply her blond hair looked white around the temples. "I shall need money, and I haven't much of my own, and I'm used to earning . . ." She broke off lamely, mortified at having to ask for an allowance. Bernard should have made this easy for me, she thought with a sudden burst of anger. He should have said something, right at the beginning, when they were planning their lives together; something that would clarify the situation. Instead, here she was fumbling for words, trying to preserve some shred of dignity.

Bernard waved his hand airily. "Oh, just put everything on my credit cards. I'll get your signature authorized, so it'll be no problem."

"Yes, but . . ." She still didn't feel entirely happy. Suppose she wanted actual cash? Suppose she wanted to buy him a present and didn't want him to know how much it had cost?

She wriggled uncomfortably. "I'd rather have money in my bank account," she added plaintively.

Bernard rose and stretched. His voice sounded angry. "What's the matter with you? Why all this fuss . . . first about a dress and now money? My financial advisers look after everything for me. They take care of my bills and my taxes so that I don't have to be bothered with this sort of thing. I don't even want to have to think about money. It bores me! My life is music—not how do I pay for a pair of shoes or a new shirt or some such trivia!"

"That's all very well for you," Jessica retorted, the bit between her teeth now, an insane desire to pursue the subject to the limits, almost as if she'd been spoiling for a fight. "*You're* earning the money in the first place and you can do as you like with it. For the first time in my life, I'm not going to be earning anything, and . . . well, it makes me feel insecure and . . . and *beholden* to you. It makes me feel like a kept woman!"

For a moment Bernard stared at her and then he threw back his head and gave a bellow of laughter. A moment later he had his arms around her, hugging her close. "You funny girl . . . you funny girl," he repeated, rocking her gently, his face buried in her hair. "Scratching like a little wildcat who does not want to be looked after!"

"But, Bernard . . ." Jessica said weakly, leaning against him.

"Is this what women's lib does for you? Makes you unable to accept a man's love?"

"No, of course it doesn't." She pushed him away slightly. "Love has nothing to do with this. Love is something you *give*—money shouldn't come into it at any point. I don't like the feeling that you're letting me spend your money just because you love me."

"Is that what your mother said to your father? I don't suppose she complained about being looked after financially, any more than my mother did," Bernard replied. "You young girls have got it so screwed up. You feel it's a disgrace if you can't pay your way like a man, while I think it's a man's duty, not to mention his pleasure, to look after a woman in every way."

Jessica broke away from his arms, her small face determined. "I don't agree. I like to be able to spend my money as I like. How can I do that if it's your money?"

"Shouldn't you have considered this before you came away with me?" Bernard asked reasonably. "You must have known you'd be giving up your career?"

Jessica hung her head, feeling childish and foolish. "I never thought," she said, almost sadly. "It all happened so quickly."

With a swift movement Bernard took her in his arms again, kissing her face with light fluttery kisses, looking adoringly down into her eyes. "I know, my love. I know," he murmured softly. "It must all be so strange for you, and you must still be jet-lagged and tired. I've been a fool to rush you like this, without stopping to consider how you must be feeling."

Jessica returned his kisses, feeling her body responding to his, though doubts still hovered in her mind. She did belong to a generation of young women who guarded their financial independence fiercely. Most of her friends had continued to work, even after they'd married and had children, and she'd always supposed it would be the same for her. If she had married Andrew, she'd have had to continue working in any case for them to afford the style of living they had both wanted. Andrew. Her parents. England. How far away they all seemed. Bernard was carrying her in his strong arms into the bedroom now, and she could feel his mounting desire. Her body was, confusedly, filled with a longing for him too, although her mind had suffered tiny thrusts of misgiving. In time she would resolve her feelings, but for now here was Bernard, soothing and arousing her with hands of magic, kissing away her fears and bringing to the surface a passion she had never known existed. She didn't even remember taking off her clothes. The next thing she knew, Bernard had placed her astride him as he lay on the bed under her, and he was thrusting upward with such strength that he was lifting her, penetratingly and violently, with each push. With his sensitive hands holding her hips in position, he took first one small breast and then the other in his mouth as she leaned over him, sucking deeply on her until she felt as if her whole body was inflamed. With each thrust the intensity increased, until she convulsed and begged him to stop. Only then did he allow himself to climax, giving himself to her with a rush of passion and a cry of joy.

Madeleine read the letter quickly, trying to understand the pedantic legal phraseology that all lawyers loved to indulge in. By the time she'd come to the third "whereunto" and "wherethrough," she reached for the phone and dialed the Devonshire number of Spindle, Coutts, and Marks. Mr. Marks came quickly on the line, shouting slightly, as if to make sure his voice carried across the airwaves of the Atlantic.

"I've heard from your father, Mr. Jake Shearman," he said in a loud voice, "but he hasn't given me any details that will help to verify the existence of your mother's death certificate."

"I see." Madeleine didn't know her father had been in touch with the law firm. Why hadn't he mentioned it to her? "What exactly did he say?" she inquired.

"Well, he asks me to fly over to visit him in America—quite out of the question, of course." Mr. Marks dismissed the idea as crazy—as if he'd been invited on a spaceship to the moon.

"Why did my father invite you over here?" Madeleine asked, mystified.

"I'm afraid I don't really know. He said it was a confidential matter, so even if I was aware of the facts, I would not be able to impart them to you," he added primly, his voice still raised to a tremulous shout.

"So what happens now?" Madeleine was deeply irritated. Why on earth couldn't Jake cooperate so that this whole business could be settled once and for all?

"I'm afraid we'll have to go ahead with bringing the case to court, to get an order of presumption of your mother's death, and you will have to appear. Even if I had the time to get away, which I haven't," he added hastily, "it's too late to cancel the hearing. That's why I wrote to you."

Madeleine's mind worked quickly. The last thing she wanted was to have to attend this court case, which would be held in Okehampton Assizes and would no doubt attract a lot of local gossip and speculation. On the other hand, she desperately needed a valid reason to go to Europe right now, and this was a trip Carl wouldn't question. She'd tell him Mr. Marks demanded her presence, and that while she was in England she'd make arrangements to hold an exhibition of her work the following summer in London. That should satisfy him; more important, it would be a perfect cover for what she really had to do.

Tonight she and Carl were dining with her father. Aunt Patti would be there. Suddenly Madeleine realized it would be the perfect opportunity to kill two birds with one stone. She'd tell them she had to go back to Milton Manor for the case, and she'd ask her father why he'd wanted Mr. Marks to fly over to see him.

When Carl returned from the bank shortly before seven o'clock, Madeleine was in their bedroom changing for dinner.

"Hi, darling," she called out when she heard his step in the hall. "Like a drink while you're getting ready to go to Daddy's?"

Carl entered their bedroom and saw Madeleine sitting at her dressing table putting the finishing touches to her makeup. She was wearing a brilliant yellow jersey silk dress, her black hair a riot of curls around her exquisite heart-shaped face, and he thought he'd never seen her look more beautiful. He went over and kissed her tenderly on the side of the neck.

"I'd love a drink," he said with feeling. "It's been one helluva day and I'm whacked!"

"Why don't you get into the shower while I fix it," Madeleine suggested, jumping to her feet. She gave him a brief loving look and then went into the living room to fix his favorite dry martini with an olive. When she got back to the bedroom he was undressing slowly, as if every movement was an effort.

"What have you been doing today?" he asked, taking the drink from her and sipping it appreciatively. The gin, sharply iced, hit his stomach explosively. Leaning back on the white sofa at the foot of their bed, he closed his eyes.

Madeleine went and stood over him, gently massaging his neck and temples in a way she knew he liked. "Oh, nothing much," she lied in a soft voice, "but I did get a letter from Mr. Marks telling me I'll have to go to England for the court case."

"Yeah?" Carl wondered why he felt a momentary stab of relief. He'd miss her as he always did when she was away, but right now the strain of having to carry on as if nothing was wrong was proving too much for him. He'd started to use sleeping pills lately, and he'd lost so much weight his trousers were in permanent danger of falling down. Madeleine was bound to notice soon. It would give him some breathing space if she was away for a week or so.

"I'll miss you, honey," he said truthfully. "I wish I could go with you, but it's impossible right now."

Her fingers, rotating gently on the nape of his neck, were easing the tension, but he still felt strung-out.

"I'll be back as soon as I can," she promised. "You know I can't bear to be away from you for too long either."

"Good," he said absently, the gin taking effect. Hank Pugsley was due to put through another transfer any day now, and Carl lived in sickening dread of the moment when he would see the signed authorization on his desk. Kimberley had a way of laying it on top of all his other papers so that he saw it first. He knew that behind her gesture of leaving it prominently displayed lay an element of psychological warfare. She despised him for his initial moment of weakness in allowing himself to be seduced by her, and now it gave her a kick to torture him every time Hank's transfer came through; remind him that if he hadn't been such a fool, none of this would have happened; remind him also that he was in her power and he'd have to do as she wished.

Would Hank's transfer come tomorrow? Carl's stomach contracted painfully. Instead of feeling easier with each successful transfer, he was getting increasingly panic-stricken. Kimberley had been lucky so far, but suppose somebody came into the computer room at the exact moment when she had the copy of the tape from Jake's office in operation. Suppose that person came up to her and, seeing the layout on the green screen, asked: "Hey, Kimberley, what are you doing?" Suppose someone met her on her way to the computer room—or on her way back—with the tape in her pocket and the details of Hank's latest transfer in her hands. Suppose . . . At this next supposition Carl's heart gave such a bound that he was sure Madeleine, stroking his neck, would feel the hammering of his pulse through her fingers. Suppose Jake were to ask one day why Brandt's Motors seemed to have stopped paying regular invoices to Michaux Internationale in Zurich . . . and suppose he then called up Hank Pugsley to ask if everything was all right. Carl squeezed his eyes closed in inner agony.

"I think we should go away for a long vacation when this is all over," he heard Madeleine say.

Carl caught his breath sharply. "When what's all over?"

"This business with the lawyers and my grandfather's will, of course. We were just talking about it."

"Yes. Oh, of course." Christ, he'd been miles away, the worry eating into him, making him paranoid. In an hour they were due at Jake's house. Better get showered and changed.

"Could you fix me another drink, Maddy?" He held out his empty glass.

"Sure." She sounded surprised. "But you'd better not arrive at Daddy's in an alcoholic stupor! You know how he likes to indulge us with his special wines." Jake considered himself something of a wine connoisseur.

Carl managed a laugh. "I know!" He imitated Jake. "At a hundred dollars a bottle, we shouldn't spoil our palates by drinking gin first."

Madeleine giggled. "If Daddy had his way, I wouldn't wear lipstick when drinking wine either, because it spreads a layer of grease on the surface of the wine and affects the taste. And he says I shouldn't use perfume! 'Destroys the delicate bouquet.' Honestly, I think he goes too far at times."

Carl smiled, longing to feel as merry as Madeleine obviously did. And then it struck him. When had he last felt really happy?

Jake Shearman's house, set in a quiet cul-de-sac off Beekman Place, overlooked the East River, far below, and was one of the few buildings that were still privately owned. Built with the formal symmetry of a doll house, it was stone-fronted up as far as the third-floor windows, and above that, red-bricked. Somehow retaining the quiet elegance of a bygone era, and far enough away from the heavy traffic of First Avenue, the area formed a quiet oasis of tree-lined streets in which purring limousines waited for their owners to appear. Madeleine had spent her childhood in this tranquil house, and when she'd left to marry Carl, Jake decided to stay, looked after by the servants who had been with him for over twenty years. After all, he said, where else could he house his possessions? The Shearmans had been one of New York's most revered families for three generations and, having originally made their fortune in tin mining, they had invested that money in priceless paintings and antique furniture and objets d'art that would more normally be found in a museum.

Now, as president of Central Manhattan Bank, Jake looked upon the Beekman Place mansion as a perfect setting for formal entertaining. The top-class ambience was something you couldn't buy in a restaurant. The new money of yesterday had become the old money of today.

When Madeleine arrived with Carl for dinner, the beauty of the house, which would one day be hers, struck her afresh, as it did every time she visited Jake. There was something so wonderfully warm and welcoming in the softly lit rooms, where French and English antiques blended together under the fine oil paintings on the walls, and where marble and gilt, natural polished floors strewn with Oriental silk rugs and raw-silk draperies at the windows, gave the whole atmosphere a rare elegance.

Jake was waiting for them in the living room where great Chinese vases full of white lilies added to the air of opulence.

"Hi, Daddy!" Madeleine swept forward, very much a fashionable figure of the eighties in this eighteenth-century setting. Her yellow dress stood out dramatically against the pastel shades of the room.

"Hello, Maddy." Jake leaned forward to kiss her, and then he shook hands with Carl, although he'd seen him at the bank only a couple of hours before. "Good to see you, Carl."

As a vintage Bollinger champagne was being poured into Waterford glasses, Madeleine looked around the room, her eyes automatically straying to the wall above the mantelshelf. It was as if she always hoped for a miracle, hoped that one day the portrait of her mother would suddenly reappear, so that she could study it, especially now that she'd seen all those old photographs of Camilla at Milton Manor. Had the artist seen into Camilla's soul, the way Madeleine herself saw into the souls of her sitters? Had he, too, found her eyes mockingly evil?

"Daddy . . ." she began, her curiosity suddenly consuming her. After all, why shouldn't she ask where the painting was?

". . . and with interest rates being what they are, I said to the President . . ." Jake had his back to her, deep in discussion with Carl.

Madeleine sat down on the sofa facing the fireplace, waiting for the men to stop talking. Suddenly she heard Jake say:

"I saw that glamour girl you've got working for you in the

lobby yesterday." He paused, his brows furrowed. "What's her name? Something to do with a diamond."

Carl shifted his feet, avoiding Madeleine's eyes, and said abruptly, "Kimberley. Kimberley Cabot."

Jake beamed as if he'd remembered it himself. "Of course! Kimberley! Like the diamond mines. Well, she said . . ."

Madeleine realized both she and Carl were straining forward, eager to catch each word. She recovered herself first, and sipping her drink with seeming nonchalance, heard Jake continue: "She said you'd had a lot of meetings in connection with third-world debts."

The atmosphere in the room instantly relaxed, grew warm, and Madeleine had a delicious floating sensation as if the champagne bubbles had lifted her bodily as well as mentally, and were making her drift upward. She heard Carl reply: "We've had a few problems, but there's nothing that won't right itself in time . . ." before she felt herself crashing downward again at her father's next words.

"Carl, that was a large transfer of dollars you put through to Ireland at the beginning of the week. Loan for a new car plant, is it?"

Madeleine watched Carl closely; maybe there was more going on than she knew about, and perhaps Jake had gotten wind of it. The muscles of her stomach tightened sickeningly and she held her breath, waiting for Carl's reply.

"Yes. The Morgan Company. They're opening a plant just outside Dublin. Oliver Morgan, from Wisconsin, is president, and he's over there now setting everything up."

"Of course." Jake nodded. "I remember now. It should bring a lot of employment to Ireland where it's most needed." The two men smiled at each other and continued to discuss business.

For Madeleine it was enough. She didn't want to spend the whole evening on an emotional switchback with Jake giving her these frights every time he opened his mouth. She tried to keep her voice light and jokey.

"Now, that's enough, you two. No more business talk! You've got all day at the bank to talk shop, so let's discuss something else."

Jake grinned indulgently. "My little girl getting bored?" But Carl looked surprised. Normally Madeleine showed an interest in what was happening and never cut short a business discussion.

At that moment Patti Ziffren arrived, alone because Sam was attending an all-male dinner at the New York Yacht Club.

"I hope you're not expecting any other guests," she remarked tartly after greetings had been exchanged.

Jake looked mystified. "No, there's just us. But why?"

Patti settled herself on an upright chair, a cigarette in one hand and a drink in the other. She surveyed them sternly. "Because I've had enough of making polite conversation to boring socialites to last me a lifetime! Today I had lunch with twelve other women. This afternoon I was with the committee for the Arts Educational Trust to discuss their gala benefit night . . . and you can imagine the jealousy there is on the ladies' committee, not to mention the bitching; and this evening I had to go to a cocktail party on the way here!" She closed her eyes, as if the rigors of socializing were too much to bear. The gentle blue vapor of her cigarette rose around her perfectly coiffured head and gaunt face, making even her diamonds look smoky, and for a moment she seemed to withdraw from them as she recalled the stress of the evening.

Jake's mouth twitched. "Patti, you don't have to go to all these things. You know you only do it because you really enjoy it."

Her eyes opened with a snap and regarded him fiercely. "You talk a lot of nonsense, Jake . . . and where are the ashtrays?" Her head swung jerkily, stiff with age, from side to side. "Why do you never have any ashtrays around, for goodness' sake?"

"One ashtray coming up!" Carl said, swiftly placing a tiny china dish by her side, a grin on his face. "This will hold precisely one butt and a little ash, and then I'll find you another one."

Patti laughed, and it was like the sound of rusty machinery that hadn't been used for years. "Thanks," she replied. "You look tired, Carl. Jake, are you working this boy too hard?"

"I'm a slave driver, Patti, you should know that by now," Jake said with a glimmer of humor.

"Yes," quipped Carl. "He chases after us with a whip! No slacking's allowed at the Central Manhattan!"

Patti looked from one to the other, and then turned to Madeleine. "And you look as if you need a break, and I'm not sure that yellow dress doesn't make you look like a ripe banana! Never mind, your hair's very pretty tonight."

Madeleine roared with laughter. "That, I must tell Calvin Klein. I'm not sure he won't sue you. But we can't all look like Marlene Dietrich on a good day, Aunty Patti."

"Impudent girl!" chided her aunt. "Marlene Dietrich has the most appalling taste in clothes!"

"More champagne, Patti?" Jake asked.

"I thought you'd never ask. And are we ever going to eat? I can't live on canapés, you know!" The exhausted socialite of a few moments before had become the ebullient scene-stealer as she held court in her brother's living room as if he'd invited thirty guests instead of three.

Patti was in her element, teasing one moment, charming the next, playing her little audience along like a fisherman trying to land a salmon but knowing he would let it go free when he did. The others enjoyed the little charade, pitting their wits against her razor-sharp repartee and gimlet mind, trying to hold their own in the face of her volley of insults, none of which were meant to hurt or be taken seriously. For Jake and Madeleine it was easy; both had known Patti all their lives and were used to her acerbic tongue. Jake gave as good as he got, while Madeleine trod more delicate ground, aware that she belonged to the younger generation and must temper her ripostes with good manners. Carl was in a more difficult position. It had taken him nearly five years to get used to Patti Ziffren at all, let alone engage in astringent badinage with her, but he had finally hit upon an act of cheerful guileless boyishness, and she loved him for it, especially when he pretended to flirt with her. Then Jake was reminded of the Patti of his childhood, a high-spirited young woman, fourteen years his senior, and the toast of New York, with young men falling over themselves to take her out. And that, Jake reflected sadly, was before a loveless marriage to Samuel Ziffren, and being unable to have children, had made Patti take cover behind a facade of asperity so that she might protect her real feelings.

"That's the third cigarette you've smoked since you arrived, Patti," Jake said with some anxiety.

"So, who's counting?" Patti retorted, and promptly fell into a coughing fit. She was still wheezing when the butler came in to announce dinner.

Jake Shearman's dining room was no less formal than the living room, hung with Brussels tapestries and furnished with Hepplewhite chairs and table. A dazzling display of silver and crystal glittered in the glow of many pale blue candles, which Patti complained made it too dark to see what you were eating, but was, on the other hand, a very flattering form of lighting, "and God knows, Jake, you and I need all the flattering we can get!" she added as she took her place opposite him.

Madeleine had decided to wait until dinner was over and the servants had withdrawn before producing Mr. Marks's letter, and her stomach tensed as the time drew nearer. Once Carl and her father had stopped talking business, the evening had become pleasant and relaxed, but she knew that as soon as she spoke about her mother, there would be acrimonious repercussions. She was about to speak, when Patti, whose eyes had been flickering around the table observing everyone with her usual acute sharpness, turned first to Carl and then to Madeleine.

"What's the matter with you two?" she demanded. "I've heard more conversation in a cemetery on a wet Sunday."

Madeleine seized the opportunity, withdrawing the lawyer's letter from her purse. "I've heard from Mr. Marks, Daddy. Here's his letter. I'd like Aunty Patti to read it too." She handed Jake the stiff white sheet of paper, which had the name of the company discreetly printed in small black lettering along the top. "Why did you write to Mr. Marks, Daddy, without telling me? What could you tell him that you couldn't tell me? I have to go to England again in a week's time, and I've got to have some answers before I go."

Jake's eyes were skimming the letter, his bonhomie vanished at the mention of the lawyer's name. In silence he handed it across to Patti. When she had read it, she looked up at him, her eyes unfathomable in her drawn face. The atmosphere in the room was suddenly charged with expectancy, an anticipation that was painfully palpable.

Carl was the first to speak, and his tone was quiet and reasonable. "Look, I think it's time everything came out into the open, don't you? It's embarrassing for Madeleine not knowing what the hell's going on, and it's beginning to put her in an awkward position with Mr. Marks. As it is, she's now got to appear in court to try to get an order of presumption of her mother's death. Wouldn't it be simpler to spare her all this and just tell her what happened?"

Madeleine's expression, as she looked across the flickering candlelit table to Carl, was one of gratitude. Carl's supportiveness meant the world to her, especially at this moment.

Patti spoke before Jake had time to reply. "I think Carl's right, Jake."

Jake looked down at his demitasse, stirring the black liquid absently with a small gold spoon. "I had hoped this whole thing could be settled quietly and without fuss," he said slowly. "I was prepared to talk to Mr. Marks if he came over."

"But why not to me, Daddy?" Madeleine pleaded. "It's not much to ask. All I need to know is when and where my mother died, and then the matter can be settled."

"Go on, Jake!" urged Patti, as if she could hardly wait for the tale to be told at last. "It'll be worse for Madeleine if she hears it from someone else."

Something cold and prickling and tingling swept across Madeleine with a suddenness that made her give a little gasp as Jake rested his elbows on the table and covered his face with his hands. The only sound was the occasional hiss of a guttering candle flame and, far away, the desolate wail of a police siren, growing louder, then fading away again.

Something was about to be revealed, a curtain of silence and a conspiracy of secrecy was about to be lifted, and Madeleine sat rigid, knowing at last that it was about to happen, while her mind silently shrieked: Tell me . . . tell me. . . .

The shock when it finally came burst upon her like an explosive shower of sparks, stinging, burning, scorching her brain.

Jake took his hands away from his face, and his eyes, as they looked into hers, were full of pain, but his voice was sharp and clear.

"The truth of the matter, Maddy . . . is that your mother is still alive."

13

"MY MOTHER'S still *alive?*" Madeleine repeated Jake's word in disbelief. "What . . . how do you mean . . . alive?"

Jake looked at his daughter as if the truth, wrenched at last from his soul, had left him raw and bleeding.

"Alive?" Carl echoed incredulously.

"She's not dead, as we led you to believe," Patti cut in in a clear, concise voice. "I'm sorry, Maddy, but under the circumstances both your father and I felt it was better to let you think she'd died when you were small."

"But why?" Madeleine felt the room spinning around, as her mind tried to absorb this unbelievable thing—that the mother she'd always thought was dead, the mother whose love she'd craved when she'd been a child, the mother whose guidance she'd longed for as she grew up, the mother whose support and encouragement she'd so wanted in recent years . . . was alive. The blood rushed to her head as angry tears blinded her. She turned to Jake, who sat in silence.

"How *could* you?" she lashed out in fury. "How could you deprive me of my mother all my life? I don't care what she did to you," she continued wildly, "I don't care how much she hurt you, you had no right to keep me from her. Oh, God, I always wanted my mother so much!" Her voice ended on a sob and she seemed to crumple and grow smaller in her chair. Carl rushed from his side of the table and put his arms around her.

"You mustn't blame your father," she heard Patti say. "He did what he thought was best, and I backed him all the way."

"Was it because she was involved in black magic?" Madeleine demanded. "Why didn't you take her away from England, then? Why didn't you bring her back to New York?" Her questions, tumbling out one after the other, caused Jake and Patti to look at each other, exchanging knowing glances. Madeleine intercepted their looks and a cold wave of fear swept over her.

"Is she . . . is she still involved . . . in witchcraft?" she blurted out wretchedly.

Patti shook her head violently, the ash from her cigarette falling into a little gray roll on the table's polished surface. "No. No, she isn't, Madeleine. She hasn't been involved in . . . that sort of thing since . . ." Her voice drifted away, and again she caught Jake's eye. Something in his expression silenced her.

". . . since you were little," Jake finished the sentence for her. "Please believe me when I say that what I did, I did for your own good, honey. You know me well enough to know that I would never do anything to hurt you."

Madeleine knew her father was telling the truth. Ever since she could remember, he'd put her first, caring for her in every way, even though the bank had always made great demands on his time. Somehow he'd managed to get home in time to read her a bedtime story at least twice a week, which was more than many of her friends' fathers did, and on weekends he'd always taken her out and spent time with her.

As she sat at the dining-room table now, looking at him, she believed him when he said he'd never do anything to hurt her, and yet . . .

"So why did you never tell me my mother was alive, Daddy?" she cried out piteously. "God knows I've asked you often enough! It wasn't until I went to Grandfather's house that I even found out what she looked like. All these years you've kept me in the dark, and so have you, Aunt Patti, and I want to know *WHY*."

"Yes," Carl broke in loyally, his arm still around Madeleine, stroking her shoulder comfortingly. "There'd better be a damn good reason for you to have kept Maddy in the dark all these years, and I, for one, would like to know what it is!"

Madeleine turned her head to look at Carl, grateful for his support, and it flashed through her mind that once they were out of this nightmare of her problems with her family and his problems with Kimberley, they'd be such a strong unit that nothing would ever be able to break them. She reached out and took his hand, and he returned her grip with a tender squeeze. A heavy silence fell on the room, and when Jake at last spoke, his tone was measured.

"You have to realize, Maddy, that you were only three when your mother and I . . . er . . . parted, shall we say. Far too young to be told anything, and like all small children, you accepted her absence at first because you had me, and a very good nanny, and of course Aunt Patti."

"But I remember asking about my mother all the time," Madeleine protested. "You wouldn't tell me anything at first, and then you said she was dead. Why did you tell me she'd died, Daddy, if she hadn't?"

"Perhaps because . . ." Jake paused, as if searching for the right words. "Perhaps because she was and always would be dead to you and me," he finished quietly.

Madeleine's dark eyes grew round. "I don't understand."

Jake leaned forward, his eyes filled with sympathy and compassion for the daughter he loved so much and on whom he was having to inflict pain. "I'm afraid, my darling, that your mother is in a mental hospital. She's been hopelessly insane for over twenty years."

The mocking eyes, hundreds of them, closed in on Madeleine, threatening her with their malevolence, terrifying her with their feral venom. It was dark. She was in a padded cell, so soft-walled and soundproofed that her cries could not be heard, and around her wrists, tight bindings held her fast. There was no escape; she had been banished from the light a thousand years ago, and held in this place where the walls were made of glittering eyes and the silence was the silence of the tomb. Her throat ached with screams that could not be heard, and in a frenzy she fought to free herself of the shackles. . . .

"Madeleine! Darling! Wake up!" Slowly, through the dark mists that enveloped her, Madeleine struggled to the surface of consciousness, aware that her nightdress was soaked with sweat and that her hair clung about her face and neck.

"It's all right, sweetheart," she heard Carl saying repeatedly, holding her flailing wrists with both hands. "You've had a nightmare. Wake up! It's all over now. You're all right, darling."

Madeleine opened her eyes and looked around to reassure herself that she really had been dreaming. "God . . . it was all so vivid," she muttered, burying her face in Carl's shoulder. "I dreamed I was my mother . . . and that I'd been held in a padded cell for years and years."

Carl turned on the bedside light, bathing the silky room in a rosy glow. Then he took Madeleine in his arms, holding her close.

"I could kill your father for springing that information about your mother on you like that tonight," he said angrily. "You've had the most tremendous shock, Maddy. I'm not surprised you had a bad dream."

"Oh, Carl . . . it was awful!" Tears streamed down her cheeks as she pressed herself close to him. "Daddy never said what made her go crazy. . . . Do you think it's hereditary? Is that why he hasn't told me about my mother before—because he knew it could happen to me too? God, I felt I was mad in that dream just now!"

"No, I don't think that was his reason. I think something happened . . . something traumatic, from which she never recovered," Carl said gently. "You found out she was involved in black magic. I suspect it had something to do with that."

Madeleine raised a tearstained face to look into his, seeking reassurance. Carl didn't know it, but she had so much on her mind at present, she felt she *could* easily lose her mind. What with Kimberley Cabot and the bank embezzlement Carl was involved in, and the deal she'd made with Hank earlier in the day, it was enough to send anyone off her trolly without being told her mother was not dead but had been totally insane for years!

"You're probably right," she said, trying to get a grip on herself, though small dry sobs still caught her breath, "but I feel scared of going to sleep again."

Carl kissed her cheek warmly and tenderly. "You'll be safe with me," he whispered, tightening his grip. "I'll see that nothing happens to you."

But as she drifted off to sleep at last, the irony of his words struck her. It was *she* who was trying to see that nothing happened to *him*.

They met at Mortimer's for lunch, greeting each other joyously and a little curiously, having exchanged all their news on the phone the previous day. Madeleine wondered if Jessica would have changed in any way, as a result of falling so dramatically in love with a stranger, even to the point of giving up her old life, and Jessica was consumed with interest to find out Madeleine's reactions to finding that her mother was alive.

"It's *so* good to see you," Jessica crowed, doing a little jig. She looked vibrantly alive in a scarlet suit with lots of brass buttons, but for once her hair was in a tight chignon and her large gilt earrings made her face look more diminutive than ever. "But, Maddy, you're looking pale," she added accusingly.

Madeleine made an attempt at flippancy. "Well, it's not every day you find out you've got a mother, when you've spent most of your life thinking you haven't!" She looked thinner than usual, and there were dark shadows under her eyes. "Anyway, let's have a drink. I'm longing to hear all your news—it sounds amazing."

"It is! And I want to hear all yours. When did Jake spring all this on you, and *why*, my dear?" Talking nonstop, Jessica settled herself at the corner table they'd been shown to, ordered a wine spritzer, and then turned her full attention on Madeleine. "Seriously, Maddy, *are* you all right? You look dreadful!"

Madeleine burst into laughter. "Thanks, Jessie. That's just what I wanted to hear. Now I feel terrific!"

Jessica snatched her arm earnestly. "You know I didn't mean it like that, sweetie. I'm worried about you. You said you were flying to England in a couple of days . . . is it to see your mother?" Jessica couldn't help shuddering inwardly as she recalled the story her journalist friend Peter had told her. It had been so horrific she'd kept it to herself all this time. She wondered how much Madeleine knew, even now. At the time, she'd pretended she hadn't been able to get hold of Peter, so that Madeleine wouldn't probe further.

"I don't know whether I'll see my mother or not," Madeleine replied honestly. The truth was, she was still using the revelation about her mother, plus the fact she had to discuss Milton Manor with the lawyer, as an excuse to go to Europe. There would be no court case now, to prove her mother dead; Jake had held the power of attorney of Camilla's estate for years, so Madeleine would inherit automatically.

"I couldn't believe it when Jake told me she was still alive,"

Madeleine continued as she slowly sipped her drink. "To think she's been in an institution all these years, with Daddy sending regular payments, and I never knew! He still won't tell me what happened, why she went mad, but I think it's got something to do with black magic or whatever it was she was involved with."

Jessica's face was inscrutable, giving nothing away. "Perhaps she just had a nervous breakdown," she said carefully.

Madeleine shook her head. "No, I'm sure it had to do with witchcraft. In any case"—she straightened her shoulders and looked more cheerful—"I'll find out now. I'll ask the doctor who's looking after her at the institution. Even Jenkins, the gardener, might spill the beans when he realizes I know she's really alive after all. Hell, I might even ask her herself!" Madeleine gave an edgy laugh with a thin vein of hysteria running through it.

Jessica frowned. "Maddy, you *are* uptight! Oh, God, I wish I could be in England when you go over. Isn't it the most maddening thing," she demanded, "that just as I arrive in New York, you buzz off to London, and I suppose I'll have left for Moscow by the time you return."

"Oh, I should think so," Madeleine replied carefully, not wanting Jessica to suspect that she intended to stay in England until a great deal more than the affair of her mother had been settled.

"Oh, damn! Then I won't see you for ages again. You must keep in touch and tell me *everything* that happens, and exactly what Camilla's like."

"I will," Madeleine promised. "And now you'll be touring with Bernard Scheller most of the time, won't you?" she added with a sudden feeling of embarrassment. It had been Andrew for so long . . . Andrew, whom she'd grown really fond of . . . Andrew, whom she'd always supposed would one day become Jessica's husband. It was strange and awkward to have to refer to a man she'd never met and who, from what she'd heard, wasn't exactly right for Jessica.

"My dear," Jessica said excitedly, "do you realize that I'll be living out of suitcases for the next five months? That's twenty-four weeks! Talk about a Gypsy existence."

"Some Gypsy," Madeleine teased, "staying in five-star hotels around the world, getting the full VIP treatment wherever

you go! Jessie, you're going to be living like a film star, so
don't expect any sympathy from me. What's Bernard like?"
she added almost shyly.

Jessica wasn't in the least inhibited about her newfound love.
"Maddy, wait till you meet him!" she breathed. "He's the
most electrifying man you've ever met. He oozes charisma. I
bet he'll knock you sideways when we all meet for dinner
tonight. He is, my dear, *totally* divine."

Madeleine regarded her with undisguised amusement. Jessica had always been given to exaggeration and dramatization,
and she seemed to have completely gone overboard this time.

"And you're not going to miss the Royal Westminster?" she
asked gently. "You worked so hard to get on in the hotel
business, Jessie—are you sure you're not going to have
regrets?"

"None," replied Jessica, a shade too swiftly. "I realized
when I met Bernard that never in my life again would I find
a love like this. You've no idea what it's like, Maddy." She
turned her round blue eyes to Madeleine, and they sparkled
with earnestness. "He's a *fantastic* man, there's no other word
for it, and he really is as much in love with me as I am with
him. Of course, I felt a dreadful pang the day I left the hotel,
but one can't have everything in life, and I reckoned that
Bernard was worth a dozen hotels, or a hundred careers."

Madeleine's smile was genuinely warm. "Then I hope you'll
be tremendously happy, Jessie, and I'm really glad for you."

Jessica grinned back, almost moved to the edge of tears by
her friend's sincerity. "Thanks, Maddy. You'll see what I
mean, as soon as you meet Bernard."

"Which reminds me . . ." Madeleine looked at her askance.
"Have you been in touch with Andrew?"

Jessica's face fell, as if a puppeteer had let loose all the strings
that controlled her smiling face. "Yes, I called him as soon as
you gave me his message," she replied sadly. "I really do feel
dreadful about him, but what could I do? We'd finished anyway, before I met Bernard, so I saw no point in telling him
what had happened. I didn't think he cared about me anymore—at least that's how it seemed when he broke it off because I went to live in the hotel."

"I think he hoped that one day you'd grow bored with hotel
life and return to him," Madeleine said quietly, "and of course

what really hurt him was that you weren't prepared to work less hard to please him, yet you were prepared to ditch your whole career to go off with Bernard."

Jessica hung her head like a woebegone child. "I *know* you're right, Maddy, and I know I behaved rather badly, but on the other hand"—her head shot up and for a moment she looked self-righteous—"why should it always be the woman who gives up her job to please a man? Whoever heard of a man giving up his job to please a woman?" Then they both laughed, Madeleine thinking of Carl and his dedication to the bank, and Jessica thinking of Bernard, to whom music was life itself. No, men were not prepared to make sacrifices in the way women were. "And it's jolly unfair!" Jessica declared, tackling her *salade niçoise* with gusto.

"So, we're all meeting for dinner tonight at Elaine's?" Madeleine asked.

"Yes. I've booked in Bernard's name, of course. Might as well ensure we get the best table," Jessica joked.

"I can hardly wait," Madeleine said with an unaccustomed touch of dryness.

"I've had enough of London," Andrew remarked morosely as he sat looking out at the wet Knightsbridge pavements. The large window of Jason and Seymour Partnership held displays of photographs and details of various luxury residential properties, from ten-bedroom mansions to bijoux mews cottages and modern apartments, representing an ever-increasing turnover in a booming market.

"You're *what?*" Sandy demanded as if he hadn't heard right. "Don't be such a bloody fool! This is where the money is. Properties are going up by fifteen percent a week. What the hell will you do if you leave London?"

"Properties are increasing in value in the country too. Old barns and cottages can be picked up for about forty thousand pounds, then you spend another fifty thousand on them, and they sell for two hundred and fifty. It's happening all over. Affluent people in the south of England are looking for weekend places more and more. I reckon we should cash in on the upsurge in country developments."

Sandy regarded Andrew with interest. "You could have a point," he said slowly, "and if we did branch into selling country property, you'd be prepared to run a country agency?"

Andrew nodded. "I've always wanted to live in the country—you know that. Of course, I'd planned to marry Jessica and set up . . ." His voice faltered and painfully he averted his gaze.

"Oh, I know," Sandy said swiftly. Then diplomatically he continued, "This is something we must discuss seriously. We'd have to get bank loans for the expansion, you know; we'd have to take on more staff, and you'd have to find somewhere to live, as well as opening up a new office."

"I'll get a small fortune for my flat in Chelsea," observed Andrew. "It cost me eighty thousand seven years ago, and now it's worth over a quarter of a million."

Sandy grinned. "And who said we're not in the right business? Jesus, I wish we could buy, redecorate, and sell, instead of just negotiating other people's buying and selling. We could be millionaires by now!"

"But think of the hassle. I'd hate to spend my time improving a place, only to sell it to the highest bidder. When I buy a house I want it to be my home." The wistfulness in his voice portrayed the hurt he felt inside. Sandy looked away, embarrassed. He'd always managed to remain fairly fancy-free himself, with as rapid a turnover of girlfriends as he had of new cars. With Sandy it was easy come, easy go, and as long as he had lots of money in his pocket and some female's bed to sleep in, he was happy. The thought of settling down horrified him, even more than the thought of being away from the bright lights. He jumped to his feet restlessly, walked around their office for a minute or so, and then turned back to Andrew. The scheme wouldn't suit him, but it would be perfect for his partner.

"I think you're right; I think we should go ahead with a country agency," he said. "It's a good idea."

"Great," Andrew replied. "I'll get the wheels in motion and go and talk to the bank tomorrow. I might as well get on with it as soon as possible, because there's no reason for me to stay in London anymore."

Kimberley gave a sigh of relieved satisfaction when she saw Hank Pugsley's transfer authorization among Carl's papers on his desk. She'd been expecting it any day now; in fact, it was overdue. She picked it up and looked at the amount. Three hundred and sixteen thousand dollars. Dated three days ago, so it had been delayed in the mail.

When Carl walked into his office a few minutes later, she gave him a knowing look. "Hank's putting through another one," she remarked succinctly. "It's late this time."

Carl threw her a haunted look and said nothing. He'd been expecting another transfer from Hank Pugsley any day now too, and he'd been clutching a faint straw that perhaps Hank wasn't going to send any more money to Switzerland. Maybe he'd decided to change his bank, or move to the West Coast . . . or perhaps he'd been arrested for tax evasion. Carl shook his head despairingly. Hank was alive and kicking and still up to his old tricks, and to suppose anything else was wishful thinking.

"I'll put it through late this afternoon," Kimberley said with quiet relish, as if it were something delicious she was going to eat.

Still Carl said nothing, as he wondered how much more he could take. For the past few months he'd felt as if he were swimming against the tide, struggling against currents that were stronger than he was, being bashed against the rocks every time he saw another transfer from Hank lying on his desk; and now he longed for the tide to turn and bring him back to a safe resting place where he could lie still and get his breath back. His eyes sought Kimberley's for a moment, searching for a tiny gap of weakness in their translucent gray depths, wondering if the strain wasn't proving too much for her too; but he was met with a solid resistance to his unspoken plea to call it a day. Her eyes held the flat stony lifelessness of a carved figure and were totally devoid of feeling. Abruptly Carl turned away, sickened by the whole business.

At lunchtime Kimberley went back to her apartment to collect the precious coded computer tape from where she kept it among the few books on her shelves; then she took a cab back to Wall Street. All afternoon she worked in a state of elated anticipation, seeing in her mind's eye the dollars flash up on to the green screen, seeing the number of Hank's current account, then the number of her own Swiss account: 23007 4810 66792. Kimberley knew it by heart now, had it engraved on her mind in numerals a foot high. No longer did she need to check in the index of her Filofax before putting through the transfers; it was right there in the forefront of her mind, like the amount that had appeared on the last bank statement she'd received from Zurich—more than two million dollars. Today's transfer would bring it up to nearly two and a half.

A smile hovered around Kimberley's mouth as she did her work and planned her fantasy, a fantasy that had begun when she'd been a twelve-year-old kid standing on Times Square; a fantasy that she was determined would take her to the shores of the Mediterranean, where she imagined the sea would be as blue as sapphires and the sky an endless dome of sunshine.

At four-thirty Carl announced he had a meeting.

"Okay," Kimberley replied. "I'll see you after . . . later," she corrected herself, in case anyone was within earshot. The minutes ticked slowly past, and her stomach knotted tighter with a mixture of nerves and excitement. At ten to five she slipped the tape from her purse into her pocket, adding the pack of cigarettes again in case anyone noticed the bulge. At five to five she ran through the operation once more in her mind; any mistakes or delays could prove fatal. At two minutes to five she went down into the deserted lobby and passed unnoticed as she stepped into the elevator that would take her to the basement, where the main computer room was situated, next to the vaults.

To her relief, it was empty; the dreaded Liz had already departed, along with all the other computer operators, and only one of the security guards, in his office along the corridor, glanced up casually as she passed. They smiled briefly, having known each other for nearly two years, and then Kimberley hurried into the computer room and took her seat at the keyboard.

First, remove the checking account disk from the computer. Kimberley did this, watching the screen go blank and dark like a television set that has been turned off. Then she whipped the foreign-transactions disk out of her pocket, and loading it carefully, watched for the screen to glow brilliant green again and for the flickering black lettering of the program to reveal itself so she could type in Hank Pugsley's details and then the secret code for her own foreign account.

Suddenly she stiffened in her seat and craned forward anxiously. Something had happened. Something was terribly wrong, and for a moment she felt a shaft of panic pass through her. Kimberley tried again, removing her tape and then reloading it with care, but still the screen remained dark. There was nothing. The screen looked back at her, just a piece of thick glass as gray and blank as the eye of a great dead fish.

Kimberley glanced swiftly around the room. She still had a few more minutes before the security guards did their rounds, so as an experiment she loaded the original disk in the computer again. Within seconds there was a happy sort of bleep and the screen sprang to life, green as freshly mown grass, alive with a mad flutter of names and figures, as the records of clients' checking accounts appeared. Kimberley stared, appalled, the color draining from her face so it picked up the green tinge of the screen. It could mean only one thing, she thought. Recklessly, in a desperate effort to prove herself wrong, she removed the disk once more and reloaded her own. Again nothing. A dead screen with not a flicker of life, a hostile square of glass that mocked her in her anguish and offered her no comfort from its sterile depths.

Tight-lipped, Kimberley slipped the disk back into her pocket, replaced the original one, and strode out of the computer room, too angry and upset to even notice the security guard beginning his round of inspection.

Back in her office, she lay in wait for Carl to return from his meeting, disappointment and frustration jostling with each other in her mind alongside fear and apprehension.

As soon as Carl appeared, she sprang from behind her desk and rushed into his office, closing both her door and his to the corridor. "Something's gone wrong with my computer disk," she said in an urgent whisper. "I couldn't put through the transfer."

Carl's face grew haggard and pale as he sat slumped, looking up at her. His voice was dangerously quiet and calm. "What happened?"

Kimberley shrugged in an exaggerated way. "I don't know, I tell you! All I know is that my computer disk has been wiped clean! There's nothing on it. You'll have to get the original from Jake's office again so that I can make another copy."

"You know perfectly well I can't!" snapped Carl. "Jake has recently introduced tighter security methods. Those master disks are kept under lock and key twenty-four hours a day, and only Jake and his deputy have access to them. There's no way I can even get near them."

Kimberley knew he was speaking the truth, and the knowledge increased her rage. "Fuck it!" she spat, keeping her voice low with an effort. "How am I going to transfer Hank's money now? What can we do? Of all the goddamn things to happen!" She began to pace up and down his office, beside herself with a fury she was finding it harder by the minute to control. Suddenly she swung on Carl, her eyes blazing. "I bet you've done something to sabotage my disk! It's been in my office all afternoon!"

Carl eyed her coldly, a creeping sense of relief stealing over him. If her disk had been wiped out, there was no other way he could think of that she could transfer Hank's money to her own account. Her scheme might be forced to grind to a halt here and now. The thought made him momentarily dizzy. Could the end really be in sight?

"I haven't even been in your office today," he heard himself say. "If you will recall, I've been in here with clients, or in the boardroom at a meeting."

Kimberley turned sullenly away, unable to deny he was telling the truth. "Then what the fuck's gone wrong?" she demanded hoarsely.

"I don't care what's gone wrong. All I do know is that tomorrow, first thing, Hank Pugsley's transfer of dollars has to go through in the normal way."

"Like hell it has!" Kimberley stormed.

"It must!" Carl insisted angrily. "The date of transfer has got to show up on his bank statement. The dollars have got to be taken out of his checking account, and if they aren't, he'll wonder why. Every month his statement shows the debit side of his account, so we've *got* to transfer the money by tomorrow. I just hope the manager of his bank in Zurich doesn't contact him and ask why this is the first time in weeks he's sent money over."

Kimberley let out a low moan like an animal in pain as she sank onto one of Carl's office chairs. Her long fingers covered her eyes in a gesture of despair. "What can have gone wrong?" she whispered. "Everything was working so perfectly."

"Too perfectly, perhaps," Carl said crisply. He didn't like it himself. Why should Kimberley's disk have been wiped clean, and who could have done it? That was the thing that worried him most. Someone, apart from himself, was anxious to put an end to her activities, and that person had deliberately sabotaged the disk.

If the end of one nightmare was over, another one might just be beginning.

14

"And this is Bernard!" Jessica exclaimed with a flourish as she introduced him to Madeleine and Carl that evening while they had drinks in the bar at the Plaza, where they were staying, before going on to dine at Elaine's.

They all shook hands, grinning self-consciously, uttering the usual social banalities and eyeing each other with curiosity.

"I've heard so much about you from Jessica," Bernard said suavely to Madeleine, "and you're even more beautiful than she described." He held both her hands in his and stood looking at her as if he found her enchanting. Madeleine returned his gaze evenly, summing him up, slightly shocked that he was even older than she had thought. There was a fine network of wrinkles spreading from around his hooded eyes, and there were deep lines at the corners of his mouth.

"Thank you," she said simply.

"Let's have some champagne!" Jessica was saying as they seated themselves at a table in the corner, away from the crowded activity of people drinking and talking. She signaled for a waiter, her gold bangles rattling on wrists that seemed slimmer than ever. "Oh, isn't this divine! I've been longing for us all to get together, and here we are at last!"

The waiter placed little bowls of nuts and green and black olives on the table, and Jessica grabbed Bernard's hand in a rush of excitement.

Carl turned to Bernard. "Do you travel a great deal?"

Bernard, having decided that Madeleine was not going to succumb to his charismatic charm, and was not even going to flirt with him, seemed to be losing interest in the proceedings.

"I'll be touring for eight months this year," he replied casually, his eyes roving around the bar area to see if there was anyone he knew. "I'm giving concerts in all the major cities, including Tokyo."

"Then we have four months off," interjected Jessica. "Touring isn't all glamour, I've discovered. It's living out of suitcases, catching planes, checking in at different hotels every few days, and as for Bernard's fan mail! My dear, he gets *sacks* of letters. But"—she squeezed Bernard's hand—"we're actually having four months' break in the spring. Did I tell you Bernard had a house in Sardinia? It's on the beach, I gather, and . . . Oh! Oh, Bernard, I've had the most wonderful idea!" Jessica's small face suddenly blazed with delight. "Maddy and Carl can come and stay with us, can't they? Wouldn't that be fantastic? The house is on the Costa Smeralda, and we could go snorkeling and sailing, and there are riding and tennis, aren't there, darling? . . . And then there's the Pevero golf course! Oh, just think what fun we'll have, and how *brown* we'll get!"

Bernard looked taken aback, and a glint of annoyance showed in his eyes. Not noticing, Jessica insisted, "Wouldn't that be fabulous, Bernard?"

He hesitated, his smile contrasting chillingly with the cold warning look he seemed to be giving Jessica. "Well . . ." His voice trailed away, his tone discouraging.

"I don't know when Carl and I will be able to get away," Madeleine cut in hurriedly. It was obvious Bernard was not going to make them feel welcome, and for Jessica's sake she felt it was better to take avoiding action.

"Of course you can get away. Don't be silly," Jessica declared impatiently. "What's wrong, Bernard? Aren't there enough bedrooms?" She was sitting very upright now, in a way Madeleine knew so well, her cheeks flushed and her attitude that of a persistent child determined to embarrass a grown-up. "We'll never get to see our friends if we can't have them to stay with us."

Madeleine, amused, took a swift gulp of her drink to hide her twitching mouth, not daring to look at Carl, who was studying the ceiling of the bar. Out of the corner of her eye she saw Bernard run a caressing hand down Jessica's arm. Then he spoke in a polite but firm voice, but as if Madeleine and Carl had not been there.

"I bought the house as a private hideaway, not for entertaining," he was explaining. "It's where I write my music; it's where I go to get away from people and have a bit of peace. I do not want people to stay." Then he turned to them as if he'd just remembered their presence, giving them a patronizing smile: his adoring fans, honored to be in the presence of the great man himself.

Jessica's flush deepened, and for a fleeting moment she looked like a disappointed child who might burst into tears, but Madeleine's eyes narrowed as she looked at Bernard, and in that instant she realized she disliked him deeply. He was an arrogant, conceited bastard, and she wondered how Jessica could have fallen in love with someone so utterly conceited and wrapped up in himself. She also knew in that instant that the feeling was mutual. A flash of hostility had passed between them as they exchanged looks, and she knew it was partly because she hadn't pandered to Bernard's vanity when they'd been introduced, and partly because he resented Jessica having close friends from her past.

"So you do all your composing when you're in Sardinia?" Carl asked conversationally. "Does it take you long to write . . . say, the theme music for a film like *Silver Apples of the Moon*?"

Bernard cast world-weary eyes around the crowded bar area, making it clear that he was sick of always being asked the same sort of questions. "It depends . . ." He shrugged nonchalantly. Then he looked at Jessica and gave her a conspiratorial wink, a look that said: Won't it be nice when these dreary people have gone and we're on our own again?

"Are you all right, darling?" he whispered intimately.

"I'm fine!" Jessica replied with a perky smile, though she still looked slightly deflated. Then she turned to Madeleine and Carl. "Now, I want to hear all your news. Carl, you're looking divinely distinguished! Still taking Wall Street by storm? And I adore that dress you're wearing, Maddy. It's to *die* for! Who designed it—Bill Blass?" Her slim little hands fluttered, hovering over the silk of Madeleine's skirt, and her smile was one of undisguised admiration. "You always look so good," she added generously.

Madeleine laughed. "Thanks, Jessie, but there's no need to overdo it."

Undeterred, Jessica continued, "God, how I wish we were going to be in London when you're there. We'll be in Moscow, won't we, Bernard?"

Bernard's brows had been gradually drawing together in a deep frown while Jessica had been prattling happily on, but now he seemed to reach flash point.

"I'm more concerned about where we're going to eat tonight," he snapped, slamming his glass down on the little table. "I've been rehearsing all day and I'm tired. I certainly don't want to hang around this place all evening, drinking. Let's go now."

Jessica rested a placating hand on his arm. "All right, darling. There's no need to get in a state." She turned to the others. "Would you mind if we had dinner a little early? Bernard suffers from low blood sugar when he's been working very hard, and he feels awful if he doesn't get something to eat straightaway."

"That's fine," Madeleine replied lightly, thinking it was less a case of low blood sugar than a case of raised temper that was making Bernard behave in this way.

Then, as she watched Jessica take his arm, looking adoringly and with concern into his face, Madeleine realized just how much her friend was in love with this talented but irascible man. She seemed bewitched and bedazzled, a satellite encircling a star with a selfless devotion. And Bernard knew it; of that Madeleine was certain. With a triumphant look on his face at having gotten his own way, he was striding out of the Plaza bar with Jessica running after him in her spike heels in order to keep up, and his head was held high as he pointedly ignored the stares and nudges and admiring whispers of the other people in the bar when they recognized him.

God help her, Madeleine thought as she and Carl followed. He's already got her running in circles, pandering to his every need. What about her own career? What about the lively independent spirit who knew exactly what she wanted and where she was going? Already Jessica seemed changed from the young woman who had told Andrew she was a person in her own right. Already there was a submissiveness about Jessica that had not been there before. By falling in love, Jessica seemed to have lost a little of herself in Bernard.

*   *   *

"I didn't like him, did you?" Madeleine said to Carl as they got ready for bed that night. It had been a difficult evening, with awkward silences and stilted conversation, so unlike the previous times she and Carl had spent with Jessica.

"He's okay," Carl said, "but I wouldn't have thought he was Jessica's type. Far too temperamental and volatile, very different from Andrew." Carefully he laid the gold cufflinks Madeleine had given him in his jewel case. "What d'you suppose she sees in him?"

Madeleine thought for a moment, sitting at her dressing table brushing her hair until it gleamed blue-black in the soft lighting of their bedroom. "Excitement, I think . . . and maybe a challenge. Andrew was the only serious boyfriend she's ever had, so maybe one of Bernard's attractions is that he's completely different. And he *is* charismatic—I'll give him that." She turned to look at Carl, a worried expression in her eyes. "I hope she's going to be happy, but I'm afraid Bernard just wants a glorified personal assistant and someone to go to bed with regularly, and that's not going to be enough for Jessica."

Carl raised his eyebrows. "Maddy, you really do amaze me sometimes." He walked over to her and placed his hands on her shoulders. Then he lowered his head so they were cheek to cheek, looking into the mirror at their reflected images.

"Why do I amaze you?" She rubbed her cheek softly against his.

"Because I always suppose you're in a dream . . . painting some great picture . . . imagining some scene . . . and then you suddenly come out with a remark that shows you're as on the ball as anyone."

Her dark eyes widened as she thought of Kimberley, thought of all the things going on at the bank, thought of her own well-laid plans to get even with a woman who had tried to ruin her happiness. Then she looked down at her hands lest her expression give something away.

"Oh, I don't know," she replied lightly, "I'm in a dream most of the time, really."

Carl kissed her ear, then ran his tongue around the lobe, tugging it gently with his lips. "Are you coming to bed?" he asked, his voice suddenly thick with longing.

Madeleine nodded, leaning back against him, feeling already the arousal of his body as he pressed himself against her.

"I agree with Bernard about one thing," Carl whispered as his hands slid to her breasts, which strained full and round against the satin of her nightgown.

"What's that?"

"I like having someone I can go to bed with regularly!"

"So I should hope!" she cried in mock horror. "How dreadful it would be if you didn't!"

"You were very rude tonight!" Jessica scolded Bernard as soon as they'd climbed into bed in their suite at the Plaza. "Madeleine and Carl are my oldest and greatest friends. Why did you behave so badly?"

Bernard rolled onto his back, his broad shoulders indenting the pillows, his head supported by his hands. "I was bored, sweetheart," he replied blandly. "Carl is a typical banker, all he thinks about is money. Madeleine is your typical rich society girl, spoiled and empty-headed."

Jessica shot into an upright position, her breasts bare above the fallen sheet, her face enraged. "How can you talk such rubbish?" she stormed, her eyes round with indignation. "Madeleine is *not* spoilt or empty-headed. On the contrary, she's a very talented artist who's had a lot of success so far, and she's amazingly shrewd. She was too polite to say anything tonight, but I don't think she liked the way you patronized her, at *all*."

Bernard turned to look at her, his hooded eyes unfathomable. "Are we going to spend the night quarreling about your little friend, or are we going to sleep?"

Jessica plumped her pillows angrily and glared at him. He seemed so changed since she'd joined him in Boston—grumpy, domineering, and demanding. Where was the tender, passionate lover who'd confessed to being lonely, whom she'd met in London?

"I don't want to quarrel with you," Jessica said fretfully, "but I don't understand why you didn't like Maddy and Carl. You could at least have been nice to them for my sake."

Bernard snorted contemptuously. "Life is too short to be nice to people one doesn't care for, and your friends committed the worst social sin of all!"

"What do you mean?"

"They were boring! Utterly, desperately boring!"

"And I suppose the sycophants who surround you aren't?" Jessica shot back. "For God's sake, Bernard, that's the most intolerant and ridiculous remark I've ever heard. Some people can't help being boring!"

"Everyone can help being boring . . . it just requires a little effort. People who socialize have a duty to be interesting. They must be prepared to sing for their supper!" he added arrogantly.

Jessica jumped out of bed and flung on her blue satin robe. "You're a conceited bastard, Bernard Scheller," she yelled, making for the door, "and if you think—"

Bernard was too quick for her. With a bound he was across the room, his naked body blocking her way, his strong arms encircling her. "Hush, hush!" he admonished. "You're getting too excited."

"I will not listen to the rubbish you talk!" Her tiny fists flailed wildly in the air as he grappled with her, eventually catching her by the wrists. Then he pulled her close until she grew still and leaned against him.

"That's better," he whispered soothingly, stroking her head as if she were a child. "What a fuss about nothing! It was only a little dinner party that turned out to be a bit dull, not the end of the world."

Unexpectedly, Jessica found herself sobbing, as if she were the child Bernard was reassuring. "I know," she wept, surprised by her own display of emotion. The whole evening had somehow unnerved her, and now she felt a deep reaction. It wasn't just that Bernard hadn't liked her friends, it was that her friendship with Madeleine represented the security she'd known ever since she'd been a child, which she suddenly seemed to have lost. Her parents had always been there in the background, loving and supporting, and now they were thousands of miles away. Her friends and all the people she'd worked with in the Golding Group were scattered far and wide too, and as for Andrew, alone in the little Chelsea flat they'd shared . . . She gave a loud sob. Up to now her life had progressed gradually from childhood to adulthood, each event and each person in it linked to the previous event or person, so that a continual chain had woven her destiny. That was until she'd met Bernard. Then her past had been severed with a suddenness that only now did she realize had been traumatic. In a matter of weeks her job, her friends, her family, and even the country of her birth were things of the past, exchanged for a man she hardly knew and for an existence which would be basically nomadic. There had been no talk of marriage or lasting commitment; nothing to replace the security she'd relinquished, nothing to give her a sense of having new roots to lay down; and suddenly, tonight, Bernard's rejection of Madeleine and Carl had made her see how alone in the world she was with him. There were just the two of them, and she was utterly dependent on him for everything.

"I wanted you to like them," she snuffled. "They're my best friends."

"Good. That's nice." He sounded as if he were humoring her. "Friends are important, darling, but don't forget that my life is very demanding and that I don't want to be surrounded by people any more than I have to be. I was trying to explain that earlier, about not wanting anyone to stay with us on Sardinia. It's bad enough having the servants, even though they've learned to keep out of my way. But people staying . . . ? Impossible! Unbearable! I can't have any distractions when I'm composing."

Jessica nodded, understanding, but the feeling of hurt and insecurity still lingered inside her. For a moment she felt a flash of panic, wondering what she was going to do with the rest of her life while Bernard worked, but she pushed the thought away.

"Come back to bed, sweetheart," Bernard was coaxing.

Back in bed, he held her in his arms, rocking her gently, stroking her hair as it lay like a stream of gold silk on the pillow. Gradually the knots of tension began to dissolve as his hands moved down her body, caressing her, arousing her, and all the while his voice, hypnotic, was repeating: "Little one . . . little one."

As Jessica's senses were lulled, her fears abated, seeming now hysterical and irrational. After all, Bernard had been tired after rehearsing all afternoon, and he'd probably have preferred a quiet dinner with her rather than having to see people he didn't know. Little by little, her disappointment and chagrin faded as Bernard's hands and lips worked their magic, touching her just where she wanted to be touched, kissing her where she longed to be kissed. Then Bernard touched himself, his eyes closed, his expression absorbed. As his strong hand smoothed and stroked his erection, Jessica became consumed with passion. An instinctive urge, part-love, part-lust, filled her with desire to give this man his pleasure, to bring him to a peak of fulfillment, knowing in those moments she would have him utterly in her power.

With a swift movement she rolled over onto her knees, and taking him in her mouth, sucked deeply. Groaning with an almost animal gratification, Bernard rocked his pelvis with deep sensuality, thrusting himself until he touched the back of her throat, extracting every exquisite sensation he could from her tongue and luxuriating in the pleasure she was giving him.

"Yes . . . oh, yes," he murmured. "Stroke my balls, darling . . ."

Jessica glanced up for a second and saw that he was looking down at himself through half-closed eyes, watching his own inflamed passion, admiring himself as she brought his precious body to a climax. He ran his tongue along his bottom lip and his hands pressed down on the flatness of his stomach. Then he relinquished himself to her ministrations, almost as if he were doing her a favor.

The doctor's face was grave. "I'm sending you for X rays, Mrs. Ziffren. How long did you say you'd had that cough?"

Patti Ziffren cleared her throat, and the sound was raspier than usual. "Oh, pretty well as long as I can remember," she said with a touch of forced gaiety. "It's only a smoker's cough, for goodness' sake! I came to see you because of my headaches. There's nothing wrong with my lungs." She pulled the white cotton wrapper across her thin body, and her eyes challenged the doctor to disagree with her.

"Well, we'll have to see about that," he said slowly. He was a young doctor who had recently taken over the practice, and he refused to be intimidated by Mrs. Ziffren. She might be one of New York's richest and most influential women, but to him she was just another patient, and a rather sick one at that.

"I'll tell you why you're getting headaches when you wake up every morning," he continued. "You tell me you smoke three packs of cigarettes a day?"

Patti shrugged bony shoulders. "Yes, probably. Sometimes less, sometimes more."

"Then every morning you're suffering from a nicotine hangover. That's worse than an alcohol hangover. You've got to give up smoking, you know. At this rate you'll be dead in a couple of years." He spoke earnestly, his face full of concern.

Patti tossed her head. "Never heard such nonsense in my life! Usually I take a couple of aspirin and then the headache goes. But it doesn't seem to be working as well as usual."

"I'm not surprised. Quit smoking altogether and then you won't get any more headaches. Meanwhile, we must have a look at that chest of yours. I'll arrange for the X rays to be done first thing tomorrow morning." The doctor didn't even ask her if it would be convenient. As far as he was concerned, Mrs. Ziffren was underweight, with skin the color of putty, and a cough that was tearing her apart.

As Patti got dressed again, she knew, with a sickening feeling of dread, that the doctor was right. She *was* killing herself by smoking, but the hell of it was that she neither wanted nor felt able to give it up. The more Jake nagged her about it, the more contrary she felt. Sam had stopped trying to persuade her years ago, so she got neither support nor disapproval from him, but one by one all her friends had given up, and in the last year or so she had begun to feel she was being antisocial. Although she lived only two blocks from the doctor, she'd ordered her car to wait for her. It was absurd, she knew, but walking home those two blocks would have left her feeling tired and breathless. A jab of panic sent tingles of fear shooting through her; suppose what the doctor said was true. Suppose the X rays revealed something. Suppose she only had a couple of years to live.

With unaccustomed weakness, Patti's eyes filled with tears as the car sped her home. She didn't want to die yet. She wanted to live so that she could eventually see Madeleine's children and watch them grow up as she'd watched her niece grow up. Life is a precious thing, she thought, reaching automatically for a cigarette. It was lit and she was dragging on it before she realized what she was doing. This is crazy, she thought, and yet, as she inhaled, her worries seemed momentarily to fade. Doctors didn't always know what they were talking about, she reassured herself. She'd have gotten lung cancer by now if she was going to. After all, cancer didn't run in their family. Anyway, what was the point of being alive at all if you were miserable—and without cigarettes, she *was* miserable. They made her calm and . . . She was seized by a fit of coughing so severe that her chauffeur slowed down, glancing over his shoulder anxiously.

"Are you okay, ma'am?"

Patti could only nod. With streaming eyes, her body convulsed by spasms, she was unable to speak as cough after cough was wrenched from her throat. For a moment she thought she was going to choke, but with a final rattle she got her breath back. Exhausted, she leaned back in the car, her eyes closed. Between her manicured fingers, her cigarette still smoldered. With a sudden movement she stubbed it out in the car ashtray, and taking a lace-edged handkerchief out of her handbag, she wiped her eyes and dabbed the corners of her mouth. The doctor was right. This couldn't go on.

The Boeing 747 skimmed through the thick gray-porridge clouds that hung over southern England, losing altitude as it approached Heathrow. In first class, Madeleine sat huddled under her blanket, feeling cold and shivery, as if the clammy chilliness of the swirling cumulus had penetrated the aircraft cabin. It had been a long night and it seemed an age since she'd kissed Carl good-bye in New York.

The smiling steward brought steaming coffee and poured out a generous cup for her. Madeleine sipped it gratefully. The next few days were going to be the most nerve-racking of her life, and a lot would happen before she could go down to the comparative peace of Devon. In the meantime, Carl must be allowed to believe that she was in London arranging her next exhibition, prior to catching the train for Milton Manor.

"Please extinguish your cigarettes and fasten your safety belts," a disembodied voice said over the loudspeaker.

Madeleine's ears started to pop and she swallowed hard, partly to relieve the unpleasant sensation but partly from nerves. Everything depended on this trip being successful, and she hoped and prayed that Hank had kept his side of the bargain. If he lost his nerve, Kimberley might still get away with everything, and that was a thought Madeleine couldn't bear to contemplate.

The plane touched down, roared along the runway with its jets screaming, and eventually came to a halt near the terminal buildings. Half an hour later Madeleine was through customs and hurrying toward the taxi rank.

"The Royal Westminster, Hyde Park Corner," she told the driver, remembering the last time she'd been to England, when Jessica had been with her. They'd chatted all the way into the center of London, discussing her grandfather and wondering what he wanted. Well, now she knew. Her mother was alive and in an institution, where Jake had been paying for her to be looked after for over twenty years now. But I mustn't think about my mother, she thought grimly. Not yet. There'll be plenty of time to think about her and decide whether I'm going to go and see her when this business with Kimberley is over. Carl comes first, and getting him out of this mess without Jake discovering what has been going on is the most important thing right now.

As the taxi rattled along the highway, getting snarled in the morning traffic from time to time, Madeleine ran through her carefully laid plans. Checking into the Royal Westminster first, although it meant she had to make the journey back to the airport a few hours later, was all part of the scheme. At lunchtime she'd call Carl and tell him she'd landed safely and would be out and about meeting people until she left for Devon. That way, if he should call her at any time, he wouldn't be surprised if the hotel switchboard couldn't locate her.

The Royal Westminster gave her the VIP treatment, including the glass of champagne while she checked in, but it seemed strange without Jessica and her bright little face, alive with its welcoming smile, her hair glinting with gold under the formal chandeliers. To Madeleine it seemed as if a light had gone out in the hotel, and at that moment she would have given anything to have her friend with her. No matter how serious the situation, Jessica always managed to inject a shaft of humor into it, and right now she would have been such a help in the dreaded task that lay ahead.

Madeleine had been given a magnificent suite overlooking Hyde Park. As she stood looking out the window, the soldiers of the Queen's Household Cavalry jingled past on their magnificent black horses, breastplates and plumed helmets glittering in the early-morning sun, the clatter of the polished hooves reminding her that before the days of cars, horses had been the only means of transport in this great old city.

Unpacking her cases, she showered, changed, and then repacked an overnight bag. She wasn't going to need much, just a nightdress, one complete change of clothes, and her toiletries and makeup. Then, pulling the telephone toward her, she lay down on the bed to make the first of her phone calls.

The first was to Mr. Marks, the lawyer.

"I'm in London for a couple of days," she told him, "and I'll be coming down to Milton Manor to see about my grandfather's property on Wednesday."

"That will be very nice, Mrs. Delaney," she heard him say. She could just imagine him sitting in his office, surrounded by stacks of dusty legal papers, his mothlike eyelashes fluttering as he talked.

"As I told you when I called you from New York, my father has given me all the information I need regarding my mother and the estate," continued Madeleine. "I will tell you all about it when I see you."

"Indeed. Well, that is very good, isn't it? And we shan't have to go to court now?"

"That is correct."

"Well, I'm sure that's a relief for you, Mrs. Delaney. I'll see you on Wednesday, then."

"Ten o'clock at the Manor. I'll be there." Madeleine hung up and then got the switchboard to get her a number in Zurich.

"Schweizerhof Hotel. Can I help you?" asked a German-sounding voice when she got through a few moments later.

"May I speak with Mr. Hank Pugsley?" Madeleine asked. Oh, God, let him be there, she thought, digging her nails into the palm of her hand. Suppose he hasn't arrived yet. Suppose he's chickened out, in spite of the plans we made.

"Hello?" she heard a man's voice say cautiously.

"Hank Pugsley?"

"Y-yes," the voice admitted, still sounding doubtful.

"This is Madeleine Delaney. I've just landed in London and I'm catching an afternoon flight to Zurich."

"Good," Hank said. "I was waiting for your call. Everything okay?"

"Everything's fine," Madeleine said, "and we're meeting as arranged in the Banque Internationale on the Bahnhofstrasse tomorrow morning at nine-thirty."

"I'll be there. It's a long street, by the way. The bank is near the center, near Barengasse Strasse. It's a big building; you can't miss it."

"Thanks." Madeleine's mouth twitched. Hank was obviously enjoying himself. He was talking in a James Bond sort of voice, clipped and secretive, and she could just imagine him sitting in his hotel bedroom, shirtsleeves rolled up, ready for action. I hope to God he hasn't got a gun with him, she thought in sudden alarm.

Hank's next remark caught her off-guard. "Why don't we meet for dinner tonight?"

Madeleine, remembering his fat greasiness, thought quickly. Having a deal with him to outwit Kimberley was one thing; having to spend an evening socializing with him was another. She tried to let him down gently so as not to hurt his feelings.

"I don't think that would be wise," she explained. "My husband thinks I'm going to be staying in London, and if one of his business contacts spotted me in Zurich, and in the company of a man, well . . ." Her voice drifted off, leaving the sentence unfinished.

Hank was quick to catch on. "Oh, no, we don't want that," he agreed. "Right, well, I'll see you tomorrow morning, and we'll cook the little bitch's goose once and for all!"

"I'll see you then." Madeleine hung up. She had two hours to kill. She closed her eyes, trying to sleep, but tension held her in its grip, and she found her mind going over and over the details for tomorrow. It was going to be a highly risky business, and if the bank in Zurich became suspicious . . . She shut her mind to the dangers; she had set out to get the better of Kimberley, and now she had to go through with it.

At twelve-thirty she put through a call to Carl, who had just woken up. "Yes, I'm fine, darling," she assured him. "I'm off to see a gallery in Bond Street," she continued, hating to lie to him, "and there are one or two in Chelsea that sound interesting. Anyway, I'll call you, Carl, when I've settled on something. Don't bother phoning me because I'm going to be out most of the time," she added firmly.

"Okay, sweetheart," she heard him say. "Take care of yourself. I hope you'll find what you're looking for."

Madeleine smiled to herself. "Oh, I'm sure I will," she said with a touch of irony, knowing Carl would think she was referring to a suitable gallery. Then she picked up her overnight bag, walked out of the hotel, and caught a cab around the corner, out of sight of the hotel's main entrance. There was no point advertising the fact she was returning straight to Heathrow.

Four hours later, Madeleine landed at Kloten Airport. She was directed by a helpful official to an adjoining railway, where, within minutes, she was on a train to Zurich. Tired and feeling strained, she sank thankfully onto a seat as the train pulled swiftly out of the station. To her amazement and relief, the journey took only ten minutes, and when she alighted she found herself at the Hauptbahnhof, in the center of Zurich. She jumped into the first of a waiting line of cabs. "The Baur au Lac Hotel, on the Talstrasse," she told the driver.

Gazing out the windows as tempting shops and inviting cafés and restaurants flashed by, Madeleine realized that apart from being one of the world's leading financial centers, Zurich was one of the most affluent cities in Europe. She could see prosperous young bankers returning home from work, hopping on clean-looking blue trams that skimmed smoothly up and down the well-kept streets, for Madeleine remembered that only "foreigners" drove their smart cars to work. Beautifully dressed women were shopping in the many boutiques that lined Zurich's principal boulevards; and then she saw it! The Banque Internationale, just as Hank had said, halfway down the main street.

The Baur au Lac Hotel, which she'd chosen from a travel brochure, since she didn't want to involve her usual travel agent, turned out to be sensational—beautiful and elegant, it was a favorite haunt of bankers and industrialists, with a pretty pavilion set in its extensive gardens and a view over the Limmat River from its windows.

Madeleine ordered supper in her room and went to bed early. Tomorrow was going to be a big day.

* * *

Jake came into Carl's office shortly after he got in that morning.

"Heard from Madeleine?" he inquired. Jake was never happy unless he knew his daughter was all right.

"She's arrived okay. I spoke to her before I left the apartment and she was in great shape," Carl replied. "She's going to be looking at London galleries today."

"That's good." Jake looked relieved. "Now we've just got to make sure Patti's all right, and our problems will be over."

"Patti?" Carl repeated. "What's wrong with her?"

"Her doctor is insisting on a chest X ray," he replied grimly. "I told her she smoked too much—she's had this terrible cough for a long time now."

"Oh, my God!" Carl looked anxious. "I hope she's going to be all right. Does Maddy know?"

Jake shook his head. "This only happened yesterday, but she doesn't want Madeleine to know anything unless . . ." He sighed deeply, breaking off. Patti was the only family he had left, apart from Madeleine, and if anything should happen to her, he knew he'd be devastated.

"I'm sure she'll be okay," Carl said comfortingly.

"I don't know . . ."

"When will she get the results of the X ray?"

"I expect they'll be able to tell her right away. I asked her to call me as soon as she knew."

"If there's anything I can do, Jake . . ."

Jake smiled absently, his eyes still troubled. "Thanks. Right now, we can only hope . . ." He broke off, as with a flourish Kimberley Cabot hurried into Carl's office, unaware that Jake was there.

"Oh!" She started, stopping in her tracks. She looked quickly from Carl to Jake, wondering what was going on.

"Good morning," Jake greeted her politely.

"Good morning, Mr. Shearman," she said demurely. "I'm sorry. I didn't realize you were in here."

Carl sat, his face a dull red now, his expression uneasy.

"What did you want?" he asked her bluntly.

Her gray eyes widened innocently, and she looked almost hurt. "There's so much work to do, I thought I'd make an early start."

Carl studied her poor-little-me-I-only-wanted-to-be-helpful look and was incredulous. She was more than convincing, and Jake was totally taken in.

"Mr. Delaney sure is a lucky man to have you as an assistant," he said, smiling down at her. "You were working late last night too, weren't you?"

Kimberley's lips curved around her teeth when she smiled, in a way most men thought deeply attractive. Carl watched as Jake fastened his eyes on her mouth, and Carl knew exactly what he was thinking. She'd had the same effect on him once upon a time.

"I try to make it a rule to clear my desk before I go home at night," she said earnestly. "That way we don't get a backlog."

Jake looked impressed. "Very good! Quite right!"

"I don't need you at the moment, Kimberley," Carl cut in smoothly. "Why don't you come back when I've gone through these transfers?"

She looked at him from veiled eyes. "Certainly, Mr. Delaney." A moment later she had slipped back to her office, closing the communicating door behind her.

Jake dropped his voice to a barely audible whisper. "Lucky you're a happily married man," he joked.

Carl's smile was sickly. "Very. You'll let me know anything you hear about Patti?"

"Yes, of course."

Two hours later the phone in Jake's office rang and his secretary said it was Mrs. Ziffren. Jake grabbed the phone with shaking hands.

"Yes?"

"Is that you, Jake?"

To Jake's horror it sounded as though Patti, who was never known to shed a tear, was crying her eyes out.

Hank arrived first at the Banque Internationale, trying to look inconspicuous in a raincoat over his suit, although it was a dry day. He hovered just inside the main door, highly visible, deeply unattractive, and obviously a foreigner. When Madeleine walked quickly into the bank, his moon face was already gleaming with sweat. With his lumbering gait, he went up to her.

"Good morning," she said tensely.

Hank didn't reply. Regarding her with anxious eyes, he looked as if he wasn't sure it was really her, she looked so different.

"Okay?" she asked shortly.

"D'you think it's going to be all right? I mean . . ." He looked around the busy bank lobby as if it scared the hell out of him.

"Watch me," Madeleine replied with more confidence than she felt, "and don't say a thing."

She wasn't sure whether Kimberley had come to Zurich in person to open her bank account the previous year. If she had, there might be someone who would remember her, so before leaving the hotel she'd put on sunglasses, a dark blue turban that completely covered her hair, and heavy makeup with thick dark red lipstick. It wasn't a likeness of Kimberley, but it gave an impression of her, and Madeleine hoped that would be sufficient. Of course, it would be a disaster if the bank teller knew Kimberley well; apart from the fact that both women were of medium height and slim, they bore no resemblance to each other at all.

Madeleine's eyes moved swiftly along the row of bank tellers, deciding which one to choose. They were all busy with a line of people waiting to draw out or deposit money, and she decided on a pale thin young man who looked particularly harassed; if he was busy, he might not have the time to look too closely at her. He had steel-rimmed spectacles, pale brown hair receding at the temples, and an instantly forgettable face. Madeleine joined the line of people waiting to be dealt with by him. Hank remained at her side, tense and silent, as if going to his own execution.

At last Madeleine reached the counter, and the teller looked at her questioningly, his gray eyes magnified by his glasses so they looked sharp and foxy.

"I'd like to transfer some dollars from my account and deposit them to another account," she said, managing to keep her voice steady.

"Your account is in this bank?" he asked in broken English.

Madeleine nodded. He passed her a slip of paper.

"Please to fill it in," he said in an expressionless voice.

Without faltering, Madeleine filled in: 23007 4810 66792. Below it she signed: "Kimberley Cabot."

"Will you wait a minute?" said the teller, snatching up the slip of paper without looking at it. Madeleine watched him go to a colleague who sat at a computer. The two men exchanged a few terse words, and the second man seemed to be tapping something into the keyboard in front of him. Then they both watched as a rippling tide of clients' names and details shimmered from the bottom of the screen to the top. While Madeleine waited, watching out of the corner of her eye, she saw them peering intently and muttering something. She knew she had perfected forging Kimberley's signature from the memo she'd taken from her office, but had she gotten the account number right? After all, it had only been by deduction that she'd decided the orthodontal-insurance number in Kimberley's Filofax was her Swiss account number. Maybe it wasn't! She felt an icy clutching in her stomach now as she stood there trying to look unconcerned. Perhaps Kimberley had gotten there first and had already removed all the money.

Something seemed to be wrong, for the teller and the clerk were still muttering to each other, and at one point the clerk looked back over his shoulder and pointed her out. Casually Madeleine opened her handbag, withdrew her gold compact, and powdered her nose. It was the sort of thing Kimberley Cabot would have done. Then the teller nodded to the clerk and vanished through a door marked "Privé." Madeleine replaced the compact in her bag, keeping her face expressionless, aware that Hank, by her side, was breathing heavily now. At any moment Madeleine expected some top bank official to appear, to accuse her of attempting to steal funds . . . of embezzlement . . . of forgery. She imagined Carl and Jake, in New York, being informed that she'd been arrested and charged in Zurich. Her heart started thumping thickly, and she could feel the blood drain away from her face. She glanced at the main doors that led to the street, wondering if she should make a run for it, but already it was too late. The teller was bounding back through the door and coming toward her. Madeleine braced herself for an interrogation.

"How much do you want to transfer?" he asked with a friendly smile.

Relief swept over her, bathing her in sweat. She was sure her face had turned scarlet.

"I'd like to close my account," she said, amazed at the coolness of her voice, and then, taking a gamble, added: "I can't remember how much I have in this account, but if you would be good enough to transfer it all to the account of Mr. Hank Pugsley . . ." She indicated Hank, still standing by her side as if his feet were glued to the floor.

The teller glanced quickly at the slip of paper he held and then wrote something on another slip, which he handed her, having discreetly folded it in half first.

Madeleine opened the paper and stared, stunned for a second by the amount he'd scribbled down. Then she pulled herself together quickly and said, "Yes, that's right. I'd like to transfer it all, please."

"Sign here, please," the teller said, and once more she scribbled "Kimberley Cabot." Then Hank gave the number of his account and it was all over.

Five minutes later they were out in the busy boulevard again, and Hank was gasping, "I could sure do with a drink!"

Madeleine glanced at the fat man as he shambled clumsily by her side, and for a moment she almost liked him; in the past fifteen minutes they'd shared a nerve-racking experience, and it had made her feel quite close to him. They could have been arrested, and it would have been very difficult to get anyone to believe their story. Now that it was over, and they'd outwitted Kimberley Cabot, she felt elated, but there was still a need for caution. She wouldn't feel really safe until she was back in England. She grabbed Hank's elbow and hurried them along the Bahnhofstrasse, past shops and inviting-looking bars and cafés.

"I could do with a drink too, but let's get away from here first," she said, glancing over her shoulder. "If they suddenly discover what I've done, they might try to come after me." As she spoke, she whipped off her turban and shook out her black curls, instantly transforming herself from an older, chic-looking woman into a wildly pretty young one. She reached in her pocket for a tissue with which to wipe off the scarlet lipstick, and then she put her sunglasses in her pocket.

"You're right," Hank cried. At that moment they saw a cab

and he raised his great beefy hand to flag it down. "Where are we going?" he turned to ask her.

"My hotel . . . the Baur au Lac, on the Talstrasse," she told the driver as she jumped in. "I have to pick up my bag to catch the next flight out of here, but we've time for a drink first," she added as Hank sank onto the seat beside her.

He looked at her dubiously. "Do you think we're being followed?" he asked nervously. He craned his neck to look out the back window.

Madeleine shot him a warning look, her fingers to her lips, indicating the driver. "I don't think my husband actually saw us," she said loudly and clearly.

For a split second Hank looked at her with totally blank eyes before he understood. "Oh! That's good! Okay, then! We don't want your husband to find out about us, do we?" he almost shouted.

They ordered two brandies in the bar of the hotel, and sat in an alcove where they couldn't be seen.

Madeleine was the first to speak. "You're flying back to the States today?"

"Yup! And you're going to England?" he inquired.

"Yes. I have some family business to attend to."

"You don't want to be in New York when Kimberley finds out what's happened?" Hank asked curiously.

"No way. And I don't want my husband to be there either," Madeleine said, sipping her brandy slowly, feeling her nerves gradually settling.

"Is he going to join you in England, then?"

Madeleine gave Hank a dry smile. "He doesn't know it yet, but yes, he is."

Hank nodded with understanding. "Good idea!" he said. "When the shit hits the fan, it's sure going to go flying all over the place!"

Jessica glanced around the hotel bedroom, shrugged her shoulders, and decided they must be in Milan. It was the old joke: this is Thursday so it must be . . . Only the joke was wearing thin as far as she was concerned.

They'd been flying from country to country, staying in city after city, living in hotels, never having time to unpack properly, and she had the terrible feeling that they were never going to *arrive*. But arrive where? she asked herself. There *was* no point of arrival, no moment when they could say: At last we're here. They were on a journey that had no ending, and all she could long for was next spring, when they finally got to Bernard's house in Sardinia. But next spring! That was still months away.

Jessica jumped up from the dressing table, where she'd been putting on her makeup, and went to look out the window. Ahead lay the Duomo, Milan's cathedral, blackened with age, as awe-inspiring as a great peaked rock, dwarfing the tourists who milled around the large square in which it stood, imposing its majesty on the historic city. Could she wait until next spring? Then what? She and Bernard would have a few months at his home, and then they'd be off again for another eight months, jetting around the world in a never-ending spin. Depression ate a great hole in her heart as she leaned her forehead against the cool windowpane and thought about how lonely and bored she felt. For a moment she almost wished it hadn't been a false alarm and that she was pregnant, but Bernard's face when she told him she thought she was going to have a baby still sent an icy chill through her when she thought of it. Bernard didn't want a baby. He'd made that very clear.

Jessica had said nothing at the time. In fact, she had been partly relieved, because she'd been wondering how she'd manage on tour with a baby; but now his reaction added to her depression. She'd always planned to have children one day, and if she wasn't going to have a career in the hotel business, she might as well get on with it now, surely. What was she waiting for? When she and Andrew . . . Jessica caught herself up short, startled to find herself thinking of Andrew again.

"Are you ready?" Bernard bellowed at that moment from the living room of their suite, where he'd been on the phone for hours. They were due to have lunch with the publicist of his Milan concert, and after that he was being interviewed for *Gente Mese* magazine before going on to rehearsals. Apart from lunch, Jessica faced the rest of the day and most of the evening alone.

"Yes, I'm ready," she replied, running a brush through her hair and picking up her purse. She joined him in the next room, where he sat surrounded by papers and notes, the phone still in his hand.

"You will have to replace the third violinist!" he was shouting at someone on the other end of the line. "I cannot work with an . . . an amateur!"

Jessica sat down opposite him, waiting for him to finish, and when he put down the receiver she jumped to her feet.

"Okay. Shall we go?" she said brightly.

"*Momento, momento . . . !*" Bernard said vaguely as he started to dial another number.

Jessica planted herself before him, her slim straight figure and long legs in their high-heeled shoes in an attitude of indignation.

"Don't '*momento*' me!" she stormed. "You asked me to go to this lunch with you and I'm ready to go. It's you who made such a fuss about our being on time!"

Bernard continued to talk on the phone, barely acknowledging her presence in the room. Jessica watched him angrily, her pent-up frustration at having nothing to do increasing her irritation. Never in her life had she hung around for anyone. Her time had always been tightly scheduled, her hours filled with work and purpose. Sitting around now, waiting for something to happen, was driving her crazy, especially as Bernard barely noticed her presence. What had happened to the ardent lover who had declared he was so lonely as he traveled the world by himself? What had happened to the pleading man who had said he needed her with him because life on his own was so desolate? What has happened, thought Jessica spiritedly, is that Bernard likes having someone in tow just in case he has an idle minute away from the sycophantic adulation of his fans—an idle moment during which he might be forced to entertain himself! He doesn't want *me*, Jessica thought furiously, he wants a bimbo with whom to decorate his bedroom! Someone who's always there looking pretty and sexy, ready to boost his ego and pander to his needs.

"If you're not ready to go to lunch, I am!" she exclaimed, flouncing toward the door.

"Wait!" Bernard commanded, raising his hand.

"What for?" she retorted. "To starve to death?"

But that night as she sat in the concert hall watching as Bernard conducted the great orchestra and his music filled the air with its unbearable sweetness, her irritation and growing resentment vanished. The magnificence of his melodies as they washed over her stirred her deeply, filling her with worship for this talented man whose music thrilled millions. *And he's all mine*, Jessica said to herself, overwhelmed by the thought. He is mine to care for and look after; mine to love and adore. I am the person with whom he spends his nights . . . At that moment she realized how envied she must be by other women. Bernard wasn't only a rich and highly successful man, he was a star in his own right, and a musical genius. She was lucky to have him in her life, she told herself as the violins sang out with pathos and the muffled drums found an echo in the thudding of her heart, and I should appreciate him more, she reflected as full-throated trumpets took up the melody and the cymbals exploded in a spine-chilling crash of excitement. Bernard is a great man, Jessica reminded herself as her eyes grew moist at the passion of the music, and I love him with all my heart and mind and soul.

At breakfast the next morning, which they had in their suite, an altogether more prosaic atmosphere pervaded as Bernard grumbled about one thing after another. The concert had been lousy. The first violinist ought to be shot. The party afterward was a disaster, and why had the car been forty minutes late to collect them afterward? He'd slept badly because the room was too hot, and he'd been awakened at dawn by road repairs going on under their bedroom window. On and on he went, finding fault with everything and everyone, until Jessica finally lost her temper. This was not the godlike creature she had put on a pedestal the previous night, but a petulant, spoiled little boy who seemed to think the world should revolve around him.

"Oh, for God's sake, Bernard, do shut up!" she exclaimed crossly. "You're *never* satisfied! You always find something to complain about. Why can't you relax? You don't seem happy unless you've got something to be unhappy about."

"Nonsense!" Bernard raged back. "I just don't like inefficiency. Look what happened a minute ago! I tried to put through a call to Paris . . . and the stupid operator cut me off." He looked as offended as if he'd been mortally insulted. "Now it means I must try again, and I have better things to do with my time than waste it fighting with stupid little girls on a switchboard."

"I'll try to get through for you," Jessica said resignedly. "Anything for the sake of peace," she added *sotto voce.*

"What was that?" Bernard roared.

"I said anything for the sake of peace," Jessica repeated sullenly. "You get so worked up about everything, and frankly, life's too short."

"No, I don't!" he retaliated. "I've a right to expect telephone operators to work efficiently . . . and I don't see why I should put up with a hot, noisy bedroom in a five-star hotel. Do you? . . . Well, answer me? Do you? Were any of the guests at the Royal Westminster subjected to massive road repairs going on right under their bedroom windows, and the central heating turned on during a heat wave?"

"Don't be ridiculous! The heating was *not* turned on last night—"

"Why do you always argue with me?" he cut in, his tone aggrieved. "Why do you never take my side when something goes wrong? I expect loyalty from you, Jessica—"

"Oh, this is bloody absurd," Jessica exclaimed, banging down her coffee cup and rising. "I'm going to have a shower." She hurried to the bathroom, closing and locking the door behind her. Bernard had made her so angry that she didn't trust herself not to throw something at him. How, she asked herself, could a mature man of such enormous talent sink to the level of behaving like a superbrat?

When she went back to the bedroom to dress, she heard Bernard talking on the telephone in the next room, as blithe and cheerful as if nothing had happened. Which was all fine and dandy for him, she thought, but she was getting a bit tired of living on an emotional switchback.

It wasn't until they arrived at their next destination, Paris, the following day, that Jessica realized the full extent of Bernard's moodiness.

They were booked in at the Hotel George V, near the Etoile, in Paris, and two nights later Bernard was to give a concert at the Théâtre Musical de Paris. As usual, they were given the best suite in the hotel, which had once been a French palace, and the full VIP treatment.

When they'd arrived from Milan it had been so late they'd gone straight to bed and hadn't awakened until noon the next day. According to the itinerary Jessica saw, it was marked as a "free day" for Bernard, but from experience she knew that didn't mean a thing. Bernard wouldn't be happy unless he was talking on the phone for hours, contacting friends, acquaintances, and colleagues, whether they were in Europe, Australia, or America, and then he'd set up meetings to check on every detail of the forthcoming concert, although there were plenty of people whose job it was to do that. Finally he'd arrange to meet a score of people in the late afternoon. It was always the same: a restless round of self-inflicted commitments that left Jessica either hanging around waiting for him or trailing along after him. Today she decided to do her own thing. She hadn't been to Paris for ages, and she would combine looking around the city again with some shopping.

Bernard's reaction to this was to throw up his hands in a gesture of helplessness. "Shopping again?" he almost moaned. "Dear God, don't you do anything but buy clothes? You must be spending a fortune with my credit cards."

"But it was you," Jessica gasped, stung to the core by the injustice of his words, "*you* who insisted I should use your credit cards! *You* who said I shouldn't make a fuss because I'm not able to earn my own living anymore and it was . . . And I am *not* spending a fortune on clothes!" Incensed, she had jumped to her feet, and was hopping angrily in front of him, her eyes blazing.

Bernard's hooded eyes swept coldly over her. "You're always buying clothes," he retorted accusingly. "Every time I see you, you've got on something different; every concert I give, it's another evening dress. Why do you bother anyway? You're not the one who's in the limelight, you know. Who's going to be looking at you anyway?" He waved an imperious hand as if to dismiss her, and went back to reading his newspaper.

"That's the nastiest thing I've ever heard!" Jessica exploded, dumbfounded by his rudeness and arrogance. "Don't you dare talk to me like that! I may not be a star, but I *am* a person! And don't you *dare* throw up in my face that you have to pay for my clothes. You know I'd much rather be earning my own living!"

Bernard shrugged as if he were already bored by the subject. "Well, stop spending so much of the living *I* earn."

Jessica grabbed her purse, whipped out her wallet, and wrenched all his credit cards from one of its pockets.

"There!" she yelled. "And there! And there!" Plastic cards rained down on Bernard, bouncing off the edge of his coffee cup and showering the breakfast table. "Take back your cards! I'd rather *die* than use them now. You're the meanest, nastiest, most . . ." Her voice trailed away as large tears of rage popped out of her eyes and splashed down onto her satin robe. She gave a loud sniff.

Bernard looked at her, his eyes crinkled, and then with a guffaw he doubled up, rocking with laughter. His shoulders shook and his face had turned scarlet with mirth.

Jessica mopped the tears from her cheeks with the back of her hand and looked at him suspiciously.

"What's so funny?" she croaked.

"You . . . you . . . Ah-h-h . . . !" He went off into another paroxysm of laughter, rolling his head from side to side as he helplessly flopped back onto the sofa.

Jessica gathered her robe closer in an effort to look dignified, but it wasn't easy, with her hair disheveled and her eyes red-rimmed. Her chest heaved in an involuntary sob.

"I don't see what's so f-funny."

"*You* are!" Bernard gasped, wiping his own eyes. "You're hysterically funny. I've never seen an adult woman turn so quickly into a four-year-old child!" He gave another gurgle of mirth. "You should see yourself! Why are you so upset?"

"Because you're being unfair, unjust, and I won't be talked to like that!"

"Come here, little pet." Bernard held out his arms to her, his eyes gentle through their deep amusement, his voice soothing. "Come to me, my little pet . . ."

Jessica allowed herself to be cosseted, although she was aware that he was manipulating her. He was kissing her face softly now, holding her close, in a way that was partly fatherly and partly like a lover, and all the time he was whispering endearments. But these swings in mood were treacherous, Jessica knew. Sometimes she wondered if he wasn't nasty to her on purpose, either to prove to himself his power over her or because seeing her upset amused him. Either way, she was beginning to feel like a dice, shaken and thrown down at regular intervals, never knowing which way she'd land.

15

MILTON MANOR was as Madeleine remembered it, except that
the seasons had changed and the soft Devonshire landscape
had hardened and grown bleak with winter, its soil frozen
and its trees long since stripped of leaves. Once again Jenkins
met her at the station, silent and morose, and drove her along
the ice-bound roads and under overhanging branches lacy with
frost.

And I've changed since I was here last, she thought as she
sat in the back of the old car gazing out the window. I, too,
have hardened like the chilled earth, by being exposed to the
biting wind of reality, and there have been moments when I
thought I would perish. She thought of Carl, in bed with
Kimberley while she visited her grandfather in this very house
last summer, and she thought of the scheme Kimberley had
put to Carl, blackmailing him into going along with it. Then
she thought of the months of self-control she had been forced
to exercise, hiding from Carl the fact that she knew what was
going on, while all the time laying a trap for Kimberley to fall
into. What amazed her most, looking back, was her own
strength. If someone had told her six months ago that she'd
have to endure this living hell while pretending to be bright
and happy, she'd have said it was impossible. Yet she'd done
it, because she loved Carl and wanted to save their marriage;
but most important of all, because she knew Carl loved her.

But it wasn't over yet. Kimberley could still bring about his
downfall.

Hunter greeted her with his usual formality, but she could
tell he was pleased to see her again, and when she glanced
around the house, it was obvious that he and the other servants had been keeping it in pristine condition. Jenkins had
also been at work in the garden, for there was not a dead leaf

or twig lying on the ground, and the paths and lawns looked orderly and neat.

"Is there anything I can get you, madam?" Hunter asked, taking her case.

Madeleine had flown from Zurich that morning, and on landing at Heathrow, had taken a taxi into the center of London, collected her things and checked out of the Royal Westminster. When she caught a train for Okehampton, she'd been away exactly twenty-four hours and there was just one message for her: would she please call her husband in New York. He'd called at six o'clock the previous evening, English time.

"I'll take a shower," Madeleine told Hunter, "and then I'd like some coffee in the library. I've got some phone calls to make."

"Certainly, madam."

The pretty chintz-filled bedroom had been prepared for her again and it was warm and cozy as she entered. A log fire crackled in the pink marble fireplace, and a bowl of Christmas roses, white and delicate-looking as porcelain, stood in a vase by the bed. The curtains had already been drawn.

Twenty minutes later, bathed and changed into a long green woolen housecoat, her hair still damp and held off her face by a scarf, she sat at her grandfather's desk in the study and dialed the number of the Central Manhattan Bank.

"May I speak with Mr. Carl Delaney?" she said, as soon as she got through.

When Carl came on the line he sounded anxious. "Maddy? I've been trying to get hold of you! Where on earth have you been?"

"I'm sorry, darling. I had to look at so many—"

"There's been a panic here, and I desperately needed to get hold of you." His tone was slightly reproachful.

Madeleine's heart skipped a beat. "What do you mean? What sort of panic?"

"It's Patti. She's not well, and the doctors insisted she have some chest X rays done—"

"Oh, my God. Is she all right, Carl?" This was something she hadn't expected; she'd been so sure something had gone seriously wrong at the bank. "What did the doctors say?"

Carl let out a long breath. "She's been lucky, Maddy. She's got a chronic chest infection, but it's not lung cancer. We've

all had a bad fright, though. Patti didn't want you to know
while we were still afraid it was something serious, but I knew
you'd want to and that was why I was trying to get hold of
you."

"Oh . . . Carl!" Madeleine felt quite drained with shock. If
anything had happened to her beloved aunt, she'd have been
distraught. As it was, relief made her feel choked, so that what
she had to say next sounded more plausible.

"Carl . . . please come to England to be with me. I feel
absolutely strung-out . . . it's scary enough, having to go and
see my mother in the institution, but thinking what might
have happened to Patti . . ." Her voice broke off in a little
sob. "Please, darling," she begged, "please come to England
to be with me?"

"Sweetheart, you know I can't get away," Carl said reasonably. "We're up to our eyes in work at the moment. It's quite
impossible."

"Listen, Carl." Madeleine wasn't having to act now. Real
desperation to get him to leave New York gave her voice a
genuine ring of fear and her hands were shaking. "You've no
idea how badly I need you here. I can't cope with having to
see my mother on my own . . . and there's this house . . .
Oh, Carl, I don't often ask you a favor, but please, just this
once . . . even if it's only for a few days, please fly to England."

"I don't think I can, much as I'd like to, Maddy—"

"Carl, you *must* come," she broke in. If what Hank Pugsley
said was true, Carl must be a million miles away from the
bank when the balloon went up. "Please, sweetheart . . . I'll
talk to Daddy, he'll arrange for you to get away."

"All right, all right," Carl said soothingly. "I'll come, darling.
Don't get in such a state. I'll fix it with Jake myself. What's
gone wrong, Maddy? You weren't worried about meeting your
mother before you left here. What's suddenly scared you?"

She let out a little sigh. "I don't know. This place maybe.
All I know is that I want you here. Can you fly over
tomorrow?"

"Tomorrow!" Carl sounded startled. "For God's sake, I can't
just walk out of the bank like that . . ."

"Please, Carl." Never in her life had she used her powers
of persuasion with more force. If only she could tell him the
truth. If only she could tell him the months of fear and misery

were almost over. But right now she had to use her own fear of facing her mother as an excuse to get him to fly over, and she prayed to God it was a strong enough reason.

"Okay," she heard him say at last, and her heart swelled with relief.

"Let me know when you're arriving, Carl, and I'll meet you," she said, "and thank you, honey. You have no idea how good I feel now that I know you're coming over."

When she'd finished talking to Carl, she put through a call to Jake. She wanted to get her side of the story in first, and she wanted her father to realize how much she needed Carl at this time.

"That's fine," Jake said when she told him. "He could do with a break anyway—he's looking very tired these days. How long do you think you'll both be away?"

That was something Madeleine couldn't answer. To see her mother and wind up the estate with Mr. Marks would probably take only a few days; to put paid to Kimberley's activities might take longer, and that was now up to Hank Pugsley anyway.

"I'm sure we won't be away long, Daddy," she said, "and you'll encourage Carl to come over here, won't you? I really need him."

"Of course, honey. Don't worry about a thing."

Madeleine let out a long sigh of relief. So far, everything was working out just as she'd planned. In the morning she'd call Mr. Marks and make an appointment to see him, and she might even call Hank, just to ask how things were going.

Mr. Marks arrived promptly at noon the next day, delighted to accept Madeleine's invitation to luncheon, which she'd issued when she'd telephoned him earlier that morning.

"So kind . . . quite delightful . . ." he muttered, eyes blinking rapidly when he saw her.

Madeleine had asked Hunter to light a fire in the drawing room and they now sat in front of it, Mr. Marks with his glass of sherry, Madeleine with a gin and tonic. She looked rested and refreshed after a good night's sleep, and knowing that Carl was on his way had taken a great load off her mind.

"You said you had some information about your late mother," he began pedantically. "Has your father been able to give you the details . . . ?"

"Yes." Madeleine smiled gently, knowing what she was going to say would be a great shock to Mr. Marks.

"Ah . . ." He paused delicately. "You have traced the death certificate?"

"There is no death certificate. My mother is apparently alive." Briefly Madeleine told him what Jake had told her. "I have these documents for you," she continued, handing him a large brown envelope. "When she became ill, my father was given power of attorney, with the permission of my grandfather, so there should be no problem about my inheriting this house now. I'm afraid she'll never come back here."

"So . . . so she's at the Meredith House Institute, is she? My goodness me! My word!" Mr. Marks was deeply baffled. "And you never knew? All these years she's been alive . . . and you thought she'd died? That must be why your grandfather never made a new will; your mother was alive, and perhaps he thought she'd get better."

"That may be the answer," Madeleine replied. "That was certainly what he wanted to tell me, so that I'd go and see her sometimes, so there'd be someone to care."

"What an extraordinary story!" he exclaimed. "I've never heard anything like it! All these years . . . and your father knew, but he never told you." He continued to shake his head in wonderment.

"It's been rather a shock," Madeleine remarked, looking at him candidly. "My husband is flying over tomorrow, and as soon as he arrives, we'll go and visit her." As she spoke, she felt her stomach muscles tighten. She was actually going to be seeing her mother within the next couple of days—the mother she'd wondered about ever since she could remember, the mother she'd so wanted when she'd been a child, the mother she'd so feared on her last visit here. In the past week or so the existence of Camilla had been overshadowed by her other worries, but now she was about to come face-to-face with the woman of a thousand eyes who kept a journal about her black-magic experiences, whom no one had talked about for more than twenty years. Madeleine shuddered violently, as if a cold wind had touched her, and Mr. Marks looked up anxiously.

"Are you all right, Mrs. Delaney?"

"I'm fine," she said quietly. Mr. Marks wasn't exactly the type of man she felt she could confide in. After he had left, and Hunter had served a light lunch, Madeleine tried to settle in front of the fire with a newspaper and a novel she'd bought at the airport, but she felt restless and on edge, as if she was waiting for something to happen. She looked around the drawing room, pretty and innocuous as any room in a typical English country house now that all the pictures of Camilla had been removed, and wondered why she still felt uneasy. The fact that she now knew her mother was alive should have lightened the atmosphere, because the living do not haunt, but still she seemed to feel a ghostly presence in the room, and after a few more minutes she left it and went into the hall. Jenkins was walking toward her with a basket of logs, and as their eyes met, Madeleine knew the moment had come when she must get him to tell her everything. She followed him back into the drawing room and stood watching as he transferred the logs from his basket to the side of the fireplace. The only sound in the room was the crackling and sizzling of the fire, and in Madeleine's head the thudding of her heart.

"Jenkins," she began, then waited for him to turn and look at her. His back view looked stern and unbending, and for a moment she wondered if he was going to ignore her. "I'd like to have a few words with you, Jenkins," she said more strongly. "You see, I know my mother's still alive . . . and I know she's in a mental home . . . and I also know it's got something to do with the black magic and witchcraft she was involved in . . ." Madeleine broke off as Jenkins spun around to look at her. She couldn't tell from his eyes what he was thinking, but there was something fearful in his look.

"Who told 'e that?" he croaked, his Devonshire accent rich and strong.

"My father told me," Madeleine replied, watching him closely, "but he wouldn't discuss what had caused it. You know, don't you, Jenkins? It was you who took from the library the diary she'd kept, relating her satanic experiences, wasn't it? All along, you've known what happened, what made her go crazy. I'm asking you to tell me now, Jenkins. Please. I'm an adult, and I shall be going to visit her as soon as my husband arrives from the States. It would help me a great deal if I knew what had happened; it would help me to cope with her . . . and the situation."

While she'd been talking, Jenkins had remained on his knees

in front of the fire, his gnarled, work-worn hands nervously rubbing the brass fender, his eyes fixed on her face.

"Dear Lord . . ." He seemed to be offering up a prayer, as if asking for guidance, and for a moment he closed his eyes.

Madeleine dropped onto her haunches beside him, her full-skirted gray dress falling into heavy folds around her feet, her black hair tinged with blue by the light of the fire. Tentatively, desperate now to get him to respond, she stretched out a hand toward him.

"Please, Jenkins. You've no idea how much it means to me to find out the truth."

She watched his face, and the deep lines seemed to deepen; there was wetness around his eyes. His mouth quivered.

"Lord bless you, miss, and you were such a bonny little girl," he said gruffly. "It would have been murder if anything had happened to you that night!"

Jostled by crowds scurrying home from work at the end of the day, Kimberley walked the last two blocks to her apartment that evening. She wanted to buy some groceries, but more important, some liquor. Her men friends had a habit of calling up unexpectedly and inviting themselves over, and she liked to keep a well-stocked bar. Not that she was expecting anyone tonight, thank God, she thought as her high-heeled boots crunched on the icy sidewalks and the piercingly cold wind bit through her clothes. She had planned a quiet evening on her own, to wash her hair, have supper, and watch a movie on TV. The sort of evening she liked to have occasionally, when she could relax and do nothing but pamper herself. She bought herself a steak, some salad, and some fruit, and then as an afterthought a section of rich dark chocolate cake from the delicatessen across the street. Hell, she reflected as she entered the lobby of her apartment house, who cares about a few extra calories! Her figure was superb, without a trace of fat anywhere. No need to worry about dieting yet.

There was a letter in her mailbox; the moment she saw the Swiss postage stamp and the familiar white envelope, her heart gave a little bound of joy. Taking the elevator up to her apartment, she let herself in and hurriedly dumped her shopping on the floor, lit one of the lamps, and ripped open the envelope with fingers that shook with excitement.

Kimberley knew it was risky, having the Banque Internationale send her monthly statements, but she couldn't resist seeing, in black and white, exactly how much money she had deposited in Switzerland. To see it made it seem more real; to count it was as comforting as counting the cookies in a jar for a small child. The words "Credited" and "Balance" were music in her ears. Each month, the "Credited" column showed how much she'd transferred into her account, and the figures under "Balance" rose steadily, the number of fat naughts increasing all the time. It reassured her to know every month that she was becoming a very rich woman. Soon she'd be able to vanish from New York, pick up the cash in Zurich, and then disappear into . . . Italy perhaps. Kimberley Cabot would no longer exist.

Eagerly she pulled out the folded statement. Maybe Hank could resist seeing how much he had stashed away, she thought, but she couldn't. She liked to check that every transfer had gone through, and then double-check the final total. Even the best banks made mistakes; no one was going to make a mistake with *her* account. Today she figured her balance must stand at three million, seven hundred and eighty-two thousand dollars. Exactly. Of course, if only she'd been able to put through the last transfer, that would have been a further three hundred and sixteen thousand dollars! She bit her lip, still deeply vexed that her computer disk seemed to have been wiped clean. It was something she still couldn't understand. The tape had been permanently in her possession; how could it have been erased? And she still had to think of a way of getting around Jake's new security methods so that she could make another copy.

Feeling an almost physical thrill, she unfolded the statement and smoothed it flat on her knee, her eyes sweeping down the "Balance" column. Then she started, eyes popping out of her head. That *couldn't* be right! Something had gone terribly wrong with the Banque Internationale's computer! It had made a mistake and she must call Zurich right away! Her heart was hammering now as her panic-stricken eyes swept down the columns. Just under four weeks ago she'd transferred three hundred and twenty-one thousand dollars . . . yes, there it was in the "Credited" column. Relief swept over her momentarily until she caught sight of a row of figures in the "Debited" column. *Debited!* her mind shrieked. But she hadn't withdrawn any money! And then she saw it—the amount she had expected to see at the bottom of the "Balance" column. Three million, seven hundred and eighty-two thousand dollars. But it had all been withdrawn the previous week! The only thing at the bottom of the column were the words "Amount: Nil. Account closed."

Kimberley slid off the chair to her knees, sobs of rage tearing at her throat. Someone had taken her money—*all of it!* She pounded the floor with her fists as tears of fury poured down her cheeks. Spitting obscenities and cursing with rage, she clawed the air and rolled on the floor, beside herself with wrath.

"My money! My money!" she moaned as a mother will cry out in anguish at the loss of her child. "My money!" Convulsed, tearing at her hair, her face twisted in a paroxysm of bitter passion, she writhed about as if demented. It was *her* money! *Her* savings! She was the one who had taken the risks and she was the one who deserved to be rich! It was her future too . . . all that she had ever dreamed or planned for. Gone! As if it had never been. The deep pain of her loss coursed like a virulent poison through her veins, and for a moment she felt capable of killing.

"I'll get him for this!" she screamed, picking up an ashtray and hurling it across the room. Then, with a violent move she kicked over a lamp and it went crashing to the ground. "That fucking bastard! He won't get away with this. I'll see him dead first," she screamed. Inflamed into a passion in which reason played no part, Kimberley thrashed around her living room, smashing what she could pick up and throw, kicking or pushing over what she couldn't. And everything she threw and kicked and punched was Carl. She'd get him for this! She'd go to Jake Shearman and all the other directors of the Central Manhattan Bank and then she'd go to the FBI and she'd bring about Carl's ruin if it was the last thing she did. Thoughts of revenge, like a towering black wave, swamped her and drenched her, carrying her along a treacherous path where she saw herself bringing about the final downfall of Carl . . . and his damned wife too. Flinging herself onto the sofa, which stood amid the destruction she had wrought, she stared into space, her gray eyes wild, her hair a tangled mess. Her mind was already formulating a plan. She had been cheated, and she'd get even. The bastard was not going to get away with it, sitting in his fucking Fifth Avenue apartment with everything he could ever want, while she slogged it out for the rest of her life behind a desk.

Kimberley closed her eyes for a moment, gathering her thoughts. She'd say that Carl had forced her to make a copy of the computer disk he'd stolen from Jake's office, because he wanted to embezzle Hank Pugsley's money. She'd say he blackmailed her into doing it—threatening to expose the fact that she'd once been a prostitute unless she did as he said. And because she'd wanted to keep her job at the bank . . . Kimberley nodded to herself, pleased with that line. Yes, it would work very well. Then she'd say Madeleine had barged into her apartment one day—which was true—threatening her.

That was it! Kimberley's inflamed mind worked frenziedly, making sure her story was watertight and making sure that what she had to say would ruin them both forever.

She went over her story again and again, until finally her rage exhausted itself and gave way to tears of sheer misery. Kimberley started sobbing at her lost fortune as if her heart would break, knowing that her dreams would never come true now. The little girl who had stood in Times Square, dazzled by the lights that blazed their tempting message of prosperity, was still inside the woman who crouched huddled on the sofa, so that now, together, they mourned their loss; the dream was but a dream. The string of lights would never become a string of diamonds now, and her tears were as much for sorrow at the little girl's disappointment as for her own.

The room was in semidarkness now, lit only by the one lamp she'd switched on when she'd come in, and through the uncurtained windows the blackness of an icy night, friendless and stark, lay like an uncharted sea. Of course, she didn't have to tell the FBI anything, she thought as she wiped her face with the palms of her hands, smudging the eye makeup. She wanted revenge more than anything, but wouldn't she be cutting off her nose to spite her face? Common sense began to prevail as Kimberley got a grip on herself and tried to control the occasional childlike sob that shook her frame. Crushed by her loss, and filled with a tired despair, she nevertheless began to realize that in making Carl and his wife suffer, she'd only be adding to her own suffering too.

If she did nothing, no one would ever know what had happened. Certainly Carl and Madeleine weren't going to talk, so . . . Suppose she left her job at the bank, got another job, maybe in modeling . . . Her fertile mind began to write a whole new scenario, with herself, as always, the central figure, the heroine.

When the doorbell shrilled in the darkness of her apartment lobby, she paid little attention at first. She wasn't expecting anyone, and she was still too couched in misery, too much in a state of shock, to want to see anyone. But it rang again, strong and persistent, demanding attention.

Slowly, stumbling over the wreckage she had created, Kimberley went to the door, accidentally tripping over the bags of groceries and liquor she'd placed there earlier. Swearing, she fumbled for the lock just as the bell rang out again. It scared her this time, ringing out with piercing loudness just by her ear, and inflamed with irritation, she grabbed the handle and jerked the door open. Too late, she realized she'd forgotten to put on the safety chain because she'd been in such a hurry to open her mail.

A second later Kimberley's terrified screams echoed and reechoed along the deserted corridors of her apartment house, heard only by those who chose to mind their own business. In the dim light she could make out the great bulky figure and sweating moon face of Hank Pugsley.

"Murder?" Madeleine repeated, shocked. "My grandfather said something . . . What was it? Oh, yes, he said something had nearly led to my death, but I don't understand, Jenkins. What happened?"

The old gardener remained on his knees in front of the fire, dabbing his watery eyes with a red-and-white-spotted handkerchief.

"You really wants to know, miss?" he asked, almost in a whisper, his rich Devonshire accent thick and pronounced. "Sir George, he hushed up the whole thing at the time, though everyone in the village knew what had happened. And your father, miss, Mr. Jake Shearman, he threatened to sue anyone and take them to court if they so much as breathed a word of what happened that night. That's why I durstn't tells you nothing when you asked before, not even when all the village people at Sir George's funeral looked at you, curious-like. But they remembered 'cos it would be hard to forget, it would."

Madeleine leaned forward, straining to hear and understand every word he said. "But I do want to know, Jenkins. I must know if I'm to meet my mother. What happened? Was there an accident?"

Jenkins shook his head morosely. "It were no accident, miss. It were the doing of the devil."

Something in the way he said it made Madeleine catch her breath. "So my mother *was* involved in witchcraft?"

"Oh, aye." The old man nodded vigorously. "Your mother, she got involved in a witches' coven. They were led by a man who called himself the 'master.' They used to meet on Friday nights, up in Warrener's Copse, where there used to be an old barn. Strange things did happen on them nights. Bad things. Put the fear of God in me, all right, did those bad things." His accent and way of speaking made Madeleine lean closer, listening intently.

"How did my mother get involved?"

Jenkins shrugged and looked down at his strong old hands as if seeking some solution to her question. "I don't rightly know," he said at last. "Maybe it was because she got low after her ladyship died. Proper hold they had on her, though. All the time your father was working in London, she was gettin' deeper and deeper in, and I warned Sir George, but he wouldn't listen."

"My grandfather knew what was happening, but did nothing to stop her?"

"As far as Sir George was concerned, Miss Camilla could do no wrong," Jenkins replied.

Madeleine was touched by the respectful way the old gardener still referred to her grandparents and her mother. "Did my father know?" she asked.

"I didn't think it was my business to go telling your father. After all, I was just the gardener here. Then, one night I went up to the barn on Warrener's Copse, over Pendlebury way, where I knew the coven used to meet, because I heard strange noises." His voice dropped to barely a whisper and his eyes took on a fearful expression, as if the memory of that night still haunted him.

"They'd just sacrificed an animal," he continued. "I could hear them chanting and I looks through a crack in the window, and I think they were smearing someone with blood. It was terrible to see the strange things that were going on. Then, all at once . . . I heard them say your name."

Madeleine stiffened, knowing, before he said it, what was coming. She could just imagine the old barn with a makeshift altar set up in the middle, surrounded by the men and women wielding phallic symbols and dancing and chanting, naked in the candlelight around the sacrificed animal.

"It was to be *you* next time," Jenkins breathed almost inaudibly.

"No!" Madeleine sprang to her feet, horror making an icy shiver crawl down her spine and her face blanch to whiteness. "No!" It was a protest, a wild cry to blot out the terrifying images that sprang before her eyes. Her own mother had been prepared to have her sacrificed!

"That can't be true," she whispered brokenly. "You must have heard wrong. That's too horrible an idea, my mother would never have . . ."

Jenkins continued as if she hadn't spoken, as he gazed at the burning logs in the fireplace. "Then I run back to me cottage, not knowing what to do, like. It was no good going to Sir George again, because he wouldn't listen. And there wasn't much time. I'd heard them talk about 'midsummer eve,' and that was just two days away."

The silence was so heavy in the drawing room that it seemed to close in on Madeleine like a tangible force, blocking out all outside sounds, as if she was at the bottom of a deep pool. Only the roaring in her ears of her hammering heart made her believe this moment was real. What Jenkins was saying had the quality of a nightmare, with her and her mother as central figures moving like ghosts in another time and age. She looked down at her hands, slim artistic hands, with only her gold wedding ring for ornamentation, and she wondered if these very hands had held on trustingly to her mother . . . a mother who had led her as a child from her cot and taken her to a place of unspeakable evil . . . a mother who had been ready to sacrifice her to some satanic god for reasons best known to herself. Had she cried out? Clung to her mother's skirts? Begged to be protected?

Madeleine closed her eyes, feeling sick. "What happened?" She spoke so low, Jenkins could barely hear her.

He turned his weatherbeaten face toward her, and in its deeply carved lines there was a certain nobility, an honesty and integrity that made her realize at that instant there was something very special about him. The faded blue eyes, still moist with emotion, looked at her with something like compassion.

"I got in touch with your father in London," he said slowly, as if measuring each word, trying to spare her the worst of the shock and agony that already she knew was to come, "and your father, he come down as quick as he could, because he didn't believe what I had to say. But he believed me, all right, when he arrived late at night, all the way from London, and neither you nor your mother could be found in the house. Sir George, he said he didn't know where you'd gone, and then your father got real worried. Rushed round the house shouting and hollering your names: 'Camilla,' he yelled, 'where are you? Where's Madeleine?' And then Sir George got anxious too, and they both looked at me."

There was a long pause as Jenkins seemed to relive that moment, probably the most important moment in his life, when a child's life hung in the balance, a child he had the power to save. Madeleine held her breath, spellbound, hanging on his words.

"I said to 'em, 'Follow me,' and I led them to the barn up on Warrener's Copse," Jenkins continued.

Madeleine could hardly bear to hear any more, feeling the cold wind sweeping across the lonely copse, seeing the barn, the candles, the altar standing ready. She closed her eyes and buried her face in her hands, and suddenly she was trembling with a barely remembered terror that flashed through her mind. A knife, chanting voices, naked flesh, and eyes, dozens of eyes, that burned like lasers into her body as she lay there . . . and a man's voice.

"Oh, Christ!" she cried out. "Oh, dear God!"

"Aye," Jenkins said ponderously. "We got there in time, your Dad and me. He ran forward and grabbed you off the makeshift altar they'd built, and I caught hold of Miss Camilla

. . ." The tears started to roll down his cheeks again and he dabbed them ineffectually with his spotted handkerchief. "I'd known her since she was a little girl too. Wild she was, that night. Screamed and raved, and it took me all me time to get her out of the barn and drag her back to the house here. You weren't harmed, though you were bawling your head off, and Sir George rang for the doctor. Your dad rang for the police."

Madeleine was crying too now, crying for the lost mother and the lost child and the terrible night which, but for Jenkins, might have ended in a heinous crime. It was as if something that had been locked inside her all her life had been revealed and had exorcised dark memories that had always been just beyond her reach before.

Jenkins continued: "They couldn't do nothing with your mother. Gone clean off her head, she had. Doctor said something about her being in a trance when your father and I broke into the barn, and the shock turning her mind, or sommat. But we'd got you out, all right, and that was the main thing." There was quiet pride in his voice now, but no more than if he'd grown a beautiful rose or planted a bed of fine lilies.

"You saved my life," Madeleine said, looking at him as he knelt with dignity, the only sign of emotion being the hand that clutched and reclutched the red-spotted handkerchief. "I shall always be grateful to you for that," she added with sincerity. "I had no idea . . . What happened when the police arrived?"

"Well, of course they'd all run off, and left the barn empty, hadn't they? Scarpered all over the country, leaving the place in a mess. There was one old woman in the village who was charged with being an accessory to attempted murder, but it came to nothing. Got into a lot of newspapers, though. Made a real stink. That was why Sir George was so angry with your dad. Had a real fight, they did. Sir George said the whole thing should have been hushed up to protect the Dalrymple family, and that the police should never have been called. I think your dad was right, myself. Those wicked people should have been caught and punished."

"And my mother?" Madeleine asked painfully. "Did she go into . . . ?" She couldn't finish the sentence. The whole thing was a tragedy: a beautiful young woman married to a wonderful and successful man, a lifetime of golden happiness with their little girl before them, and then a dark nightmare casting its shadow over them all, ruining Camilla's life and causing Jake such deep suffering.

"Miss Camilla was sent to hospital for treatment, but it didn't do no good," Jenkins said, answering her unspoken question. "She must have been at Meredith House going on twenty-two years now. She don't know anyone, of course. Don't even know who she is herself," he added sadly.

Madeleine looked up, surprised. "You've been to see her?"

"I go from time to time," he replied shyly. "I takes her a few flowers from the garden."

"Thank you, Jenkins. Thank you for everything," said Madeleine, rising. "I shall always be grateful to you for caring about my mother, and me, when I was small. Also for all the years you gave to my grandfather. I think the Dalrymple family owes you a big debt of gratitude."

He looked embarrassed, bundling his handkerchief into his pocket, then rubbing his hands before the blazing fire as if to warm them.

"I want you to know," Madeleine continued, "that I'll see that you're always looked after. Do you own the cottage you live in?"

"Why, no, it's part of the estate, ma'am," he mumbled, looking startled. "Sir George just let me and me wife live in it while I worked here."

"Then I'll get the solicitor to draw up the necessary papers, making you the owner," said Madeleine, "and apart from the bequest my grandfather left you, I'll give you sufficient income to live comfortably when you retire."

Scarlet in the face, hands shaking, Jenkins thanked her. She could see he was overwhelmed.

"I just hope I can go on working the garden when you sells the house," he added. Then he turned and looked out the drawing-room window at the stretch of lawn with its outer edges fringed by great elms and oaks and beech trees. "I loves that old garden, I do," he said simply.

Madeleine nodded, understanding. "You can rely on me to do all I can to persuade the new owners to keep you on. I'm sure it won't be a problem, and at least you can be sure of a roof over your head, and your own bit of garden, for the rest of your life."

"Yes, ma'am. Thank you very much, ma'am. The wife will be right pleased." At last he turned to her with a beaming smile before walking slowly to the door. Then he stopped, and gave Madeleine a final grin.

"I'm right pleased to have got that lot off my chest at last, too," he said with relief.

Madeleine held Carl in her arms as if she could never bear to let him go. "God, I've missed you," she whispered, pressing her cheek to his. "Thank you for coming over. You've no idea how badly I need you."

"Well, I'm here now, sweetheart!" He hugged her back and she thought how tired and strained he looked. Jake was right, Carl badly needed a break, although only she knew why.

"Did you have to abandon everything to fly here?" she asked as they clambered into the back of her grandfather's old Riley, which Jenkins insisted at driving at thirty miles an hour.

"More or less. I was able to delegate a lot, and Jake was very good about the whole thing. It's a particularly busy time of year, though; I'd never have gotten away if I hadn't been married to the boss's daughter!" Carl joked.

Madeleine felt inward relief. It looked as if she'd managed to get Carl out of New York in time. If he hadn't mentioned anything, then the balloon obviously couldn't have gone up yet. All she had to do now was keep Carl in England with her for perhaps another week, and with any luck it would be safe for them to return home.

"How's Aunt Patti?" she asked cheerfully.

Carl grinned. "You'll never believe this. She's given up smoking."

Madeleine's face lit up. "No! Really? Thank God for that! How on earth did she manage it?"

"A hypnotherapist was recommended to her. Apparently he has a high rate of success, and after only one session with him she threw away her Marlboros and walked out, saying she'd never smoke again."

"That's fantastic! Do you really think she'll stick to it? It would be wonderful if she did."

Carl sounded positive. "She got one hell of a fright, you know. Really thought her number was up! I don't think she'll touch another cigarette as long as she lives. Already she's started to complain about other people smoking!"

Madeleine laughed. "Now, that *does* sound like Aunt Patti."

Soon the car was turning up the drive that was so familiar to Madeleine now.

"So this is Milton Manor," Carl exclaimed. "I must say it's impressive-looking. Are you sure you want to sell it, darling?"

"Yes, and I've spoken to Andrew about it. He thinks he's already found a buyer, though he wouldn't say much at this stage. But as I told him, the best gardener in the world goes with the property, so whoever buys it is very lucky." Madeleine smiled at Jenkins as she got out of the car, and he beamed in response. It was as if a great weight had been lifted off his shoulders in the past twenty-four hours, and Madeleine knew it was because he'd told her everything.

"Who is he?" Carl whispered when they were alone. "He's like a little garden gnome."

Madeleine burst out laughing, amused by the accuracy of Carl's description. Then she grew sober, relating what he'd told her the previous day. Carl listened with growing horror, hardly able to believe his ears.

"You mean in this day and age . . ." he said incredulously. "My God, the whole thing sounds medieval. I can hardly believe it. You mean you were going to be killed as part of some satanic ritual . . . and that your mother was a part of it?" He shook his head. "Thank God for Jenkins, then, and thank God for your father. I'm not surprised he refused to tell you all this. It's a terrible story."

"I know," Madeleine agreed. "It explains so much, and I can understand why Daddy wouldn't have it mentioned . . . and I'm scared, Carl. What's she going to be like? Apparently she won't have any idea who I am. Jenkins said she doesn't know anyone, but I'm still nervous of having to meet her. That's why I wanted you here." It was true. She'd used her fear of meeting her mother as an excuse to get Carl away from New York, but now it had become a reality. Without Carl by her side, she didn't think she could go through it.

"Whatever happens, I'll be with you, Maddy," he assured her tenderly. "It's probably just as well she doesn't know anything. Imagine how she'd feel if she did."

They went up to bed early that night, to Madeleine's pretty bedroom, where one of the maids had lit a fire and turned on the softly shaded lamps. The flower-patterned counterpane had been folded back to reveal an inviting downy nest of pure white linen and lace, and when Madeleine saw it she felt a sudden stab of desire. How long had it been since she and Carl had made love—really made love, away from the pressures of the bank, which had hung over them both like a towering shadow? She sat down on the chaise longue that stood before the fire, gazing into its glowing depths, wondering if Carl felt the same. Or did he still think of Kimberley and remember what she'd been like in bed? Madeleine forced the thought out of her mind and concentrated instead on the logs that flamed and flickered before her.

Carl undressed, and putting on his blue silk pajamas, came and sat down beside her.

"Are you all right?" he asked, looking at her profile, wondering what she was thinking.

Madeleine stretched out to caress his thigh. The silk felt sensuous beneath her fingers, and her hand slithered higher.

"I'm fine," she said softly, "but I've missed you." As she spoke, she could see the stirring of his passions, and looking deeply into his eyes, she slid her hand higher still. Carl took her hand and held it tightly.

"God, I've missed you too," he replied, and Madeleine could detect that same quality of desperation she'd noticed before, during that weekend at Oyster Bay. It was not the desperation of frustrated passion, but of a deep sadness and regret, as if he could never undo what he had done, and as if he'd lost something precious he'd never find again.

"I love you, Carl, more than you'll ever know," she said softly as she looked at his beloved face in the flickering flames of the fire. "You know that, don't you?"

Carl put his arms around her, his eyes shut. "And I love you too, Maddy," he said simply.

They kissed with tenderness, her hands cupping his face as his tongue gently explored the softness of her mouth. Then he removed the long velvet dress she'd worn for dinner, slipping it off her shoulders and revealing her perfect breasts, pulling it down over her slim hips, his hands caressing her skin as he did so, his mouth leaving a fiery trail of kisses.

Madeleine whispered with longing, "Oh, Carl, I want to feel you inside me."

"Maddy, my darling Maddy . . ." Carl kissed her deeply, as if he could never bear to let her go. She relaxed, melting in his arms, blocking her mind to everything except the strength of him, the heat of his body, and the sound of his voice. Together they lay in front of the fire, their bodies glowing pink in the firelight, their breathing the only sound in the room.

"My love . . . Oh, God, my love," Carl cried out as he entered her. She was clinging to him with a fever of passion now, wanting him to fill not only her body but also her mind, to wash away the pain and anxiety that had blighted her for so long, to restore the trust and belief that it was only her he loved and to give back to her the peace of mind that once she'd taken for granted.

"Love me . . . love me forever," she begged between her kisses.

"I'll love you as long as I live," he vowed, thrusting deeply inside her. "Take me, Maddy. Take me. I'm all yours."

In the dim red light she could see the outline of his golden body as part of her body now. They moved in unison, transported to a level of such intoxication that they were unaware of their surroundings, heedless of the ringing of the bedside phone. As wild, tumultuous waves of piercing pleasure drove Madeleine to a fevered desire for fulfillment, Carl climaxed with a wrenching rush that left him shuddering and calling out her name.

Beached, as if giant waves had thrown her high and cast her down again upon some distant shore, Madeleine lay dizzy and drained by the violence of her emotions. Then, as if from a long way away, she heard Carl speak.

"Is anyone going to answer that damned phone?"

She became aware of the incessant shrilling of a bell, but then it stopped and she snuggled closer to him, feeling the pounding of his heart as he lay struggling to get his breath back. A few minutes later there was a tap on the bedroom door.

Carl raised his head and looked unbelievingly toward it.

"Yes, what is it?" he shouted.

They could hear Hunter's voice, clear and concise. "I'm sorry to disturb you, sir, but there is an urgent call for you. It's from a Mr. Shearman at the Central Manhattan Bank in New York, and he says he must speak to you immediately because something has happened at the bank."

16

IT WAS in Sardinia, where the turquoise sea lapped along the sun-drenched platinum beaches and the perfume of wild thyme and rosemary and rock myrtle lingered in the air, that Jessica realized with a shattering suddenness that she was no longer in love with Bernard.

The previous week, after the concert in Tokyo, Bernard had decided in a temperamental flurry of anger that he wished to return to his home, bringing to an end his tour then and there.

"I'm tired," he declared petulantly. "I can't be expected to continue week after week like this! I'm not a machine! I am exhausted."

Jessica felt torn between longing for a break herself and thinking Bernard was behaving unprofessionally.

"But you're abandoning the whole tour!" she told him. "What about all the people who've bought tickets? What about the organizers? The advertising? It's going to be a major disappointment for all the people who admire you."

"Why should I care about those people?" he shot back. "My health is more important, and my creative ability! To hell with other people. I couldn't care less."

Jessica remained silent, seeing what a bad mood he was in and knowing it would do no good to argue; this was a very different Bernard from the man she had fallen in love with. Gradually, over the weeks, she had had to cope with his moodiness and irascibility, and it was dawning on her that maybe this was what he was really like. Had she only imagined him to be good-tempered and considerate, blinded as she'd been by love? Or had he merely put on an act at the beginning, in order to seduce and ensnare her?

Now, a week after they'd arrived at the Villa Roccia di Volpe, she was sure that was what had happened. Accustomed to switching on the charm when he met friends or fans, none of whom he ever had to spend a long time with, he was unable to maintain those more pleasant facets of his character for any length of time, and Bernard, thought Jessica, stripped of his veneer of charm, was a very different person.

Unable to sleep one morning, Jessica rose at dawn and wandered through the cool white marble rooms to the veranda, where, wrapped in a misty dawn, lay the Cala di Volpe bay, its turquoise waters as smooth as silk. She curled up on one of the large bamboo seats and watched, with unseeing eyes, the first gray veil of dawn spreading itself over the landscape.

How could she have fallen out of love? Her head spun at the impossibility of the thought, and yet increasingly she'd grown tired of having her independence taken away from her, grown bored with not having a life of her own, and most of all, perhaps, become fed up with always having to dance to Bernard's tune. A smile flickered across her face at the unintended pun—Bernard's tune indeed!

In the garden of the villa, where tall cypress trees and exotic shrubs and flowers grew lush and ripe in the rich soil, Jessica could hear the gardener, who came every day, setting up hoses to water the rough grass. Soon the steady and soothing *phut-phut* of sprinklers filled the morning air.

Going into the kitchen, Jessica decided to make herself some coffee. When she got back to the terrace, it had grown lighter, and already the heat of the coming day was rising in warm bands, carried inshore by the trade winds. The scent of marjoram, sweet and pungent, mingled with the perfume of wild rosemary and myrtle, and from the shrubs came the soft shrilling of awakening cicadas. This is idyllic, she thought, propping her bare feet up on the low stone wall that edged the terrace, as she absorbed the beauty of the island's dawn.

And then, as if she had foreknowledge of what was going to happen, she knew that it would be very difficult to leave this place. Already she loved the villa, the gardens, and beyond, the beach, with its strange-looking rocks sculptured by thousands of years of wind and water. A part of her would remain here forever, she thought emotionally, rooted deep into the soil like the olive trees. On this island her soul had been touched by the beauty of nature, and she dreaded saying good-bye to it all. And yet a part of her knew that that was what was going to happen sooner or later.

At noon Bernard appeared, tousle-haired and naked under his toweling robe. Jessica, who was sunbathing after a swim, opened her eyes and smiled, longing for him to smile back so that she could reassure herself that her love for him was as great as ever; but he scowled instead, seating himself in the shade of a striped umbrella, cursing someone who had just phoned him from Rome, awakening him.

"But it's nearly lunchtime," Jessica pointed out reasonably. "You're missing the best part of the day by sleeping all morning."

"Nonsense! Anyway, I was working until late last night on the concerto I'm writing." Bernard glanced around angrily, as if displeased with everything he saw.

"What's the matter, Bernard?" Jessica suddenly demanded. She knew she was treading on delicate ground, because when Bernard was in this sort of mood, questioning him only made it worse, but something inside her couldn't resist needling him, almost as if she wanted to bring this whole discordance between them out into the open.

"Nothing," he replied sullenly.

"There must be something wrong. You're like a bear with a sore head!" With slim brown hands she pushed her blond hair back from her face, peering at him through the loose curls that floated around her face. "People don't get bad-tempered for no reason. Are you feeling ill?"

He gave a snort of annoyance; then, raising his voice, he bellowed to the servant who was setting the table for lunch: "Bring me some coffee and make sure it's strong!"

Jessica ignored the fact he was ignoring her, and reaching for the bottle of tanning oil, she remarked dryly: "Perhaps you're drinking too much coffee. It's supposed to make people feel stressed."

"Don't talk to me about feeling stressed," Bernard snapped. "You're the one who's stressed."

"I'm not!" She sat bolt upright with indignation. "Why should I be stressed?"

"That's what I want to know." His eyes narrowed as he regarded her, making her feel vulnerable and exposed, though she wasn't sure why. It was true she was edgy. She felt she was nearing some crisis in her life; half of her felt as if she was running away from whatever it was and the other half of her seemed determined to bring it to a head.

"It's just that . . ." she began, but then she paused. How do you tell someone, after you have given up everything to be with him, that you think you are no longer in love? It sounded crazy. It *was* crazy! There was no way it made sense, but right now, neither did she, she decided. Something was falling apart inside her and she no longer knew how to hold it together. Why had she fallen out of love with Bernard when she'd been so besotted with him such a short time ago?

Later, as she lay on the terrace reading, she could hear Bernard in the music room, playing his latest composition on the piano. The music came floating on the still air, stirring her emotions, sending little thrills up her spine. She closed her eyes, letting the sweet cadences wash over her, and gradually she began to feel all her senses melt like ice in the sun. Her body became languorous and her blood seemed to flow thickly through veins suffused by desire. Her hand touched her breast accidentally as she put down her book, and a thrill, strong and vibrant, shot through her, making her realize how much she desired Bernard. The music continued, seductive and rapturous, winding its way like tendrils around the strings of her heart, invading her mind with images that cast her loose on an endless sea of rapture.

"Oh, I do love him," Jessica thought as she lay in a state of hot desire. "Of course I love him. He's the most wonderful man I've ever known . . . passionate, with such tender feelings . . . brilliantly talented, a genius. I love him with all my heart." Deep happiness flooded through her as she realized how lucky she was to have a man like this in her life, a man who could transport her, and millions of other people, with his music to heights of feeling they had not thought possible. So what if he was a bit temperamental? He was a creative artist, and one had to make allowances. No doubt Beethoven and Chopin and Rachmaninoff had had their bad-tempered moments too. Jessica smiled, making allowances for Bernard, as she always did. One couldn't expect someone as talented as he was, she told herself, to be like other people.

The music continued, the top notes fluttering teasingly, and then the melody flowing in the minor key, almost moving her to tears. A moment later the major chords, strong and powerful, made her smile again, and so she lay on the terrace, letting the strains manipulate her as the clouds above were being manipulated by the winds—swept forward, then held back; tossed about, then scattered until they disappeared altogether.

Then came a crashing, grating discordance, a shouted oath, and the falling of something heavy. Startled, Jessica opened her eyes and sat up. She could see through the windows into the music room, and to her horror, she could see Bernard throwing something at a frightened servant who stood too petrified to move. Bernard was yelling abuse at her, and the sight sickened Jessica. Then Bernard pushed over a chair in rage and went storming out the front of the villa.

It was as if a bucket of ice water had been thrown over Jessica, awakening her from her beautiful reverie. Shocked, she crossed the terrace, where the stones were so hot they burned her feet, and, entering the music room, looked around, dismayed. So much damage had been done in those few seconds. Sheets of music lay scattered, a table as well as a chair had been overturned, spilling books onto the floor, and a vase of flowers lay smashed, the water a spreading pool on the terra-cotta floor.

"What happened?" Jessica exclaimed, aghast.

The servant, a young local girl, was clutching her cotton skirts, a terrified expression on her face. Then she dropped to her knees and with trembling hands started to pick up the pieces of the broken vase.

"Are you all right?"

The girl whimpered and touched her head, where a bruise was starting to swell up on her forehead.

"You're hurt!" Jessica hurried forward, helping the girl to her feet. "Leave this mess . . . I'll see to it. You go to the kitchen and put some ice on your head."

The servant looked at her doubtfully, then shook her head in protest. "I'm okay," she whispered in a heavy Italian accent.

"You leave this to me," Jessica said firmly. She'd been used to dealing with staff of all nationalities at the Royal Westminster, and this girl reminded her of many of their chambermaids. Jessica guided her in the direction of the kitchen.

"Lie down for a while and put ice on the bruise. Now, don't worry—everything will be all right."

"It often happens . . . for no reason," whispered the servant.

"Then I think you should find work in another villa, where the people are kinder, don't you?" Jessica suggested briskly. Inside, she was seething with rage. How dare Bernard treat anyone like that! After she had cleared up the mess, she walked slowly back to the terrace, and it was at that precise moment that she knew exactly what was wrong with her relationship with Bernard.

He reappeared at lunchtime and blandly took a seat under the awning on the terrace as if nothing had happened. Jessica had no idea where he'd been for the past hour and she didn't really care; he was sipping his glass of iced Frascati as if he were unaware of her presence, and so she set about planning what she would say to him.

Now that she knew the truth about her feelings, her instincts were to flee, to get away from Sardinia and Bernard and the whole terrible mess she'd made of her life, and to go and hide somewhere quiet where nobody knew her. She'd been such a fool, she thought. How could she, an intelligent, successful woman of twenty-six, who'd been holding down a highly responsible, highly paid job with a great future, have made such an utter fool of herself? At the time, it had all seemed so right! But from falling madly in love with Bernard, which had blinded her to everything else, she now had to face the fact that the mists of infatuation had cleared and the stark truth had presented itself before her.

Bernard suddenly spoke. "Shall we have a swim before luncheon?"

"I'd rather talk," she replied. Bernard looked over to where she sat cross-legged on a lounge, a vividly colored sarong showing off the glorious tan of her shoulders and arms, her blond hair swept up on the top of her head in a tumble of unruly waves and curls. Her candid blue eyes were looking intently at him and her small mouth was, for once, serious.

"I might as well have another drink, then." He poured himself another glass of Frascati, and then, as an afterthought, offered some to her. Jessica shook her head.

"What do you want to talk about?" he asked.

Her voice quavered slightly. "You and me."

"I imagined so." Thoughtfully he sipped his wine and then said in a quiet voice, "I think I know what's coming."

"You do?" The faint sound of her gold bangles tinkled in the warm, still air. "You mean you've realized . . . ?"

"That you are no longer in love with me? Yes. Yes. I've realized, Jessica." He sounded weary, tired, as if he knew the score. "I was afraid of this happening," he added almost sadly.

"But I don't understand. Why do you think . . . ?" She became lost for words, confused, barren of thought. How could he know? She was sure she'd given no hint of her feelings during those moments when she felt she had nothing in common with him, but then, of course, she had also shown him her feelings when the magic of his music had lifted her to unbelievable heights of ecstasy.

"Tell me what you feel," he urged, leaning toward her, his eyes penetrating, the whole strength of his great personality focused on her at that moment, so that she felt like a tiny insect being looked at through a giant microscope.

Jessica looked back at him, faltering, wavering under the power of his gaze. "I think . . ." she began, then cleared her throat. "I think it's your music I'm in love with . . . not you." The last words were a whisper, barely audible.

Bernard nodded, seeming to understand her completely. "Like some people fall in love with the character an actor plays, and not the actor himself," he suggested.

Jessica pounced on the explanation. It so perfectly described how she felt. "That's right. That's exactly how I feel. When I hear your music, I'm totally carried away . . . transported—"

"It's not unusual," Bernard cut in. "That's why my wife left me. She adored my music but couldn't stand me or living my kind of life. Music can be a very dangerous and potent thing, Jessica, as you have found out. It can have more effect on human emotions than anything else on earth, because it is the language of the soul. Through music, any mood can be conjured up, haven't you noticed? Play a certain type of music, and everyone jumps to his feet and wants to dance. Play another kind, and everyone weeps. And play the type of music I compose, and you affect the heart and soul of the listener. That is what has happened to you, Jessica: the music has carried you away, but the reality of life, when the music stops, is something different."

Large tears trickled down Jessica's cheeks at the wisdom of his words. They were so true. Always an emotional person, she had let herself get carried away by the music, imposing on its creator all the beauty and the passion he'd brought into existence, without stopping to examine the man himself. She hung her head, feeling so childish, so utterly stupid, like an adult who'd just realized Santa Claus didn't exist.

"That's why I didn't ask you to marry me," she heard Bernard say. "I realized when my wife left me that marriage wasn't for me. Sooner or later, women always get fed up with me and my life-style. Music may be the food of love, as Shakespeare said, but unfortunately one needs something a little less romantic to keep one going on a day-to-day basis." He smiled wryly and reached out to stroke her shoulder. "Little Jessica, a born romantic," he murmured. "It is for women like you that I write my music. No one prosaic would be so affected by it."

Jessica stared at him, the tears drying on her bronzed cheeks, leaving little streaks of salt. "You thought this might happen?"

"I hoped it wouldn't." Bernard sounded sincere, and he continued to gaze at her thoughtfully. "But I could see all the signs coming on as soon as we started traveling. Living out of suitcases isn't anyone's idea of romance. I know that only too well."

"It isn't the traveling," Jessica protested, "it's just that you've become . . . well, a different person from the one I knew in London. I don't seem to know you anymore."

"You never did know me, Jessica. That's the whole point. There wasn't time. You came away with the person you thought I was, because of my music. When you got to know the real me, it was a different story. No man can live up to the dream lover a woman creates in her mind."

Jessica shook her head, still bewildered. Bernard seemed to understand what she felt, and was expressing it better than she could ever have done. "I don't know what to do," she said dejectedly.

"You can stay, or you can go home," he said gently. "It's up to you. But remember, if you stay you will have to put up with the real me, and the way I live. I can't pretend to be the romantic hero of your imagination in order to keep you happy. My job is to write music, make records, go on tours; it is as exacting a life as a lawyer's or a financier's. There is very little time for romance."

"But in bed . . ." Jessica faltered, painfully averting her eyes. "You were passionate in bed when we first met; you said you loved me. Were you acting then?"

He took her hand, holding it between his own two strong ones, smoothing her slender fingers. "I am a man like all men, Jessica. Of course I fell in love with you, and I did everything I could to get you to go to bed with me. It was wonderful and, believe me, I enjoyed every moment of it as much as I hope you did, but . . . men are different, darling. Once the chase is over and the conquest has been made . . . what is left but to repeat the act again and again until both the man and the woman are bored by it?"

Jessica looked up swiftly, angrily, wanting to deny his words, but he silenced her with a look before she could say anything.

"Relationships have to be based on reality," he continued. "They are not symphonies or grand operas, they are a part of real *life*." He stressed the word as if to reach through the tangled dreams that filled her head and obscured her real feelings.

"I understand," she said slowly.

"Think about it. There is no need to rush into a decision. You may find you can continue as we are, or you may find that reality is too painful, or too unpalatable, and if that is the case, you must go." He spoke without self-pity, as if he'd set the rules of the game and was perfectly happy to abide by them.

Jessica had guessed it would be difficult to leave the island, and now, as she packed her cases, a sense of finality lay over her like a black shadow, cold and bleak, a sentinel on the closing chapter of something that had started with a starburst of love and laughter and wonderful prospects. It was midafternoon and her flight was taking off at five-thirty. Dry-eyed and numb, she methodically folded her clothes and stuffed paper into the toes of her shoes, going through the motions like a sleepwalker, while the villa lay wrapped in the sultry silence of the afternoon and Bernard remained in his music room.

Resigned to the fact it was all over, Jessica calmly fastened her cases and went out onto the terrace for the last time. It was the magnificence of the bay she wanted to look at once more, so the memory of its aquamarine waters and surrounding lush greenery would remain with her always.

The only sound that broke the silence was the cicadas shrilling madly in the long grass. Feeling a sense of relief that it was nearly over, Jessica leaned on the parapet looking down to where the water gently lapped the shore, and then she heard it. Bernard's music—evocative, haunting, stirring, creeping into her being like a vapor, weakening her senses as she leaned against the warm stones, filling her with intense feelings that clamored to be assuaged. Raising her head, she looked up at the blue density of sky, and then, dizzily, she closed her eyes as the music seared her senses and ripped into her heart. With a quick bound she was across the terrace and through the glass doors into the music room. Bernard was sitting at the piano playing his latest concerto, a faraway look on his face as his hands moved over the keys.

"Don't you dare try that trick on me now!" Jessica shrieked, waving her small fists above her head. "That's the lousiest thing I've ever heard of. You *know* the effect your music has on me! It simply isn't fair!" Large tears splashed down her cheeks as she fought for control.

Bernard looked up at her, a knowing smile spreading slowly across his face. His hooded eyes bore into hers as he continued to play.

"You like this piece, do you?" he asked quietly.

"You know I do, damn you!" she yelled, quivering with rage. "You . . . you deliberately set out to upset me . . . and I think it's really nasty of you!" Angrily she wiped away the tears and tried to pin up her topknot, which had come undone and was cascading down over her shoulders. "Don't you dare do this to me!"

Bernard's mouth twitched. "My darling. I'm not doing anything to you, you are doing it to youself. I come in here to work on my music, and you get all excited and say I am playing dirty tricks on you." As he spoke, he continued to play, filling the room with rising cadences and swelling chords that thrilled with a promise of ecstasy.

Jessica clamped her hands over her ears. "Stop it! Stop it at once! I hate you, Bernard Scheller! You're a very dangerous man, do you know that?" She turned and ran out of the music room, still blocking her ears. Bernard threw back his head, laughing richly.

Jessica's high heels could be heard clattering on the marble floors, and then there was silence. The smile faded from Bernard's face and he sat looking reflectively through the glass doors to the terrace and bay beyond. He should have known Jessica better than to imagine she could be seduced into staying. Even by his music.

The plane rose from the runway like a powerful bird heading out to sea, breasting the stiff breeze, setting course for the northwest. Below, Sardinia lay like a topaz in an aquamarine setting, growing smaller all the time as Jessica sat watching out her cabin window. She looked at it for the last time, hardly able to bear the thought of the broken dreams she was leaving behind. She'd never be able to return; there was too much that reminded her of her own weaknesses and failures and the fact that she'd allowed herself to be overpowered by emotion. That was all over now. She'd said good-bye to Bernard for the last time, and now she had to look ahead. The dreams had gone, vanishing like stars behind a cloud. Only one thing remained, and that was something she would be sharing with the rest of the world: Bernard's music. It would live on after all the hopes and desires it evoked had faded away.

Carl's legs felt like lead as he crossed the bedroom to pick up the phone. A call from Jake, at this hour of night, saying there was something wrong at the bank, could mean only one thing. Cold sweat ran down his back, and in spite of trying to control himself, his hand shook as he reached for the receiver.

"Jake?" Somehow he managed to sound casual. Madeleine had come to lie on the bed to be near him, but he turned away so she wouldn't see his face.

"I'm sorry to disturb you . . . it must be quite late in England, isn't it?" Jake inquired genially.

"Er . . ." Carl was thrown. "Well, it's fairly late, but not to worry. How's everything?" He had the receiver pressed to his ear, hoping Madeleine wouldn't be able to hear what her father was saying. Stupid, really, he reflected. This was something he wouldn't be able to keep from her, not once it blew up in his face.

"It's about your secretary . . ." he heard Jake say. "There's been a bit of trouble, and I thought you ought to know."

This was it. The moment he had been dreading, the final terrible exposure of what he and Kimberley had been doing. It was obvious she'd been caught, and within no time now the net would close in on him. He knew what Jake was going to say even before he said it.

"I'm afraid Kimberley Cabot's been arrested, Carl . . . this afternoon. It's been a terrible shock, but I'm hoping we can keep it out of the newspapers, for the sake of the bank."

Carl sank weakly onto the edge of the bed, feeling as if someone had punched him in the stomach. "Arrested?" he echoed faintly.

"That's right." There was a long pause on the line as Carl sat there seeing the ruins of his life spread before him like a sea of wreckage. He'd really done it now. His marriage, his career, his whole future lay demolished . . . and he had only himself to blame. That one unguarded moment, when he'd felt lonely, had paved the path to his own destruction, and now he must face those fatal consequences.

Jake's voice broke into Carl's thoughts. "She's been charged with larceny . . ."

I know, I know, Carl's mind screamed in silent despair. You don't have to tell me; over three million dollars' worth of theft. Aloud he said, "What happened, exactly?"

"What is it?" Madeleine was asking. She was sitting on the bed beside him, trying to attract his attention. "What's going on?"

Carl spoke into the phone. "Hang on a minute, Jake. Madeleine wants to know what's happening." Carl cupped his hand over the mouthpiece, and managing to avoid catching Madeleine's eye, outlined briefly what Jake had said. Then he turned his attention back to the phone. "You were saying, Jake?"

"Give my love to Madeleine! Now, about this girl, Kimberley, it seems she had a boyfriend called Hank Pugsley . . ."

I know, thought Carl.

". . . and he had a grudge against her . . ."

He would have, Carl reflected.

". . . so he called in the police and had her arrested for stealing . . ."

Like three and a half million dollars, Carl said to himself.

". . . some jewelry from his apartment . . ."

"*What!*" Carl clutched the phone, frowning deeply.

"Stealing some jewelry from his apartment," Jake repeated. "He was particularly upset about a pair of diamond earrings that had belonged to his mother."

"But . . ." Carl paused, stunned with confusion. How could Kimberley have been such a fool? She'd been clever enough to think up a scheme that would rob Hank of millions, and then she'd gotten caught for petty larceny by pinching some earrings from his apartment. *I didn't even know she'd been to his apartment recently. Since when had she been seeing Hank again?*

"So she's been arrested?" Carl asked lamely. Madeleine, he'd noticed, had wandered away from the bed and was brushing her hair at the dressing table as if she'd lost interest. Maybe I'll get away with it, Carl thought for one wild elated moment, but then he knew he was kidding himself. Kimberley was probably laying the blame for everything on him, right at this moment, and it was only a matter of time before the world knew of his involvement. Maybe it would be better if he told Jake everything now. Get it over with. Carl's mind worked quickly, wondering if confession might not be better than waiting to be found out.

Jake continued: "Yes, she's being held at the local precinct now. They searched her apartment earlier, I gather, and found the stuff hidden under her mattress," Jake said, breaking into Carl's thoughts. "They'll probably keep her in custody overnight and charge her in the morning."

"Jake," Carl began slowly, "there's something . . ." How was he going to tell his father-in-law what he'd done? How on earth could he begin to explain what had happened? And yet the temptation to unburden himself, at last, of the secret that had tormented him for months now was so great he gripped the phone and started to speak again. At that moment, as if she'd been listening after all, Madeleine came hurrying across the room and took the receiver from Carl.

"Hi, Daddy. Don't you want to say hello to your only daughter?" she demanded gaily. "You interrupt my first evening with Carl to talk business, without a thought for me! Don't you want to know how I am?"

Jake laughed, always amused by her banter. "I wouldn't dare talk to Carl and *not* ask how you are," he responded.

Madeleine kept him talking for a few more minutes and then said, "Is that all? Is there anything else you have to tell Carl?"

"No. That's it. I just didn't want him to call his office and find that his secretary was missing because she was in jail! Sorry I disturbed you, darling."

"That's all right, Daddy. Just don't do it again," she joked. When she hung up, she turned to Carl and looked at him with an expression he didn't understand.

"You had nothing further to say to my father, Carl," she said pointedly. "Kimberley has been arrested, and I have a feeling that's the last you'll hear from her."

"I didn't take his stuff. I haven't even been to his apartment for about a year," Kimberley insisted.

As she sat at the table in the interrogation room of the police department, she felt a mounting sense of fury. Hank Pugsley had set her up, and she'd walked right into his fucking trap! The bastard was too clever to get her for robbing him of his dollars, because he'd incriminate himself, so he'd thought up this scam instead, leaving the evidence himself under her mattress.

I wish to God I hadn't lost my head when he came to see me the other night, Kimberley thought with clenched teeth. If I'd kept my cool . . . but I was so sure he'd come to kill me and so thankful when he appeared friendly, that I was caught completely off guard. She remembered the terror she'd felt when she'd seen him looming large and threatening in the corridor outside her apartment door. She'd screamed, certain now he'd found out what she'd done, sure it was him who had taken back all his money and somehow managed to close her Swiss bank account. The sound of her cries, high-pitched and loud, echoed in her own head as they reverberated down the passage.

"Hello, Kimberley," Hank had said gently, as if she hadn't made a sound, as if he'd seen her only a few days before. She'd stopped yelling when she saw he wasn't going to hurt her.

"Can I come in for a little drink? Long time no see." Hank inched his bulky form through the door, and automatically Kimberley stood to one side, wondering how she could ever have slept with this great slob of a man. Without replying, she led him into the wreckage of her living room, picking up her shopping bag of liquor as she did so. Hank ignored the mess and dropped heavily into one of her suede armchairs.

"So, how have you been?" he asked conversationally.

Striving to keep calm, wondering now if he *did* know she'd been systematically stealing from him for months, she replied, "Okay. And you?"

"Oh, I'm just fine." He sounded quite perky. "Have you got any Scotch? I've had a long day and I could do with a drink."

"Yes. Okay." Kimberley went into the kitchen to get some ice, her mind in a turmoil. Perhaps it *was* Carl who'd taken everything out of her account, after all. Maybe Hank had just dropped in for a drink, for old times' sake, and had no idea what had been happening. He'd certainly been very friendly, she thought rapidly, the ice cubes burning the tips of her fingers as she put them into a bowl, and he wouldn't have come there to be friendly if he suspected anything. Kimberley decided to be nice to him.

"Here's your drink," she said, smiling as she handed him his Scotch on the rocks. "Will you excuse me for a moment? I just want to freshen up."

Hank nodded benignly, like a sweating mandarin. Even the glass was sweating in his chubby hand. A few minutes later, Kimberley reappeared, her red hair brushed so that it fell in curls around her shoulders, and she'd slipped into a cream silk robe that fell open at the front, revealing her snowy cleavage.

"I'm sorry about the mess," she said lightly. "I was just about to clean up when you arrived."

Hank spoke softly, almost in a whisper. "That's all right. Don't worry about it. It's you I came to see. I've been thinking a lot about you recently."

Kimberley's heart skipped a beat, and she tried to keep her hand steady as she poured out a drink for herself. "You have?" she asked, sounding coy.

"Sure I have. Why shouldn't I? We had some good times together, babe."

"We sure did."

"In fact, you've been on my mind a lot recently." Hank gulped noisily at his drink and handed her the empty glass to refill. "Last time I saw you, you were planning to be a model. How did that work out?"

Kimberley poured more whiskey into his glass and added some ice. "I've done a little work, mostly fashion for the trades, but I'm hoping to get a new agent soon. I've met one, and she thinks I could make the cover of *Vogue*."

"Is that so?" Hank sounded genuinely interested. "Well, you know, babe, you can count on me if you need anything. I'm not in the fashion world, as you know, but I do have my contacts."

"That's very kind of you, Hank." She curled up on the sofa, covering her bare feet with the skirt of her robe.

"You'd like to be rich one day, and successful, wouldn't you?" Hank asked reflectively, never taking his eyes off her face.

Kimberley shrugged and gave a little brittle laugh. "Who wouldn't?" Then she thought about the three million dollars that had been hers, *hers*, and a shadow passed over her face. She'd never, as long as she lived, get over the loss of that money.

"Anything wrong, babe? Anything troubling you?"

She glanced nervously at Hank, forcing her stiff face into a smile, willing her mouth to turn up at the corners. "No. Why should there be? Tell me your news, Hank."

"Ain't much to tell. Business is as good as ever. Get a bit lonely at times, of course." In the semidarkness, his eyes seemed to glint lasciviously.

"Perhaps we can do something about that."

"Perhaps we can," Hank replied. "Are you sure I'm not disturbing your evening? Perhaps you're expecting someone?"

Kimberley was surprised by his consideration. She didn't remember him being that thoughtful in the past.

"No. I'm not expecting anyone." Suddenly she rose, longing for it to be over, longing to be alone with her misery and her heartbreak at her loss. "Shall we go, then?" With a nod of her head she indicated the bedroom.

"I'll finish my drink first, babe. You go right ahead," Hank replied.

Kimberley was lying on the apricot sheets, naked and with her hair spread out, when Hank entered the bedroom. He sat down on the side of the bed and undressed slowly. His weight made the mattress sag, and as Kimberley lay there looking at his back, she gave a little shudder of revulsion. But at least he was being nice to her, so he couldn't suspect a thing. She closed her eyes with a sense of relief that was even greater than her sense of disgust.

Two days later she had been arrested as she was leaving for the bank. Under her mattress the police had found a gold watch, two pairs of gold cufflinks, an antique silver cigarette case, and a pair of diamond drop earrings. She was charged with stealing them from Hank Pugsley's apartment.

"Hank Pugsley came to *my* apartment!" Kimberley told the policeman who was questioning her, with increasing desperation. "He must have planted the jewelry then. He was angry with me because I wouldn't let him stay all night. This is his means of revenge."

But she knew it wasn't. It was Hank's revenge for something much greater, and she knew he wouldn't rest until he had exacted his pound of flesh from her. She also knew there wasn't a damned thing she could do about it.

Carl eyed Madeleine nervously. "Why do you say that?" he asked. "Why do you say I won't be bothered with Kimberley anymore?"

"Daddy called to say she'd been arrested, didn't he?" Madeleine said, feeling nervous now that the moment had come to tell him everything.

"Yes, how did you know that?" Carl looked at her, startled.

Madeleine leveled her gaze at him and said with a flicker of a smile, "Because I helped set her up."

"You *what?* How do you mean? What do you know about Kimberley Cabot?"

"Everything, Carl. Everything." Her voice dropped to a whisper, and for a moment she averted her gaze, unable to let him see the pain in her eyes. "I've known for a long time now what went on between you two."

Carl's face flushed dark red, his skin suffused so that the veins stood out at his temples. "How?" The single word, dragged from his dry throat, asked a million questions.

"I happened to be in the washroom in your office one day, when I heard you and Kimberley quarreling . . . and I heard what she was doing and how she was blackmailing you . . ." The pain in Madeleine's voice was raw now, and she was finding it difficult to choose the right words.

"Oh, my God," breathed Carl, looking at her with anguish.

"And I heard her tell you that what you were doing was safe . . . that you'd never get caught . . . that Hank would never find out." Tears filled Madeleine's eyes now as she remembered the shock and agony of that day. Then she told Carl all that she'd overheard.

"At first I didn't know what to do," she concluded, "but then I remembered hearing you say to Kimberley that you loved me." She turned to look at him then, her eyes suddenly blazing with passion. "If I hadn't believed that was true, Carl, I'd have left you immediately."

"Oh, Maddy . . ." Wretchedly he held out his hand to her. "It's such a mess . . . such a goddamn awful stupid mess! I never stopped loving you, not for a moment. I hope you'll always believe that. If it hadn't been for you, I don't know what I'd have done. I never loved Kimberley. It was one of those crazy things . . . no more than a one-night stand that went hopelessly out of control. Then when she sprang this ultimatum on me . . . well, I sort of panicked. I should have told her to go to hell."

Madeleine took his hand and squeezed it tightly. "I know, Carl. I can understand how you felt. The most important thing is that my father should never find out any of this. Things would never be the same again if he were to know what Kimberley did, with your help."

"But what about Hank? Will he be content to have Kimberley charged with petty theft, when she's got three million dollars of his?" Carl protested desperately.

"She *had* three million dollars of his," Madeleine corrected him. "Hank and I took the money out of her account in the Banque Internationale last week, and transferred it to Hank's account." Carl's mouth fell open in utter astonishment as Madeleine told him about getting Kimberley's bank-account number out of her Filofax and then learning to forge her signature.

"This is unbelievable," he said at last, shaking his head. "You, Maddy, who have always been such a dreamer . . . I always believed you were so impractical, so in need of protection . . . and now you tell me you and Hank actually met in Zurich when I thought you were looking at London art galleries . . . and you took the money out of Kimberley's account and gave it back to Hank?"

Madeleine nodded, the color slowly coming back to her cheeks. Her relief that the long, drawn-out ordeal was nearly over, and that Carl was no longer in danger was making her feel quite light-headed. If Kimberley, out of spite, were to accuse Carl of embezzling funds, she'd no longer be able to make it stick. Hank had his money back and he'd say it had been in his account all the time.

Suddenly Madeleine thought of something. "Carl," she asked, "did Kimberley try to put through a transfer a couple of weeks ago, only to find her computer disk was blank?"

Carl's eyes widened and he looked at Madeleine incredulously, as if he couldn't take much more.

"Yes," he croaked. "Why?"

Madeleine gave a smile of deep satisfaction. "Brilliant! I'm so glad it worked."

"What did you do? I remember she was wild because Hank was transferring a lot of money to Switzerland that day, and she couldn't get her hands on it. She had no idea what had gone wrong, though."

"I don't suppose she did," Madeleine replied dryly. How well she remembered the visit she'd paid to Kimberley Cabot's apartment that Saturday afternoon. She'd asked for some coffee, and sullenly Kimberley had gone into the little kitchen to make it, leaving Madeleine alone in the living room. She'd overheard Kimberley say to Carl that she kept the copy of the computer tape she'd made in her apartment for safety's sake, and Madeleine's eyes had flickered around the room hopefully. It was probably locked away, but as she had glanced at the books on the shelves, she suddenly saw it, recognizing it because she had seen many tapes like it in her father's office. She could hardly believe her luck. Moving swiftly, she'd slipped the disk inside her jacket, and holding it there, wandered into the kitchen on the pretext of chatting with Kimberley. As soon as the girl's back had been turned, she'd slipped the tape onto the counter beside the microwave oven, casually drawn a dish towel over it, and then switched on the microwave. Distracting Kimberley by remarking on everything in the kitchen, she had been able to switch off the microwave again, retrieve the disk, and then wander back to the living room, where she replaced it among the books, without Kimberley's ever being aware of what had happened.

Carl looked blank. "I don't get it."

"I read somewhere that a famous TV comedian kept all his jokes on a disk," Madeleine said. "Everything was fine until he left it in the kitchen and his wife switched on their new microwave."

"You mean . . . ?"

"Exactly. The tape was erased."

Carl drew in a deep breath. "So you made Kimberley's disk blank? You wiped out the computer code . . . everything?"

"Everything! I must say, I'd have loved to see her face when she got a blank screen."

"My God . . ." Carl, shocked and amazed, sat gazing at Madeleine as if he couldn't believe all he'd heard. That his gentle and artistic wife had been strong enough to outwit Kimberley Cabot was a stunning revelation. "And I never knew you had any idea what was going on. All this time, my main worry was that you would find out," he added.

"That was one of my worries too," admitted Madeleine. "I was afraid you'd find out I did know everything! I knew you'd never have been able to carry on without Kimberley suspecting something, if you got wind of the fact I was aware of what was happening. I wish I could have let on sooner, Carl, for both our sakes, but this was the only way."

Carl could only hold her hand in both of his, so deeply had he been affected by finding out what Madeleine had done. Later there would be a time for laughter and tears and explanations, but right now he just felt the need to be close to her.

The cold blue light of a wintry dawn was stealing through the chinks in the bedroom curtains when at last they lay down together, the terrible misery and anxiety of the past few months washed away by their talking. When at last the sun rose, weak and milky over the Devonshire countryside, Madeleine lay with her eyes closed and her hand still in Carl's. She was exhausted, but she had never felt so happy or so close to Carl. His words of love and his appreciation for what she'd done still echoed in her mind, and she thanked God that the long ordeal was over.

17

THE FAMILIAR sight of the lofty flower-filled lobby of the Royal Westminster Hotel made Jessica's heart give a great lurch. It seemed to her as if she'd been away a lifetime, and yet nothing had changed. The same hotel staff in the same dark green uniforms were going quietly and efficiently about their work, and there was the usual hustle and bustle of comings and goings, the same stacks of luggage, the same expensive smell of polish and perfume, and leather and lilies, and the same muted murmuring of voices in a dozen different languages. With a sense of *déjà vu*, Jessica paused and looked around, hoping against hope that she might be able to return to work here, feeling in many ways as if she'd never left, as if the whole episode with Bernard had been some extraordinary dream. She glanced at the revolving glass doors, almost expecting to see him stride through, his hooded eyes taking in everything. Then she looked over to the cluster of seats arranged under the oasis of plants and remembered sitting there talking to him. Had it all really happened? It seemed that another person in another time had clicked her way in high heels across the gleaming marble floor, brimming over with enthusiastic love for a man she hardly knew, and now that same person, feeling considerably older and wiser, stood here wondering what she could recapture from the past.

On the phone yesterday, the general manager, Kenneth Wolfson, who had always liked her, had said he could see her at eleven-fifteen. Jessica's hopes had soared, seeing herself back in her old position, back in harness, her mistakes forgotten as quickly as possible. She had only one idea in mind: to get back to work and resume her old life. Only by doing that could she hope to obliterate her sense of failure and foolishness. That morning, as she'd driven up from her parents' house in Sussex, she swore to herself that never again would she be so impetuous or crazy. Letting her heart rule her head had proved fatal, and she might even have lost her career because of it.

Jessica glanced at her watch. It was ten past eleven. By the time she got up to the executive offices on the third floor, it would be time for her appointment. With a mounting sense of excitement she got into the elevator. Already she was feeling a part of the place again. As she passed a console table outside Kenneth Wolfson's office, she gave the arrangement of flowers a proprietary look and paused to straighten a bloom. How did I ever imagine I could exist without this life? she thought.

Kenneth Wolfson greeted her cordially, looking just the same, with his shining clean pink face and sharply pressed Savile Row suit. A pleasant aura of Paco Rabanne after-shave moved with him like a perfumed shadow.

"Well, this is a nice surprise, Jessica," he said, shaking hands with her. "I didn't think we'd see you again for a long time."

In spite of her resolve to keep cool, Jessica found herself blushing to the roots of her blond hair as she took a seat opposite him. Suddenly she felt more nervous than when she'd gone for her first job interview when she'd been eighteen.

"I didn't think I'd be back either," she replied, trying to sound jokey. "I'm afraid it was all a great mistake."

Kenneth Wolfson smiled kindly. "I'm not going to say I told you so. Let's just be thankful things are not worse. For example, you could have married Bernard Scheller, or had a child with him."

"I know." Jessica nodded with fervor. "It's been awful, but it could have been much worse, I suppose. I just wish I hadn't got so carried away in the first place."

"It's all part of the learning experience, Jessica. My generation had to live by our mistakes. We didn't have the chance to discover things were wrong before we got married, and afterward it was too late. We were lumbered." He sighed again, as if he spoke from personal experience.

"So I was wondering . . . ?" Jessica began hopefully, her eyes wide and candid, her mouth curving in an eager smile.

"Yes. I asked you to come and see me this morning because I wanted to explain the situation to you."

Something in his tone sent a chill through her, a premonition that it was not going to be easy to persuade him that she really intended to get back to work again.

"I promise you I won't go off like that again," she said earnestly. "I know it was a kind of madness, but I've got it out of my system now and I really want to resume work in the hotel business again, more than anything."

Wolfson leaned back in his opulent leather chair and his hands fiddled with a letter opener shaped like a dagger. Without looking at her he said slowly, "It's not your reliability I'm referring to. I know you're a professional to your fingertips and I appreciated the way you were prepared to continue last time until we found a replacement for you. Why I wanted to see you myself is that I wanted to tell you that I'm afraid we don't have any vacancies in the hotel at the moment."

Jessica's face fell, distress showing in every feature. "There's *nothing?*" she gasped.

"Not a thing, I'm afraid. Every position is filled, and I honestly can't say when a vacancy is likely to occur again. I'm really sorry, Jessica. There's nothing we'd have liked more than to have you on board again." His smile was genuinely sympathetic as he noticed how upset she looked.

"Do you think there'll be anything going on in any of the other Golding Group hotels? Oh, I can't *bear* this!" she wailed.

"I made a few inquiries on your behalf yesterday," he told her, "but head office said there was nothing available at present, except for the job of deputy banqueting manager at their Dubai hotel, but you haven't got the qualifications for that anyway. You're purely on the sales side, and right now all those posts are taken."

Disappointment hit Jessica like a body blow. Never for a moment had she imagined she'd be unable to get another job in the Golding Group; even if it wasn't in the Royal Westminster, she had been certain there'd be something in one of their other hotels.

"Oh, God . . . I wish I'd never left now!" she exclaimed. "How could I have been such a fool?" She wrung her hands despairingly. "How could I have been so crazy? I've thrown away my career . . . my whole future . . . everything I worked for!" Her little red pointed nails stabbed the air dramatically and she looked ready to burst into tears.

"I'm awfully sorry, Jessica," Wolfson said in an effort to sound soothing. "I really am. If anything comes up, I'll let you know immediately. In the meantime, why don't you take a break? Have a little time to yourself?"

"I've just had a break," Jessica responded spiritedly. "Such a long break that I'm bored to tears. I want to get some work or I'll *die*."

Kenneth's mouth twitched. One of the things he'd always liked about Jessica was the way she dramatized everything, making it sound sensationally interesting even when it wasn't.

"It might be worth your while applying to one of the other hotel groups," he suggested. "They might have some vacancies."

"I'll try, but it won't be the same. Oh, are you *sure* you couldn't squeeze me in somewhere?" Jessica's blue eyes were beseeching.

"I wish I could, my dear." He shook his head sadly.

"Well, that's that, then." Regretfully she rose. "If you hear a loud bang in the corridor, you'll know I've shot myself!"

He laughed outright. "Don't make too much mess on the carpet, then. We're short-staffed when it comes to cleaners, if not sales representatives. Good-bye, Jessica, take care of yourself"—he shook her hand warmly—"and the best of luck."

"Thanks. I need it!" Pretending to be lighthearted in order to disguise how deeply depressed she felt, Jessica pranced down the corridor, out of the hotel, and into the street, where the Hyde Park Corner traffic swept relentlessly past, numbing her senses with its roar.

Damn. Damn. Damn, she thought as she hurried down Knightsbridge in the direction of Harrods. She didn't know where she was going or what she was doing, so flattened did she feel, so utterly deflated. She had no job, and nowhere to live. The fact that she had no boyfriend either was a minor consideration by comparison. Men she could live without, especially right now. Work she could not do without, and she couldn't bear the idea of burying herself in the country. Her parents were very sweet, but life didn't exactly buzz in Surrey.

Then she had a brilliant idea. She'd fly over to New York to see Madeleine! That would cheer her up. She'd spend a couple of weeks catching up on everything with her best friend, and then she'd think about getting another job.

* * *

In the sleepy village of Sherston, the people awoke to a morning of sparkling frost and chill mists that swirled around the old thatched-roof cottages and plucked at the icy ground. Up at Milton Manor, servants were lighting fires, drawing back the thick curtains at the windows, preparing breakfast in the large country-style kitchen. Jenkins, in his best serge suit, shiny at the seat and elbows, hovered expectantly in his cottage nearby, having given the Riley a good polish. Today he was driving Madeleine and Carl over to the Meredith House Institute to see Camilla, and he felt quite nervous—"Dodgy like," he'd informed his wife.

"Then why take them?" she'd demanded. "They can drive themselves, can't they?"

"It wouldn't be right," Jenkins insisted. "Miss Madeleine is goin' to need someone who knows what's what. Mr. Delaney, he won't be much good; when I sees him last night he was more worked up than her!"

Mrs. Jenkins protested, "But 'e's her husband!"

"Aye, but I knew Miss Camilla, and 'e didn't. If anything goes wrong, I wants to be there, to protect Miss Madeleine like."

"What could go wrong? I thought you said her mother was like a cabbage . . . didn't know no one."

Jenkins nodded in agreement. "That's right, but you never know. At the sight of her daughter, something might come back to her," he added darkly.

Madeleine and Carl were waiting in the hall when Jenkins brought the car to the front door. Wrapped warmly in a thick red coat and black leather boots, Madeleine got into the back, holding Carl's hand all the time.

In the last couple of days they'd grown closer than ever, their relationship strengthened by Madeleine's ingenious scheme that had removed Kimberley from their lives and proved to them both the solidarity of their marriage. Nevertheless, she felt very emotional at this moment. The time for wondering about Camilla was almost over, the mystery almost unveiled. In an hour she'd come face-to-face with her mother, and she couldn't help wondering what she'd find. What sort of woman would she be, who could have been prepared to offer up her child as a sacrifice to some satanic god? Involuntarily Madeleine shuddered, and Carl slipped his arm around her shoulders.

"You don't have to go ahead with this," he said gently.

"I know," she agreed, "but it's something I feel I must do. Lay the ghost once and for all, put an end to over twenty years' speculation and doubt. I also want to satisfy my curiosity too, you know. If I don't see my mother now, I'm going to be wondering for the rest of my life what she was really like."

"You will remember, won't you, darling, that she was a very sick woman and that these evil people only got a hold of her because she was in a very vulnerable state at the time? She couldn't have been herself on the night she took you up to the barn—she couldn't have known what she was doing," Carl assured her.

Jenkins cleared his throat from the front of the car, with a scraping sound. "Mr. Delaney is right," he interjected. "Miss Camilla was a lovely young woman before they cast their spell on her and led her astray."

"Those are the words my grandfather used," Madeleine said. " 'Led astray.' Even so, I find it impossible to understand. How any woman could do such a thing . . ."

Carl hugged her tenderly. "Try not to think about that side of it. Try to remember that you are going to visit a woman who had a total breakdown a very long time ago and who has been virtually catatonic ever since."

"I'll try," Madeleine said doubtfully.

Meredith House looked surprisingly ordinary—a large red brick building set in spacious grounds, hidden from the main road by a high wall. Security gates, manned by a uniformed guard, were the only hint it was not the estate of some rich landowner. The long curved drive, bordered on each side by high rhododendron bushes, was well-kept and the lawns in the hazy winter morning were smoothly mown and looked well-cared-for. A few people, huddled in thick coats against the sharp edge of the wind, walked briskly in pairs, and a nurse in a dark cloak pushed an elderly woman in a wheel-chair.

Madeleine's heart plunged with a swift surge of pain before resuming its thick beating. Then she got out of the car and walked with a firm and determined tread toward the entrance. Carl followed, and Jenkins came slowly after them, a few creamy Christmas roses from the garden of Camilla's old home clutched in his hand.

The institutional smell of disinfectant and floor polish assailed Madeleine's nostrils as she entered a large square hall sparsely furnished but with a pleasant and warm atmosphere. A wide staircase led up to the floor above, and on either side of the hall, passageways led to a series of private rooms, all with numbered doors. Madeleine hesitated, wondering where to go. There was no reception desk or obvious information office, and she was just about to turn to Jenkins for help when her elbow was suddenly gripped from behind and squeezed almost fiercely. She let out a small cry as panic engulfed her. Whoever had come up behind must have recognized her, and she spun around fearfully, half-expecting to see the deranged face of her mother. Then she let out a gasp of relief.

"Daddy!" she cried. "Oh, Daddy, what are you doing here?"

Jake, smiling and distinguished-looking, put his arms around her and hugged her close.

"You didn't think I'd let you go through an ordeal like this without being here, did you, Maddy?"

Madeleine leaned against him, relief weakening her limbs and almost reducing her to tears. "Daddy, I'm so glad to see you. But how did you know . . . ?" Then she looked questioningly at Carl, who grinned back at her. It was he who had told Jake she was going to visit Camilla today! Carl who had asked Jake to fly over so that she could have him by her side now.

"Thank you, Carl," she whispered gratefully. She knew he would have preferred to avoid seeing Jake so soon, in case he got drawn into discussions about his ex-secretary's activities, but for her sake he'd asked her father to come.

"I thought you'd need Jake at a time like this," Carl whispered.

"I've already seen the matron," Jake said. "Camilla's in her room now. Shall we go and see her?"

Madeleine looked up into her father's eyes, feeling again like the little girl who'd once depended on him for everything.

"Daddy?" Then she hesitated.

"What is it, Maddy?"

"I know everything now, you know, about her belonging to a satanic organization, about her being a witch and offering me as a sacrifice, and I know if it hadn't been for you and Jenkins I might not even be alive today." Her voice had sunk to a whisper.

Jake looked down at her, a troubled expression in his dark eyes. "Now you know why I wouldn't have her name mentioned, why I never wanted you to know. I was afraid of the psychological effect it might have on you. Imagine! A child finding out her mother was prepared to watch her being killed as part of some ghastly religious ritual! The truth was so terrible that Patti and I decided to say your mother had died. . . . It wasn't such an awful lie, was it? After all, from the moment Jenkins and I rescued you and broke up the ceremony, she has in fact been dead to the world. She doesn't know what's happening, and they tell me she never will again."

"How did you bear it, Daddy?" Madeleine asked.

Jake didn't answer at first, and the lines of his face were deeply scored, but then he smiled again, and bending forward, kissed her cheek. "Because I had you, sweetheart," he replied simply. Then he added quietly, "Shall we go?"

Madeleine nodded, and while Carl and Jenkins waited in the hall, she and Jake mounted the stairs to the second-floor room where Camilla awaited her husband and her daughter, although she was not even aware of it.

The peal of the front doorbell echoing in Milton Manor brought Hunter, who had been down in the cellar selecting bottles of wine for the weekend, rushing, panting, to open it. On the worn stone steps stood a petite blond in a fluffy cream wool coat and black woolen stockings and high-heeled black boots. She was stamping her feet to get warm, her head cocked to one side. Hunter was instantly reminded of a Highland sheep. He'd seen them on a holiday in Scotland once, all long slim black legs prancing from rock to rock, while their bodies looked like woolly balls and they had a way of looking at you with their heads on one side that was almost human.

"Is Mrs. Delaney at home, please?"

Hunter raised his eyebrows, noticing a local taxi behind her, with the driver unloading a lot of luggage. He remembered the young lady now. She and a gentleman friend had stayed at the Manor earlier in the year.

"I'm sorry, but madam is out," he said, then added carefully, so as not to give offense: "Is she expecting you, madam?"

"No. That's the whole idea. I'm surprising her. I called her in New York and they told me she was here! Will she be out for long?"

"Several hours, I should think. She and Mr. Delaney have gone visiting," he added diplomatically.

The little figure clapped black-woolen-covered hands in delight. "Perfect! I can get installed before she comes back, and then she'll get the shock of her life when she finds me here!"

She certainly will, Hunter thought, but he said nothing. Years of training as a butler had long since taught him when to speak and when to keep his mouth shut.

Blue doll-like eyes smiled into his, sparkling with fun. "Do you remember me? I've stayed here before and my name's Jessica McCann, and I'm Mrs. Delaney's oldest and best friend, and I *promise* you she'll be delighted when she sees me. I'd hoped to spring a bit of a surprise on her anyway, but as she's out it's even better. Wait until she walks in!" Jessica hopped from foot to foot with anticipation while the driver carried her cases into the hall. Then she handed him the fare plus a generous tip. Hunter was still hovering with deep consternation, not knowing what to make of this extraordinary young lady, when she turned to him, her face serious and concerned.

"Look, I know you think I'm mad, but I really do want to surprise Mrs. Delaney. She thinks I'm on the other side of the world. I haven't come to steal the silver or anything, and I promise you she really will be glad to see me when she gets back."

Hunter's resistance crumbled. With a weak smile he ushered her into the hall. "Would you mind waiting in the library, madam?" he suggested. "There's a nice fire in there, and perhaps you'd like a cup of tea while a bedroom is being prepared for you?"

Jessica's eyes widened with appreciation. "Hunter, you should work in a five-star hotel. You're wasted in a private house. You'd make the most fabulous majordomo!"

Looking startled, Hunter led the way to the library, lost for words.

"Thank you," Jessica said, removing her large woolly coat,

which he took from her with as much reverence as if it had been made of priceless sable.

"Hunter, could you do me a big favor?" she begged, clasping her slim hands together. "Could you hide my luggage?"

"Hide it, madam?" His resonant tones filled the library.

"Yes, you know! Put it out of sight somewhere. Then, if Mrs. Delaney returns before my bedroom is ready, it won't give the game away."

Hunter's mouth twitched against his will. "Very well, madam."

As Jessica sat by the blazing log fire in the library, she looked around with interest. The carved ceiling and old stone mantelshelf and walls lined with books from floor to ceiling gave the room an atmosphere of quiet tranquillity that made her feel instantly at home. Milton Manor was just the type of house, she thought, that she'd like to have if she ever went to live in the country. There was something solid and gracious about it that appealed to her, and when she went to look out the window, the charming gardens looked inviting in spite of the frost. On the lawns, large black rooks flapped about like clerics in a hurry, and Jessica smiled to herself, somehow reminded of her own secure childhood in the countryside. It was all very reassuring.

Hunter brought her tea, impeccably set out on a silver tray with Rockingham china.

"Your room will be ready in a few minutes, madam. I am most sorry for the delay. Is there anything else I can get you in the meantime?"

"No, thank you," Jessica replied, more impressed than ever by his manner. He was exactly the type of person they were always looking for at the Royal Westminster: polite without being servile, anticipating guests' requirements without bullying them into having something they didn't want, friendly but never familiar.

"Have you ever thought of working in a hotel?" Jessica asked suddenly as Hunter added another log to the fire.

"I've always been in private service, madam. I wouldn't mind working in a small, shall we say, exclusive hotel, but I don't think I'd like to work in a big place. They're so impersonal, I always think." He stood waiting for her to give that almost imperceptible indication, known to all well-trained servants, that the conversation was about to be politely terminated. Jessica, who had spent the past seven years learning the finer points of dismissing staff from one's presence without appearing to do so, smiled knowingly. The man was a treasure. If Madeleine had any sense, she'd take him back to America with her.

When Jessica had drunk her tea, fragrant Lapsang souchong with a thin slice of lemon, she decided to freshen up before Madeleine returned. Hunter had told her where her bedroom was, so, slipping out of the library, she crossed the hall, making for the staircase. The drawing-room and dining-room doors were open, revealing tantalizing glimpses of the rooms beyond. She hadn't noticed the extent of the beauty of the house on her last visit because she'd been too upset at having to tell Andrew about her promotion; but now, as she wandered into the rooms, she realized just how exquisite they were, with their big bay windows overlooking the gardens and their handsome marble mantelshelves and ornate plaster ceilings. Just the sort of place that would . . . Suddenly she clapped her hand over her mouth, stifling a gasp. She'd just had the most wonderful idea! A staggeringly fantastic, amazing idea! Oh, why hadn't she thought of it before? She clasped her hands in an ecstasy of excitement; her idea was so perfect it *must* be made to work! Leaping up the stairs two at a time, she paused at the top, making a quick calculation. Counting the top floor as well, there were probably eighteen or nineteen bedrooms; of course, there wouldn't be enough bathrooms, but they could easily be put in. . . .

With excitement rising in her like a fever, she rushed into the bedroom she'd been given, and opening the little *secretaire* in the window, grabbed some sheets of thick cream writing paper embossed with the address of Milton Manor in dark blue. Sitting on the chintz-covered bed, she started doing some calculations. On her last visit, she remembered Andrew telling Madeleine she'd probably get over half a million pounds for the sale of the place; add to that various conversions and redecorating, installing a commercial kitchen with the best stainless-steel equipment from Germany, plus crockery, cutlery, beds, three sets of bed linen and blankets . . . On and on the list grew, until at last she drew a thick line along the bottom of the figures and started to add them up. Taking a deep breath, she finally arrived at the total. It would cost about seven million pounds to turn Milton Manor into the five-star exclusive country hotel of her dreams. Her calculations continued as her ambitions soared. The running costs would be heavy too: heating, lighting, first-class staff, a Rolls-Royce to collect guests from the station, flowers in every room, superb food and wines . . . Hugging herself with delighted anticipation, Jessica continued to sit on the bed daydreaming. She was certain she'd have no trouble in raising the money from backers; after all, her experience in the Golding Group would show that she knew what she was doing. But first she had to tell Madeleine she wanted to buy the manor, though that wouldn't be a problem; she knew Madeleine had been wanting to sell it from the moment she inherited it.

Cream paint and green linoleum, discreet grilles on the windows, and locks on the doors distinguished Meredith House as a mental institution. Not that there was anything resembling a prison about it, Madeleine reflected as she followed her father along a corridor. The atmosphere was more that of a private nursing home with strong security.

Room number eighteen was not locked, except at nights. Jake opened the door and entered quietly, followed by Madeleine. Seated in an armchair by the window, her hands folded on her lap, was a middle-aged woman, plain and dumpy, her gray hair cut short, her blue eyes lifeless. Like an empty husk, with all life gone from it, Camilla gazed vacantly before her, unaware of her visitors' presence.

"Hello, Camilla," Madeleine heard Jake say.

The woman's face, as devoid of makeup as it was of expression, showed no signs of having heard him.

"I've brought Madeleine to see you," Jake continued, and there was pain in his voice. The lovely young woman he had married, and the mother of his child, seemed to bear no resemblance to this zombielike creature whose eyes never flickered. "Do you remember Madeleine?" he asked, peering into her face though he knew it was useless. Camilla was not capable of understanding anything, and perhaps, he reflected, for her own sake it was a good thing. But the waste of it all, his heart cried out wildly. He had lost a wife and Madeleine had lost a mother, and all because of some evil people who had sought to take command of Camilla's mind and her spirit. Whatever demon had insinuated itself into her being, brainwashing her into believing in satanism, had long since lost its power, but the empty shell that had survived filled him with pity. Jake reached out and took her hand. All that remained was an ineffectual, ordinary-looking woman who no longer even knew who she was.

Tears suddenly sprang to Madeleine's eyes, childish tears that had not been shed since she'd been a lonely little girl wanting her mother. Then in her imagination Camilla had been like a fairy queen, warm and loving, and she'd made up wonderful stories about her. In recent months the pictures had changed and grown dark and sinister and fearsome; now it was something of an anticlimax to be faced with this broken woman who was lost to the world, and was a threat to no one . . . nor a comfort either.

Jake broke the silence. "I'm afraid she's always like this, darling."

"You've been here before?" Madeleine looked up at him in surprise. "I never knew that."

"I come every few years, and of course I keep in touch with the doctors, in case there's any change."

Madeleine glanced at the blank face, embarrassed to be talking in front of Camilla like this, as if she wasn't there at all. "And she'll always be like this?" she whispered.

"I'm afraid so." Jake sounded full of compassion. His rage had faded and died over the years as he'd come to realize it was useless to blame Camilla for what had happened. Her mind, already emotionally frail after the death of her mother, had been corrupted and finally destroyed, and she had ended up being as much the victim as the perpetrator of evil.

Madeleine rested her slim hand on Camilla's shoulder, longing to bridge the emptiness between them, wishing fervently she could make contact.

"Hello . . . hello, Mummy," she breathed softly, the tears spilling down her cheeks, but Camilla moved her head away to look out the window and did not appear to have heard.

"Don't be upset, sweetheart," Jake said, putting his arm around her. "I think she's quite happy . . . where she is."

They stayed a few more moments and then slipped out of the room again, still unnoticed by Camilla.

Madeleine took Jake's arm as they walked slowly back along the corridor. "Daddy, can I ask you something?"

Jake smiled and there was a touch of weariness in his expression. "Anything you like, Maddy. I've no more secrets from you now."

"Why did you never marry again?"

"Because your mother and I are still married."

Madeleine turned to him, horrified. "What? You never got divorced?"

"How could I divorce her, Maddy? Think about it. It was the trauma of Jenkins and me breaking up the ritualistic ceremony, when she'd been put into a trance, that sent her over the edge. I've always felt a sense of guilt about that. We had to do it to save you, but it undoubtedly wrecked your mother's already delicate mental state." Jake sighed, as if the burden of knowing this had lain heavily on his shoulders for a very long time.

Madeleine paused halfway down the corridor and looked up at him, her face full of sympathy.

"Oh, Daddy, that must have been dreadful for you. I'm sure you're not to blame. If my mother was that near the edge of insanity, anything could have tipped the balance."

"You may be right, Maddy. Anyway, I couldn't divorce her then. She was no longer with us in the true sense of the word, and to have divorced her would have been like betraying her when her back was turned."

Madeleine squeezed Jake's hand. "Did I ever tell you that you're a very special person," she whispered, "and that I'm the luckiest girl in the world to have you as a father?"

"You haven't told me lately," Jake replied with a teasing smile.

Carl was waiting for them down in the lobby. Without letting go of Jake's arm, Madeleine reached forward and took his hand.

"Everything all right, Maddy?" he asked anxiously.

She nodded. "Yes, and I'm glad I came."

Jenkins, who had left his roses with a nurse to give to Camilla, was standing in the drive chatting with the chauffeur who had driven Jake from the airport.

"Carl, why don't you go with Jenkins, and I'll go in Daddy's car," Madeleine said pointedly. She wanted to find out from Jake if there were any more developments about Kimberley, and it would be better if Carl was not involved in the conversation.

Carl, understanding, winked imperceptibly at her. "Fine," he agreed. "See you back at the house."

Madeleine settled herself comfortably beside Jake in the back of the hired limousine. "So, how's everything at the bank?" she asked.

"We're busy, as usual," replied Jake. "I'll be glad to have Carl back in New York, of course, although I think he needed this break. He's looking much better."

"Yes, I think he is. What's happened about that girl who was arrested? Carl told me she'd been charged with stealing." Madeleine spoke evenly, her eyes fixed on the tangled hedge-rows as the car sped along the country lanes.

There was a moment's pause; then Jake spoke. "Kimberley Cabot, you mean? Oh, she's being held on a charge of robbery and I think she'll be convicted. What a fool! She had such a good job at the bank, and she risked everything for a thousand dollars' worth of jewelry! After this, she'll never get a decent job again. Anyway, Carl will be pleased to hear that his old assistant, Averil Fielden, is coming back to work for him. She missed New York, apparently, and can't wait to get back."

Madeleine let out a little secret sigh of relief. Jake spoke of Kimberley as if he had already half-forgotten her.

"That will please Carl," she said lightly. "He was sorry when Averil left."

Jessica heard the scrunch of tires coming up the gravel drive just as she finished her calculations. Peering out the bedroom window, she saw Madeleine come into the house with Carl and Jake, and a minute later their voices, laughing and chatting, could be heard coming from the drawing room below. Brimming with excitement, she slipped out of her room and down the stairs. She could just imagine their surprised faces when they saw her.

Pushing open the drawing-room door, she struck a pose, arms outstretched.

"Hi there, everyone!" she called out gaily.

There was a stunned silence as the others turned to look at her. Madeleine was the first to recover.

"*Jessica!* What on earth are you doing here?"

"That's not much of a welcome," chided Jessica, running over to hug her.

Carl and Jake greeted her with amazed affection, exclaiming as Madeleine had done: "What are you doing here?"

Jessica stood in the middle of the large room, her hands on her hips, making an effort to look insulted.

"You'd think you weren't pleased to see me! I come from England, remember? I *live* here! . . . Well, er . . . I do now," she added lamely.

Madeleine looked at her anxiously. "You mean . . . ? What's happened to Bernard?"

"Bernard, for all I know, is still throwing the china at his servants on Sardinia."

"You've left him?" Carl asked wonderingly.

"I have indeed left him, my dear," Jessica said flatly. "The whole thing was a ghastly mistake, right from the beginning. I must have been mad, quite mad! Anyway, I'll tell you all about it later. What I'm longing to hear right now is your news, Maddy." She glanced at the others. "And why are you all here?"

Madeleine slipped her arm through Jessica's. "We've been visiting my mother," she said quietly. "I'll tell you all about it later." She'd already made up her mind that not even her best friend would ever know what had been happening in the past few months. That was something that only she and Carl would share.

At that moment Hunter brought in afternoon tea, setting the silver tray on a round table in front of the fire. He was followed by one of the maids with plates of sandwiches, scones, and a homemade walnut cake. Jessica clapped her hands in delight at the sight.

"Perfect! Every detail is perfect!"

Madeleine looked at her questioningly. "How do you mean?"

Jessica laughed and shook her head mysteriously. "Oh, it's nothing, really. I was just thinking how pretty the tea things looked."

After tea, Carl and Jake wanted to walk in the gardens, in

spite of the cold, so Madeleine and Jessica sat by the fire catching up on all their news.

When Madeleine had described Camilla and repeated the dreadful story Jenkins had told her, Jessica looked at her thoughtfully for a moment. Then she spoke.

"I've known all that for some time, you know, Maddy. My friend Peter Thorn, who works on the *Evening Standard*, told me all about the sacrificing ceremony in the old barn, because he reported the incident. Of course, I couldn't tell you—it was all too horrible, and I knew you'd be terribly upset."

"My God, I'd no idea you knew."

"Oh, I can be discreet sometimes." Jessica grinned.

"Now, are you going to tell me what happened between you and Bernard?" Madeleine asked, intrigued.

Jessica's face grew pensive and there was suddenly a sheen of unshed tears in her eyes.

"I've made the most awful mess of my life, Maddy," she confided in a low voice as she curled up on the chintz sofa. "I must have been mad to give up everything and rush off with Bernard. He wasn't at all like I'd expected—he was grumpy and demanding. I lost my feeling of independence and I had nothing to do. Oh, God, it was awful! I suddenly realized I'd fallen out of love with him as fast as I'd fallen *in* love. It was all a disaster."

"Jessica!" Madeleine remonstrated gently. "How could you make a terrible mistake like that? What did Bernard say? Wasn't he upset . . . or angry?"

"Oh, he understood. His wife left him for the same reason, I found out. You see, I fell in love with his music, and I thought he *was* his music, and then when I found out he was quite different, not a bit like I'd imagined . . ." Her voice trailed off as she looked at Madeleine, her expression beseeching. She was longing for her friend to understand and sympathize. To her relief, Madeleine smiled warmly.

"It must have been awful for you," Madeleine said. "Thank God, at least you didn't marry him. This way, hopefully, you can get back to your career and, as Dad always says, 'put it down to experience.' "

"That's just it," Jessica wailed, dashing a tear away from her cheek, "I've blown it, Maddy! I can't get my job back and there aren't any vacancies at all in the Golding Group. I've been such a fool! Right from the beginning. Why didn't I stay with Andrew? Why wasn't I content to just work in the Royal Westminster without having to claw my way up the ladder? Now I've got nothing, nothing at all. No job and no Andrew." She was silent for a moment, gazing disconsolately into space. "I really regret losing Andrew now," she added softly.

Madeleine looked at her with astonishment. "You do? Are you sure that isn't because everything else has gone sour? You had no hesitation about hurting him, right in this room, the last time you were here, because you wanted to give your all to the hotel. Jessie, are you sure you *do* know what you want, honey?" She hated talking harshly to her friend, but she was worried. Jessica, who had always seemed so together in the past, now looked as if she were about to crack up.

Jessica's reply surprised her. "Yes, I know what I want now, Maddy. As far as Andrew is concerned, it's probably too late, I'm afraid, and I do have some pride. I'm not going running to him. But as far as work is concerned, I've had the most brilliant idea!" She dabbed her eyes with a small lace hand-kerchief and sat bolt upright.

"You're planning to sell this place, aren't you? Well, I'd like to buy it."

Madeleine looked at her blankly. "What on earth do you mean?"

"I want to raise the money to buy this house and turn it into an exclusive five-star hotel. Oh, Maddy, I've been making the most wonderful plans while I was waiting for you to get back, and you know how I've always dreamed of having my own hotel!" Jessica spoke earnestly and excitedly. "The potential is fantastic! All the house staff could stay on . . . and we could build tennis courts, a swimming pool—"

Madeleine broke in with a touch of anxiety. "Jessica, do stop and listen to me for a moment."

"What's the matter? You *are* planning to sell the house, aren't you?" She looked crestfallen, seeing her wonderful new dreams smashed before her eyes. "Don't tell me you've changed your mind?"

"It's not that." Madeleine looked distressed. "What I'm trying to tell you is that Milton Manor has already been sold."

"Sold!" Jessica looked ready to weep again. "You can't mean it, Maddy! Oh, that's dreadful. How can you have sold it so quickly?" She sounded almost reproachful.

"I'm really sorry. Once the solicitor knew I had the legal right to sell, I put it on the market." Madeleine opened her mouth as if to say something else, then changed her mind.

"What were you going to say?" Jessica asked, noticing how abruptly her friend had stopped talking.

Madeleine flushed uneasily. "Nothing. Just that the house has been sold. I think the contracts were exchanged yesterday."

"Oh, hell." Jessica sat disconsolately, her brow gathered with aggravation and misery. Nothing was going right for her these days. She'd been a headstrong fool, and now she was having to pay the price. She'd let Andrew slip through her fingers and she'd walked out on the best job she'd ever have. How could she have done it? she asked herself as she curled up more tightly on the sofa in her anguish. How could she have walked away from everyone and everything she knew and cared about—and that included her parents as well as her friends—for a perfect stranger? What lunacy had swept all else away so that she could pursue the dangerous madness Bernard's music had evoked? Like someone drugged on melody, bewitched by cadences, besotted by the strains of a sensual rhythm, she had let his music dull all her other senses; she'd become deaf to all other warning sounds and blind to what was obvious, and when the harmony had disintegrated and the music had stopped, nothing was left but the discordance of her own feelings and the frustration of knowing that she had no one but herself to blame.

Madeleine was looking at her watch. "Will you excuse me, Jessie? I've got a few important phone calls to make. Carl and I are flying back to New York in a few days and there are some loose ends I want to tie up first."

"Of course. Go ahead." Jessica forced herself to sound cheerful.

As Madeleine hurried out of the room, Carl and Jake returned from their walk, stamping their feet and clapping their hands for warmth. Madeleine drew them into the library for a few minutes, speaking rapidly and quietly.

"The Central Manhattan could finance the project," Jake whispered when she'd finished talking.

"Are you going to call him now?" Carl asked.

Madeleine nodded. "Go and chat up Jessica, will you? She's rather low and needs cheering up."

At dinner that night, Madeleine announced that she and Carl were holding a luncheon party the following day, before Jake flew home.

"Who's coming?" Jessica asked. "Do you know any of your neighbors?"

"I've invited someone called Alice Stewart; she was a lifelong friend of my mother's and she's awfully sweet."

"It'll be nice to see her again," Jake observed.

"And you say her son, Philip, is coming too?" Carl asked.

"Yes. Apparently we met as small children, although neither of us remembers," Madeleine said with a smile.

Jessica let out a groan. "Oh, I get it! You're setting me up with a blind date, aren't you, Maddy? Oh, God, you're hoping I'm going to like him and forget all about Andrew and Bernard!"

Madeleine's mouth twitched. "No, I'm not. Philip isn't your type at all. I was actually hoping you'd hit it off with the new owner of Milton Manor. He's coming too."

Jessica cast her eyes to heaven. "This is going to be more than I can bear," she declared dramatically. "How could I possibly even *like* him? He's bought the one house in England I want, and now you're expecting me to be friendly with him? Honestly, Maddy!"

The next morning it was colder than ever. The winding lanes that led to Milton Manor stretched like glittering trenches through the frozen countryside, and icicles hung like crystal stalactites from the eaves of thatched cottages. At ten o'clock a large van trundled up the drive to the front door; painted on its side was: SEWELL. REMOVALS AND STORAGE. OKEHAMPTON.

"They haven't come to take the furniture away already, have they?" Jessica demanded, looking through the window.

Madeleine looked puzzled. "No. I haven't arranged for anything to be moved until next week. I wonder what they want!"

A minute later, Hunter came into the library, where they

were sitting. "There's a delivery for you, madam," he said. "An item that Sewell's have been storing for many years, I believe."

"What is it, Hunter . . . and who asked them to bring it here?"

"I did, darling," Jake said, coming into the room at that moment. "Get them to bring it in here, Hunter."

"Very well, sir,"

"What is it, Daddy?" Madeleine repeated. "I didn't know we had stuff in storage here."

"This is something I had shipped over from New York a very long time ago. I had it put in storage, since I didn't want to upset your grandfather by letting him know I didn't want it," Jake explained.

Two men in overalls came staggering through the doorway, and Madeleine could see they were carrying a canvas wrapped in sheeting. She looked questioningly at Jake, and slowly he smiled and nodded.

"Is it really . . . ?" she asked.

"Yes, my darling. I thought you'd like to have it now."

The deliverymen propped the canvas against the wall and Madeleine stepped forward and lifted away the covering. There, in colors as fresh and vibrant as if it had been painted yesterday, was the portrait of her mother that she remembered from her early childhood.

"Oh, Daddy," she breathed, gazing at it. It was a masterpiece, a perfect example of the work of Philip de Laszlo, showing the sweetness and innocence of the young Camilla, in a creamy lace dress, with a cascade of pearls falling from her neck. This was the Camilla that Madeleine had based all her imaginative ideals on; this was the vision that had inspired a thousand childish fantasies, and now Jake had given her back the mother of her dreams.

"Thank you, Daddy," she said, a catch in her voice. "I always wondered what had happened to it."

"I'm glad you're pleased," he said, also moved by emotion. "This is the way we should both remember her—she is really like this inside, I believe. The other Camilla was possessed by some terrible evil force, but this is the woman who was my wife and your mother."

"Yes," Madeleine said softly. "I shall hang it in the living room at home in New York." Then she turned to kiss him impulsively.

Alice Stewart and her son arrived at half-past twelve, and within minutes she and Jake were chatting away as if they'd seen each other only a few weeks before.

"My dear man," Alice flattered him, "you look more distinguished than ever, and of course Madeleine is the image of you!"

Jake roared with laughter. "Well, I can tell that *you* haven't changed, Alice!" He turned to Philip. "Did you know that in her day your mother was the most outrageous flirt?"

Philip grinned. "She still is!"

Everyone was talking and laughing while Hunter served glasses of champagne from a silver tray, when Jessica, who was being rather quiet, suddenly looked at Madeleine.

"I hear another car arriving," she observed. "Is it . . . ?"

"Yes, it's probably the new owner." Madeleine went over to the window and looked out. "Yes, it is." There was a certain satisfaction in her voice.

"Oh, I'm going to hate him!" Jessica exclaimed. "This is dreadful."

"Oh, it could be a lot worse," Madeleine said casually.

"I don't see how—" began Jessica, peering over Madeleine's shoulder. Then she let out a shriek and turned scarlet. "But it's Andrew!"

Madeleine nodded knowingly and smiled.

Jessica was bewildered, her eyes round. "But I don't understand . . . Why didn't you tell me? What does he want this big house for?"

Madeleine laughed. "Why don't you ask him yourself?"

"But, Maddy . . ." Jessica clutched her arm in apprehension. "Does he know I'm here?"

"Yes, of course he does. Stop panicking! When you told me you wanted this house for a hotel, I called him, and he was just in time to stop the sale by telling the other buyers I'd changed my mind and wanted to keep it. Then, with backing from the Central Manhattan Bank, which Daddy and Carl arranged, Andrew bought it himself . . . for you! You can have your hotel, Jessie, and Andrew as well! But I think you'd better let him tell you that part himself!" Madeleine said, pushing Jessica gently but firmly into the hall.

Jessica clasped her hands together, looking scared. Then she watched as Andrew came up the front steps. "Oh, my God, Maddy! I don't believe this! You mean . . . Andrew wants me back?"

"Go and greet him, Jessie—you're being hopeless!" Madeleine teased, giving her friend a final push. Then she went back into the drawing room and closed the door quietly behind her.

"Everything all right?" Carl murmured, seeing her conspiratorial expression.

Madeleine crossed her fingers. "I think everything's going to be just fine!" she replied, "and I've got a feeling that we'd better ask Hunter to put some more champagne on ice!"